FROM BEYOND OUR WORLD, THE DARK POWER OF FAERY REACHED OUT TO CLAIM ITS OWN. . . .

At the end of the Edwardian age, Emily Desmond, the headstrong daughter of an eccentric astronomer and a famed Irish poetess, succumbs to the terrible seductive call of the horns of Elfland.

In the years before the Second World War, Jessica Caldwell, a fiery-tongued artist, holds the dark power at bay with the aid of a demon lover and two mystic vagabonds.

And in the glittering world of present-day Dublin, Enye MacColl, an independent young writer, battles the living embodiment of her darkest fears with cutting-edge science and a samurai sword.

"The decade is still young, but *King of Morning, Queen of Day* carries such a rich wealth of language and story, of character and concept, that I don't doubt it will rank among the best works the genre will produce over the next ten years. This is a brilliant book; do yourself a favor and read it."

—Charles de Lint,
author of *Moonheart*

D0012018

Read these other fine fantasy novels,
available wherever Bantam Spectra Books are sold:

KING OF MORNING, QUEEN OF DAY

Ian McDonald

BANTAM BOOKS

NEW YORK • TORONTO • LONDON • SYDNEY • AUCKLAND

KING OF MORNING, QUEEN OF DAY

A Bantam Spectra Book / June 1991

ISBN 0-553-29049-5

Published simultaneously in the United States and Canada

Bantam Books are published by Bantam Books, a division of Bantam
Doubleday Dell Publishing Group, Inc. Its trademark, consisting of the
words "Bantam Books" and the portrayal of a rooster, is Registered in
U.S. Patent and Trademark Office and in other countries. Marca
Registrada. Bantam Books, 666 Fifth Avenue, New York, New York
10103.

PRINTED IN THE UNITED STATES OF AMERICA

OPM   0 9 8 7 6 5 4 3 2 1

PART I

CRAIGDARRAGH

*We have followed too much
the devices and desires of our own hearts.* . .
—The General Confession: Book of Common Prayer

To My Faery Lover

Oh, would that we were many things,
My golden-shining love and I;
Bright-flashing scales, a pair of wings
That draw the moonlight down the sky,
Two hazel trees beside the stream
Wherein our fruit in autumn drop,
A trout, a stag, a wild swan's dream,
An eagle cry from mountaintop.
For we have both been many things:
A thousand lifetimes we have known
Each other, and our love yet sings.
But there is more that I would own.
Oh, would that we could naked run
Through forests deep and forests fair,
Our breasts laid open to the sun,
Our flesh caressed by summer's air,
And in some hidden, leafy glen
My striving body you would take;
Impale me on your lust and then
Me Queen of Daybreak you would make.
And we would dance and we would sing,
And we in passion's fist would cry;
Loud with our love the woods would ring,
If we were lovers, you and I.
If we were lovers, I and you,
I would cast off all mortal ills
And you would take me, Shining Lugh,
To feast within the hollow hills.
For the world of men is filled with tears
And swift the night of science falls
And I would leave these tears and fears
To dance with you in Danu's halls,
So let us cast our cares away
And live like bright stars in the sky,

Dance dream-clad till the break of day,
For we are lovers, you and I.

—Emily Desmond
Class 4a, Cross and Passion School

Emily's Diary: February 14, 1913

Hail to thee, St. Valentine, Prince of Love. Hail to thee on this, thy festive day!

We, thy adoring servants, praise thee!

We stole the statue of St. Valentine from its niche in the corridor by the Chapel and smuggled it up to the dormitory. If the Sisters were ever to find out what we did to it we would all be expelled, every last one of us, but I have made all the girls take blood oaths of utter secrecy, and we will have it back in its rightful place before even Mother Superior comes on her rounds. At the last stroke of midnight, the first stroke of St. Valentine's Day, we stood the statue on a chair we had placed on a table and decorated it with the snowdrops and crocuses I had instructed the others to collect in botany class. We placed a crown made from chocolate wrappers on his head and, with much giggling, Charlotte and Amy got the thing they had made out of stolen modelling clay and erected it in front of the statue. Then we all performed the St. Valentine's dance in our *déshabille* and went up one at a time to kiss the clay thing and dedicate ourselves to the service of love. Then we sat down in a circle around the statue to read, by the light of one small candle which we passed around, the love poems we had written. Everyone thought mine was the best, but then they always think my ideas are the best; the whole St. Valentine's Day celebration was one of my ideas.

Charlotte told me that Gabriel O'Byrne, the grounds-man's son, had told her that he had been trying to give me a letter for over a week but hadn't been able. I wonder, she said, what it's about? and nodded at the clay thing she had made for St. Valentine.

I should wonder: as if I didn't know, from the way

Gabriel O'Byrne stops work every time I pass, and doffs his cap and smiles at me. All that waving and smiling. Well, she can just tell him I don't want any letters from Gabriel the groundsman's son. I don't want his dirty little affections; I want, I deserve, better than him. I deserve a faery prince, a warrior hero, strong-thewed and iron-willed, with raven black hair and lips like blood.

Edward Garret Desmond's Personal Diary: February 15, 1913

After three weeks of sleet, snow, and lowering clouds, last night the sky was at last sufficiently clear to permit me my first view of the newly discovered Bell's Comet through the Craigdarragh eighteen-inch reflector. For all its doubtless charms and graces, County Sligo is not blessed with the most equable of climates for the astronomer; namely, those clear-as-crystal skies beloved of the astronomer-priests of ancient Mesopotamia and noble Greece. And since the notification of this object's entrance into our theatre of interest in December last's *Irish Astronomical Bulletin*, it has been a source of major frustration to me (my dear Caroline would declare that I have become positively ratty on the subject) that I alone of all the country's—no! damn it! *Europe's* astronomers—have been unable to observe the phenomenon. That is, until today. At about four o'clock, as I was taking my usual ill-tempered post-afternoon-tea turn about the rhododendron gardens, generally bemoaning the nation of Ireland and the county of Sligo in particular, its winds, weathers, and climates, bless me if the wind didn't blow (capriciously as ever in this part of the globe), the clouds part, and a glorious golden late-winter radiance suffuse the countryside! Within half an hour the sky was clear blue all the way to the horizon, a sight so gladdening to the heart that I at once returned to the house and informed Mrs. O'Carolan that I would be taking supper in the observatory that evening.

It was some time before I was able to locate the subject

of my observations in the eighteen-inch reflector; the comet had moved across a considerable arc since first observed by Hubbard Pierce Bell of the Royal Observatory at Herstmonceux. Finally it lay squarely within my cross hairs and I was without doubt the only man in Ireland for whom this was a novelty.

In my excitement at finally being afforded the opportunity to observe Bell's Comet, I had forgotten how cold the night would be on account of the clear sky. I was shivered to the very pith of my bones. But, oh! Most estimable woman! Most worthy servant! With typical foresight and wisdom, Mrs. O'Carolan came through the frost to provide me with rugs, comforters, a steady stream of bricks warmed in the kitchen range, and, most welcome of all, a bottle of potín, a present, she maintained, from the widows of the parish. Thus fortified, I returned to my labours with enthusiasm.

No tail had yet developed, Bell's Comet being still beyond the orbit of our Earth. I noted positions, luminosity, apparent and proper motions in my observer's notebook and made some sketches. On returning to the telescope, it seemed to me that the object's luminosity had altered, a thing I at the time dismissed as a defect of vision in adapting to the Stygian blackness of space. By now the cold had confounded all Mrs. O'Carolan's ramifications, and for the good of my health, I decided to take a series of timed photographic exposures through the telescope and withdraw indoors to the comforts of hearth and wife. I was familiar with the local meteorology, as an astronomer must be, and I knew that this clear, cold weather would linger for several days.

This morning, on developing the plate, I noticed the anomaly. To be certain that it was not an imperfection in the emulsion (a series of such imperfections had caused me to terminate my arrangement with Pettigrew and Rourke Photographic Suppliers of Sligo, a pretty bundle of rogues, indeed), I quickly produced a full set of prints from all the exposures. Patience is the keystone of professionalism; the amateur would have hurried the job, and in his haste smeared the photographs so badly as to render them worthless. I bided my time, and when the little alarm clock rang was therefore able to see immediately that what I had recorded was no photographic error, but an unprecedented, and quite extraordinary, astronomical phenomenon.

The track of Bell's Comet was quite clear to see, arcing across the paths of the more familiar constellations. At regular intervals this arc was punctuated by what I can only describe, for want of a more elegant term, as blobs of light—concentrations of luminosity so intense they had actually burned away the photographic emulsion. Every other inch or so another of these blobs occurred at regular intervals along the comet's track. For a full minute I was so astounded by my discovery as to be incapable of rational thought. Then I gathered my wits and concluded that Bell's Comet must be emitting bursts of intense light. From the photographs, I calculated these to occur every twenty-eight minutes, a burst of light of such infinitesimally short duration and brilliance as to assume the luminosity of a major planet. Quite extraordinary!

Leafing through Hubbard Pierce Bell's article, I was unable to find the slightest mention of any fluctuation in luminosity. Such a phenomenon could not have been overlooked; the only possible conclusion was that it had not *at that time occurred*.

Delicious irony! That I, the last astronomer in Europe to observe Bell's Comet, should be the discoverer of its most fascinating secret! I have dashed off a hasty letter to Sir Greville Adams at Dunsink Observatory claiming the discovery; this evening, God willing, I will observe again.

Is it unprofessional (and, more to the point, unscientific), I find myself asking, to feel elation at the possibility of being the discoverer of a major astronomical event? (Might even the comet be renamed Desmond's Comet? I would even consider double-barrelling acceptable, but only as a last resort: Comet Bell-Desmond.) And there you have it. A quite inappropriately proprietorial attitude toward a lump of stellar matter! Terrible indeed to be reduced to an excitable schoolboy by the vainglorious thought of being the toast of the astronomical societies.

To matters more mundane, and sobering. Typical of Caroline to puncture my mood of ebullience by choosing luncheon today as her platform to raise the unpleasant issue of Emily's schooling. Now, I do not deny that Emily's problems at Cross and Passion are important, and that I, as a father, should be deeply concerned with the improvement of her academic standards; indeed, it is of paramount importance if daughter is to follow father down the noble highway of science. However, there is a time and a place for everything, and Caroline's insistence that we discuss this at length over luncheon so soured my mood of geniality that it is quite impossible for me to develop the tranquility of mind necessary for the proper contemplation of the heavens. *Priorities!* Like mother, like daughter. Neither, alas, knows the importance of *priorities*.

Emily's Diary: March 6, 1913

I heard them again last night, I'm sure I did—the Hounds of the Gods, out there among the trees. I heard them give tongue, like the baying of dire wolves it was, as they caught the scent of their quarry. I heard the cries of their faery master. Like the songs of nightingales they were, sweet and lovely. Rathfarnham Woods rang with their song. I imagined the woodland creatures fleeing from their footsteps: *Make way, make way, make way, for the Wild Hunt of the Ever-Living Ones!* But what could have been their quarry, out there in the rain-lashed wood? What was the scent the hounds tasted that set them baying so? Surely nothing so ignoble as the vulgar fox or badger that O'Byrne sometimes shoots when they raid the school chicken runs, nothing as common as that. Perhaps the noble stag. That would be quarry worthy of the Riders of the Sidhe. Maybe one of Lord Palmerstown's herds, or, is it possible? a *faery* stag from the pages of legend and story, the stag that is hunted and killed each night by the Wild Hunt only to rise again with the morning sun? Or, most romantic of all, one of their own kind, a manhunt, a faery warrior fleet-footed and daring, laughing as he slips tirelessly between the trees of Rathfarnham, making sport of the hounds and the spearmen dogging his footsteps.

Charlotte in the next bed asked what did I think I was

doing, sitting up all hours of the night looking out the window, didn't I know that I'd get in trouble if Sister Therese caught me? And just what, she asked, was I looking for out there in the pitch-blackness anyway?

"The hunt of the Ever-Living Ones, chasing a golden-antlered stag through the forest of the night with their red-eared hounds. Listen! Can you hear them, baying out there in the night? Can you hear the jingle of the silver bells on their horses' harnesses?"

Charlotte scrambled out of the sheets and knelt beside me on my bed. We looked out through the barred window and listened as hard as we could. I was certain I heard the call of a hound, very far off, as if the Night Hunt had passed by and moved onward. I asked Charlotte if she had heard anything.

"I think so," she said. "Yes, I think I heard something, too."

March 12, 1913

The Royal Irish Astronomical Society
Dunsink Observatory
County Dublin

My Dear Dr. Desmond,

A few lines of admiration and appreciation (and, I must admit, envy) on your success concerning the periodicity of Bell's Comet. For once the quixotic climate of that wretched county of yours has done you a service: interest having waned while you languished beneath your blanket of Celtic mist, yours was indeed the sole eyepiece in the United Kingdom to be trained on the comet at the precise moment it began to display its unique behaviour. Some gossoon from some wretched little city-state university in Germany has lodged a counterclaim; quite frankly, I suspect it is purest jealousy. These Huns will attempt anything to outdo His Britannic Majesty. So, the claim is yours, indisputably and unequivocally, and as a result, all those telescopes that turned away in search of celestial pastures new are turning back with wonderful haste to Bell's Comet. Alas, your name will not be joined with that of the comet's discoverer, but your fame, I think, will be the more enduring for having disclosed an unprecedented astronomical phenomenon. A flashing comet! Quite remarkable!

I have checked your calculations of rotation, angular momentum, velocity, and periodicity against my own observations (forgive my presumption in so doing), and have found that my figures correspond with yours to a high degree of accuracy. However, I am at a loss to furnish some hypothesis which might account for a rotational period of twenty-eight minutes but a maximum luminosity period of only two and three-eighths seconds. In our orderly universe, as strictly controlled and time-tabled as Great Southern Railways, such paradoxical behaviour is deeply offensive to we gentlemen of astronomy. Any hypothesis you might provide to explain this phenomenon would find wide general appreciation, and, should such a time arrive when you might wish to make it public, the lecture theatre at the Society is at your disposal. For the meantime I once again congratulate you on your achievement and encourage you to return to your studies.

Yours Sincerely,
Sir Greville Adams

Emily's Diary:
March 18, 1913

Alone in my small bower, I write, a dell among the woods of Rathfarnham. A secret place, a private place, a place where I am enfolded by tree branches like caring arms. A woman in green; this is my leafy bower. It took me a long time to find my place among the trees on the hillside, so close to Cross and Passion that I can almost reach out to touch the chimney pots, yet whole worlds away from Latin and Greek and French irregular verbs. Here I can be on my own, all alone, and lie down on the soft green moss and let my mind roam. Out across the land it goes, ripping up the fields and farms and houses of Rathfarnham, sowing in their place tall green trees—noble oaks and beeches. Look! There goes Cross and Passion, chimney pots and all, torn up and thrown away. Where it was is a gentle glen lit by shafts of soft sunlight, and deer look up, startled nostrils twitching, sniffing the air for the scent of the hunter. And here in my green bower, I am the poet-queen, dreaming of odes and lays and love songs, idylls and elegies and laments for mighty sons fallen in gory battle.

If the Sisters ever found me here, there'd be such trouble. But then Emily's always in trouble, isn't she? Trouble trouble trouble. They just can't leave me alone to be and do what I want. Well, only one more week in that cold old dormitory that smells funny, as if things have been locked up and left to die and rot, and then I'll be home for two weeks. Two weeks, such bliss! I know I'll miss the other girls, but in Craigdarragh the daffodils will be tall and golden on the lawn and the blackthorn will be blooming, and the may, and the alder; there will be birds singing in Bridestone Wood and all the trees will be putting on their newest green, all for me. I'm glad I'm spring born, when the earth is being born, too. I love it the years when Easter falls so I can have my birthday at Craigdarragh. I wonder, will Mummy have a party for me? I wonder, if I asked her nicely, would she allow boys to come? Parties are no fun without boys.

From the Private Notebooks of Constance Booth-Kennedy: March 23, 1913

The spring in Dublin! Most miraculous of seasons! Especially after the dreariness of February. Honestly, it never seemed to end this year. Twelve months of February; wind, cold, and sleet. Dismal. But how uplifting to see the early blossom in St. Stephen's Green and the new, bold green on the trees along Merrion Road. Even that Dublin wind, which, blowing in off the Irish Sea in midwinter, can strip the black lead from the palings around Trinity College, seemed as gentle and refreshing as a zephyr. And I am glad to see that Caroline is as refreshed and renewed by the change of season and scenery as I. Her spirits visibly rose by the mile on the train to Amiens Street Station, and since arriving in the capital, why, what a transformation! Once again (and not before time, I think), she is the gay and vivacious creature I recall so well from school days. I know for a certainty she will be the toast of all Dublin at the reading tonight: here's to Mrs. Caroline Desmond, the lady poetess of Drumcliffe! Her visit to the Gaelic Literary League is long overdue. Edward, though quite a dear in his own wee way, can be the most infuriating of men, especially when he goes into one of those trancelike states of his and, for days on end, shuffles around the house and gardens in carpet slippers muttering arcane *abracadabras* which we are meant to treat with a hushful reverence due deep musings upon the higher mysteries of the universe. This time it is some aery-faery nonsense about travellers from another star riding through space on the tail of a comet. No wonder poor Caroline was so easy to prise away from home. The man is getting worse, I declare.

A leisurely dinner at the hotel with a few friends from the Literary League, followed by a short, pleasant walk to University College, and finally, the triumphant reading of her latest collection, should restore a proper perspective to Caroline's life. Willie will be there. I must introduce him to Caroline. I'm sure he'll be quite entranced by her. Perhaps the next time he is over in the West I might arrange for a little soiree at Rathkennedy for Caroline, poet to poet. The atmosphere in Craigdarragh is so musty and stifling and *scientific*.

March 29, 1913

Craigdarragh
Drumcliffe
County Sligo

My Dear Lord Fitzgerald,

Many thanks for your letter of congratulation. It is most gracious of you, especially as I consider myself to have, in a sense, robbed you of your dues; after all, but for your winter sojourn in Nice, it could as easily have been yourself observing through the Clarecourt telescope as I through the Craigdarragh.

Therefore, I feel it only politic to inform you, a fellow astronomer and close colleague, that I have developed a theory on the nature of Bell's Comet which, I may say without fear of exaggeration, will rock the entire scientific community to its core, not merely the Irish Astronomical Society. Indeed, I have been invited to address my theories to that body on the eighteenth of April. However, with regard to the solidarity between us as brother astronomers in this benighted outpost of the Empire, I feel it is only proper that I should share this hypothesis with you before facing that lions' den of whippersnappers and ossified intellects in Dublin. Might I therefore extend to you an invitation to visit us here at Craigdarragh; would the fifteenth of April allow sufficient time to amend diaries and make arrangements? Please let me know at your earliest convenience if this date will not serve; it will be no difficulty to arrange another.

I conclude by expressing my fondest hopes that you will be able to visit our humble home. Both Caroline and I extend the warmest welcome, and, as ever, our thoughts and prayers are always for your good self and the Lady Alexandra, who is as close to our hearts as to yours,

I remain,

Your Obedient Servant,
Edward Garret Desmond, Ph.D.

Emily's Diary: April 2, 1913

Craigdarragh. Since crossing the threshold I have gone around hugging every wall, window, and door in the place! Mrs. O'Carolan can hardly believe what she is seeing; she goes around muttering under her breath that she always knew it ran in families. Dear Mrs. O'C! I almost hugged *her* when I saw her waiting on the platform at Sligo Station. Oh dear, the look she would have given me!

It is all as I imagined it on the train up from Dublin. Complete and perfect in every detail, the people, the faces, the places. The people: Mrs. O'Carolan fat and fusty and kind; Mummy a poet and an artist and a tragic queen out of legend all rolled into one; Daddy worried and hurried and so busy with his telescopes and sums I'm sure he's already forgotten I'm here. And the places: the red of the early rhododendrons, the blue sea, and beyond it, like a cloud, purple Knocknarea. Woods, mountains, waterfall: wonderful! Today I visited the Bridestone up above the woods on the slopes of Ben Bulben. How good it was to be alone and at peace. Up there, with only the wind and the song of the blackbird for company, it is like nothing has changed for a thousand years. It was easy to imagine Finn MacCool and his grim Fianna warriors hunting the leaping stag with their red-eared hounds through the woodland glens, or the sunlight glinting from the spear points of the Red Branch Heroes as they marched to avenge a slain comrade.

Perhaps reality was too much for me after months with nothing to call upon but my imagination: I could have sworn that I was not alone as I came down from the Bridestone through the green woods; that there were shadowy shapes flitting from tree to tree, unseen when I looked for them, giggling at my foolishness. Ah, well, I have always thought it was an enchanted faery place.

The Bushes
Stradbally Road
Sligo

Dear Mrs. Desmond,

Thank you for inviting Grace to the surprise party you are holding in honour of Emily's fifteenth birthday; I am delighted to accept on her behalf. She is looking forward to the twelfth with mounting excitement. A grand and gay time will be had by all, I am certain.

With regard to transport out to Craigdarragh, I have arranged for Grace to travel with the O'Rahilly twins, Jasmine and Briony, in the O'Rahillys' motor car. Reilly the chauffeur will see to it that they get themselves up to no mischief and are home by a decent hour.

Yours sincerely,
Janet Halloran

April 9, 1913

Clarecourt
Ballisodare
County Sligo

My Dear Edward,

I shall be only too delighted to accept your invitation to Craigdarragh House, and am honoured to learn that I will be the first recipient of the most eagerly awaited event in the astronomical world at the moment, the secret of Bell's Comet.

However, I fear that the fifteenth is impossible for me. I am required at the House of Lords for the reading of a piece of legislation close to my heart, the Irish Home Rule Bill, and what with trains and steam packets and the like, I must leave on or around the fourteenth. Would the twelfth be acceptable? Please let me know. I am most eager to visit, as this business in London will prevent me

from attending the meeting of the Royal Irish Astronomical Society. My intention is to travel on the train which
will arrive at Sligo Station at 6:16 P.M. I look forward to
seeing you then. Until the twelfth, then, my warmest
regards to you, your wife, and your charming daughter.

Sincerely,
Maurice: Clarenorris

Dr. Edward Garret Desmond's Personal Diary: April 12, 1913

Another domestic furore! Honestly, I am beginning to feel
I am no longer master of my own household! I bring the
Marquis of Clarenorris home from the station and what do
I find? My home and place of work overrun by shrieking,
silly schoolgirls! Caroline's idea—a surprise birthday tea
for Emily. Result, the house is in an uproar. Why was I not
informed of this? I am quite certain that I notified Caroline
of the changed dates of Lord Fitzgerald's visit. Sometimes
she seems to go out of her way to upset my plans and
arrangements.

To his endless credit, Lord Fitzgerald showcd no embarrassment at the girlish proceedings and indeed took the
whole debacle in exceedingly good spirit; nevertheless, I
was only too glad to hurry him out to the observatory,
where, with the aid of telescope and photographs, I took the
opportunity to explain to him my hypothesis concerning this
object erroneously named *Bell's Comet*. This he received
openly and without prejudice, asking me perceptive and
informed questions. However, it is more than the Marquis's
favourable ear I must win. I have need of his considerable
fortune also, if the second stage of my investigations, which
I have tentatively christened *Project Pharos*, is to be
brought to fruition.

Domestic memo: I must remind Mrs. O'Carolan to waken
Lord Fitzgerald at six thirty and provide him with a
substantial breakfast; the worthy Marquis has far to go
tomorrow. Also, I must have a man up from the town to

look at the electricals: tonight's unexpected current failure was somewhat disconcerting, and judging by the shrieks and cries from the drawing room, caused great distress to the young folk at the party.

Memorandum from Mrs. Caroline Desmond to Mrs. Maire O'Carolan

Dear Mrs. O'C,

Another one! Last night, just after supper, for the space of a good thirty minutes or so. Now I know, Mrs. O'C, that you know as much as I do about the mysteries of electricity, which is precisely nothing, but you have the advantage over me in knowing virtually every soul between here and Enniskillen. Would it be possible for you to find among this host of acquaintances and relatives *someone* who could come and have a look at the wiring or the junction box or whatever is the matter with the infernal thing? I do not, positively *not*, want a repeat of Tuesday's catastrophe. First Emily storms out in tears and tantrums muttering how *embarrassing* it all was, *little children's stuff*, and how she'd wanted *boys* there, like an *adult* party; not cakes and ginger ale and blindman's bluff. How sharper than a serpent's tooth, indeed, Mrs. O'C! And as if that wasn't enough, the lights go out and I am left trying to calm a roomful of hysterical, screaming girls. The trials of parenthood, Mrs. O'C. That aside, Mrs. O'C, do give it a try, will you? Edward promised to get a man up from town to do something on Wednesday, but you know how utterly useless he is about anything that isn't a million miles away in the depths of space. If you can't sort it out, it'll mean my tedious brother Michael calling out to have a look and going on and on and on about the grand all-electric future the Sligo, Leitrim, Fermanagh, and South Donegal Electrical Supply Company is going to provide for us. The man cannot even change an incandescent bulb!

Incidentally, only cold meats and salads for supper, if

you please; Emily and I will be over at Rathkennedy House all of today. We hope to be back here by about eight o'clock.

Excerpts from Dr. Edward Garret Desmond's Lecture to the Royal Irish Astronomical Society: Trinity College, Dublin, April 18, 1913

Therefore, learned gentlemen, it is clearly impossible for these fluctuations in luminosity to be due to the differing albedos of the spinning surfaces of Bell's Comet, as my mathematical proofs have demonstrated. The only—I repeat, *only*—explanation for this unprecedented phenomenon is that the emissions of light are artificial in origin.

(General consternation among the Learned Fellows)

If artificial, then we must address ourselves to the disturbing truth that they must, *must*, gentlemen, be the works of intellects, minds, Learned Fellows, immeasurably superior to our own. It has long been held that we are not the unique handiwork of our Creator; the possibility of great civilizations upon the planets Mars and Venus, and even beneath the forbidding surface of our own moon, has been many times mooted, even in this very lecture hall, by respected gentlemen of science and learning.

(Heckler: "Intoxicated gentlemen of absinthe and bourbon!" Laughter.)

What I am proposing, if I may, Learned Fellows, is a concept of a whole order of magnitude greater than even these lofty speculations. I am proposing that this artifact, for artificial it must be, is evidence of a mighty civilization *beyond our solar system,* upon a world of the star Altair, for it is from that quadrant of the sky that the object called Bell's Comet originates. Having ascertained that the object was indeed no lifeless chunk of stellar matter, I attempted to ascertain its velocity. As the Learned Fellows are doubtless all too aware, it is difficult in the extreme to calculate with absolute mathematical precision the velocity of any astronomical phenomenon; nevertheless, with persistence and application, I estimated the object's velocity to be in the close proximity of three hundred and fifty miles per second.

(Murmurs of amazement from the Learned Fellows)

Moreover, during the four-week period during which I kept the object under daily observation, or as regularly as the climate of County Sligo would permit, this velocity decreased from three hundred and fifty miles per second to one hundred and twenty miles per second. Clearly, the object is decelerating, and from such behaviour only one conclusion is possible—that the object is a spatial vehicle of some form, despatched by the inhabitants of Altair to establish contact with the inhabitants of our Earth.

(Heckler: "Oh, come now!")

While the exact design of such a spatial vehicle is beyond my conception, I have some tentative suggestions with regard to its motive power. That most estimable Frenchman, M. Jules Verne, has written most imaginatively . . .

(Heckler: "Not one half as imaginatively as you, sir!")

. . . thank you, sir, of how a great space gun might propel a capsule around the Moon. Intriguing though this notion is, it is quite impractical as a means to journey from Altair to our Earth. The velocity imparted by such a space gun would not be sufficient for the journey to be completed within the lifetimes of the voyagers.

(Heckler: "Will this lecture be completed within the lifetimes of the Learned Fellows?" Laughter.)

Therefore, I would suggest, if I might do so without interruption, Learned Fellows, that the vehicle accelerates and decelerates through a series of *self-generated explosions*, of titanic force, which propel the vehicle through transtellar space at the colossal velocities necessary to traverse such an immense distance. Of course, such starcrossing velocities must be shed to rendezvous with our Earth at the completion of the journey, and I would suggest that the immense flarings of light we have all witnessed are the explosions by which this vehicle slows its headlong flight.

(Heckler: "Are we in any seriousness meant to accept these fanciful vapourings over the Astronomer Royal's reasoned and cogent arguments?")

Learned Fellows, I cannot with any degree of scientific certainty speculate . . .

(Catcalls, booing. Heckler: "Scientific certainty? What scientific certainty?")

. . . what such a propulsive explosive might be; certainly no earthly explosive would possess sufficient power for its weight to be a practical fuel for such a transtellar journey.

(Heckler: "Oh, certainly!")

However, I have conducted a spectral analysis of the light from Bell's Comet and found it to be identical to the light of our own familiar Sun.

(Heckler: "Of course: it's reflected sunlight, man!")

Could it be that extrasolar stellanauts of Altair have learned to duplicate artificially the force that kindles the Sun itself and tamed it to power their vehicles?

(Heckler: "Could it be that the Member from Drumcliffe has learned to duplicate artificially the spirit of the mountain dew and used it to fuel his somewhat overwrought imagination?" Uproarious laughter.)

Learned Fellows . . . gentlemen . . . please, if you would pay me the courtesy of your attention. Since it is now clear that we are not unique in God's universe, it is therefore of paramount importance, even urgency, that we communicate with these representatives of a civilization immeasurably nobler than our own. Therefore, in September of this year, when Bell's Comet makes its closest approach to Earth . . .

(Heckler: "I don't believe it! Learned Fellows . . . a fact! A cold, hard fact!")

. . . I will attempt to signal the presence of intelligent life on this world *(laughter, growing louder)* to the extrasolar intelligences of Altair.

(General laughter and derision: cries of "Poppycock," "Shame," "Withdraw." A rain of pamphlets falls upon the platform. The president calls for order. There being none, he declares the meeting adjourned.)

Emily's Diary: April 22, 1913

It is all most unpleasant. Ever since Daddy's return from Dublin there has been the most horrid atmosphere in the house. He has locked himself up in his observatory and works as a man possessed, growling like an angry dog at the least annoyance. Mummy has warned me not to disturb him. She need not fear—I have no intention of going near him until his mood has sweetened. Whatever it was that happened in Dublin, it has so soured the atmosphere that my Easter has been quite spoiled.

Well, maybe not completely. Oh, this sounds foolish, this sounds like whimsy, but last night I looked out of my bedroom window and saw lights up on Ben Bulben, like the lights of many lanterns there on the slopes of the mountain, as if there were people dancing there by lantern light. When I was young, Mrs. O'Carolan told me that years ago, when a betrothal was announced, the people of the parish used to celebrate it by dancing in a ring around the Bridestone and the man and the woman would plight their troth by joining hands through the hole in the middle of the stone. Could what I saw have been a faery wedding? Could noble lords and ladies and moon-silver stallions have stood around to watch by faery light as the King of the Morning and the Queen of the Daybreak joined hands through the ancient troth stone? How wonderful, how romantic! As I leaned out to watch, I imagined I could hear the whinnying of those faery horses, and the playing of the elfin harpers and the gay laughter of the Host of the Air. *I do believe that there are strange and magical things in Bridestone Wood!* Real magic, magic of stone and sky and sea, the magic of the Old Folk, the Good Folk who dwell in the Halls Beneath the Hills, a magic we see, and feel, and touch . . . but just for a moment, and then it is gone again. How easily such things are lost! How easily the cold light of day dissolves away the magic of the night, like mist. This will be my last night in Craigdarragh; tomorrow I must return again to Cross and Passion. Though I love the other girls, even now I am counting the hours until I am home again in the greenwoods of Craigdarragh, under the wise shadow of ancient Ben Bulben, where the faery folk will be waiting for me.

April 26, 1913

Craigdarragh
Drumcliffe
County Sligo

My Dear Lord Fitzgerald,

I am deeply, deeply grateful for your letter of the twenty-fourth inst. in which Your Lordship pledged support for my project to communicate with the transtellar vehicle from Altair. I am glad that Your Lordship was spared the embarrassment of my humiliation before the Society: Christians to the lions, my dear Clarenorris, were none such as I in that lecture theatre. Yet, like those early martyrs, my faith is undiminished, my zeal for the successful persuance of Project Pharos is greater than ever: we shall teach these arrogant whippersnappers a thing or two when the star folk come! And I am delighted, no less honoured, to hear that Your Lordship has submitted a letter of support for my propositions to Sir Greville Adams, though I regret that, for all Your Lordship's cogent argument, it will achieve little: the gentlemen of Dublin are stunted in mind—intellectual dwarves compared to we revolutionary thinkers of the West.

Now ensured of support, we may proceed apace with Project Pharos. Enclosed are blueprints for the signalling device. Nevertheless, I will here summarise in my own hand the principles of said device, lest my enthusiasm in draughting the designs has rendered my diagrams a trifle hard to comprehend.

The device takes the form of a cross of floating pontoons supporting electrically powered lanterns. The cross must necessarily be of immense size: I have estimated that to be visible from the perigee position, the arms will have to be five miles in diameter. This of course necessitates the use of the pontoons. An artifact of such dimensions could never be constructed on land, but on sea it is a relatively simple task to construct on such a scale, and possesses the additional benefit of the signal being clearly distinguishable from the humbler lamps of civilization, namely, Sligo town. Electrical supply for the pontoons can be cheaply provided by my brother-in-law, Mr. Michael Barry, of the Sligo, Leitrim, Fermanagh, and South Donegal Electrical Supply Company. How useful it is to have relations in positions of influence!

Here, Your Lordship, I must beg leave to conclude. I once again thank you for your kind patronage of this experiment, which will surely be regarded by history as one of the epochal events of the millennium. I will keep Your Lordship closely informed of further developments, particularly with regard to the blueprints, which are in the hands of Gilbey, Johnson, and O'Brien, Architects, of Sligo town; and also of my efforts to compile a code with which to signal the presence of guiding intelligence to the Altairii, as I have termed our extrasolar visitors. Finally, I would wish God's richest blessing upon yourself and all at Clarecourt, especially the Lady Alexandra, who is never far from our affections here at Craigdarragh.

I remain,
Your Humble Servant,
Edward Garret Desmond, Ph.D.

Emily's Diary: May 26, 1913

Such a strange thing, today. I almost hesitate to set it down in these pages. I am still not certain that the whole incident was not a dream . . . Yes! I am certain. However strange, however uncanny, it happened, it was real, and I shall set it down for all time in these pages so that I will always remember that it happened.

I was up at the bower in the woods above Cross and Passion after evening chapel. It was lovely and bright, a gorgeous late evening, everything just as full of life as it

could be; bees and butterflies and birds and everything. I
thought I'd like to read some poetry. Mummy'd just sent me
one of Mr. Yeats's books of poems. With it in my hand I
slipped away across the back field. I'm sure no one saw me,
but I kept having that funny feeling you get when you are
sure someone is watching you but you can never catch who
they are. I would look behind me every so often, but I still
couldn't see anyone or anything. But I still kept getting that
peculiar prickling-between-the-shoulder-blades feeling. I
should have gone back then, I suppose. If I'd known then,
I would have.

Even in the bower the funny feeling would not go away.
Funny *feelings*. There was another one, sort of like the one
you get just before a thunderstorm, that something is going
to happen, as if every leaf, every flower, every blade of
grass is humming with a power that might at any moment
burst in release. But it wasn't a scary feeling, this other
one—not like the invisible eyes. It felt safe and comforting.

I was reading poetry from Mr. Yeats's book, and I must
have been far, far away in it, even with all the funny
feelings, because I never heard him coming up on me. All
of a sudden I heard the crashing of branches and leaves and
the light was cut off by this big shadow at the entrance to the
bower—the huge, horrible, frightening shadow of a man,
blocking the way. It was Gabriel, the groundsman's son. He
was standing there in front of me, looking at me. Not a
word did he say, not a muscle did he move. He just looked
at me, and that was horrible because the way he looked was
as if he was saying all the horrible, horrible things I knew
he wanted to do to me. I was too scared even to scream, let
alone move to get away from him. Everything was spinning
in front of me.

And then there was a sound, just like a bee buzzing
against my cheek. I felt a tiny puff of air, as if stirred by an
insect's wings, and there was an arrow between his feet.
Right between his feet, an arrow, out of nowhere. Then it
was as if he had seen the most awful thing he could
imagine. I have never seen such a look of shock and horror
ever before. I have never seen anyone run as fast as he ran
away, shrieking and screaming and wailing.

I looked behind me and still I cannot quite believe, dear

diary, what I saw. Standing there was a fair-haired man with a small harp. He had little rags tied all over him—in his hair, in his beard, to his clothes, to his arms, his legs, his toes, his fingers. Even his little harp had coloured rags tied to the tops of its strings. He was blind—I could see that at once. He had no eyes. He had never had eyes. Where eyes should have been, there was smooth skin growing over empty sockets.

Beside him was a red-haired woman dressed in a sort of harness made out of leather straps. She carried a huge bow as tall as she was, which was not very tall, smaller even than I am, and the wood of that bow was marvellously painted with spirals and twisted, twining animals. At her waist she wore a quiver of arrows.

I stared so long, diary—I just could not believe what I was seeing. Then, without a word, the blind man and the woman turned and walked away, back out of the bower, up into the woods, and I heard the song of the ragman's harp drifting on the still evening air.

As I have written, it all seems now like a dream, or a nightmare. I just don't know which is more disturbing—if it was real, or if it was a dream?

Dr. Edward Garret Desmond's Personal Diary: May 28, 1913

Work is proceeding apace on the signalling device. The labourers are addressing themselves to their tasks with an enthusiasm I would like to attribute to a desire to communicate with higher intelligences but I think is rather due to Lord Fitzgerald's generous purse; the little I have managed to scrape together from the estate is paltry in the extreme compared to the Clarenorris fortunes.

Already the first pontoon sections have been floated into Sligo Harbour and the lanterns tested and found to operate satisfactorily. Such successes are heartening after the delays and confusions of the early weeks. The plan is to assemble the cross from 170 pontoon sections, each one hundred

yards long. This sounds a daunting proposition, given the
sober truth that astronomical mechanics wait for no man,
but the sections have been largely preassembled in the town
boat yards and only remain to be floated and bolted into
their finished form. Observing the great legion of labourers
(of which there are no shortage in this poverty-blighted
county), I have no fear that Project Pharos will not be
completed by the time the extrasolar vehicle attains perigee.

My outstanding concern—that of devising a universally
comprehensible mode of communication with which to
converse with the Altairii—has recently been resolved to
my complete satisfaction. It is a universal truth that the laws
of mathematics are the same upon the worlds of Altair as
they are upon this one; to wit, the ratio of the circle's radius
to its circumference, which we call *pi*, must be as familiar
to the Altairii as to us. Therefore I have designed an
electrical relay whereby one arm of the cross will flash its
lights twenty-two times for the other's seven, this being the
approximate fractional ratio of *pi*. Such a signal cannot fail
to attract the attention of our stellanauts and pave the way
for more intimate conversation, a code for which I am
currently devising using primes and exponents.

May 31, 1913

Craigdarragh
Drumcliffe
County Sligo

My Dearest Constance,
    Just a brief note to express my thanks for your
generous invitation to the boating party at Rathkennedy.
Of course I shall be there. Few things are more delightful
to me than an afternoon on Lough Gill aboard *Grania*,
and, coupled with a reading by Mr. Yeats, you temptress,
how can I resist? Since our little soiree at the Gaelic
Literary League, I have looked for an opportunity to meet
him again. My dear Constance, wild horses wouldn't
keep me! I wonder, however, might I bring Emily? She
will shortly be returning for the summer, and I know

nothing would thrill her more than to hear Mr. Yeats reading his own incomparable verse. I sent her copies of *In the Seven Woods* and *The Green Helmet and Other Poems*, and she has devoured them as a starving man would a crust of bread! To actually meet this Olympian figure . . . I can assure you that she will be on her very best behaviour; no repeat of the histrionics at her birthday party. She conducts herself exceedingly well in adult company; quite the little charmer. It has been said by others that she reminds them of me, but it sometimes seems to me that she is a little too eager to grow up. Please do give it your consideration. Emily would be thrilled if it is acceptable. If the request is within your powers to grant, I will write to Emily to inform her, and I thank you once again for your kindness and hospitality. It will be good to meet Mr. Yeats again.

Yours Sincerely,
Caroline

Emily's Diary: June 29, 1913

Oh, to be in Craigdarragh now that summer's here! It is the little, magical things that make the summer for me: Michael and Paddy-Joe, Mrs. O'Carolan's sons, scything the front lawn; the sound of their scythes reaping the tall grass; the smell of bruised hay; the sagging tennis net run out for another year; old Dignan the gardener trying to creosote straight tram lines; the smell of sun-warmed wood and old, peeling paint in the summerhouse; the sound of opera from the garden when Mummy takes her big black deckchair with the sunshade, her phonogram and her workbooks out into the sunken garden (how she can work with people screaming at each other in Italian I do not know), the house filled with clicks and creaks and strange little animal sounds, as if it were stretching back into the life and heat of summer after months of hibernation; early morning light streaming through my window onto the counterpane; outside, the quiet rustle of the *Irish Times*. I always know that summer has truly arrived when Daddy has his alfresco breakfasts at the table by the rhododendrons. And just to make everything perfect, there is the promise of a boating trip on Lough Gill with Mummy's friend Mrs. Booth-Kennedy, and of actually meeting with Mr. William Butler Yeats, the greatest poet who ever lived! It is as if everything is in some great, benign conspiracy to make this the most perfect summer yet.

To prepare myself, I have been rereading all my copies of Yeats; sometimes aloud outside in the gardens, because they seem to perfectly match each other—the wonderful words, the magical summer. Poor Paddy-Joe and Michael, what must they think when they see the daughter of the house pirouetting, barefoot, among the rhododendrons, reciting *The Lake Isle of Innisfree*?

The weather is exceptional; since the day I came home from Cross and Passion there has not been one cloud in the sky. I love the weather when it is like this, when every day is the same as the one before and it seems that they will go on like this forever—day after day after day of perfect, unchanging blue, when the sun rises at four in the morning and sets so late that it never gets properly dark at all and the whole world seems suspended somewhere beyond time, changeless, like a flower in a glass paperweight. The air feels strangely charged, as if This World and the Other-world are at the closest points of their orbits and the friction of their passage is being translated into a lazy, sensual magic. It is quite impossible to concentrate on anything for more than a few minutes without my imagination flying away like mayflies above the minnow-burn—one minute hovering in one place, the next, somewhere else, so fast you would think they had the gift of instantaneous movement. With everything so pregnant and potential, it seems impossible that there has been no faery manifestation; yet every day since I came home I have gone into Bridestone Wood, expecting, hoping, *wanting* to see something. But there is nothing! Not even that sensation of *watching* I remember from the spring, and again, that time in the bower, just before. . . .

Perhaps the problem is that I am expecting too hard. Faeries have always been tricksome, flighty creatures.

Maybe when I stop wanting something to happen, then something will happen, but oh, how difficult it is not to want the thing which deep down in your heart you want more than anything.

Mummy has been working in the garden—how, in this heat, I don't know. All I want to do is flop about in a sun frock, but she is hard at it, researching a book. Not a book of poetry this time, she told me, but a proper book, a serious book. It will be called *The Twilight of the Gods*, she thinks, and it will be about how Christianity has dethroned the old, elemental gods of the Celts, first driving them underground to become the Host of the Hollow Hills, the *sidhe*; and ultimately, to reduce them into leprechauns and pookahs and brownies and Trooping Faeries. That seems to me like a sad and terrible end for the old gods who could be many things at once—young and old, male and female, human and animal. Much better, I told Mummy, for them all to have died in some great and noble last battle than to dwindle and shrivel like the old generals at Kilmainham Hospital with their medals and bath chairs, changed into green-gaitered pixies guarding crocks of gold. Mummy agreed, but said that the secret of the Old Gods was that they were never totally defeated by Christianity; they merely changed form again and went more deeply into the land. Irish Catholicism, she maintained, contains many elements that are not Christian at all but stem directly from the old pagan religions. Many Irish saints are just old gods and goddesses sealed with the Pope's stamp of respectability, and the so-called Holy Wells, like the one at Gortahurk where Mrs. O'Carolan goes for her rheumatism, are nothing more than old Celtic votive sites to the water spirits. Old sacrificial stones were often decorated over with new Christian symbols. There is a standing stone in a village in County Fermanagh where an old deity has been converted into a bishop, complete with bell, crozier, and mitre! And many of the Church festivals, including Christmas, Michaelmas, and Halloween, are the old Celtic festivals of Lughnasadh and Samhain, Christianized, tamed and stripped of their old pagan power, like lions in a circus with their teeth pulled.

So sad, that the great days of the gods and fighting men should have dwindled away to nothing. But when I think about it more, I can see Mummy's point—perhaps Christianity, in all its arrogance, did not succeed in putting a ring through their noses and leading them down the aisle to kneel before the cross. Perhaps it liberated them from the shapes and characters people had forced upon them, and allowed them to be at last what they wanted to be, free from the cares and responsibilities of the world to hunt and play once again through the endless forests of Otherworld.

If Otherworld was never lost, merely hidden as if it had pulled a sky-coloured cloak around it, then perhaps it may still be attainable to those with the sensitivity to seek it. Perhaps it is close at hand to those who sincerely desire it.

And then, today, confirmation. The woods were smothering: the leaves seemed to trap the heat beneath them in a dense, stifling blanket. Bridestone Wood was filled with a sense of exhausted stillness—not a bird sang, not a leaf stirred. The only motion in the entire wood was the drifting balls of thistledown turning lazily in the still, thick air. There was a spirit in the trees I could not name—not the feeling of watching, nor the electric prickle of something about to happen. A more diffuse sensation of waiting seemed to draw me deeper into the wood until I came at last to a small glade I am quite sure I have never seen before. Bridestone Wood is not a very big wood—a few acres on the side of Ben Bulben—and I was certain I knew its every nook and cranny, but this glade was new and unfamiliar to me. Here the air was so still and heavy it seemed almost that I parted a curtain as I entered the dell. The leaves of the oaks light-dappled the carpet of grass; one shaft of hazy, dusty light illuminated a small mossy stone. On top of the stone I found them—two pairs of wings, like a butterfly's, though no butterfly ever flew on wings so large, so delicate. Like dragonfly's wings, they seemed, like lace, finer than the finest Kenmare needlepoint, and the precise colour of oil on water.

Faery wings. I imagined a tiny figure, no larger than my hand, climb up on this rock, drop a pair of old, used-up wings to the moss; imagined the new, crumpled buds of new wings unfolding from her shoulders, opening, drying in the sun as she sat there, waiting, fluttering them from time to time until they were strong enough that, with a soft whirr, she would leap from the stone and be carried away into the leaf-dapple.

I carried them home and pressed them between the pages of a botany book. I pondered about whether to tell Mummy. She had been brought frequently to Craigdarragh as a child—her mother and Daddy's mother were cousins. I wonder, did she ever see things in the woods—strange, wonderful things, things from a world not ours at all, but altogether more wonderful and magical. I think this because when I read her poetry, I can see the magic in it—I can hear the faraway horns and hear the baying of the hounds of the Wild Hunt. I think Mummy must have experienced something, but like the old standing stones she told me about, her childhood glimpses of Otherworld must have become overlain with the trappings and ornaments of this world. That is why she writes about them in her poems and books; only there can she hear the horns of Elfland blowing from faraway.

Dr. Edward Garret Desmond's Personal Diary: July 2, 1913

I pause here in my records of Project Pharos (which is proceeding to my complete satisfaction, though I have not yet received replies to one-tenth of the invitations I have sent to prominent members of the astronomical community to witness the greatest event of this, or, dare I say? any other age: the establishment of communications with a race from another world) to comment upon a lesser matter, of a personal nature, which is causing me not inconsiderable distraction. I refer, of course, to the increasingly irrational behaviour of my daughter Emily. Since her return from Dublin she has floated around Craigdarragh as if in a daydream, paying only the scantest attention to her father and his epochal work, her head filled rather with fantastic notions about faeries and mythological creatures haunting Bridestone Wood. I can not comprehend, much less tolerate, my daughter's absolute insistence upon the objective truth of these fantastical notions. And as if this were not enough, she has now intimated to me that she wishes to borrow one of my portable cameras with which I am charting the progress of the Altairii vessel to take a series of photographs of these "faery folk" at play in the woods around the demesne. Is she doing this out of spite for me and my rational, scientific philosophy of life in a pique of adolescent rebellion? We had the most fearful row, Emily insisting that she was not a little girl any longer, that she was a woman and that I treat her accordingly; I arguing with gentle persuasiveness and calm rationality that to be treated like a woman, she cannot revel in childish hysteria. Alas, nothing was resolved, and I fear that, as in every other decision regarding our daughter, Caroline will refuse to support me and side with Emily.

But that I had more time to spend with Emily! Maybe then she would not have wandered heedless into these realms of fantasy and whimsy! I fear I have not of late been a proper father to her, but the advent of the star folk of necessity turns all our human relationships on their heads.

Finally, the electrical fluctuations that bedevilled the house at Easter have resumed and are more frequent and of longer duration. I shall have to have words with Mr. Michael Barry of the Sligo, Leitrim, Fermanagh, and South Donegal Electrical Supply Company, and with his dour employee, Mr. MacAteer. The disruptions to my work at this advanced stage of the experiment are bad enough. What is intolerable is that the electrical supply for the pontoon lanterns should be unreliable, and fail at the most inopportune moments!

Finally, and I mean quite finally, as in the proverbial dromedary's straw, for several weeks the tenant farmers have been complaining of attacks on their poultry runs—as if I were somehow responsible for their domestic security. Well, what do I discover this morning but that the same damn vermin has broken into the Craigdarragh pens, and in an act of sheer, wanton destruction, ripped the heads off five birds. As if my burden were not heavy enough. Alas, I have not the time for a detailed investigation of the distractions; the demands of the Altairii are paramount.

Emily's Diary: July 3, 1913

Yesterday was the hottest day yet; it was so unbearable in the gardens that we were forced inside, where it was at least tolerable. Only Daddy seemed unaffected by the heat, bustling around on his funny businesses like it was a cool April morning and not the hottest day of the century (so the *Irish Times* said), while Mummy and I flopped around expiring on sofas, begging Mrs. O'C to bring us *another* jug of iced lemonade.

It was too hot to sleep last night. After what seemed like hours of tossing and turning and trying to force myself to go to sleep (which only makes you all the more awake), I gave up the struggle and got up. There was still light in the sky. Whether it was the light of the sun just set or about to rise I do not know: all the clocks in my room had stopped at different times. There was a bright moon, just past full. I don't know what made me open the window; perhaps I hoped for a cool and refreshing breeze off the mountains, but if anything, the air outside was heavier and more stifling than in my bedroom. Everything was purple and lilac and silver, and still; so still. It seemed like a midsummer night's dream come true.

Then it was as if a silent voice had called my name: *Emily.* I had to go out there, into the night. I had to. I remember noticing that the Westminster chimes on the landing had stopped at ten to two. As I tiptoed downstairs and out the french windows in the dining room, I heard the voiceless voice call again: *Emily.* Outside, the air seemed to embrace me. The perfume of flowers was overpowering—gardenias, night-scented stock, honeysuckle, jasmine. Everything was as still and silent as if time itself had stopped, not the Craigdarragh clocks. I crossed the sunken garden and the tennis court. Where clematis, sweet pea, and hollyhock screened off the summerhouse, I stopped. I could feel the compulsion inside me, but I resisted. It was a foolish thing to do, for the more I resisted, the stronger and stronger it grew, until it overwhelmed me. I untied my shoulder bows and stepped out of my nightgown. As I did, it seemed to me that the entire garden had been holding its breath and now released it in a gentle sigh. I did not feel ashamed, or afraid—not then. I felt free, I felt elemental, I felt as if I was not naked at all but wrapped in a cloak of sky.

The voiceless voice called me toward the gazebo, grey and silver and shadow in the moonlight. Under the eaves glowworm lights flocked and buzzed. But these were not glowworms, for glowworm lights are cold green and these were blue and silver and gold. It seems strange now (many things seem strange now about that night, though they seemed as natural as air then), but I was not afraid. The voiceless voice called me forward again, and as I drew closer, the lights swarmed away from the summerhouse eaves and hung in a moving, dancing cloud before me. I gingerly stretched out a hand—not in fear for myself, but rather that I might frighten them away. One detached itself from the flock and settled onto my palm. It allowed me to lift it up in front of my face, and I saw that it was not an insect at all but a tiny, tiny winged girl, no larger than a fly, glowing all over with silvery-blue light. Then she leapt from my hand and the cloud of lights moved away from me, between the screens of hollyhocks, toward the rhododendron garden and the woods beyond. I followed on; I had no doubt that I was being led.

The faery lights led me over the stile across the demesne wall and into Bridestone Wood. And there the magic, so long anticipated, so deeply desired, was waiting for me. Bridestone Wood was alive as I have never known it before— every twig, every leaf, every blade of grass breathed the old magic of stone and sea and sky. My heart hammered in my breast and my breath faltered, so strong was the call to come away, come away. The lights led me onward, inward. The woods were thick with floating thistledown which brushed softly past my body. The perfume of green growing things was as overpoweringly heady as the flowers in the Craig-darragh gardens. The grass beneath my bare feet sparkled with dew but I did not feel cold—I did not feel anything except the need to penetrate deeper, closer. And the deeper I went into the wood, the faery lights increased in number. There were glowing sparkles in bush and tree and leaf, and more than lights. Half glimpsed in the shadows and the faery flicker, then gone again, I thought I could distinguish faces and forms, half human, half plant—faces like open flowers, like leaves, like patches of silver lichen and wrinkled bark. Onward I went, and inward. I cannot now recall the specific moment when I became aware of their presence; their manifestation must have been gradual—a slow stirring together out of air and moonlight and shadow. At first I thought they were night birds or bats—they were close, but not so close as for me to be able to make them out clearly. Then they were all around me, clinging to the harebells and the brambles and the ivy and the branches of the trees, springing into the air as I pushed past: the faeries.

They were of a size that would stand comfortably in the palm of my hand. All were naked and as innocent as babes in Eden. Of course faeries, like angels, know neither shame nor conscience, though I was surprised to see that they were not all female, as I had always thought. They had both females and males. The males were wild, eldritch little creatures, with pointed ears and teeth; dark slits of eyes, like cats; and a great fierce mane of dark hair. Their wings were like those of bats, as opposed to the sheer gossamer ones of the females. For their small size, they seemed to have disproportionately large genitalia. Also the females, though altogether more delicate and diaphanous, each possessed large pairs of breasts that hung almost to the waist.

In my spellbound state, I did not realise how far I had come—to a place on the side of Ben Bulben where a rock face had, at some distant time in the past, broken and littered the slopes with large, sharp-edged boulders. In the dell at the foot of the cliff, among the moss-covered rocks, the guiding cloud of faery lights dispersed to roost on the branches of the trees, as if a constellation of stars had fallen from heaven and caught there. I looked around, not certain what to expect; then, from afar, I heard the silver notes of a harp. And suddenly, I could see them. All of them, everywhere. Suddenly every flower was a face, every stone a pair of eyes. I saw the leprechaun on his cobbler's stool amid the cool moss of the dell. I saw the pookahs—creatures the length of my forearm with the body of a boy

and the head of a horse—capering agilely through the trees.
Among the roots squatted things like tiny fauns, with the
legs and horns of a ram and bright, human eyes. In the
distance I saw the figures of the woman archer and the blind
harper, whose music filled Bridestone Wood, floating like
the drifting thistledown through the trees. And beyond
them, almost hidden by the moon shadows, were the Lords
of the Ever-Living Ones: the antlered helmets of the Wild
Hunt, the moon-silvered spearpoints of the Host of Sidhe.
The music swelled until the woods rang and I felt my heart
would burst. And then there was silence—profound, absolute silence, and stillness. And far off, among the trees,
there was a golden glow. It drew nearer, and as it approached, the host of the faeries let out a bubbling murmur
of awe. Heads bowed, knees bent, spear points touched the
moss. The golden glow entered the clearing and I saw that
it was a wheel. It was five-spoked, much as I have always
imagined a chariot wheel to be, rolling by its own power. It
rolled toward me, enveloping me in its golden glow. I felt
an overwhelming need to kneel before it. Inside the light I
saw that the wheel was not just one thing, but many things
at once: a golden salmon, a spear of light, a swan with a
silver chain around its neck, a radiantly beautiful man with
the green branch of a tree in his hand. The words of wonder
and awe seized in my throat. I reached out a hand to touch
the magic and mystery. The golden light blazed up before
me . . . and the next thing I remember, I was back again
beside the summerhouse where I had dropped my nightgown, alone and naked and cold. My feet were like two
blocks of ice in the heavy dew. It is strange, but I remember
feeling guilty and embarrassed as I pulled on my nightgown. The sky was beginning to lighten to the east; dawn
would soon be rising over Glencar. I shivered and shuddered in the cold before the morning.

I do remember one more thing. As I slipped back through
the french windows up to my room again, all the clocks I
passed stood at quarter to four.

Emily's Diary: July 7–12, 1913

The good weather broke last night in a tremendous thunderstorm. It started unassumingly enough—just rumbles and grumbles out beyond Knocknarea—then the sky gradually filled with black and before we knew it, lit up with lightning. The thunder rattled the windows and the storm was upon us. I have never seen the like before, trapped and roaring in the glens and valleys around Ben Bulben. Mrs. O'C was sure the world was going to end, and every time the thunder roared, I found myself agreeing with her.

It definitely spelled the end of the marvellous weather. When I looked out my window this morning the mountain was covered in grey cloud and a dismal, dreary rain was falling. I was stuck in the house all day doing jigsaws in the library and playing with the cat. How easily entertained are cats! A little scrap of wool and they are amused for hours. Lucky cats. I am bored, tired from doing nothing, and depressed. When the weather broke, it felt like the magic broke with it. Was it all just a Midsummer Night's Dream?

July 8

Still raining. Looks like it will never end. How much rain can there be in a cloud? I had always imagined that as they rained, clouds dwindled until eventually they rained themselves away to nothing. Evidently not.

I've been thinking—about the faeries; about the magical Otherworld so close to our own, and yet so far away; about what Mummy said about the Old Gods not really dying, only changing into the shapes of their enemies. All sorts of thoughts whirled around in my head like a kaleidoscope, wanting to fall together into a pattern that would make sense—a theory, a *hypothesis* (Daddy would be pleased. Here I am, thinking like a scientist)—but they wouldn't. It is as if there is one magical, golden key that holds them all together and I cannot find it.

One positive thing out of today: after all my badgering and beavering (like the drop of water that wears away the mighty stone, as Daddy keeps reminding me), and, I don't doubt, a little help from Mummy (I'm sure I heard voices raised in the breakfast room when I got up this morning), Daddy has relented and let me have the use of one of his cameras—a leather-bound brown folding portable.

July 9

On appearances only, today is no better than yesterday, but I could feel a change in the air, in that same way you know by feel when it is going to clear up and when it is going to rain all day. By three o'clock there were patches of blue coming in from the Atlantic, and, miracle of miracles, the odd stray beam of watery sunlight. These were still far from perfect conditions, but I had no intention of losing another moment to the weather. Armed with camera and notebook, I went up into Bridestone Wood to hunt faeries. Nothing. They must be even more sensitive to the elements than we are. It was not a totally fruitless day. At teatime I noticed, as if for the first time, the carved Dutch wooden globes Daddy keeps on the dining room mantelpiece. They are hollow wooden balls painted with old maps of the world which open like Russian dolls so that the smaller globes nestle within the larger. Noticing them made something go click! in my head and all those thoughts and ideas that had been flying around loose in there began to fall together.

July 10

No faeries today, either. But I could feel them as I have never felt them before at Craigdarragh—that spooky, electrical sense of *presence*.

I am developing a theory about the faery: it is that our world and Otherworld lie one inside the other, like the concentric spheres of the carved Dutch globes, along different planes of being. In many ways they are alike, though I think that to us, Otherworld seems a little smaller than our world. Perhaps to Otherworld it is our world that seems the smaller. Both follow the same path around the Sun, and (here lies the significant difference) both turn, but at very different rates. In our world a day is twenty-four hours long; in Otherworld, a day can be a year from dawn to sunset. Daddy would be pleased with my next piece of reasoning: I consulted the atlas in the library and thought it all out very scientifically. Because the periods of rotation are different, there may be times when our world's axis is inclined at a different angle from that of Otherworld, with the result that the surface of Otherworld touches, then passes through, the surface of our world. This area of intersection starts as a point, increases to a circle. Then, as the orbits progress and the axial tilts come back into line again, the zone of interpenetration diminishes again to a point. This, I think, is why Otherworld has always been associated with things of the earth—with hollow hills and the underworld. Mummy's book makes the point that the legendary entrances to Otherworld have always been through caves and lakes. It would also explain why supernatural events are associated with the equinoxes and solstices—because it is at those dates that the shift of the axes occurs! I think that the geography of Otherworld must be very different from our World. I think there is much less sea, much more land—the Otherworldly Tir Nan Og is always placed in the far west, where we have only the empty Atlantic.

The more I think about my theory, the more it opens up before me, just like one of the magic gates to Otherworld, the moon-shadowed path that leads to the Land of Ever-Youth. I am so excited, it is as if after a long, hard climb, I have come to a high vista from which I can look out over a whole new landscape.

July 11

The weather is better, brighter; there is a strong breeze off the Atlantic carrying fast white clouds upon it. I went up to the wood with a sense of expectation and was not disappointed. I saw a pookah—one of the little horse-headed men. It took me quite by surprise—all of a sudden, it just appeared out of the brambles. By the time I had recovered

from the surprise and unfolded the camera, it had vanished.
But at least I know that they are around. Better luck
tomorrow.

I am thinking today about the faeries—how in the old
days there were many manifestations of the same person;
how they could be a salmon and a rowan and an eagle and
a great golden cauldron all at the same time. This leads me
to wonder if maybe these latter-day faeries—the pookahs
and the leprechauns and the Trooping Faeries—are also
forms of the same mythological characters. But they seem
to me much less highly sophisticated than the early,
elemental personas, almost as if they have degenerated
rather than developed. This seems strange to me, so I have
been doing a little more reading. The Teaching Sisters
would be horrified if they knew I had been reading Charles
Darwin; yet it was to his *Origin of Species* (strangely
enough, one of Mummy's contributions to the library, rather
than Daddy's) I went for help. What I read there only
confirmed my suspicions. Creatures do not devolve into less
sophisticated forms, but evolve into more developed, gen-
eralised ones. Which leads me, dear diary, to my most
startling conclusion yet. These smaller, more specialised
species of faery are the early, primitive, less evolved forms;
the ancient, elemental shape-shifters who were many bodies
with one person, they are the later, more highly evolved
manifestations. Which can only lead to one conclusion:
*Time in Otherworld runs in the opposite direction to the way
it does in our world.*

July 12

Success today! In the morning, I came up quietly on a group
of Trooping Faeries at their toilet, washing themselves in
the late dew still lying in the bells of foxgloves, and
managed to take a couple of photographs. I cannot say if
they will come out—I am no photographer—but I hope so
much they will. It is so important that I have evidence. I
received the impression that the faeries knew I was there
and *allowed* me to photograph them. But, if time runs
the other way in Otherworld, then what I did will already

have happened to them; to them, the time I start to take photographs is the time I suddenly stop.

The whole of Bridestone Wood feels strange today, as if it were not the place I have grown up beside to know and love, but a part of the ancient wildwoods of Otherworld somehow imposed onto our world. The trees seem very tall, the air full of the sounds of birds—raucous calls, flapping wings.

After luncheon I glimpsed the faery archer. This time there was no misunderstanding; she knew I was there and waited, smiling, for a full minute while I fumbled with the camera before she went leaping off through the undergrowth. Toward teatime, I stumbled across the trail of the Wild Hunt itself and followed them for the better part of half an hour. Alas, all I will doubtless have to show for my efforts will be a few blurred images of antlers silhouetted against the sky.

I am thinking about what I said yesterday about time running the other way in Otherworld. It seems to me that this might be an explanation for the mechanics of *magic*, though it makes my head spin, thinking too long about it. For example, we *wish* for something in our present (which is the same as the faeries' present, this point where our worlds pass each other). The answer comes in our future, which is their past, because the faeries, in their future, which is our past, cause things to change about and set events in motion so that at the proper time—in our future, their past—that wish will come true. This is why magic is just what it is—*magic;* why there is no apparent link between cause and effect, because, in our direction of time, there isn't, but to the faeries, everything is done in accordance with their arrow of time, and their laws of cause and effect. In their past, they see the effect, the wish comes true, and so in their future, they must arrange things so the past comes true. But I have the feeling that the faeries are not as strictly bound by the laws of past and present as we are; that is why, in our world, they can be both future and past forms, because they can be whatever they have remembered they were, and whatever they hoped to become.

See? I said it made my head spin if I thought too long and hard about it.

July 22, 1913

Rathkennedy
Breffni
County Sligo

My Dearest Hanny,

A thousand and one apologies. It is much much too long since I last wrote to you, much less saw you. The fault, I fear, is entirely mine, and I cannot even plead having been up to the proverbials in work. Alas, I am purely and simply the world's worst at writing letters.

Anyway, customary salutations to you, your health, your wealth, your happiness etc., and without further ado, I shall get down to the real meat of this epistle.

My dear Hannibal, you really *must* drop whatever you are doing *at once* and come up to Sligo. There is something happening here that is so extraordinary and exciting that . . .

I am getting ahead of myself. Much less confusing if I were to spell things out in the natural order in which they occurred. Freddie says I am always doing that, rushing off everywhere and nowhere at once.

As you may know, the other Constance, my cousin on the Gore-Booth side of the family, had invited William Butler Yeats up to Lissadell for a few weeks. Well, of course, what with us being Brethren in Arms of the Gaelic Literary League and Green Flag Nationalists, I couldn't let the occasion go unmarked. So I had Beddowes and the boys from the estate buff up the brasswork and slap a lick of paint on old *Grania* (you remember? The venerable family steam launch) and throw a little boating-party cum picnic cum poetry reading. Among the *literati* I'd invited was Caroline Desmond (yes, *those* Desmonds, though she has nothing to do with that contraption bobbing up and down in Sligo Bay) and her daughter Emily, already at her tender years an ardent admirer of Willie's poetry and philosophy. Yes, contrary to what you may have read in the newspapers, there is some sanity and good taste in the household, needless to say, all firmly attached to the distaff. Well, the day went capitally. The weather was perfect, old *Grania* chugged along without bursting a boiler, no one decided to bless the lough with seasickness, Beddowes didn't have to fish any of the old spinsters of the League out of the drink with a fishhook, Willie was his usual Olympian self, the wine was actually *cool* this time, no one was ill from overeating and heatstroke at the picnic on Innisfree, etc. Nothing out of the ordinary here, you are thinking. Patience, my dear Hanny. Patience. It wasn't until *Grania* was within sight of the Rathkennedy landing stage that the maroon went up. Willie had, inevitably, gathered a small group of sycophants around him and was regaling them with some learned gobbledygook about Celtic mysticism and the New Age when out of absolutely nowhere, Hanny, this Desmond girl, little Emily, produced a set of photographs which she claimed show legendary creatures inhabiting the woods around her home. Well, of course, with the ensuing uproar, I had to see what the excitement was about. Poor Willie was almost apoplectic, and, well, I hesitate to use stronger words, bless me! if she wasn't telling the truth. Ten photographs, and notes on where, when, and how taken, down even to the prevailing weather conditions! Some, I will admit, left a lot to the imagination—patches of shadow that could as easily have been the branches of trees as the antlers and spear points of the Wild Hunt of Sidhe which they were claimed to be. But others were less equivocal—two of a brazen hussy dressed only in leather straps, carrying a bow the size of herself, with a smile somewhere between the Giaconda's and a Montgomery Street madam's. More convincing yet, one showed a congregation of six little woodland nymphs washing themselves, for the love of heaven, Hanny! in the petals of a foxglove. And, most irrefutable of all, the final two in the sequence—the first, of a little naked mannequin with the head of a horse, and one of herself smiling at a tiny, winged woman sitting in the palm of her hand, combing her long hair with minuscule fingers.

My dear Hanny, what can I say! I have seen the evidence myself and I am convinced of its veracity. Had it been presented by an accomplished photographer, I might have hesitations, but these are the handiwork of a fifteen-year-old girl!

Well, of course, Willie has been in a fine old flap ever since, and wants to arrange a series of interviews, preferably under hypnosis, with Emily to finally prove the existence of a mystical world apart from, but adjacent to, our own. Even before I heard the word *hypnosis* mentioned, I had thought of you, Hanny; after all, you are the country's leading investigator of the strange and supernatural. Willie hasn't the first idea about mesmerism, let alone how to go about an investigation scientifically, so I suggested you to him with a few of your credentials and he insisted that you be in attendance. I know you'll hardly need asking twice, but please hold your horses one moment before throwing things into cases, telephoning the station, etc., and I'll summarise the arrangements.

Caroline Desmond has suggested the weekend of the twenty-seventh of this month as a provisional date. Telegram me, will you, and let me know if it is acceptable. She's offered to accommodate you, but I said there was more room at Rathkennedy, and anyway, we were old friends. Hanny, dearest, there's too much we have to talk about! *Do* say you can make it—I'm dying to see you again. It must be over three years since our paths last crossed.

Erin Go Bragh!
Connie

Excerpts from the Craigdarragh Interviews: July 27, 28, 29, 1913, as Transcribed by Mr. Peter Driscoll, Ll.B., of Sligo.

(The first interview: 9:30 P.M., July 27. In attendance: Mr. W. B. Yeats, Mr. H. Rooke, Mrs. C. Desmond,

Miss E. Desmond, Mrs. C. Booth-Kennedy, Mr. P. Driscoll. Weather: windy, with some rain.)

Yeats: You are quite certain that Emily is in the hypnotic trance and receptive to my questioning, Mr. Rooke?

Rooke: Quite sure, Mr. Yeats.

Yeats: Very well, then. Emily, can you hear me?

Emily: Yes, sir.

Yeats: Tell me, Emily, have those photographs you have shown me been falsified in any way?

Emily: No, sir.

Yeats: The recorder will note that scientific research has proved that it is impossible for a subject to lie under hypnosis. So these are genuine pictures of faery folk, then?

(No reply.)

Rooke: You must question the subject directly, Mr. Yeats.

Yeats: Forgive me, a momentary lapse of memory. I repeat, Emily, are these photographs actual representations of supernatural beings? Faeries?

Emily: Faeries? Of course they are faeries—the Old Folk, the Ever-Living Ones.

Yeats: The recorder will let it show that the subject, on being questioned a second time on the veracity of the photographs, again verified their genuiness. Therefore, having established the validity of the photographs, could you tell me, Emily, on how many occasions these photographs were taken?

Emily: Three occasions. Once in the morning. Twice in the early afternoon. Three days. Then . . .

Yeats: Go on, Emily.

Emily: It was as if they didn't want me to take any more photographs of them. They were distant and aloof, like there was a cloud over the sun. They drew apart from me, hid themselves in the wood. I haven't seen them now in many days, Oh, why do they hide themselves from me? I only want to be their friend.

Yeats: Thank you, Emily. That will be all, for now.

Rooke: Excuse me, Mr. Yeats, one moment. Might I ask

a couple of questions before we close? Emily, on what date did the first manifestation occur?

Emily: The first night was the sixth of July. I remember—I wrote it in my diary. It was the last night of the very hot weather. I'd been home from Cross and Passion about ten days. I heard them call my name, and when I went out to look, the garden was full of lights. They led me into the wood. I'd never imagined there were so many of them, or that they were so beautiful.

Rooke: And can you remember what the state of the moon was that night?

Emily: I remember it was very bright—just past full. But oh so bright!

Rooke: July the sixth. I would estimate about thirty minutes past full. Hmm. And the dates of the subsequent manifestations, Emily?

Emily: The eleventh, twelfth, and thirteenth.

Rooke: Thank you, Emily. Back to you, Mr. Yeats. I have no further questions.

(The second interview: 9:50 P.M., July 28. In attendance: as above. Weather: wind gusting from the west, with showers.)

Yeats: This encounter you mentioned yesterday (*consulting notes*) on the night of the sixth of July—was this your first experience of this nature?

Emily: No.

Yeats: There have been . . . forgive me . . . have there been others?

Emily: Yes. One other.

Yeats: Would you tell us about it?

Emily: It was at school, up in Rathfarnham Woods. I'd always felt that they were there, up in the woods. At night I could hear them hunting. I could hear their dogs hunting, I could hear the jingle of bells from their horse bridles and falcon jesses . . . hunting. It was up in the dell.

Yeats: The dell?

Emily: (seeming to grow impatient) Yes, the dell. My dell, my place, my private place where I could be alone with myself, where I could shut away Cross and Passion and the Teaching Sisters and be still enough to feel the magic.

Yeats: Please, continue.

Emily: There was danger there, from the one who had sent me letters, the one who said he loved me. They came and they drove him away before he could hurt me.

Yeats: What—the faeries? I don't understand. Emily?

Emily: One was the archer woman, the one I took a photograph of. She was as close to me as you are. Her bow was taller than she was. She isn't very big, you see, even smaller than I am, and I remember she had an arrow nocked. She fired it at him—not to hurt him, but to scare him—and he ran away. The other was the harper. The blind harper. It is as if he was born without any eyes. There is only blank skin where the eyes should be. He's very tall and thin, and he has little rags and ribbons tied all over him—to his fingers, his beard, his hair, the strings of his harp, everywhere. I used to wonder why he had those little rags tied all over him, but now I see! They're to help him see where he's going. They're like a cat's whiskers—; they're moved by the wind and the leaves and the branches and can feel the diffcrent movements and know where he is. *(Murmurs of amazement in the room. Here several persons began to speak at once but were hushed by Mr. H. Rooke.)*

Rooke: And could you possibly tell me upon what date this . . . ah . . . event occurred?

Emily: It was the second of April.

Rooke: I see. That's most interesting. Excuse me, Mrs. Desmond, but I presume that your husband, being in the line of investigation that he is, would be in the possession of such a thing as an astronomical almanac or calendar? Could I possibly ask the loan of it for a minute or two? *(Here Mrs. C. Desmond retired to the library to fetch said almanac.)* Thank you. Let me see,

the second of April, 1913 . . . damnation, what's
happening?

C. Desmond: I'm so sorry—it's another of those pesti-
lential electrical failures I mentioned to you yesterday.
Mrs. O'Carolan . . . Mrs. O'Carolan, lamps, please.
If you wish, we may continue by lamplight.

Rooke: Thank you, Mrs. Desmond, but before I can
further pursue my inquiries, I have a little research I
need to do, and, unless Mr. Yeats has anything further
he wants to ask, I rather think we have put poor Emily
through quite enough for one evening.

(The third interview: 3:30 P.M., July 29, 1913. Present:
as above, with the addition of Dr. E. G. Desmond.
Weather: cloudy, threatening rain from the West.)

Emily: (her face ecstatic) Oh, can't you hear them? Can't
you feel them? Oh, I thought I'd lost them, affronted
them, and they'd hidden themselves away from me,
but they've returned, they've come for me. Oh, can't
you hear them, calling through the woods and glens,
across the mountainsides? They are the fairest of the
fair, the sons of Danu; there are none to compare with
the comeliness of the dwellers in the hollow hills: no
son of Milesius, no daughter of proud Maeve aslumber
on cold Knocknarea. Their cloaks are of scarlet wool,
their tunics of fine Greek silk. Upon their breasts they
wear the badge of the Red Branch Heros, upon their
brows circlets of yellow gold; their skin is as white as
the milk of mares, their hair as black as the raven's
wing. The glint of iron spear points is in their eyes and
their lips are as red as blood. Fair they are, the sons of
Danu, but none so fair or so noble as Lugh of the Long
Hand. Strong-thewed he is, golden-maned, golden-
skinned; clad in the green and the gold of the Royal
Dun of Brugh-na-Boinne. He is Lugh, King of the
Morning, Master of the Thousand Skills. There is none
to compare with him in music or archery, poetry or the
feats of war, the hunt, or the tender accomplishments

of love. (*Here Dr. Desmond blushed.*) We are riders on the wings of morning, he and I, dancers in the starlit halls of Tir Nan Og. And with the sun setting we rise in the shape of swans, joined at the necks by chains and collars of red red gold, and journey through the night to the Land of Sunrise where we embark again upon our wondrous journey of love. We have tasted the hazelnuts of the Tree of Wisdom. We have been many things, many shapes—wild swans upon the Lake of Coole, two arbutuses twined together upon a bare mountainside, white birds upon the foam of the sea. We have been trees, leaping silver salmon, wild horses, red foxes, noble deer; brave warriors, proud kings, sage wizards . . .

Yeats: Entrancing. Quite entrancing. Ah . . . thank you, Emily. That will suffice for the moment. Mr. Rooke, have you any questions you would like to put?

Rooke: Just one or two, if you will indulge me. Emily, could you tell me, when did you start your last period? (*General consternation.*)

Yeats: Mr. Rooke. Please!

Rooke: My apologies if I have offended any sensibilities, but this line of questioning is critical to my investigation of these manifestations. Emily, did you hear the question?

Emily: The eighth of July.

Rooke: And are they regular? I mean, is there a regular period of time between them?

Emily: Always the same. Twenty-nine days.

Rooke: So, the previous one would have begun about, say, the sixteenth of June?

Emily: Yes.

Rooke: And the next one would be due, then, in, let me think, eight days' time, on the eighth of August? About the new moon?

Emily: Yes.

Rooke: And how long is it since you felt the returning presence of the faeries?

Emily: Since last night. I felt them, in my sleep last night—their presence out there in the wood, calling to me.

Rooke: Tell me, Emily, have you been feeling in any way physically out of sorts? Dizziness, light-headedness, stomach cramps, as if they were warning signs that a period is due? During a period, do you ever experience peculiar changes of mood and feeling? For example, have you ever felt sad and depressed and then, seemingly for no reason, found yourself suddenly buoyant and elated? When you become aware of the presence of the faeries, do you ever experience any kind of, how shall we put it, sensual, sexual excitement, or arousal?

E.G. Desmond: I insist that this stop at once! I will tolerate no more of this humiliation, this prurient titillation! No, I will not tolerate it. My daughter is not some sideshow, some circus freak for your idle amusement! I will not stand for any more of this cheap and tawdry voyeurism masquerading in the guise of science and learning! Good Lord, we stand poised upon the brink of a new age, an age of communion with minds immeasurably superior to our own, and in my very home I am subjected to occult, superstitious bosh, and my daughter to the filthy indulgence of jaded appetites! My daughter's adolescence will not be soiled and sullied with your gleeful prying into her most private intimacies! Good day to you, gentlemen. I wish for you all to leave. At once, if you please. Mrs. O'Carolan, be so good as to fetch these people their coats. Caroline, I wish to speak with you immediately, in the library.

The Beau English Club, Nassau Street, Dublin

"Well, I see the papers have hold of it now."

"Yes, I picked it up in the *Irish Times* this morning. Full column, on the front page, by the Lord Harry."

"You know, of course, what they're calling it?"

"You mean, Desmond's Downfall?"

"Haven't heard that one. Heh, that's a good one. Very good. Most droll. Where did you pick that one up?"

"The *Independent Irishman.*"

"That Fenian rag. Never read it myself. Mind you, Desmond's Downfall, that is a good one. Another brandy?"

"Don't mind if I do. Most civil of you. You know, it shouldn't surprise me in the least if the English papers didn't pick up on the story. 'Eccentric Irish Astronomer Attempts Communication with Star Men.' Love that sort of thing, the English. Could be circulating worldwide within the week."

"God forfend. Imagine it, though—scruffy old Desmond with his eighteen-inch telescope on the front page of *Le Soir* or the *New York Times*. 'Desmond's Downfall: Exposed.'"

"Don't know how old Maurice ever got himself sucked into this one."

"I'd have thought better of him myself. Mind you, Charlie, he's always had a reputation for espousing weird and wonderful causes. What about all this lobbying for that Home Rule Bill and votes for women? A queer fish in the aristocratic goldfish pond is our Maurice Fitzgerald."

"I blame it all on breeding, myself. You know, like cocker spaniels, inbreeding and all that. Congenital idiots. House of Lords is full of them. Educated idiots in ermine. No wonder old Maurice goes baying at the moon, or Bell's Comet, or whatever."

"It'll be the ruination of him."

"That it surely will. Do you know how much that floating pontoon thing is costing?"

"Wouldn't like to guess."

"Wouldn't like to spoil your luncheon."

"Still, I'd like to know how Desmond wangled that old bird into parting with the Clarenorris fortune for such a ludicrous scrape."

"Ah, he has a silver tongue, has Dr. Edward Garret Desmond. Could charm the birds off the trees."

"Certainly charmed that fine woman of his off the Barry family tree. He's well in there, Barry linen fortunes and all that. No stone, our Edward."

"Heh, heh. Fine woman she certainly is, that Caroline Desmond. Damn fine poetess, too. Read some of her stuff in *Eire Nua*—not, I hasten to add, that it's the sort of thing I read regularly. This 'Celtic Twilight' stuff baffles me—woolly-minded mysticism—but what I read of her was excellent. She has the magic touch, right enough."

"Well, Desmond's old silver tongue let him down badly at that farce of a lecture."

"Ah, that was O'Neill, wasn't it? He's a demon for the wit, is O'Neill."

"He queerly sharpened it on the good Dr. Desmond."

"A good thing, too, if you ask me. That lecture was the most ludicrous thing I have ever heard. Extrasolar civilizations, comet-riding star travellers . . ."

"Ridiculous. Tosh, gibberish, and flapdoodle."

"Isn't it? I do hear that he's invited astronomers from all over Ireland, and beyond, to be present when he switches this pontoon thing on."

"You going?"

"Fishing's good, this time of year. You?"

"Wild horses, and all that."

"Still . . ."

"Still what?"

"Still, what if he's right?"

"Come now, you yourself checked his figures and proved beyond any shadow of a doubt there were errors in his mathematics you could drive the Ballybrack omnibus through."

"Charlie, both you and I have been gentlemen of science long enough to know that mathematically proving or disproving something often has not the slightest effect on whether it actually happens or not. What if, I say, despite all the errors, the fantastic speculations, the astonishing expenditure, the ludicrous electrical signal—what if, after all, he is right?"

"Well, you don't need me to tell you the consequences . . ."

"What little credibility the R.I.A.S. has managed to salvage from this fiasco would go straight out the window. We would be laughingstocks."

"At least."

"But now, consider this carefully. If he never gets to complete his experiment, then no one will ever know whether he was right or wrong, will they?"

"Are you implying what I think you're implying?"

"Now, I'm not talking anything as unsubtle as a little judicious sabotage from the local Bould Fenian lads. Heavens, no. I'm not even talking troublesome and annoy-

ing labour disputes. No, a little economic leverage should
do the necessary dirty work. His resources are, shall we say,
stretched?"

"Short arms, long pockets."

"Precisely. You know, I've been thinking, it's been a
devilish long time since you last had that admirable chap,
the Marquis of Clarenorris, down at Temple Coole for a
weekend wild-fowling. Come to think of it, I wouldn't mind
getting a little in myself, before all the good shooting's
done . . ."

August 2, 1913

Clarecourt
Ballisodare
County Sligo

My Dear Dr. Desmond,

I have searched for every possible alternative to this
letter, delayed until the last possible moment in hope that
it would not be necessary, but situations have developed
in such a way as to leave me no other choice. Please,
prepare yourself for the receipt of the worst possible
news.

It is with the greatest sorrow that I inform you that I
can no longer permit myself to be involved in, or
associated with, Project Pharos. I regret further that I
will be able to provide no additional funding for the
completion of the stellagraph, or any other aspect of the
project, and must insist that my name be withdrawn from
all documents, accounts, communications, papers, etc.,
connected with it.

I am deeply sorry for this obvious dashing of all your
bright hopes, and at the very least, I owe you the courtesy
of an explanation for this decision.

Believe me, Dr. Desmond, I have not chosen this
course of action out of any lack of faith in your
experiment or hypothesis—I remain firmly convinced
that the object called Bell's Comet is indeed a vehicle
from another star. Rather, it is situations and events in

your immediate household, over which you, unfortunately, have had no control, that have made it impossible for me to continue to be associated with you.

I refer, of course, to those recent events involving Mr. W. B. Yeats, the celebrated poet; one Mr. Hannibal Rooke, a so-called supernatural investigator; Constance Booth-Kennedy and your wife and daughter; in what the popular press is calling the Craigdarragh Case. I fully understand that these "faery photographs" and purported otherworldly encounters are as offensive and embarrassing to you as they are to me; however, please consider (and I can trust you that this will go no further) that I am already under considerable pressure from my peers because of my support for Project Pharos; the recent events threaten to damage my reputation to the point where I can no longer remain a credible figure in the fight for Irish nationalism in the House of Lords. There are issues at stake here larger even than the advancement of science and learning—issues with direct bearing upon the future of our nation. Permit me to be blunt: it is not seeming for the leader of the lobby for the Irish Home Rule Bill in the House of Lords (where, dear God, support is paltry enough) to be seen to be associating with people who believe there really are faeries at the bottom of the garden!

I had hoped that time would draw its veil over this Craigdarragh Case, but quite the reverse has happened—public and press interest, already high from the construction of the stellagraph, has been fanned into veritable incandescence by reports of photographs of faery folk, from within the same family. No; I am afraid only one course of action was open to me, which, loath though I was to exercise, I nonetheless have taken: I have had to resign from any involvement and association with Project Pharos.

I do sincerely hope, my dear Dr. Desmond, that even at this late stage, funds will be forthcoming (though, alas, I cannot foresee from where) for the completion of the project. Certainly, if successful, it will bring more lasting glory upon Craigdarragh than a whole legion of faeries.

Once again, I am most sincerely sorrowful that situa-

tions should have forced me to such a pass. Would it had
been otherwise.

Faithfully,
Maurice: Clarenorris

August 3, 1913

Blessington & Weir, Ltd.
Commercial Bankers
119 Merrion Road
Dublin

Dear Dr. Desmond,

We have recently been in receipt of a letter from you
requesting the creation of a mortgage facility for the
completion of your project to the sum of £22,000 against
the deeds of your property, Craigdarragh House.

We are pleased to inform you that your application has
been successful; a meeting has been arranged between
our Sligo representatives, Mooney, Talbot & O'Brien,
Marine Finance, Ltd., and their solicitors, and yourself
and your solicitors, to formalise the agreement. Please
telephone us to confirm the date and the arrangements:
our number is Dublin 3617.

We at Blessington & Weir are glad to have been able to
aid you in the completion of your work, and we await
your communication in the near future.

Sincerely,
Caius E. Blessington,
William Weir the Younger

Dr. Edward Garret Desmond's Personal Diary: August 4, 1913

The heady sensation, like that of fine old claret, that comes
when one plucks triumph from the very brink of disaster! I

am not ashamed to say that I despaired when I received the news of Lord Fitzgerald's withdrawal from the project for the flimsiest of motives. Thunderous words such as *treachery* and *betrayal* struggled with nobler sentiments more proper a member of the peerage as the thought churned over and over in my mind: *This is the end, Desmond—all come to naught and ashes.*

But now, since the settlement of the mortgage (Blessèd Muse, that touched me with such inspiration in my darkest hours) and the payment of all my most pressing creditors, everything is changed. It is like a particularly fine spring after a long and dismal winter. Amazing, the total change of mood and character effected by the deposit of a few pounds sterling in the vaults of the First Sligo Farmer's Bank! Now work has resumed; the last of the 176 pontoon sections was completed in the shipyard today. Already the central cross is being assembled in Sligo Bay. Not being much a mariner myself, I made my inspection by telescope from the cupola atop the old Pollexfen Shipping Line office and was filled with a most immodest pride to see out there an object which, alone I think of all man's achievements, will be visible from interplanetary distances. In addition to the work on the pontoons, a small steam tug has been chartered from the harbour commissioners to lay the electrical cable. Incredibly (normally, I would hesitate to use quite such hyperbolic language, but for once, I feel justified in its usage), the great task looks like it will be completed by the allotted date, despite a body blow that would have crippled any man of lesser conviction, lesser zeal, lesser evangelistic determination than I. Mr. Michael Barry has been in daily contact concerning the connection of the stellagraph to the county grid. I have had replies from many members of the astronomical community, both at home and from beyond our shores (though I will permit a small disappointment to cloud my general jubilation, for of those I invited, less than a third have bothered themselves to respond, either positively or negatively). The newspaper interest, already stoked up by the so-called Craigdarragh Case, is hungry for the least newsworthy morsel and I am making daily trips into Sligo to give progress reports to the assembled hacks and scribblers. In short, everything seems set for my triumph in every possible sphere—astronomical, personal, financial, social, public. If only the weather will hold!

Emily's Diary: August 28, 1913

Sometimes they are distant; sometimes they are close. As our world and Otherworld turn within each other, so we pass into and out of contact with each other. For many days they were absent—the woods were empty of story and song; sea, stones, and sky were just those, lifeless things, the elemental spirit gone out of them. Each time they leave I am desolate. I fear that they will never return, but, for all their legendary fickleness and flightiness, they have kept faith with me. Again, they have returned from Otherworld to haunt Bridestone Wood. I can feel them; I can hear them, calling for me with harp and flute and the songs of summer, calling me away, away, away from the mortal world, into the dream and the never-ending dance.

But I am afraid, undecided. There is a part of me that wishes nothing more than to lose myself in the magic and the light of the world's beginning, that would cast off all human restraints like an ugly garment and be the bride of the Bridestone. But there is also a part of me that holds back, that clings to this world, afraid of the light beyond the shadows. There is a part of me with the voice of a tiny devil that whispers, "But what do they want with you? Why do they trouble themselves to stir from the endless delights of the forests of Otherworld and make the crossing to this world? Why do they seek you, Emily Desmond? These are faery folk, the Sidhe, the Dwellers in the Hollow Hills— their motives are as inscrutable to you as the changing of the seasons or the tides of the sea. How can you be sure that they do not mean you ill? Can you trust them?"

There. That is the question that lies at the heart of all my doubts and fears, like the rotted kernel of a hazelnut. *Can I trust them?*

I am torn; between caution and abandon, between mistrust and the call of the harps of Elfland. Do I go to them and let them do what they will? Do I stay, and perhaps with the turning of the years, lose even the memory of their music? My heart tells me go, my head cautions *stay*.

In the end, I know my curiosity will drive me to find out what they want with me. To know the answer, I will have to go to them.

Extracts from Edward Garret Desmond's Notes and Commentaries on Project Pharos toward an uncompleted paper to be submitted to the Royal Irish Astronomical Society.

. . . On August 8 at 12:15 A.M. it was observed that the transtellar vehicle had ceased generating explosions, having shed sufficient velocity to match the pedestrian pace of our solar system. Its final proper motion was approximated to be fifteen miles per second.

The vehicle maintained course and velocity over the days preceding perigee. It was not until the night of September 2 that conditions were suitable for the experiment to commence. That night the sky was clear, Sligo Bay uncommonly calm, and the extrasolar vehicle two days from perigee of 156,000 miles. At 9:25 P.M. the signal was activated, and for a period of two hours the primary communication code was transmitted—that is, *pi* expressed as the approximate ratio of twenty-two over seven. This sequence was repeated every two hours for two hours until local dawn at 6:25 A.M. Simultaneous with the operation of the stellagraph, the vessel was closely observed through the Craigdarragh eighteen-inch reflector telescope. No change in luminosity was observed.

After nightfall on the following day, September 3, it again being clear and calm, the floating stellagraph was again activated, transmitting the *pi* ratio for an hour, then changing to the natural exponent *e* expressed as the approximate fraction of nineteen over seven. As before, this cycle was repeated every two hours for two hours. As before, the spatial object was closely observed through telescopes—both those of the experimenter, and of the invited witnesses in Sligo town.

No response was observed from the transtellar vessel on these dates.

On the third night, September 4, communication was once again attempted.

Dr. Edward Garret Desmond's Personal Diary: September 4, 1913

I anticipated last night with the thrill of a child at Christmas. I could hardly wait for darkness to descend and my attempts to communicate with the Altairii to commence. My to-that-date lack of success had in no way discouraged me; as a gentleman of science, I know that triumph is not always immediate. I was confident, however, that this night I would succeed in breaking through their alien silence.

At the prearranged hour, Mr. Michael Barry down in the Harbour Commissioners office operated the floating stella-graph and transmitted my recognition signal. From the observatory dome I could see the floating cross of pontoons filling all of Sligo Bay, flashing our proud message of will and intellect to the star travellers.

Then the first of the night's calamities occurred. At 10:23 P.M. the observatory was plunged into the most profound darkness. By now accustomed to these failures of the electrical supply, I lit the oil lamps I had installed with just such a contingency in mind. Then Mrs. O'Carolan came rushing in from the main house in a terrible to-do, flustered and flapping and gabbling about having heard on the telephone that the current had failed in Rosses Point, too. Alarmed, I abandoned my telescope and reached the window just in time to see the lights of my fine floating stellagraph plunged into extinction. Just as abruptly, the glow from Sligo town vanished, as if some vast hand had snuffed it out. As I was later to learn from the pages of the *Irish Times*, the electrical supply was blacked out from Donegal Town to Enniskillen to Ballina for a period of four hours. At the time, ignorant as I was, I was greatly fearful, imagining that my signal attempt had brought some dreadful star doom down upon our Earth.

Then the second peculiarity occurred. The star vehicle, which I had kept under observation in my telescope, suddenly emitted a pulse of light bright enough to be visible with the naked eye. It continued to emit these bursts of brilliant light at the rate of one per minute until 12:16 A.M., at which time the object flared so dazzlingly that I was momentarily blinded, though I have learned from witnesses that the entire sky seemed to turn white. When I regained my customary clarity of vision, I was unable to find the vehicle in my telescope eyepiece. It had vanished as utterly as if it had never been. No conjurer vanishing a lady into thin air upon the Dublin stage could have matched such a feat of prestidigitation, and the vacuum of space is thinner by far than the most rarefied of airs.

I searched the heavens frantically for some trace of the great star vehicle—some nebula, some nimbus one might expect in the aftermath of an explosion. Nothing. It might never have existed. As I was pondering upon what fate might have befallen the valiant star travellers (and rueing bitterly that it had befallen them before I had made contact with them), Caroline burst in upon me to inform me of the most dreadful news of that calamitous evening: that Emily had been found wandering in a state of great distress upon the Sligo Road by a police constable.

From the Report of Constable Michael O'Hare, Drumcliffe R.I.C. Station

Upon the night in question I was proceeding upon my bicycle along the Sligo Road toward Rosses Point, where there had been concerns expressed by certain well-to-do householders at the sudden failure of the electric supply. At approximately eleven thirty, as I was passing the point where the boundary wall separating Bridestone Wood from the Mullaghboy estate comes down to the road, I heard a noise like crying and sobbing coming from the foot of the forest wall. I advanced with caution, and by the light of my bicycle lamp saw a young lady huddled in the ditch in a state of great and obvious distress. She was quite unclothed, which somewhat unnerved me, and covered in cuts and bruises, as if she had been running through briars and brambles. I was unable to offer consolation to the young lady, so great was her distress, but for the sake of decency and the coolness of the air I persuaded her to cover her modesty with my police cape. I decided to take her to the O'Bannon residence, Mullaghboy, not a quarter mile distant, where a doctor might be fetched. The young lady would not, however, consent to be moved from the side of the road. I attempted to glean some inkling of what dreadful thing might have happened to her, but she would not so much as give me her name. I persisted with my questions, and, between sobbing fits, she mentioned the name of some person, possibly of foreign extraction or origin, whose name I took to be Lew. More significantly, she spoke of violation, stolen maidenhood, ravishment, and unfaithful lovers. Clearly, some form of indecent assault had been made upon the unfortunate young lady. It was therefore imperative that I remove her to a safe place from which I could summon the necessary medical, police, and priestly assistance. Knowing that any attempt to force her to accompany me would only increase her distress, I finally persuaded her to mount my bicycle and with her as passenger, I cycled to Mullaghboy House, where Mrs. O'Bannon recognised the young lady as Miss Emily Desmond of the neighbouring household, Craigdarragh. While I went to fetch Dr. Campbell from Dromahoe, she telephoned to inform Mrs. Desmond of her daughter's plight.

September 8, 1913

The Sligo and Leitrim Impartial Reporter

POLICE HUNT FOR MYSTERY
ATTACKER CONTINUES

The search for the mystery assailant of the Drumcliffe schoolgirl, Miss Emily Desmond, has been extended to include the Bundoran and Dromahair constabularies. Following house-to-house inquiries in the Drumcliffe area concerning the movements of the locals on the night of September 4, Inspector Patrick Gorman of the Sligo police, spearheading the manhunt, now believes that the mystery attacker is not of this locale. Though he would not comment on how widely the dragnet for the assailant might eventually be cast, Inspector Gorman did not rule out the involvement of police forces as far afield as Galway and Athlone.

Miss Desmond, daughter of the celebrated local figure Dr. Edward Garret Desmond of Craigdarragh House, was most brutally and viciously violated in the vicinity of local landmark Bridestone Wood in the parish of Drumcliffe. The constable who discovered Miss Desmond upon the road described the attack as "Frenzied—that of a madman, or wild beast." Miss Desmond is currently recuperating from her ordeal at the Fitzwilliam Street clinic of Dr. Hubert Orr, the renowned Dublin psychological practitioner. Dr. Desmond was today unavailable for comment upon the incident, save that he had every confidence that the police were exercising all possible diligence in their efforts to bring the attacker to justice. However, it has come to the notice of this newspaper that, prior to the assault, there had been several slaughterings and mutilations of chickens and small livestock on the Craigdarragh demesne.

Local women have been advised by the police not to travel unchaperoned, especially after nightfall.

Extracts from the casebooks of Dr. Hubert Orr, Fitzwilliam Street Clinic, Dublin.

My physical examination of the patient proved that she had indeed been subjected to repeated and forceful sexual penetration, without doubt upon the night in question by person (or persons) unknown. As yet it is impossible to ascertain if conception occurred; the patient is too deeply shocked to supply information concerning her periods. I shall recommend that she remain here at the clinic until some degree of certainty is possible. It will be some time before she will be capable of receiving the news if it proves positive.

Rape is a particularly detestable crime—it is a violation of the whole person. The physical damage may be small (though not to be dismissed) compared to the wounds inflicted on the mind; it may take many weeks of counselling in a conducive atmosphere before she is ready to return home, and many more until she is fully healed from the experience, if ever.

The psychological wounding may be deeper than I thought. My initial presumption was that Miss Desmond's youth would have blessed her with a natural resilience; that, like a rubber ball, she would rapidly spring back into her natural character. Rather, it seems that her tender years have rendered her all the more emotionally fragile and vulnerable. Since her arrival with us she has not spoken a word. Though she submits meekly to Nurse O'Brien's and my medical examinations and treatments, she has maintained an unbroken silence under all conditions. That she hears and responds to my questions is apparent, but she refuses adamantly to answer them with even so much as a nod or shake of the head. She is eating, but meagerly, and never in the presence of the staff. Nurse O'Brien reports that her favourite occupation is sitting by the window for hours on end, looking out at nothing. Long after darkness has fallen, she may be found in the same chair by the window, staring into the street. In the absence of concrete answers to my gentle probings, I am forced to hypothesise, a thing I am loath to do. Is her blank preoccupation a self-inflicted, selective amnesia, a hiding away of the pain of violation behind multiple locked doors, or is it an obsessional playing over and over and over the events of that September night, a memory burned like a brand so deep into her mind that it colours every thought, every feeling, every experience? Certainly, it is not healthy, but faced with a stone wall of silence, I am unable even to begin to help.

The silence has at last broken, but only partially; light streams through the cracks in the masonry but the wall still stands. The key that partly released her from self-imposed incarceration was a simple request for her diary. Nurse O'Brien entered her room yesterday morning and found Miss Desmond sitting up in bed, wringing her hands in agitation. When Nurse O'Brien asked what was wrong, Miss Desmond replied that she wanted her diary. Nurse O'Brien at once summoned me, and the question was repeated to me. I replied that I was not in possession of her diary, would some loose paper and a pen suffice? Miss Desmond insisted that she wanted her diary, her own diary, and would accept no substitute. By this stage she was becoming quite forceful in her demands, and I deliberately fostered her anger and frustration to prevent her from lapsing back into her near-catatonic state again. Finally, she agreed to be content with a pen and some foolscap in return for a promise that I would obtain her diary from her mother at my earliest convenience.

Several volumes of those diaries arrived last post this evening and I will shortly study them for the key that will fully unlock the mind of Emily Desmond.

At present she is answering some direct questions, mostly of the "Are you hungry?" "Are you thirsty?" "Do you want me to open a window?" kind. Questions that impinge too closely upon the rape she meets with a blank silence. Her sensitivity and subtlety are phenomenal. My least attempt to steer the conversation in that direction causes her to retreat into sullen, withdrawn silence. Yet it is these very subjects that must be brought to mind and dealt with openly if we are to progress to a true psychological healing.

To the Man On The Clapham Omnibus, Emily would seem to be making a first-rate recovery—she is writing in her diary every day, expresses an interest in the outside world, and will engage in casual conversation. She is restless indoors and has expressed to Nurse O'Brien a desire to go on a shopping expedition to Clery's to buy a new autumn outfit. At the end of the week, weather permitting, I may prescribe short walks in the clinic gardens, or Fitzwilliam Square. Certainly, while the current labour unrest continues to make the streets and squares unsafe for any citizen, there will be no shopping expeditions. Current civic woes aside, I am not convinced that Emily's recovery is as total as she would have us believe. There is, for want of a more exact term, a leadenness about her features, her gestures in unguarded moments. Her general demeanour is colourless and unanimated. Her conversation displays the same concealed accidie. Though she no longer refuses to answer point-blank any question bearing on the night of the rape, her replies are reluctant and often evasive. She refuses to accept the rape as having been an actual event, at times treating it as if it had happened to someone else, at others incorporating it into her elaborate fantasy life as some terrifying supernatural experience divorced from everyday reality.

My role is clearly now that of guide and shield: guide from this stage of denial through possible subsequent anger and depression into acceptance and regeneration; shield from the revelation of current events that could catastrophically retard her progress. The first of these traumatising events is the news of her father's failure, disgrace, and doubtless financial ruin in the wake of the collapse of his experiment to communicate with purported extrasolar beings. The second, and perhaps the more devastating, is the confirmation of her pregnancy. This second event cannot be long concealed; she is young, but by no means naive. I can only hope that I can guide her to the point of acceptance before she guesses herself.

Always in the science of psychology there is one set of symbols, one golden key, that opens the patient's mind and unrolls it like an ancient map of a far country to the explorer of the psyche. At last, drawing on the notes I have taken from Emily's diary, I feel I am close to unlocking that chest. Repressed sexuality is the key. The monastic regime of the Teaching Sisters at Cross and Passion has been well testified to in both the diaries and in conversation with Emily. Doubtless the juvenile dalliance in illicit sexual play inevitable in such establishments, coupled with the attentions of the young Mr. O'Byrne (how forthright Emily is in her diaries! Nothing withheld, nothing concealed!), would certainly drive her need for sexual expression deep into the subconscious and seal it there under layers of guilt. Such volcanic forces are not so easily penned: her sexual desire, her need to escape from what she perceives as social restraint, found expression in her creation of the imaginary Otherworld, a place without restraint, restrictions, without recognisable social *mores*. This Otherworld, a country created in considerable detail, for which she has formulated a sophisticated rationale, is a place of symbol and analogy, where her need for sexual, sensual, emotional, and artistic self-expression may be indulged without fear of censure, without guilt. Many of the kings, warriors, goblins, faeries, poets, harpers, even lovers, with which she populates it are clumsy recapitulations of her mother's mythological studies, the works of W. B. Yeats, the folklore of the locality as imparted to her by Mrs. O'Carolan the housekeeper, and her own "literary" aspirations. It is a ripe and ready medium in which to sow the seeds of sexual frustration and guilt, and for them to reach fruition into a personal, even sinister, symbolism and significance.

Is it therefore proper to conclude that the events of the night of September 4 may not have been rape at all, in the purely legalistic sense of the word; that Emily may in fact have deliberately gone searching for a partner, a "faery lover," and found instead an experience which turned so sour for her that she could only reject and deny it?

It is important also to incorporate the role of the father in any hypothesis. At an early age, Emily clearly idolised her father, yet at the time of the Craigdarragh incident she had grown hostile to both him and his work. That the rape commenced with the night of her father's hoped-for vindication of Project Pharos cannot be insignificant.

Emily's response to her fifteenth birthday is crucial here. Again, from her diaries, it is obvious that she considered herself to be a woman in the fullest sense of the word. Her father, perhaps in response to needs and motivations of his own, refused to consider her anything but a little girl—sexually and emotionally immature, utterly dependent, a child. Certainly her retreat into the imaginary Otherworld of distorted mythology and superstition can be seen as a strike back against her father and his rigorous, rational, scientific world view. Tragically, even at this late stage, her diary entries hint that she was desperately striving for his approval, while at the same time attacking his vision for her life, and punishing him for his supposed inadequacies as a father. That she should have succeeded is the capstone to the entire tragic episode.

However, I am utterly at a loss to proffer any explanation for the photographs of the faery folk.

September 12, 1913

Craigdarragh
Drumcliffe
County Sligo

Dear Mother Superior,

Just a brief note to inform you that Emily will not be returning to Cross and Passion School in future. Alas, the poor child has recently suffered a major breakdown of health, and after a spell in Dr. Hubert Orr's renowned Fitzwilliam Street clinic, will shortly be returning home to Craigdarragh to convalesce at length. It will be many months, I fear, before Emily fully regains her health. However, her education will not suffer—a governess is being hired to school her in a style better suited to her particular disposition. May I take this opportunity to thank you, Reverend Mother, for what you have done in the past for my daughter: education truly is a gem beyond price in this modern world, and I know that the private tutor we will be hiring for Emily will build soundly upon the solid foundation laid at Cross and Passion. In parting, then, I would ask for your prayers for Emily's safe and full recovery. As ever, my own thoughts and prayers are all for my misfortunate daughter.

Sincerely,
Caroline Desmond

September 24, 1913

Minutes of the A.G.M. of
The Royal Irish Astronomical Society

The minutes of the previous A.G.M. having been read, accepted by the House, and signed by Mr. President, the meeting then moved to the first topic on the agenda: a motion proposed by the Member for Temple Coole that the Member for Drumcliffe be expelled from the Society.

Proposing the motion, the Member for Temple Coole stated that the activities of the Member for Drumcliffe had brought the Society into disrepute both nationally and in the international astronomical forum. The Member for Temple Coole further deplored the member under censure's blatant self-publicity and courting of the press, as well as his indiscriminate abuse of his privilege as a Member to use the name of the Royal Irish Astronomical Society. In order to recoup some credibility from the Sligo fiasco, the Member concluded, the Society had no other option than to dissociate itself forthwith from the Member for Drumcliffe and his activities.

Seconding the motion, the Member for Aghavannon said that the Member for Drumcliffe's work had not been true to the high standards of mathematical and scientific rigour demanded of members of the Society; that in the persuance of his Project Pharos and his hypotheses on the nature of Bell's Comet, he had done irreparable damage not only to the Society which had opened wide the arms of astronomical fraternity, but to Scientific Method as an entity, and that, for the preservation of what the seconding Member deemed "The Temple of Science," the Member for Drumcliffe be expelled from the Society.

Mr. President then threw the motion open to debate from the floor.

The Member for Queen's University agreed with the Member for Aghavannon that the science of astronomy itself had been brought into disgrace, and added that a motion of censure also be passed upon the Member for Dunsink, the then Secretary of the Society, for encouraging the Member for Drumcliffe to publicise his theories in the lecture hall of the Society in the first place.

The Member for Derrynane declared that any Member who openly associated himself with "mediums, ghost hunters, table tappers, ectoplasm swallowers, and other such charlatans" had no place in the Royal Irish Astronomical Society.

The Member for Elaghmore, while reminding the assembled Members that he had tried to keep an open mind on the veracity or otherwise of the Bell's Comet controversy, deplored what he termed as the Member for Drumcliffe's "dog-in-the-manger" attitude, in that, while freely associating himself with the name and intellectual stature of the Society, his intent had never been to share any possible glory with his fellow Members.

Member for Slane commented that the member for Drumcliffe had received an offer from the Irish Rugby Football Union for the lights from his floating pontoons. He trusted that the Member for Drumcliffe would take great gratification in knowing that future generations would thank him for providing floodlit rugby at Lansdowne Road.

There being no further speeches from the floor, the President then moved for a division. The votes have been cast. The motion for expulsion was passed by 125 votes to seven.

Dr. Edward Garret Desmond's Personal Diary: October 3, 1913

Yesterday evening I took myself down to the shoreline at Lissadell for a beachside walk—the first time in the weeks since the catastrophe that I have felt able to bear the sight of my stellagraph. Are the gloomy miasmas and vapours at last lifting; or, as I rather fear, am I growing accustomed, even comfortable, to darkness exterior and interior? There it floats still. Looking out upon it from the shore I was overcome by a colossal sense of disbelief that this fabulous engine should exist at all—that I should have any connection with it whatsoever, let alone that of creator and inspiring light. The sensation is that of long months of hallucination from which I have at last awakened into a grey and thankless world. Had I indeed misinterpreted a perfectly natural phenomenon? Was there, had there always been, a fundamental flaw in my calculations?

Reckonings cloud my horizon. Certainly, I can expect a letter from Blessington & Weir imminently. I still entertain increasingly vain hopes that the salvage from the stellagraph will prove sufficient for Craigdarragh not to have to be sold. Even more than the reckoning with Blessington & Weir, I dread my personal reckoning with Caroline. She will have no mercy. Alas, we have grown too far apart in these past years. Once I could have trusted her to stand by me. Now I can no longer be certain that she will not be howling with the rest of the dogs to lick up the blood of Ahab. She alone possesses the power to save me; the Barry fortune could buy a dozen Craigdarraghs. But I fear that even in these extremest of circumstances her uncle will not relent, should she even have the will to approach him.

And Emily? None of us will ever know the true circumstances of the vile ravagement that took place, but in part, I know myself to be responsible. In a sense, I am punished for my sins, for my inadequacies, for my willful dereliction of the duties and responsibilities of a father toward a daughter. I was not a father to her, and the consequences were dreadful. And now Craigdarragh itself is threatened because of that same arrogance and conceit. Ashes; ashes and cinders; that is all these past five years are to me now.

"Hello? Mary? Is that you? This is me. Hello, Mary. I can hear you clear as a chapel bell, can you hear me? Yes, a wonderful day it is altogether. No, no hurry, they'll be out for hours yet, both of them. I'm keeping rightly myself. And yourself? Oh now, I am sorry to hear that. Water from the washing well at Gortahurk. Five drops, and as much house dust as will cover a florin. Rub the paste well into the afflicted area. Every time, Mary. Miraculous powers, have the waters of Gortahurk. Five drops, that's right. As much as will cover a florin.

"Things? Well, Mary, not so good. Not so good at all. Well, far be it from me to gossip on the doings of me betters, but, well, things is in a terrible state of chassis. A terrible state of chassis indeed, and, in a sort of sense, I suppose I might be to blame for it all. Yes, of course I'll tell you all about it, Mary. It all began this morning when I collected the post from Mr. Conner the postman—such a nice gentleman, he is. Of late the Master's been most insistent that I separate all his letters from Mistress Caroline's and deliver them straight to his study. Well, I don't know how it happened, it must have been behind another thicker letter addressed to Mistress Caroline is all I can offer, but anyway, there I was, tidying away the breakfast crocks, and there she was, opening her mail with that Indian ivory letter opener of hers—never seen a woman receives as much post as the Mistress—when all of a sudden I hear the clatter of that letter opener of hers falling to the table and she's holding up this letter with a look on her face like she's learned she's going to be hung; whiter than the Lilliput Laundry advertisement, she was. Sat like that for two full minutes, like she was the one made of Indian ivory, then all of a sudden she lets out this terrible screech: 'Edward!'— the Master, you know—and she's up and out of the room with a look on her face I certainly don't want to see again this side of Judgement. Well, Mary, as you know, if something is troubling the Master and Mistress, Maire O'Carolan wants to know what it is. It was only the tiniest of peeks, but it was enough, Mary! I thought I'd been struck and turned to stone. Mary, the letter was from a firm of bankers in Dublin, saying that unless Dr. Edward Garret Desmond paid them—listen carefully now, Mary—the sum of *twenty-two thousand pounds* by the end of December, they would repossess the house and estate. What had the foolish man gone and done, Mary, but mortgaged ten generations of Desmonds to pay for that monstrosity down in the bay!

"A fight? I'll say there was a fight. Mary, the time they'd finished I reckoned I'd be sweeping up broken delft and wiping blood and hair off the wallpaper from now to Michaelmas. Well, I've been keeping my head down, Mary, out of the firing line, but the atmosphere is, well, shall we say, *smouldering?* The Barry millions? You mean you don't know the story? I'll tell you how much Caroline Desmond has to her name. Nothing. Not one brass farthing. After her father died, he willed control of the linen company to his brother and put all his children's money in trust, into stocks and shares and bonds and things like that that are money but aren't any real use. To release any of their inheritance, the Mistress would need the signature of her Uncle, and the old blackguard of a Presbyterian refuses to do that. Why? Because she married a Catholic. That old black-mouthed Orangeman won't speak to her, won't even sit in the same room as her, so the Master can kiss farewell and adieu to the Barry millions bailing him out.

"What's to happen? Well, one thing's for certain, it's no time for Miss Emily to be coming home. Oh yes, on the five o'clock train, Wednesday. Yes, dreadful. Poor child; I always feared for her, you know. I always feared that with those parents of hers she would come to some harm. I prayed for her every night. I even went on a solemn novena to Our Lady for her protection. Now, Mary, don't be saying things like that. Are you as wise as God? Well, then, keep your heathen opinions to yourself. I know that God always answers prayer. Still, it's no time for her to be coming home, expecting a baby and all. Hadn't you heard? That . . . that . . . animal, poor child, he left her with a baby. And all of the age of her, too. Evil times, indeed. You only have to look at the state of the country—those atheist Socialists running amok in Dublin, those heretic Protestant Unionists rampaging in Ulster. The likes of you and me should be pitying those poor souls who have no faith to give them moral guidance and strength.

"The house? Well, unless there's a miracle, and I'm hopeful, still praying, Mary, it'll all have to be sold. House, lands, everything. Well, Mary, I'm sure that whoever comes after, there'll still be need for a housekeeper, but all the same, it wouldn't do any harm to be keeping an ear to the ground, if you know what I mean.

"You know what I think? It's a curse. I do most certainly believe that. Someone, or something, is willing sorrow and misfortune on this household. There has not been one minute's good luck within these walls since the year turned. Bad luck—you can feel it, Mary, sometimes. Why, it's almost like a physical presence. You can feel it pressing down on you like an oppressive vapour. No, I'm quite serious; there is a heavy, dark atmosphere in this house. Everyone who comes notices it. Not that there've been too many of those—visitors, I mean.

"Oh: here, Mary, I'll have to go . . . I can hear the master's car on the gravel. I hadn't thought he'd be so quick. In his current humour, I wouldn't want to be caught using the telephone. Yes, I will, surely, next free day I get. And good-bye to you, too, Mary."

Emily's Diary: October 12, 1913

I was glad, very glad, to be leaving the Fitzwilliam Square Clinic. The atmosphere in Dublin has grown sour and suspicious. On every side groups of men are taking names and arms and banners to march beneath: Irish Volunteers, Irish Citizens' Army, *Fianna, Cumann na Mban, Sinn Fein*, as well as the locked out workers. The streets are angry, the climate discontented. How far this autumn of dis-ease is from impatient swallows flocking about Craig-darragh, woods full of the voices of the rooks. It makes me all the more eager to return. In the mornings the gardeners in the square sweep the paths and set fire to their little piles of leaves and the smell is enough to transport me, instantly: I am there. Blackthorn walking sticks in the hall stand; from the kitchen wafts of vinegar and pickling spice, baking pies and apples stewing with cloves; a particular golden light that shines into parts of the house it somehow never reaches in any other season; the hot stone jar down the bed and the equinoxial gales rattling the roof slates.

The sadness of the romantic imagination is to be ever disappointed that the reality never matches the imagining of it. Always in reality there are the shadows where the light will never reach, the wallpaper peeling by the skirting board, the hall stand missing a cherub and with a cracked tulip tile.

I have said I was glad to be leaving Dublin; I did not say I was glad to be home.

They did not even come to welcome me. Their only daughter, and they sent Mrs. O'Carolan in a trap with Paddy-Joe. Oh, yes, it was good to see Mrs. O'C and Paddy-Joe again, and their delight in seeing me was honestly transparent—Mrs. O'C could hardly speak a word; she must have wrung out an entire week's supply of handkerchiefs.

From my first glimpse of the familiar pillared facade, I could feel it. Craigdarragh had changed. It was more than the inevitable disappointment of romantic idealism; I felt that the entire spirit of the house had been changed. The autumn light no longer shone into those inaccessible places; it had been defeated by shadows. Oh, Mummy and Daddy greeted me lovingly enough, there on the steps. Mummy cried and Daddy harrumphed and harrahed into his beard though it was clear to all that he was on the verge of tears himself, but there was a tautness, a reserve between them, and especially toward me, as if I were a guest in a house full of secrets. I can best describe it as a darkness behind the eyes, a preoccupation with something that consumed all their energy in its concealment.

And in Craigdarragh the blackthorns leaned against the hall stand, the apple-cinnamon-bramble perfume of Mrs. O'Carolan's tarts seeped out of the kitchen into every corner and cranny, and the October sun through the cupola cast a rose of light on the stairs, but it felt infected. It felt tired and decaying, as if the autumn had entered and filled the rooms with its placid dying.

At supper tonight Mrs. O'C excelled herself; all my favourites, and I think it gave her more delight in the serving of them than I took in the devouring, but in spite of her best efforts, what should have been a joyous occasion was tense, taut, tiring. Whenever Mummy and Daddy asked me about the clinic and Dr. Orr and the general state of Dublin, it was evident that they had no real interest in my answers—they asked merely because it was polite to ask. Whenever I asked about what had been happening at home, they gave me very straight, very considered answers. When I said that they seemed a little distant, Mummy replied that so much had happened to me, so many hurtful and terrible things in so short a space of time, that it was almost as if I were a new Emily; that they knew only how to treat the old Emily, and that was no longer suitable for a woman in my *ahem* position.

I said that the new Emily was the old Emily, that I was more like shoots and leaves on an old tree than a whole new person. Daddy cleared his throat then, in that way of his when he is going to say something he does not want to have to say, and said that they had a lot of *readjusting* to do. My own mother and father treating me like a stranger at my own table.

Readjusting to what? I asked, and then I realised. They were ashamed of me. Ashamed. I was the final disgrace. By now it was all over the county—see her, Emily Desmond, pregnant, and not even an idea of the father, much less married. Shameless, shameless. What kind of people would let that happen to a child of theirs? what kind of parents?

Never mind that this child was forced upon me, never mind that I was violated, *raped*. Why were they afraid to say the word? All they could see was Dr. Edward Garret Desmond, the once-respected astronomer, on one side and Mrs. Caroline Desmond, the renowned poetess and Celtic scholar, on the other, and a big wobbling bulge in the middle.

I looked at them, at the expressions of mock concern on their faces. Suddenly I hated them so much, I wished them dead and damned on the very spot. I screamed something, I cannot remember what, sent dishes knives forks cruets and all Mrs. O'Carolan's good work flying, and rushed off to my room.

I can still remember the pale, staring faces. In my room I paced up and down, up and down. I wanted to be angry,

I enjoyed being angry, I kept being angry because there was so much more of the anger I had wanted them to see. I found things to be angry at: stupid, inanimate things which took on stubborn wills and minds of their own—my left shoe, which stuck when I tried to kick it off, so I pulled and pulled and pulled until the laces snapped, then threw it against the wall, bringing down the lamp. I picked the lamp up and threw it down again. If it had to fall, it would fall when and where I chose it to fall, and it broke into two pieces.

I couldn't sleep. My head was bursting with that top-of-the-neck pain you get when you are too angry to be capable of expressing it. Hours passed. Realising that I would in all likelihood be awake to see the dawn, I decided to read something. I do not know what it was that made me choose that book: *The Countryside Companion to the Wild Flowers of Britain and Ireland*. Summer and its wildflowers were long dead, and botany was never my strongest suit, yet I felt compelled to read the book. Propped up in bed, I opened it where the paper naturally fell and something slipped out onto the counterpane—something gossamer and moonlit and light as a breath.

The pair of faery's wings.

I picked them up delicately in my fingers, laid them on the palm of my hand, looked at them for a long time. Then I closed my hand and crushed them into dust.

This morning I did not want to see them. Whatever apology they offered, whatever apology they demanded, they would only have made me angry again. On the excuse of morning sickness, I rang for Mrs. O'Carolan to bring me breakfast in my room, which she did. At least I have one friend in Craigdarragh.

I went to the bathroom to wash, and as I did, I saw a thing contemptible in its familiarity in the light of a totally new revelation. At the end of the landing by the linen press was the small door that led to the old servants' staircase and their quarters in the attics. In all my living memory it has been locked shut; Mummy says that the floorboards are not safe. Mrs. O'Carolan keeps a small bed-parlour beside the potato store—the heat from the range is good for her rheumatism, she insists. The rooms under the eaves have not been used

since before I was born. This morning, the door stood the
tiniest, the very least crack ajar. How could I not explore?

Such treasure that had been buried in those servants'
rooms and forgotten! The first room was filled with old
cracked albums and crumbling boxes of photographs: soft,
blurry daguerreotypes of upright moustached gentlemen in
caps and bloomers proud beside their new bicycles; ladies
who somehow looked cool and elegant in ruffled silks and
taffeta on what must have been a stifling summer day;
sportsmen in tweed jackets and knee boots leaning on
staves; fox hounds too quick for the lens a blur about their
feet; little boys in sailor suits, about to burst into tears; gents
with hands thrust nonchalantly into pockets, lolling about
the enclosure at the Sligo Races; tinker families posed
self-consciously in their doorways, surly and unwashed
looking; girls in first communion dresses standing shyly in
front of Drumcliffe High Cross. Boating excursions, tennis
parties, expeditions by jaunting car to local beauty spots,
windswept family picnics in the dunes at Strandhill, wed-
dings, baptisms, Easters, Christmases: all those times, all
those moments, captured and frozen. I flicked through box
after box of dusty, sepia-toned memories pressed like
flowers in a Bible . . . and I stopped. The photograph
was of a girl of about thirteen, standing by the sundial in the
sunken garden. On the face of the sundial was something I
could not quite distinguish; it had moved just as the
photograph had been taken and the plate was blurred, but it
looked like a tiny person, no more than a foot high. The
caption read: *Caroly: Wood nymph: The Time Garden,
August 1881*.

In the next room watery light through the streaming
skylight cast strange, rippling shadows over the bare floorboards. Everywhere were piled trunks, up to the ceiling in
some places. When I opened them they turned out to be
filled with old clothes.

But what clothes! In the first I opened were pure silk
hunting stocks; white kid gloves still folded in their tissue
wrappings; voluminous skirts split for sidesaddle riding;
whips, crops, sticks, and over-the-knee hacking boots; hunting
pinks and dubbined britches stiff with French chalk. One
trunk held nothing but hats for every conceivable occasion,

from the most sober to the most preposterous: black
Brussels lace funeral veils; bird of paradise concoctions
bursting with fruit and feathers for the Fairyhouse Races;
smart straw boaters, ribbons still crisp and clean. In another
I found fringed parasols, painted Chinese fans, and mis-
matched pairs of pearl-studded opera gloves; in a third,
party dresses and ball gowns, all as fresh and clean as if
they had only last night been discarded after the Dublin
season and laid in their trunks by Mrs. O'Carolan. But best
of all, most beautiful of all, was what lay within the trunk
directly beneath the skylight: a Chantilly silk wedding
dress. I have never seen a dress so beautiful before, and I
never shall again. When I am to be a bride, I shall be wed
in such a dress of Chantilly taffeta and creme organdy. I
lifted it out of its folds and held it against me; there was no
mirror in the trunk room so I could only imagine how I
looked. It felt made for me, hidden away in that trunk in the
old servants' rooms all these years, waiting for my discovery. But I did not try it on. Somehow, the idea of it actually
touching my flesh disturbed me.

It was the third room that I adored most of all. Pushing
open the door, I saw a figure in the middle of the bare floor.
It gave me quite a start before I realised it was only the
reflection of my silly self in a full-length mirror. Even now,
as I try to write down my impressions on entering it, I find
that the only way to do justice to how the room revealed
itself to me is to recall it as a series of photographs. Sepia:
that was the first and overriding impression—of a creamy
brown light that seemed to be made up of memories of
things past. Stillness: motes of dust hung suspended in the
rays of chestnut light; the rafters were festooned with
bunches of flowers, set there to dry and desiccate in the still
air, long forgotten. A strange perfume haunted the room,
ubiquitous, unidentifiable, like the ashes of roses. The
ochre light was broken into planes and shafts by the rafters
and hanging posies of flowers. In one corner was a
beekeeper's hat, veil, and smoke can. In the shadows where
the sepia light did not reach, indistinct stepped pyramids
were revealed by my inspection to be rolls of piled
wallpaper. There in the shadows, the scent of sun-dried
paper, soft and yellow and musty, was magical.

I do not recall how long I stood there as the room revealed itself to me; I was, for the most part, simply overwhelmed. That in the fifteen years I have spent exploring every nook and cranny of this house and grounds I should never have known of these hidden rooms before amazes me now, but then, I stood spellbound, setting the bunches of drying flowers swaying with a touch, tracing the patterns of the old wallpapers and friezes.

I would have stayed longer, but in the distance I could hear Mrs. O'C calling me to lunch. That time already! With reluctance I closed the door and took one last look back into the room of dried flowers. I saw something. I am certain I saw something. No trick of the light, I saw reflected in the mirror the Chantilly lace wedding dress, standing, as if before an altar, and where the body should have been, was sheaf upon sheaf of dried flowers.

October 26, 1913

Craigdarragh
Drumcliffe
County Sligo

My Dear Dr. Chambers,

I trust that this letter, coming as it does after so long a period since our paths last crossed, will not prove too great a surprise; I sincerely hope that it finds you in the best of health and fortune. Perhaps you recall the occasion of our last meeting—five years ago, at the testimonial dinner in the Glendalough House Hotel for our old beloved Headmaster, Dr. Ames. Certainly, the evening is still vivid in my memory. We were seated opposite each other and I recall enjoying a most stimulating conversation on the Home Rule question and the problem of Ulster, those most perennial of chestnuts which have, once again, reared their shaggy heads. I had meant, many times, to congratulate you on your appointment as successor to the post as Headmaster of Balrothery Endowed School. The oversight was most remiss of me;

permit me to extend my sincerest best wishes for your past, and undoubted future, successes.

It is in your official capacity as Headmaster that, truth be told, I am writing to you. Please excuse my forwardness in so doing. Only the most extreme of circumstances, you must understand, would force me to such a pass. Alas, you cannot but be aware of the unfortunate lot that has befallen the Desmond household these past few months. The popular press doubtless penetrates even as shady a cloister as Balrothery Endowed, and, as a consequence, I am forced to put Craigdarragh and its lands onto the open market and content myself with a humbler estate in life. To this end, I am inquiring concerning the possibility of a teaching position at the school. I understand that you have experienced difficulties in recruiting staff of a suitable calibre in the disciplines of the sciences and mathematics—disciplines with which I am most intimately acquainted by dint of my former profession. I would consider it the greatest personal favour if you were to hold me in consideration should such a vacancy occur in the near future. You will need no assuring over my academic credentials, which are impeccable, and I know I can trust you to treat any slur the public domain may have cast upon my character with the contempt and disregard it so properly merits. I am sure that you will need no convincing that my services can be of enormous benefit to your establishment and, in concluding, may I express the fervent hope that you will look favourably upon my petition, and wish you the best of health, wealth, and happiness.

Yours Sincerely,
Edward Garret Desmond, Ph.D.

Emily's Diary: November 5, 1913

I am getting lazy and lackadaisical. I have not been keeping you up-to-date, dear diary. It has been almost ten days since I last made an entry in your pages. I can make all manner of excuses—my moods, my feelings, this general lethargy which seems to have filled my bones with lead; this thing in my belly. Sometimes I feel I am nothing more than an elaborate fold of flesh wrapped protectingly around this tiny, inhuman thing. Sometimes I feel I am a great fat lazy bubble of warm oil, tautly stretched, ready to burst at the slightest tap. But the truth is that the honesty of your pages, the openness of your secret heart, frightens me. You reproach me; you demand that I confess.

So, if I must confess, I will confess. And what sin shall Emily confess this day? Sloth? Already confessed, set down in blue ink, and absolved into the receiving paper. Anger, perhaps? Yes, *anger*, diary.

They were so apologetic, so careful and chary lest the least little word would cause me to once again tip over the breakfast table and storm off to my room. Everything was explained to me in very slow, very deliberate, very simple words, as if I were a foreigner, or an idiot.

I can still see the smile on Mummy's full, moist lips; still hear the smug politeness in her voice as she said, "Emily, we are going to have to move from Craigdarragh. I know it won't be easy for any of us—we all love this house dearly—but with the money your father will receive from the sale of the lands, we'll be able to find a nice little place somewhere close to Dublin where we can all try to be a family once again, with the governess I promised for you so you can continue your education, and maybe even a nurse for the baby."

I imagined this *nice little place*, some *desirable gentleman's town residence* in Ballsbridge or Palmerstown—a red brick terrace with steps to the front door and servants in the basement and smoke pouring out of the chimneys with nothing to see from the window but other chimneys pouring out smoke, and rooftops, and telephone wires. A place where the wild spirit of the land has been chained up and tamed and smothered under *respectability* and *properness* and *progress* so long it has died and rotted without anyone ever noticing. Horrible! Horrible! I jumped up and knocked over my chair, screaming, "No! No! No! No! You can't sell Craigdarragh. You can't sell my home. You can't. You can't make me go to Dublin. I'll run away, just you see . . ." and I was halfway out of the room before the simultaneous replies came: "The notices have already been posted in the newspapers," and "Where do you think you could go in your condition, girl?"

Anger, diary, anger, and a growing, crushing grey cloud of misery. I suppose I had always considered it somewhere in my heart to be an inevitability that Craigdarragh would have to be sold. But being an inevitability does not make it a joy. Dying is the inevitable of inevitables, but that does not make it into a thing to be looked forward to. My only respite from the anger and the sense of despair growing day by day, hour by hour, was in the attic rooms—particularly that room I have named the Room of the Floating Flowers. There especially is a spirit of serenity and tranquility, a sense of beauty and wonder waiting to be discovered. I find myself drawn to that spirit, but also I fear it, for it is the spirit of the old magic, the magic of stone and sky and sea. Strange—that which repels me is also that which attracts me, perverse creature that I am.

I have discovered a splendid and totally idle amusement: with a pair of Mrs. O'Carolan's sewing scissors, I snip out the beautiful and complicated floral patterns on the rolls of old wallpaper and borders. Having cut out the twining vines and stems and climbing roses and ornate foliage and fantastical birds half living, half flame, I then move the shapes around on the floor, arranging and rearranging and mixing and mingling and combining them into funny little hybrid creatures: flowery chimeras; cloudy dragons; ugly, funny little basilisks made from tangled foliage; goblins and sprites woven from flourishes and curvets. It was the patterns themselves that suggested the pastime to me; they seemed to me somehow incomplete in themselves—parts of a greater pattern that had been separated and trapped, immobile, powerless, on the printed paper. All I provide is the connection between long-sundered parts.

Remarkable—when I am sitting on a cushion on the floor, busy with scissors and glue pot, the time just vanishes. Before I know it the latticed rectangle of pale autumn sunlight has moved from the left wall across the floor to the other wall and Mrs. O'Carolan is calling me for supper. Perhaps time is flowing faster up there in the attic.

Perhaps the accumulated mass of the past gathered there is pulling time out of the future faster, like a weight on a line. Or perhaps, more mundanely, it is only that I am getting older every year and that it is the accumulated weight of time behind me that is unreeling the years with ever-increasing speed. What a horrible thing it must be to grow older and find that ever-decreasing number of years hurrying you faster, faster toward your grave, as if time were impatient to be rid of you.

I have deliberately hesitated in writing down the events of the Harvest Mass, not because it is the pinnacle (or should I say, rather, pit?) of this confession, but because what I saw there disturbed me so—disturbs me still.

I have always loved the great festivals of the Church. At those times, on those days, I feel the Church succeeds in bringing the spiritual realm and the worldly together. The flickering light of the Advent candles; the patient tolling of the iron bell, out across the winter fields, calling all the people to celebrate the death of the year and the birth of the Redeemer; the sombre pallid sorrow of the Paschal drama, pure, stripped of all colour and decoration, contrasted so wonderfully with the joyful celebration of resurrection and rebirth on Easter Day. When the Church reaches back to its ancient, elemental roots, heaven and earth seem closest. Most especially at the Harvest Mass, with the stacked sheathes of barley, the careful piles of apples and pears, the baskets of gooseberries and blackberries, the hampers laden with scrubbed carrots and parsnips, leeks the size of your arm, golden heads of onion and cauliflower, bushels of oats and rye; sacks and mounds of potatoes. *Mountains* of the noble potato are watched over by corn dollies and woven straw St. Brigid's Crosses. All celebrate the goodness, the holiness, of the earth we walk upon. For me it has always been the highlight of the Church Year. This year, as on every other Harvest morning, I was up with the lark getting myself ready. I dressed in my very finest, all earth colours, choosing russets and browns, tans and mustards and fir greens from my wardrobe. There wasn't much that would fit around my bump, but nevertheless, by ten thirty I was downstairs in the hall waiting for Daddy. When he came out of the drawing room, pulling on a pair of driving gauntlets, he was most surprised to see me.

"Emily," he said, "what are you doing?"

"I'm going with you to the Harvest Mass," I replied.

"My dear," he said, and from the words *my dear,* I knew nothing good was going to follow. "My dear, you can't come this year. I'm sorry, you'll have to stay behind."

I bit back the fury.

"Why can I not come?" I asked. Then out of the drawing room came Mummy, tying the ribbon on her Sunday hat in a bow beneath her chin, and the fury almost overwhelmed me, because Mummy never, never, goes to chapel. The one small battle she won over the Pope was that I would only go to Mass when and if I wanted to; she herself remained resolutely Protestant.

"Emily, darling," she said, "you're looking very prim this morning."

"She wants to go to the Harvest Mass," Daddy said, and Mummy looked at me as if I were a sick lamb or a lap dog and said, "But darling, dearest, you can't possibly go in your condition. Emily, darling, you don't know what you might catch, and, well, you wouldn't want to do anything that might hurt baby, would you? Just give it a miss this year, darling, all right? There'll be other years."

As if I were a lap dog, or a sick lamb. I was too furious to be able to do anything but stand there, dumb, stupid, while they got into the car and drove off. Mrs. O'Carolan waved shamefacedly and guiltily from the tip-up seat in the back. I watched them turn through the gates and down the road to Drumcliffe crossroads. Mummy's words whispered over and over and around and around in my head. But not the words she said; the words she meant. *"Darling, dearest, we can't possibly let you be seen out in your condition. I mean, what would the tenants, the priest, the neighbours, my friends think, for heaven's sake, if they saw an unmarried pregnant girl of not even sixteen sitting as bold as brass in the very House of God?"*

It was that decided me. I would not be shut away and hidden, a sordid object of sin and shame. One thought rang in my head as I stormed down the drive and along the road to the crossroads: I would be there, in the front pew, on my knees before my parents and the entire parish and God Himself. They were ashamed of me; they blamed me for what had happened; they held me responsible. A painful stitch in my belly wanted me to give up and stop, but it only stoked my fury all the more. I marched the mile and a half to the chapel in twenty minutes.

Father Halloran was about to start his homily (doubtless another tirade against the godless Protestant Unionists in the next county and the atheist socialists in Dublin); the people were rising from the prayer for the preacher as I entered. All I really remember is staring. Father Halloran was staring at me, and, seeing him staring, the parishioners turned around to see what had commanded his attention. My own father was blushing with embarrassment; rising from the pew to come to me, hurry me out. And myself; staring—not at the craning necks and turned heads, but at the centrepiece of the Harvest display. At the heart of the corn sheaves and plaited breads and St. Brigid's Crosses, there, *her,* all Chantilly silk and creme organdy, the bride's dress filled with dried flowers.

November 8, 1913

Advertisement in the *Irish Times*

Carswell & Greer: Estate Agents
For Sale
(By private contract or auction)

Craigdarragh House
&
Estate

We are delighted to be offering for sale this superb property in Drumcliffe, County Sligo, comprising of a superior Georgian country residence set in two and one half acres of mature landscaped gardens, together with its 180-acre estate.

Situated eight miles from the town of Sligo upon the

south-facing slopes of Ben Bulben Mountain, adjacent to
the local beauty spot of Bridestone Wood, the property
offers all the charm of the rural life with the conveniences
and comforts of urban sophistication, and would, in our
considered opinion, make the perfect country seat for a
discerning gentleman farmer—perhaps a retired military
officer or colonial administrator.

Craigdarragh House dates from 1778 and was constructed in the Palladian style by Mr. James Gandon, later
architect of the Dublin Custom House, and is a superla-
tive example of his early work in the smaller country
house *metier*.

The ground floor interior by John Adam comprises of
a Classical entrance portico, a spacious hall with hung
staircase, one of the few examples of its kind in the
western counties; a main drawing room enjoying superb
views across Sligo Bay; a dining room; two studies; a
small library; a games room with billiards table; a
morning room with attached conservatory; a kitchen with
scullery and housekeeper's bed-sitting room; larder; and
laundry room. The first floor interior, by the same
architect, contains two master bedrooms at the front of
the house, each commanding fine vistas of sea and
mountain; three secondary, or guest, bedrooms; two
bathrooms, a W. C., and a nursery. The spacious attic
contains domestics' rooms, storage, and shelving, and
may be reached by means of a concealed servants'
staircase.

All is tastefully decorated, and much is period and in
exquisite condition.

Exterior features include a stable block and stable yard
with small hay loft, a disused gate lodge and two and
one half acres of finely landscaped grounds, including
rhododendron walk, sunken garden, Italian garden, walled
kitchen garden, gazebo, and grass tennis court. Approximately fifty yards from the main house, close by the
demesne wall, is a small observatory.

The sale will also include the estate of Craigdarragh,
comprising of 180 acres of farmland, fifty acres of which
consist of the woodland known as Bridestone Wood, and

the remainder being divided between three tenant farms of sixty, forty-five, and twenty-five acres respectively.

The tenancies are held under secured ninety-nine-year leases registered since the 1881 Act, and the rentable values set by the Fair Rent Court range from five guineas per acre per annum for the richer lowland leases to fifteen shillings per acre per year for the poorer hillside farm.

The tenant farmers also enjoy rights of foraging and coppicing in the estate woodlands and rights of communal grazing on the common hillside beyond the demesne wall. The prospective buyer will please note that these tenancies, though renegotiated under the 1903 Act, have been held by the same families for at least seventy-five years and that the farmers can be considered exceptional and trustworthy tenants.

The vendor has instructed us to advise any interested parties that house and estate are intended to be sold as an entity: offers for the estate alone will not be entertained, offers for the house and gardens only in the event that, no purchaser for the entire property being forthcoming, the tenant farmers exercise their option to purchase their tenancies. However, we are quite certain that there will be no shortage of parties with an interest in the property as an entirety.

Quite simply, a property of this quality must be personally inspected to properly appreciate the value for money it represents. Potential purchasers may arrange for personal tours of the property either through our Dublin office, our Sligo branch, or through the estate owner, Dr. Edward Garret Desmond; telephone Sligo 202. Without doubt, Craigdarragh is one of the finest and most desirable properties to have featured on the open market in recent years, and, together with the proven profitability of the tenant farms, consideration will only be given to offers in excess of £23,000.

Dr. Edward Garret Desmond's Personal Diary: November 16, 1913

Like a rock rising from a troublous sea, this diary represents solidity and solace in these confusing times. To be able to write down, clearly, coherently, all one's clashing thoughts and feelings, to be able to order all one's confusions into disciplined ranks of blue copperplate—that is a great comfort in a bleak and chilly season. I take small comfort from the current closeness between Caroline and me. We both understand it is an artificial thing, a mutual defense against Emily's increasingly disturbing behaviour. Emily, Emily, what to do about Emily? Her terrible, sudden fits of fury have mercifully ended, only to be replaced with a withdrawn, sullen, silent depression. Nevertheless, I do not hesitate in writing down here that we are both terrified of our own daughter. She only comes down from her room to eat, two meals per day, surely not enough for one who is eating for two, and she is picky in the extreme in her menu. A meal she has enjoyed on numerous other occasions will be rejected, untouched, while she will devour with enthusiasm such things as parsnips and spinach, which she did not even grace with a sneer before. Our gentle (and not so gentle) coercions have failed. Even Mrs. O'Carolan's unsubtle bribery will not get her to unlock her door and communicate with us. If only we could make her understand that we only have her health and the baby's in consideration. It has come to such a pass that I am afraid that sometimes her prolonged absence suits us rather too well; denied her silent, sullen presence, it is all too much of a relief for Caroline and me to temporarily overlook her existence. So greatly does she overshadow our lives that, like the climate, like the view out of one's window, overfamiliarity has bred indifference.

Yet I suspect—no, I *know*—that she is considerably more active than she would have us believe. Why, in the dead of night, have I not on more than one occasion been awakened by the sound of footsteps in the old servants' quarters above that we have reopened for the inspection of prospective buyers? And have not many of the visitors I have conducted around the house been surprised to find little snippets and cuttings of what seems to be old wallpaper arranged so as to suggest spritelike nymphs and dryads? And in the strangest corners of the house: the bottom of the bath, the pelmet in the library, tucked into the drawing room chandelier—even behind the glass of the watercolour of Croagh Patrick from Clew Bay in the dining room.

More perplexing, and irritating, is to come down in the morning to a day's work to find that objects have been moved in the night: my books all rearranged on the shelves, my lacquered Japanese wastepaper basket upended over my globe of the heavens like a ludicrous fez; my electric reading lamp shut in a drawer and my fountain pen strewn across the carpet in its component parts. Caroline, too, has experienced these mysterious rearrangements—her work-books went missing only to be discovered days later by Mrs. O'Carolan stacked in the broom closet, and Mrs. O'Carolan herself has complained of finding kitchen utensils in places she never left them, of batches of dough left overnight to rise rammed down the plug hole of the scullery sink, or salted with Vim. Most astounding of all was to discover my antique Indian brass orrery, normally resident in the observatory, rusting in the rain in the middle of the tennis court. The thing weighs nigh on three hundred-weight, and takes all of Paddy-Joe's and Michael's strength, with the assistance of Dignan, to even budge it, let alone a four-months-pregnant fifteen-year-old! There is clearly something at work here that delights in confounding me. I do not know what it is. I cannot even begin to formulate a hypothesis—any conceptions I have are so outrageous as to be instantly dismissable. I can see that I will have to break, soon, and forcibly, if needs be, Emily's silence, and demand the truth from her.

December 2, 1913

Balrothery Endowed School
Balrothery
County Dublin

My Dear Edward,

It was with the greatest regret that I received the news of your misfortune. Please forgive me for not having responded with my sympathies sooner; however, I delayed writing for the most honest of motives—that of wishing to verify all the facts before being the bearer of good news. It is with the greatest delight to know that I am, in some small way, helping a fellow Old Boy out of difficulty that, on behalf of the Board of Governors, I am able to offer you the position of Master of Mathematics at Balrothery Endowed.

Mr. Foley, the previous head of department, died most tragically and unexpectedly at midterm, and his passing left a considerable gap in our Mathematics department. Fellow masters have been covering as best as possible, but what with examination classes and university candidacies, our resources have been somewhat stretched. Your letter of request came at just the God-sent moment, and on behalf of the Board of Governors, and the entire Teaching Staff, I am glad to welcome you back to Balrothery Endowed.

I realise, of course, that it may be some time before you are able to take up the position, what with the vicissitudes of moving home and family to Dublin, but our need is somewhat pressing, and I am wondering if it would be possible for you to take up teaching duties at the beginning of the new term, on January 4?

You'll find Balrothery Endowed still the same friendly school we so fondly remember, even on the other side of the gown. Many of the masters, like your good self, and my good self, are Old Boys, and we still draw pupils from the very finest class of family, of either denomination. I think you will be pleased at how little the school has changed since you and I walked its corridors.

In conclusion, I would be grateful if you would write at your earliest convenience to confirm your acceptance of the position, and if there are any ways in which I or the staff can assist your move and subsequent settling in, feel at complete liberty just to name it. My congratulations on your success, and my every good wish for your future at Balrothery Endowed.

Sincerely,
Oswald Chambers, M.A., Dip. Ed.
Headmaster

Emily's Diary: December 21, 1913

In the night I can hear them, the tiny, whispering, tearing noises as they rip themselves free from their wallpaper and fold themselves to slip through the gaps under the doors, behind the skirtings, between the floorboards; folding and unfolding, folding and refolding as they scurry through the sleeping house, touching, exploring, testing, feeling. When I get up to turn on the light and catch them in their foldings and unfoldings, the soft, secret rustlings, they press themselves against the walls and become paper patterns again; they slip under the carpets. And by day I see them everywhere, and nowhere—a flicker of movement; a swift, sudden darting in the corner of my eye that freezes into immobility whenever I turn to look; a looming shadow over my shoulder that, when I spin around, is only a pattern acid-etched into a glass lamp globe.

I know what it is they want from me. They want me to embrace the old magic that has come out of the wood searching for me. They want me to take the hands they reach out toward me, and lead me away. And that both terrifies me and thrills me, because I know there is a part of me that still cries out, *Yes, yes, take me away with you. I have had enough of being human. Dress me in Chantilly lace and creme organdy and sweep me away into whatever you will for me and the baby.*

Now I understand why, when I first saw that dress, I did not try it on; to have put it on would have been to accept them and their will for me. To put it on would have been to make myself the Maid of the Flowers, the Queen of Morning. I dared not take more than a passing glance in a mirror for fear that She would be waiting there for me, the wedding dress filled with dried flowers. But She is no longer confined to mirrors. She has grown strong, broken free of Her constraints. Looking out the french windows in the drawing room I have seen Her floating, mist-hidden, in the sunken garden. Another time, I saw Her in the summerhouse and the sense of beckoning that overcame me was so powerful that without a thought I was out in the early December drizzle and rushing down the rhododendron walk toward the summoning figure. It was a vain pursuit, of course. I found only cobwebs, and dead moths and the dry woody scent of ancient summers. After stern warnings, Mummy and Daddy forbade me to go outside again until after the baby has come. I do not need to go outside to be in no doubt about where She is beckoning me; from attic to house to gardens to summerhouse, She is leading me, step by step, toward Bridestone Wood. Just before dark yesterday I glanced out my bedroom window and saw Her by the stile across the demesne wall into Bridestone Wood. This morning, looking again, I glimpsed Her through the cold grey mist, a half-seen phantom gliding between the nearer trees at the edge of the wood, beckoning, calling.

This is the essence of my dilemma. Do I accept that call or do I reject it? Dr. Orr and his clinic convinced me of one view of the world; my memories and experiences tell me a different view is true. They cannot be at peace under the same roof—oh, sometimes I feel I am going mad! Everywhere I hear voices, shouting—a voice in every wall, every door, every piece of furniture, shouting, "Decide! Decide! Decide!" Which is it to be, the world or the wildwoods? Choose the world and I dissolve all the magic and mystery and beauty into a foggy limbo of delusion. Do I want to think of myself as a person visited by delusions? Choose Otherworld, and I leave all that Dr. Orr taught me about myself lying discarded, like outworn clothes, on the floor. Decide! Decide! Decide!

The old servants' rooms are no longer the safe and magical sanctuary I once rejoiced in. The time before last I went up they were filled with a sense of watching, of waiting, of hungry anticipation so menacing that I could progress no farther than the Room of Forgotten Memories, torn between attraction and repulsion. Louder the voices called: *Come away, oh human child, to the water and the wild* . . . Louder, the voice of my denial thundered back at them, until I could bear no more, and in a frenzy I picked up the nearest object to hand and blindly smashed it to the floor. Glass shattered . . . and it was as hushed as the great silence before creation. Broken on the floor lay the framed photograph entitled: *Caroly: Wood Nymph: The Time Garden, August 1881.*

I had won one small tactical victory, but the inevitable conflict could not be long postponed.

And it was not.

For a week after the smashing of the photograph I had resisted returning to the attic—a week in which the supernatural forces about me seemed to double and redouble their assault as Craigdarragh prepared itself for a final, desultory Christmas. The flicker-shimmer of the Wallpaper People in the edge of my vision was a constant, distracting blur and I was subject to continual headaches. The magic mounted like approaching thunder as the token tree went up, hung with candles. The token streamers were stretched across the drawing room ceiling, and the hall decked with posies of ivy and mistletoe, the door with its holly wreath. In the deep night the entire house would tremble and shudder, as if shaken in a slumber. I knew it would only end when I finally confronted the decision and made my choice. I wondered about the broken photograph in the Room of Forgotten Memories, how my mother had chosen Caroline the toast of Gaelic Literary League over Caroly with the Wood Nymph in the Time Garden, and came to understand why she had left those attic rooms locked all these years. More than anything, I would have loved her to have shared that time with me, but I knew she could not for fear that she might find those doors she had thought so firmly locked and barred had in truth been ajar all these years. So it was that, after long and painful deliberation, I found that there was no choice to be made at all, and, long after the house was asleep, climbed the narrow staircase to the old servants' quarters, oil lamp in hand.

It was strong in those rooms that night, stronger than I have ever felt it before—a riptide that would sweep me away if for one instant I ever lost contact with the sure foundation of reality. It took all my physical and mental strength to slow its inexorable attraction to an advance of one cautious step at a time. The face of my mother looked through splintered glass at me. Suddenly feeling the need for some defence, I stooped and picked up a long shard of glass, my dagger. The door into the next room opened before me. A mad moonlight, shivered by racing clouds, patterned the floor. Step by step, I was drawn through the room of the discarded clothes into the Room of the Floating Flowers.

Beyond the door, the mirror awaited me. I looked within. There was the Maid of Flowers, in the empty doorway behind me. I whirled, quick as thought, and this time it was no illusion. The folds and pleats of chestnut silk rustled in the softly moving air; the flower heads whispered among themselves. I could have touched it . . . I almost did. My fingers were reaching out, and then I saw what I was doing, realised the consequence of my action, and lashed out with the dagger of glass from the broken photograph. With an almost human cry, the fabric ripped from breast to thigh. Inside the torn bodice I saw white roots, tangling, twining, *moving*. I started back in alarm, and out they came. Out of the rolls of wallpaper and the borders and friezes and covings where they had been trapped, the Wallpaper People came, strands and whorls of printed foliage, tearing themselves away from the paper—the sprites, the hobgoblins, the dragons and basilisks and salamanders. They flocked about me, mobbed me; like bats they flittered in my face, caught in my hair. I tried to pull them free and tear them into pieces but they were too many. In desperation I slashed and cut with my glass dagger. I will never forget the horrid, squeaking cries they made as I cut and slashed them with the sharp glass. I cut and cut and cut my way toward the door and into the Trunk Room. I tried to slam the door shut on the Wallpaper People but they were too sprightly, too thin; the few I trapped in the hinge writhed and flapped most horribly. I winced—something had grazed my cheek. A paper hobgoblin flapped away from me and I realised that it had cut me exactly as a sheet of paper, carelessly handled, will lay open flesh. I snatched at the hobgoblin and tore it to pieces but the Wallpaper People were swift to learn this new and dreadful tactic and they mobbed me with renewed vigour, cutting, slitting, gashing. I could not sweep them away from me. I lashed out futilcly with my blade and all the while the room beat like a wolf-skin drum as thc trunks in which the clothes were stored rattled and thumped impatiently on the bare wood floor. I fled, hiding my face in my hands, into the Room of Forgotten Memories. Scenting blood, the Wallpaper People came after me. Blood ran from my lacerated hands down the sleeves of my nightdress. I could not close the door or they would have been at my mouth and eyes. I stumbled blindly across the room, scattering piles of old photographs. Above and beyond the insistent drumbeat and bat chatter I heard voices calling, the voices of the people in the photographs, those voices from long ago, all calling the same words—*Choose . . . choose . . . choose . . . choose . . . choose. . . .* I found myself again looking at the broken photograph of my mother. She regarded me with a terrible look of accusation. The storm of voices and flapping wings peaked to a crescendo around me. For a moment I thought I had tumbled finally, exultantly, into insanity, and she was there, before me, the Maid of the Flowers, in the doorway to the servants' staircase.

The riptide of panic, confusion, shouting voices, and flocking, snapping paper demons tore at me, tore away the underpinnings of reality to which I had anchored myself. In an instant I was swept away, into the Otherworld. Suddenly everything was clear, everything shone with a tremendous light. I knew what I wanted more than anything in this world or the other. I lunged forward and embraced the Maid of the Flowers in my arms. At my touch all the false life went out of it. It fell in folds around me, and I felt that I was drowning in cascades of flowers and wet, black, smothering earth. The stench of humus clogged my lungs, unclean soil filled my mouth and cheeks so that I could hardly press past it the words, "Yes! Yes, I will, yes."

I was in the Room of Floating Flowers, before the mirror that stood in the middle of the bare floor. The floors, the walls, the ceiling, the glass skylight admitted a wind-driven moonlight, and all were covered with Wallpaper People. I stooped to touch one, apprehensive that it might leap for my eyes. It was inanimate and immovable, as if it had been painted there. I looked into the mirror. I beheld myself, the Maid of the Flowers, the long-expected Queen of the Morning, dressed in this garment which had been prepared for me from beyond time. I traced the edge of the gash my blade had torn, and the beautiful fabric hung away, baring me from breast to loins. My pregnant belly bulged through the ripped taffeta. I posed, I turned, I spun and wheeled, glorying in the sight of myself in my wedding dress, its folds soft against my skin, scented like spring, like sky. A giddy exultation, almost a drunkenness, burst over me. I raced to the skylight, threw it open, leaned out to bask in the warmth of the moonlight and survey my domain. To the left the land fell away toward the dark sea in parcelled farms and holdings. To the right Ben Bulben rose like a stone dragon breaking from beneath the surface of the sea. Before me, the garden twinkled under frost, its boundaries with the woodland soft, indistinct, as its designer had always intended. And beyond them were the woods. I gasped. Suddenly the house and the gardens became a small ark lost in an ocean of treetops. To my amazed vision, the woods broke the boundaries of the demesne, the land, and even the ocean. They stretched on forever into another country, another landscape. As I beheld, I heard, far off, the horns of the Wild Hunt and the baying of the red-eared hounds of the Ever-Young. I knew what it was they hunted, what it was they had always hunted, through Rathfarnham Woods, through Bridestone Wood, across the slopes of Ben Bulben and the hillsides of my dreams. Soon, very soon, they would come to take me from the dross and drear and ashes of this world into the endless light of Otherworld. Soon, very soon, I would, *I will*, break apart and cast off my human shape and name and history and all their limitations, and, a current in the sea of dreaming, ever moving, ever changing, immortal, inhuman, become legend.

December 28, 1913

Glendun
Blackrock Road
Blackrock
County Dublin

My Dear Connie,

At last, the hour of synthesis! Months of hacking my way through the jungle of false leads and speculations surrounding the Craigdarragh Case have finally ended; I am at last emerging from the general murk, and may even be able to proffer a tentative hypothesis.

Recent research in England into supernatural activity has uncovered a close relationship between emotionally or sexually troubled adolescents and psychic activity—phantom noises, the odd poltergeist, strange lights in the sky, bizarre changes of temperature in different parts of the home. I don't think it would strain the definition of supernatural activity too far for it to include the faery manifestations of the Craigdarragh Case, and it seems appropriate for them to be expressions of Emily's repressed sexuality lashing out from her subconscious.

This was the point I was striving to draw out in the interviews in inquiring about the regularity of Emily's periods. Many thanks for the copy of the transcripts. This whole endeavor would have been sunk without trace if not for some documentary foundation upon which to build them. *Menarche* can be a most disturbing time. For some girls, it may be so alarming that it leaves a permanent psychological scar. My intention was to establish a link between Emily's periods—those times of emotional, sexual, and physiological stress—the faery manifestations, and the electrical disturbances. These latter are far from the insignificant irritations the Desmonds made them out to be. More about them later. For the meantime, the correlation between these elements is exact enough to be extremely significant, though as with everything in this uncertainty-dogged discipline, a fraction short of the incontrovertible. Further, the fact that her periods coincide to an abnormally high degree with the New Moon (in all religions and mythological structures, a time of enormous symbolic and mystical significance), only reinforces my conclusions all the more.

The blessèd Yeats would no doubt have us believe that County Sligo (for that matter, all Ireland) is aswarm with faery warriors and mythological heroes only waiting to be discovered, have their photographs printed on the front page of *Stubb's Gazette*, etc., etc. My approach would be less literal. Whereas he would maintain that the faeries already existed and were only observed by Emily, I would argue rather that the faeries had no existence at all until Emily observed them; that is, that she in fact created them. The power of will over matter has long been attested to by our navel-contemplating mystic cousins on their snowy Tibetan mountainsides; their contorted psyches can apparently create material, living objects purely by force of will. If they are merely exercising for their own amusement a talent latent within all of us, perhaps it is not so surprising to find it hiding out in deepest County Sligo.

So far so good? Right. Then I shall lead you a little further into the realms of speculation. Taking all the above into consideration, I wonder, is it possible, at a deeply subconscious level, far beyond any yet tapped by hypnosis or even theorised by the good Dr. Freud, that the human mind is in direct contact with the intimate fabric of nature? That there is an underlying mental structure to the universe with which certain individuals, at certain times, under circumstances, can come into direct contact? (Pardon the purple prose, Connie, but the King's English has yet to devise expressions adequate for expressing this primordial structure.) If, as philosophers insist, reality can only be what we perceive it to be, is it possible that, in contact with this subjective sea of being, the very nature of it, and thus of our reality, may be changed?

By now (I hope), my reasoning should be becoming

clear to you, Connie dearest. Emily's frustrated sexual desires and fears touched upon this ancient reality-shaping consciousness deep below any sentient level of her mind and that power, acting through her personal symbolic mythology, gave the ultimate shape of her fancies and fantasies. I cannot help but wonder, would the Olympian Yeats be fair tickled to learn that he was, in a sense, responsible for the creation of his own symbolism? Or would he be horrified? Rather the latter, I think.

Yet there are inconsistencies in applying this theory as a universal panacea. This is the problem with research in this damnable field. Nothing is ever cut, dried, and pickled in formalin. It is like fighting the sea—you think you have one bit pinned down, and up pops another. Nothing plays by the rules, if, indeed, there are any rules to play by. The most glaring inconsistency is this: if the faeries were the wish shapes of Emily's repressed sexuality, why then did they turn on her and rape her? (I am convinced that, popular press notwithstanding, the perpetrator was not of earthly origin. The timing of the incident is too pat; the location, the entire symbolism, is too appropriate to be coincidental.) I do have a plausible offering. Tell me what you think. Back to the deep levels of the preconscious mind, if Emily was capable of giving form and shape to her subconscious desires, could she not also be capable of giving shape and form to her subconscious fears and dreads? For in the deep levels of the mind, fears are as uncontrollable as desires. So I would argue that at the moment of her greatest desire, for sexual, *romantic* fulfillment, all the fears, dreads, and guilts she learned from the Sisters at Cross and Passion (I am under no illusions about even "enlightened" convent schools) transformed her dream lover, the Lugh figure from the interviews, into her nightmare violator, punishing her for her sins.

I haven't forgotten about the electricity. Things really start to become *outré* here. Please bear with me. I have no evidence for what I am about to say, nor even know whether it is scientifically allowable, but I believe that Emily generated her mythological forms out of electricity. In this world, or Otherworld, you cannot get something for nothing. Something must power the transformation. The scientists tell us that matter and energy can neither be destroyed nor created; but may they be mutually interchangeable? Improbable, even impossible, in this level of reality, but at the preconscious level, the primary level of the universe, this might be more easily achievable than one would imagine. Mere unconscious reflex could cause Emily to draw upon whatever source of energy was convenient to generate her faeries.

Indeed, she may have been unconsciously drawing upon this power to create faeries for quite some time. For your delectation and delight, I enclose this rather intriguing cutting from the press:

May 27, 1913

Irish Independent Morning Edition:

MYSTERY POWER FAILURE STRIKES DUBLIN!

The Dublin Electrical Company has still to provide an explanation for the mysterious current failure that plunged the entire south side of the city into chaos between the hours of six and seven o'clock yesterday evening when domestic supplies were cut off, causing widespread public consternation.

Transportation was brought to a standstill. The electrical failure immobilised trams, which then created further congestion as other road users and vehicular traffic piled up around the stranded cars. Adding to the general chaos, telegram and telephone services were suspended for the hour, effectively isolating South Dublin from the rest of the country and the Empire.

As of yet no explanation has been received by this newspaper for the power failure. Scientific opinion is utterly baffled, and a spokesman from the Dublin Electrical Company has stated that during the period of the failure all the Company's generators at the Ringsend plant were operating at full capacity and the gauges in the plant registered that full voltage was being supplied. The Company engineers are at this moment checking and rechecking the transformers (which reduce the voltage supplied by the generators to a level safe for domestic usage), and though it is assumed that the cause of the failure will be found in the transmission system, Mr. Norman Parkinson, the Company spokesman, says that he has not ruled out sabotage by some extreme nationalist group.

Intriguing, no? And how similar to the notices a few months later when a massive electrical failure coincided with the disappearance of Bell's Comet. Which leads me to my most outrageous observation of all. If Emily could generate a host of the Sidhe out of stolen electricity, she could as easily have generated the astronomical object Dr. Desmond maintained (and still maintains) was an otherworldly space vehicle. It is only a matter of scale and projection, after all, and the scientists tell us that energy is many, many times more plentiful in the void than upon this earth. There are just too many coincidences between the faery and the astronomical for any other conclusion to be tenable. In the words of Conan Doyle's admirable Holmes, when we have exhausted the possible, whatever remains, however impossible, must be the truth. Emily created both faery host and Altairii, the former to fulfill her own emotional and sexual needs, the latter to punish what she clearly saw as her inadequate father—the father whose work came fair and square first and foremost in his life.

So, what now? Is there an end to the Craigdarragh Case with the conception of the baby? (Further thanks for keeping me so well informed as to the goings-on over there in Drumcliffe. More direct inquiry would be impolitic, given the turn of events.) I think not. From what you have told me, Caroline Desmond fears that the faery manifestations may be returning, though it must be noted, without the attendant electrical disturbances. The child in Emily's womb may be responsible for this. What she is carrying is, in a sense, half human, half mythical, and I feel it may be acting as a kind of taproot into the energy of this preconscious symbolic domain. It may be utilising the energy inherent in all things animate and inanimate on the earth—living things, growing things, stone, sea, sky. (Did you know there is a potential difference between the bottom of the atmosphere where we poor humans grub out our existences, and the outer- most layers, of some twenty-five thousand volts? Power enough, and to spare, to generate whole legions of the Sidhe—power being constantly siphoned and shaped through Emily's unborn child.

So, in closing (this letter has, I fear, like Topsy, just growed and growed), the final question must be, what of the child Emily Desmond bears within her? Be it mortal, be it god, I can only say that it will stand forever before her as a haunting reminder of that Otherworld which, for one single, searing second upon that hillside, embraced her, and which she has irretrievably lost.

Yours,
Hanny

The Lost Girl

(From the *Comhaltas Ceoltoiri Eireann* sound archive: Belgrave Square, Monkstown, Dublin. The MacNamara Collection of Oral History recordings, 1921–1939. Archive B34/6: Mr. Gerard Brennan of Drumcliffe Parish, County Sligo, farmhand on the Cunningham demesne, Rossnaree, speaking in the Sweet Briar public house: August 29, 1927.)

'Twas as foul a night as I can remember. The wind was blowing straight off the Atlantic; take the polish clean off the toe of your boot, it would, and the rain, the rain! Soak you to the bone in one second, it would; the kind of rain it was you hear beating on your windows of a night and in your warm bed you say to yourself, "Pity the poor soul has to be out in that," little thinking it might be yourself.

There were, let me think, yes, eight of us. Yes, eight; my- self, the brother Dermot; Old Tomas; the O'Carolan boys, God be kind to them, both of them dead in the war; Noel

Duignan, the big fellow, clever with his hands, if you catch my drift; Mr. Cunningham, and Dr. Desmond from down at Craigdarragh. His it was the daughter who had run off. Run off, on a night like that, and she five months' pregnant! 'Twas a great scandal in the village at the time, you must understand, the Desmond girl's pregnancy. Now, I know all of you read about the rape case in the papers, how they never got hide nor hair of the boy as did it. It must have unhinged her a little, affected the balance of her judgement. She always had been a queer bird, that Emily Desmond— queer bird from a queer nest, given to daydreaming and wandering off by herself into the woods, head full of all manner of nonsense. Is it any wonder, I ask you, that what happened happened? Brought it on herself, I say. Asking for trouble. But what can you expect, with parents like hers? Marry your own kind, that's what I say; oil and water don't mix. The mother, she was of the other persuasion; always acted like she thought she was too good for our village. She wrote the poetry, so you can imagine what kind of a woman she was. The father, Dr. Edward Garret Desmond, he was a fine gentleman, but given to great and eccentric notions. You've heard no doubt of Desmond's Downfall, also known as Desmond's Disgrace, Desmond's Despair, Desmond's Disaster. Well, 'twas a big story in the newspapers at the time. That Dr. Desmond. Wired to the moon, all of them. Anyway, there was a financial scandal, and he'd been forced to sell Craigdarragh. Ten generations of Desmonds grew up within those walls, and now they're gone, sold out to some foreigner from across the water. The end of the Desmonds. Well, I reckon young Emily couldn't face the leaving and in her half-crazy state of mind ran away, on the very worst night of the year, to hide herself in the woods. Anyway, up to Rossnaree comes the good Dr. Desmond, such a panic you've never seen, and I for one wouldn't condemn him, not on a night like that. So, Mr. Cunningham turns out the boys and tumbles us out of our cosy beds. We dressed as best we could in oilskins and sou'westers and rain capes, but I tell you, even standing there in the stable yard waiting for the lady of the house to light the lanterns for us, we were mortally soaked through to the skin, and half frozen to death, what with that vicious wind howling through every crevice in our oilskins.

'Twas about, let me think, yes, eleven o'clock when we set out; eleven o'clock certainly, because I remember Mrs. Cunningham standing in the kitchen door and asking us what time we would be back so she could have the tea and fruit loaf waiting for us. And Mr. Cunningham says, we'll be back when we're back, and with that off we set, our lanterns swinging to and fro in the wind and the night as black and foul as the very pit of hell itself. The plan was for us to search the southeast end of Bridestone Wood. Dr. Desmond had already been on the telephone to the police station and Sergeant O'Rourke and the boys from the village were going to work their way down from the northwest. The idea was that we'd meet up somewhere in the middle. That was the plan, but within minutes we were all separated from each other, and I don't mind telling you, this fellow was afraid. It was bad enough, what with the rain and the howling wind and me not able to see two feet in front of me, prodding out my way with this big stick I'd cut from the coppice. But the worst part of it was never knowing what I was going to find—whether the girl would be alive or dead, or what. Grim it was, grim. And I'll tell you more, say what you like about idle superstition; there's not a man here is going to tell me there wasn't something strange going on in that wood that night. All those weird shadowy things moving out there among the trees just beyond the range of my lantern light, those crashing sounds in the brambles and dead bracken that always stopped when I stopped myself to listen. I tell you, it was enough even to scare Big Noel Duignan, and he the bravest fistfighter in all Sligo. Been on the circuit across the water, he had, fought for fifty-guinea purses, and he himself told me he was shaking like a kitten. But worse even than the shadows were the voices. At first they were the voices of Big Noel and the others, and I called out to them, but they would not answer. Then I thought maybe it was the lost girl, and I called out her name. No answer. Then I stood still a moment just to listen and I could hear them clear over the howling of the wind and the lashing of the trees and the beating of the rain—voices whispering and laughing, so close I should have been able to see who they belonged to, but wherever I turned my lantern I saw only the shadows, like something huge and dark flying between the trees. Well, I had no intention whatsoever of staying there one minute longer than I had to, so on I pushed, and then all of a sudden I saw this light, far off among the trees. It seemed miles distant at one moment, then so close you could reach out and touch it the next, and I thought to myself, *'Tis the faeries. This is the pixie light of the faeries come to lure me to their kingdom under the hill.* I was petrified. Couldn't move a muscle, not even to blink, I was so scared. Then there was a crashing and clattering like doomsday itself and out of the bushes came—well, who should it be but Sergeant O'Rourke himself. And says he, "What do you think you're doing standing there like a buck eejit with your gob open, you stupid bugger? Don't you know you've been wandering around in circles for the past ten minutes, long after everyone else's met up and moved on?" He gave me a police whistle and pointed me up the slope, where the rest had gone on, and he shouted in his best peeler voice, "You see anything, you blow like buggery, for you could shout yourself hoarse and we'd never hear you in this storm."

So, up the slope went I, thrashing at the briars with my stout stick and calling out the girl's name, for all the good it would do in that din, not able to see more than two inches in front of me, slipping and sliding and be-jasusing and cursin' like a bloody heathen, God forgive me. I think I must have climbed for half an hour, then all of a sudden I was out of the trees on the slopes of the mountain. The wind was cruelly fierce now—near blew me clean away, it did—and I was so wet by now it'd've made no difference if I'd chucked off my oilskins and gone up that mountain bare-arse naked. My hands were so cold and numb they could scarce hold the lantern. Looking about me I saw strung out across the hillside the lamps of all the other lads who'd come out to search for the lost girl. I stood a while taking my bearings. I had the feeling of something in front of me—something huge and dark, cold and hard, which I could not see. I edged forward, cautious as a cat on a precipice, God alone knows why. I suppose it was that wood had spooked me. Then, all of a sudden, I knew what that dark shadow was. 'Twas the Bridestone.

Well, that brought me up proper and short, for this night the thing seemed twice as tall and thrice as wide as Ben Bulben itself, and think what you may, but that night, that block of stone felt almost alive, as if all those strange feelings that had been following me through the wood were coming from this heathen slab of stone. Well, my friends, there I was, standing like an idiot in front of this great stone, and it humming like a bee, I swear, with the rain just streaming down me, when I heard the sound. 'Twas the sound of someone crying—someone not more than two steps from me, else I would not have heard them over the wind. I knew this was no trick of the night. This was mortal flesh and blood. Raising my lantern high, I ventured forward with what small boldness I could muster, and 'twas there that I found her, the lost girl, sheltering in the lee of the big stone.

Well, a proper sight she was, sobbing and weeping and shivering and muttering over and over to herself these words, "Why don't they come? Oh, why don't they come, why don't they come?" Just those words, over and over and over. A sight she was, hair all lank and plastered flat by the rain, and dressed in nothing but what seemed in my poor lantern light to be a old wedding dress, torn and slashed most terribly. Barefoot she was, not a word of shoes or stockings.

So, what did this fellow do? Blowed his lungs out down that police whistle, that's what he did. And all across the hillside those little bobbing lights froze stock-still, and then came running toward me. I don't think the girl even knew I was there until I started blowing the whistle. She looked up all startled and I saw her eyes looking square at me and, boys, I don't mind telling you, what I saw there fair knocked the blow out of me. Her eyes were empty, boys. Nothing there. Nothing. Not even sockets. Just darkness—a dark, empty space, with things like, well, I don't know, like faraway stars, shining in them. I can see it yet, my friends.

At the sight of all the rest of the lads arriving posthaste, she upped and ran, like the billy-o. I tell you this, if she'd been a filly in the Sligo Races, I'd've made a bob or two out of her. I shouted at her to come back, but, well, that was a waste of time, with the wind roaring and howling so I could hardly hear myself. So I set off after her. She went up those slopes like a prize greyhound. Never seen anyone so fleet of foot, and her five months gone. There was I, slipping and sliding and be-jasusing trying to keep up, and she was getting farther and farther ahead of me. I looked up to see where I was, for I'd lost track of my bearings again, not being a creature graced with a great head for heights, and what I saw then, well, I don't mind telling you, it queer froze my heart. It was like mist, like a thick fog, pouring off the top of the mountain. Like a great river it was. Why, it seemed to me it was almost solid, rolling down the slopes of the mountain. But it was red, Red fog. And in a wind that would have torn any normal fog to tatters. Now do you understand why I stood paralysed in mortal fear? No natural fog, this. The Desmond girl, she stopped the same as I had, and she looked at this red fog spilling down the mountainside. Then she turned and looked at me, at all of us, struggling up that hillside in the pelting rain, and the look on her face was as if she was seeing the thing she had wanted most in all the world. Like an angel's, that face— like a sinner at the gates of heaven. That look I will never forget—no sir, not as long as I live. Then she turned and walked very slowly, very deliberately, into the red fog.

It swallowed her up, as completely as if she had never been, and then the fog, that unholy fog, I tell you, it stopped. Stopped dead. And, just as it had come spilling down the hillside, it rolled back again, up the slopes, over the top of Ben Bulben, and vanished. Of the girl who walked into the fog, the Desmond girl, there was not a trace. We went back there the next day and went over every inch of that hillside and didn't find so much as a hair. And that's as true as I'm standing here. And if you think I'm a liar, you ask of the others who were there that night. They will all testify my story is true. But, you ask, as I ask, and ask myself often, what of the girl? What happened to young Emily Desmond and her unborn child? Who knows? Who will tell what happened to her? No one.

PART II

THE MYTHLINES

So we set our eyes not on what is seen, but on what is unseen.
For what is seen is temporary, but what is unseen is eternal.
—2 Corinthians 4:18

1

Twenty miles gone and nothing to be done. Through rain, and rain, and pissing rain, and anagrams. The pissing rain had started two miles out of Dundalk, just where the road paid nodding acquaintance with the Catholic cemetery. With eighteen miles and the mountains before him, Gonzaga had lapsed sullenly into Nagmara. The smaller, darker man always reverted to speaking in anagrams when he was not happy. Solving the anagrams provided Tiresias, who was taller, thinner, and greyer, with a welcome intellectual diversion from the brainless formalities of boot before boot, mile after mile, through rain, and rain, and pissing rain. Where feather rags of cold, sodden cloud reached down the hillsides to touch Ravensdale Wood, Farmer Mulvenna of Jonesborough passing with his pigs and his new Ferguson tractor on his way over the border to Newry town bent down from his proud and lofty seat (a Ferguson tractor was an object of veneration in Jonesborough in 1930-something) to offer two saturated tramps a lift. If they didn't mind sharing with the pigs in the trailer, that was.

"Sir, beggars cannot be choosers," Tiresias had declared. "And, my dear Gonzaga, are we not the most mendicant of all that brotherhood? And is not the pig the most blessed of animals? The heathen Chinee consider doubly blessed the house that harbours a pig beneath its rafters, a sympathy unequivocally echoed by the citizens of these Four Green Fields of Ours. Do we not invite the fine pink gentleman to be our co-domiciliaries? Is it not a commonly maintained belief that, alone of all creatures, the noble pig was blessed by its Creator with the ability to see the wind? And, therefore, is it not fitting that we should also share with them this transport of delight, sharing, already, as I do, the gift of the discernment of things unseen?"

"Do youse want a lift, or do you want to stand there in the rain all afternoon gabbin'?" asked Farmer Mulvenna of Jonesborough. Gonzaga was already grubbing around in the muck and straw on the floor of the trailer for small, forgotten items for his sack. As Yeoman Mulvenna, his pigs, and his passengers jolted proudly onward to Newry town, Tiresias discoursed briefly on Chinese Taoist thought with relation to the Two Principles, illustrating his lecture with instructive fables from the Ching Dynasty. "You are aware, my dear Gogo, that in China the beggar was a person of some consequence? Many were members of mendicant guilds, and I cannot but think that it would serve us well to emulate their example. It was the established practice for a member of a medicant order to bang a gong or blow a trumpet or in some other fashion contrive to make a general nuisance of himself until the citizenry paid sufficient for him to desist his efforts. Some, would you believe, Gogo, used to swing dead cats around their heads on a rope, doubtless causing not inconsiderable distress to the very great number of feline fanciers particular to that dynastic period. Indeed, Gogo, so well organised were the beggars of Classical China that a token annuity to the guild coffers from a merchant or householder would grant immunity from their solicitings for a whole year. I would dearly love a cup of Earl Grey, Gogo—dearly."

"Ha,a! Fnoud eno!"

Gonzaga's filth-smeared face smiled up from between the pink vaulted backs of Farmer Mulvenna's pigs. Between his fingers he held a Free State penny. He wiped it clean, waved it triumphantly beneath Tiresias's nose, then thrust it into the depths of a much-worn, more soiled trooper's knapsack.

Twenty miles of rain, and nothing to be done, and rain, and anagrams; not one single worthy soul generous enough to save a tramp's shoe leather by offering him a lift. In the temporary respite offered by the walls of a ruinous castle that stood picturesquely by the waterside, Gonzaga began to snuffle, nose to the ground, in search of further treasures for his sack. "On any other day, in any other weather, at any other season," intoned Tiresias, watching the rain fall from the grey sky. Nothing found, they pressed on through countless millions of raindrops along the coast-hugging road, past the pines that demurely screened the seafront summer residences and the habits of their moneyed tenants from rude gazes. Before them rose the steeples and smokes of the village that was their destination, and beyond and above, the slopes of the mountains. Tiresias bade his colleague wait a moment while he admired the view.

"Comparable to the Corniche of Monte Carlo, or that oft-gloried road that wends south out of Naples, under the breath of Vesuvius, to Sorrento, would you not agree, Gogo? However, my boots are killing me. Or, to translate directly from the Irish, more grammatically than idiomatically, 'the boots they do be killing me.' "

They took a rest on the steps of a small obelisk erected with startling abruptness in an otherwise unremarkable cow pasture by the road.

"Erected in memory of Major Robert John Ross, who, in the War of 1814 with the colonials, actually succeeded in capturing and burning the White House, but not before he had helped himself to the presidential repast, still hot on the table, and liberated the presidential wine cellar. Apparently, it was quail on the menu." Tiresias read from the legend engraved upon the stone as, grumbling and gasping, he eased off his boots; left, then right. "Oh, Gogo, ah; the simple ecstasies are the most profound. Oh . . . ahhh . . ." Gonzaga picked up flakes of stone shed from Major Robert John Ross's stab at immortality and inspected them minutely before discarding them over his shoulder.

"Time, methinks Gogo, for a quick survey, after which

we shall partake of the marvellous restorative qualities of Earl Grey's unexcelled *chai*." From a waistcoat pocket Tiresias unfolded a pair of thick, square spectacles. Harlequin colours swirled and ran in the lenses. Wire frames were carefully hooked over scrofulous ears.

"Scofu? Snexu?"

"A modicum of time, if you please, while my weary old visual systems acclimatise . . . yes, there's something manifesting. The mythline flow follows the geomorphological landscape quite closely. Evidently there was no human settlement and mythic activity before the landscape stabilised after the Ice Age. I can distinguish a tangle of minor nodes along the river valley and there seems to be an octave of decayed myth-echoes along the shoreline. The place we're gracing with our singular posteriors is the focus of one such old, decayed echo, in all probability the site of an Old Stone Age hamlet. This whole place is quite a jumble. I'm trying to sort out the major octaves from the minor harmonics. Yes . . . yes, I've got them now. Here, Gogo, see where I am pointing?" Gonzaga hunkered and squinted along Tiresias's quavering forefinger. The old man was indicating a low, flat-topped mountain at the edge of the mass that formed such a picture-postcard backdrop to the village in the valley.

"Draloch snexu?"

"Major chordal nexus," Tiresias confirmed. "Right on the summit." The square glasses were unpeeled from the prominent proboscis, adoringly folded in vellum, and returned to the next-to-heart pocket. "Good comrade, how about that long-promised cup of liquid nectar? Time aplenty tomorrow for the setting about of ordained businesses. Tonight we rest, we recreate, we take our easance and pleasure in Rostrevor Village." Oily locks that had not seen the comb for over a generation nodded at clouds ripping and tearing under the weight of their own rain. An aqueous, ochre evening light spilled down the mountainsides and poured over the village. "See, dear Gogo, even the elements themselves have deigned to smile upon us."

"Wentyt slime gneo, dna gnithno ot eb edno," grumbled Gonzaga, reaching into the wet grass and pocketing a discarded cap from a bottle of Cantrel and Cochrane red lemonade. He took a small metal cylinder from the webbing bandolier he wore slung across his shoulder, opened the cap, tipped a few grains of black tea into the iron pot that swung from his belt. "Oyu ekam erif. Ym tfee thru."

2

Pig paws, pig faces, big pig men, bog men, up for the day from Mullingar and Kildare, plonked around the tables like sides of fatty ham, wedged apoplectically into straining tweeds and moleskins. They always sat as far from their women as the geometry of the tables would permit. Faced with lard dumplings swaddled in floral print, with cheeks like two tins of condemned veal, they could hardly be blamed for wanting to put as much distance as possible between themselves and their darling wives. What is it about Irish womanhood that aspires to the condition of massive mono-bosoms and mono-bottoms? What is the secret source of that peculiar bouquet of Eau de Farmer's Wife that envelops them, a heady amalgam of middle-aged secretions and fat heated by its own compression to the point of spontaneous combustion?

Jessica hated Tuesdays with a cordial loathing: Tuesdays, when the shopping specials disgorged their wobbling hordes of red-cheeked rurals onto the platforms of Connolly and Pearse stations and herded them like prize Landrace pigs toward the glittering sties of Clery's, Brown-Thomas, Switzers. Watching their jowls shudder as their teeth chomped down another forkful of meat and two veg, she imagined a little ditty running around and around behind their piggy eyes: *Yum yum, pig's bum, cabbage and potato; yum yum, pig's bum, cabbage and potato* . . .

The better class of client—the solicitor, the bank clerk, the accountant, the broker, the department store floor-walker—took his custom far beyond the reach of farmers and their wives on Tuesdays, and for the deprivation of their tips and their ritual, depersonalised flirtations, she despised the pig people. Tuesdays she would forever associate with the smell of boiling cabbage in big vats and the rhythmic chomp of rural mastication.

Bang through the swinging doors into the steam heat and stench of the kitchen. Clatter of plates into the sink; a glance at the clock, which seemed to be running slow, seemed not to have moved one iota, seemed to be running backwards; a sigh, a stretch against the cool of the refrigerator, a long "Oh God," an unrequited lust for a Woodbine cigarette and then a swift reverse out through the banging swinging doors with four more platefuls of Shopper's Special Luncheon. Swinging in as she went swinging out was her best enemy, Fat Lettie, with the inevitable taunt: "I think the bog man on table number six fancies you. He was asking after you—when you get off, and all . . ."

Swinging back in as Fat Lettie went swinging out, she made her riposte: "Kindly inform the gent on table number six that he has a face like a shite that's been stuck down the jax three days."

In, and out again. Fat Lettie: "You're a foul-mouthed hoor, Jessica Caldwell."

Swing, bang. "You should open your legs and let your arse do the talking, Lettie dearest—it makes a lot more sense."

And, on the return pass: "Well, at least my Eammon will be coming to pick me up in a motor car and take me out to Phoenix Park for a concert, Jessica Caldwell."

Two tables served, three cleared, and one bill later: "In the Defence Forces, isn't he, your Eammon? What's it like, doing everything by numbers? Skirt up, two three; knickers down, two three . . ."

"You bitch, Jessica Caldwell. At least I've got a boyfriend."

"And so've I, Lettie dear, and not some pissy toy soldier either—a real fightin' man, he is, a rebel boy of the Irish Republican Army."

"You are such a liar, Jessica Caldwell."

Jessica Caldwell was not a liar. She was a creator of imaginative fictions. If persons had not enough wit to recognise an imaginative fiction—come, let us not quibble, a *lie*—when they were told one, the more fool they. She could not be responsible for people believing her sorry, imaginative fictions. Lying was as natural to her as song to a bird.

"Ladies, ladies, this is a public restaurant. The customers have come here to enjoy their luncheons, not to listen to you two going at it like two Montgomery Street harridans." Brendan the head cook, as the only man in the kitchens, held an authority out of all proportion to his position. Doors banged, doors swung, and a tight and smoking silence endured until at last the clock woke from its meanderings and declared six o'clock. The peace and cool of Mangan's back alley was almost sacramental. Jessica shook the day from her hair and stretched in a warm, vagrant sunlight the exact colour of Etruscan terra-cotta. A bird threw a snatch of song over the chimney pots and chipped roof slates. Jessica smoked a long and luxurious Woodbine while in stations named after dead patriots pig men and blowsy women slumped softly, sleepily, against each other, full to the watch pockets with Shopper's Special Luncheon in trains taking them back to Mullingar and Kildare and every hole in the hedge in between.

An immense evening was unfolding itself over the Georgian avenues of South Dublin like a backdrop for some extravagant production of *Aida*. The tram paused to deposit Jessica at the end of Belgrave Road before lumbering on toward the Victorian pomposities of Palmerstown. Piano music; Jocasta practising Mozart. Did she never tire of arpeggios and glissandos and diminuendos and all those other tedious Italians? At the age of five, Jessica had whispered to her father that she thought the front door looked like a smiling face, which delighted him so much it had become a piece of family legend; the brass welcome to number twenty. She waved to Jocasta,—sorry, Jo-Jo, it sounded more arty—the sister she did like, who returned a nod and a smile. Clattering down the stairs came Jasmine, a.k.a. The Shite, the sister she did not like, sullen, spotty, and bulgy in her Girls' Brigade uniform.

"I'm supposed to bring a new song for the singsong tonight," she said. It was almost an accusation of something.

"I know a great song you can teach them. It goes like this:

> I stuck my finger up a woodpecker's hole,
> And the woodpecker said, 'God bless my soul!
> Take it down, take it down, take it down,
> Take it down!' "

Exit The Shite, scandalised. Jessica mistrusted people who had too much religion, especially when those people were five years her junior.

"Jessica Caldwell!" The roar came from the paternal sanctorum at the top of the stairs. Jessica loved her father's study only slightly less than she loved him; the triple latticed windows with their generous views of the garden and the trees of Palmerstown beyond, the cupola that cast its lotus of light over the writing desk and draughtsman's table—for as long as she could remember, her impression of the study had been one of light and warmth. Charlie Caldwell was a designer of fine linen and tableware for Doheny and Nesbitt's exclusive interior furnishings range. President Childers ate his dinner off a Charlie Caldwell plate, and had it served to him on a Charlie Caldwell tablecloth. His father before him had been a designer of tableware. His proudest boast was that his finest designs had gone down with the *Titanic*. Also like his father before, C. Caldwell cast himself forthrightly in the tradition of the Protestant Radical, two philosophies he considered severely undervalued in the new Ireland. The waxed-oak shelves of his study were stocked with books he felt reflected his dual heritage and which never failed to raise tuts of disapproval from Mr. Perrot, the clergyman, on his rare visits to the house. Mr. Perrot had always been disapproving of the Caldwell family. Anyone who called their children Jessica, Jocasta, and Jasmine was obviously suspect of heterodoxy. A valiant, and to date victorious battler against encroaching baldness, Charlie Caldwell attributed both his success in holding his hair and his intellectual vigour to Dwyer's Electrical Scalp Massage (Why go Bald?).

"Jessica Caldwell, you are the most foul-mouthed little hellion it has been my misfortune to hand rear. Do you have to offend Jasmine's tender sensibilities?"

"Ah, the way she goes on you'd think she had a lemon stuck up her backside."

The guffaw of laughter almost sent the draughtsman over backwards in his Chippendale chair. "So, how was your day in the service of Mr. Mangan?"

"Fuc . . . bloody awful. Dad, why . . ."

"Why can't you go to college to study to be an illustrator? A fine waste of money that'd be when you end up getting married to the first man you see and having babies. All that time and money down the drain."

"Jocasta's going to be a concert pianist. Is she a waste of time and money?"

"Jocasta has a great talent."

"And I don't? I can draw as well as you. Better."

It was an old, entrenched argument. Jessica argued it now purely for the sake of arguing. As soon as she had enough money from Mangan's Family Restaurant, she would apply herself to college to study illustration, and pay for it of her own sweat, see if she didn't. She was Destined for Greatness. It was written by a greater hand than C. Caldwell, Esquire's.

"Are you going to be in for dinner?"

She still did love her father, dearly.

"Well, I'd arranged with Rozzie and Em . . ."

"Abandon me to the wrath of your mother, would you, ungrateful child?"

She leaned over the desk and kissed him on the not-quite bald patch.

"Aw, Dad, for a mean ould bugger, you're a honey."

Down in the hall, heading for the front door ("'Bye, Jocasta; sorry, Jo-Jo,"), she encountered The Shite locked in incomprehensible intercourse with a pennant on a pole.

"Don't forget verse two:

And the woodpecker said, 'God bless my soul!
Turn it round, turn it round, turn it round,
Rotate it.'"

Christian Brothers' School overshadowed Heytesbury Street like Purgatory over Pleasure. The houses facing it maintained a spirit of defiant disarray—basement yards piled with decrepit mangles and juggernaut perambulators; tarnished brass and rusting palings; geraniums condemned on windowsills to the contemplation of their own corruption; white, crumbly dog turds; and greasy paper bags. Jessica knew her mother thought Roslyn Fitzpatrick and her family were below the salt, despite the good Old Norman name and the fact that Rozzie, with Jessica and the third member of their clique, Emma Talbot, sang the occasional pious trio in church to the general edification and pleasure of all. Jessica's mother's opinions were generally of little importance to Jessica, who thought of herself as one who did not judge by outside appearances, but by the heart. Like Jesus. The front room of number thirty-eight was piled with ragamuffin furniture and Victorian prints of supposedly inspirational nature. Between Gentle Jesus Meek and Mild leading a Junior Life Boy along the straight and narrow path and a framed Biblical chronology from Eternity through Creation, Redemption, and Apocalypse to Eternity again, the wireless glowed and hummed and picked "The Billy Cotton Band Show" out of the ether.

"Anne-Marie next door says Father Cumper makes you say twenty Hail Mary's and five Our Father's for listening to the BBC," Rozz said. She made the same pronouncement every time they tuned the wooden wireless away from Radio Eireann; it added a little clandestine frisson to their listening. Feet beat time to the punchy rhythms of saxes and clarinets; the girls flipped the soft, shiny pages of *Picture Parade* and *Film Fun* and talked about boys. Rozz was in love with Bing Crosby, King of the Crooners, but settled for a roving Hoover salesman. He had recently been elevated from Permission to French Kiss to Permission to Undo Bra, but Permission to Slip Hand Down Knickers was some months distant. Em had not progressed beyond the first tight-mouthed kiss in the back of the tuppennies in the Carlton Picture House, but then she had only been going out with her apprentice tiler from Haroldscross for three weeks. A Byzantine atmosphere of intrigue surrounded the affair. If her mother ever found out she was going out with a Catholic . . . Further comment was unnecessary. Jessica remained the sole unenthusiastic gooseberry.

"Oh, come on, Jessica, you'll have to get off with someone soon or it'll heal up down there."

"Eduardo in the Cagliostro fancies you. I saw him

looking at you the other night. I would say he definitely fancies you."

Eduardo Cagliostro was a curly-headed Italian Adonis, who unfortunately knew it. He was the son of an immigrant fried food shop owner. It was commonly supposed he slicked back his hair by dipping his head in the fryers. He was a classic smoulderer—on a good night, he gave off more smoke than the hot fat. He was every inch the Latino until he opened his mouth; a first generation Italo-Irish, he had inherited none of his Mama's lilting cadences. His Rathmines accent was as thick as a toilet seat. Jessica despised him and never wasted an opportunity to publicly humiliate him for his hubris. But it was getting to look like it was Eduardo Cagliostro or the Little League of Decency and Purity.

"What makes you think I haven't got a boyfriend? In fact, I have. I've been going out with him for four weeks and three days now, but I can't tell anyone about him." Minor lies boomed and rushed in her head and fused into major, then epic, lies, the familiar prelude to a feat of sustained improvisation. "His name's Damian. He's tall and very handsome, of course, and he has hair as black as a raven's wing. I don't know his surname; he couldn't tell me. In fact, I don't even know if Damian is his real name. He says he can't trust anyone, not even me. He has to be careful. It's difficult to arrange meetings. He can't meet me in the usual places everyone goes, he can't risk being seen, so it's usually after dark, on a particular bench in the park, or down an alley. He leaves messages for me at Hannah's Sweet Shop. He can't ever come to the house. I can't risk Mum and Dad seeing him." She took a deep breath.

"You see, he's on the run. He's a volunteer in the IRA." Hoots of derision greeted her disclosure. "No, it's true, I swear to God. He was in the Tipperary Brigade but he's on a special mission in Dublin. That's all he'll let me know about it, but I think there's someone high up in the Free State government he's been sent to kill. He's got a gun—a Webley revolver—he carries it with him all the time, in case he's ambushed by the Specials and has to shoot his way out. He's let me see it. He carries it under his army greatcoat, which he says he got from a soldier he shot in the Galtee

Mountains. He won't let me touch his gun, though; he says it's not right for women to handle weapons. I think that's so old-fashioned and romantic of him. He's twenty-two and he's absolutely gorgeous. I think it's because he's a hunted man. He says he wants to elope with me and live together on the run, but I tell him that's silly, and then he gets all sad because he's thinking that this night might be the last time he'll ever see me—tonight might be the night he gets gunned down in the streets by the Special Branch.

"I don't know where he goes or where he comes from. He says it's safer for both of us if I don't know, but I do know that he's in the IRA because of his older brother who fought in the Civil War and was captured and executed by what he calls Free State Traitors. When he talks about his brother he gets very pale and quiet and dangerous."

The April 1934 copy of *Film Fun* caught her in full extemporary flight; mouthful of Mae West.

"You're such a *liar*, Jessica Caldwell."

She waved two fingers in the face of her accusers. "Up your bums. It was a bloody good lie. I almost had you believing it, didn't I?" Billy Cotton's Big Band BBC Beat battled futilely against the Catholic evening gloom descending the slab walls of Christian Brothers' School.

Waiting for the eleven o'clock tram, she noticed there was still brightness in the sky. A sure promise of summer, this blue lambency in the far west, the smoking chimney stacks of Dublin silhouetted against it like the palisades and siege-engines of the army of heaven. Dark crescents and scimitars darted between the angular shadows; the swifts, returned from the lands of the heathen Moor and Berber, cut and creased the violet night. She imagined how Dublin would seem through their eyes. The streets, the alleys, the entries, the roofs and chimney pots, the stone Hibernias and marble harps and wrought-iron Celtic crosses would lose their human meaning and flow into a seamless landscape of canyons and valleys, of cliff faces and shallow ledges. Recalling the Saturday matinee Westerns, she saw Dublin become a great Monument Valley of buttes and mesas and badlands through which she swooped and veered. Through red-brick canyons lined with ledges, over hogback rooftops, circling volcanic chimney mouths, she would fly, looking down into a valley of shining trees where ponderous smoky animals lurched in predestined and invariable courses. She caught sight of her own face, looking up at the flocking swifts.

The tram drew up in a spray of blue sparks. Jessica swung onto a seat at the back. Her mother always told her to sit by the door so she could jump up if anyone tried to, well, you know, try anything. She was still perplexed by her experience of the point of view of a bird. She had always enjoyed a vigorous imaginative life, and if lately she had found her dips into the stream of consciousness becoming more powerful and insistent, she had always known on which side of the dividing line between reality and imagination she stood. But this had been real. She had been there, for one moment; she had seen as the swifts saw, been as the swifts were. Her inner and outer Dublins, the visible and tangible *Baille Atha Cliath* of reality and the invisible, intangible *Anna Livia Pluribelle* of the heart were beginning to lose their separate identities and blur: *Ballia Liviatha Cliabelle*.

The conductor was swinging his way up the tram, clicking his ticket machine. Jessica remembered that she had spent her fare home on a copy of *Picture Parade* from The Boulevard newsagents on Camden Street. Seat by seat the bulbous conductor loomed closer. Jessica improvised a barrage of lies, none of which stood the least possibility of convincing the conductor, when she remembered her emergency sixpence. Mother's wisdom—the fund of final resort was tucked into her stocking top. Her attempts to surreptitiously slip it out only attracted the attention of the young dark-haired man in the heavy coat (surely too hot for a night like this) in the seat opposite. He smiled. Jessica scowled, wrestled with straining elastic, one hand down the inside of her skirt. Got it got it got it . . . . The tram swayed over a set of points. The sixpence fell to the floor and rolled under the dark-haired man's seat. Jessica commuted her *shit* to a sigh.

"Pardon me," said the young dark-haired man. He bent down to rummage among the cigarette ends under the seat. The flap of that ridiculously heavy coat fell open. Tucked into the waistband of his trousers was an oiled black revolver.

There was a light on at the top of the stairs when she came through the smiling front door of number twenty. It did not seem a good omen. Father's in his study late at night, all's ill with the world. He opened the door, called her up in his I-don't-want-to-wake-the-rest-of-the-house voice.

He did not look like any kind of a honey.

"I had a telephone call this evening."

"That's nice for you."

"From Mr. Mangan. Apparently your performance was overheard by the entire lunchtime sitting. He gave me to understand in no uncertain terms that this was the last, the very last, time he was prepared to put up with this kind of behaviour."

This was another well-established front of entrenched warfare.

"Oh, come on, you're not serious . . ."

But he was serious.

"Really, Jessica, it can't go on. The swearing, the lying, this compulsive vulgarity. It's only a matter of time before you insult some customer. We really will have to do something about it."

"You're always saying that."

"Which is my failing. No, this time, I have done something about it. I have made an appointment for you to see a specialist in problems of adolescents, a psychologist, a Dr. Rooke."

"Are you saying that I'm a problem adolescent? Jaysus, Dad."

He sighed, hands cast up in a gesture of resignation.

"The appointment has been fixed for Saturday morning. Eleven o'clock."

"For fuc . . ." Then she saw the look of beleaguered defiance in his hands and eyes, and because she did love him, said, "Oh, all right, I'll go. It might be a laugh. You never know . . ."

3

Anyone who calls my aged secretary Miss Fanshawe's beloved Scottie Cromlyn a "little frigger" to Miss Fanshawe's hatchet face is worthy of my undying admiration, and a certain degree of professional respect. I had been looking forward to this meeting with Jessica Caldwell.

The picture her parents had painted prepared me for some kind of monster, foul-mouthed and vituperative, a compulsive liar and braggart. Imagine my surprise to find in my waiting room (oblivious to Miss Fanshawe's darkest glower) not some Dublin fishwife all chapped cheeks and puffed lips, but a girl of almost angelic beauty and demeanour (apart from a distinctly unangelic pout to the lips and shine to the eye) who spoke with a delightful soft South Dublin slur.

Every psychologist must, to some extent, be a master of subtle dissimulation and gentle deceit; ours would be a stimulating locking of horns—her innate talent against my professional training. I had no doubts that I would emerge the victor.

She succeeded in unnerving me at the very first test. I was administering a standard set of Rorschach inkblots. Jessica studied the first card from every conceivable angle before announcing, "A pair of kittens." The second card, after a fraction of the effort, produced the same response: "a pair of kittens." The third: "a pair of kittens." The fourth, the fifth, the sixth, the same reply. I reminded her to say the very first thing that came into her head.

"That is the first thing that comes into my head."

"Each one reminds you of a pair of kittens?"

"Yes. Anything wrong with that?"

"Well, is there anything else they might remind you of?"

"Like what?"

"Well, this one, reminds me of, well, it looks sexual to me."

"It doesn't look sexual to me. It looks like a pair of kittens. How does it look sexual to you?"

"Well, it reminds me of a woman's vagina."

"You dirty old bugger. If my mother knew she'd sent me here to look at dirty pictures . . ."

We proceeded to the word association test. It was even more farcical than the Rorschach inkblot test. Jessica clearly had the measure of me and manipulated the roles of questioner and questionee with such consummate skill that I became the one making lewd and suggestive replies and she the one pursing her lips and tutting, "Oh, Mr. Rooke!"

But maybe the old dog still has a turn or two.

"Well, Jessica, it's clear to me we aren't going to get anywhere with the regular psychological tests, so what we'll do is, if you're agreeable, I'll put you in a light hypnotic trance and we'll go back to events and incidents in your childhood, something you may have long forgotten, or buried in your subconscious, that might explain why you seem to need to engage in this kind of antisocial behaviour."

"I don't know about this," she said. "How do I know what you mightn't get up to when I'm under your power and totally helpless? For all I know, you could have five girls a day in here, obeying your every wish and whim."

I bridled with outrage, then saw the devilment in her eyes.

She settled back in her chair, legs spread wide, fingers locked behind her neck. "Quite frankly, mister, I don't mind what you do. You just have to look at me with those mad, mad eyes of yours . . ."

In fact, she did not have to look anywhere near those mad, mad eyes of mine. I used my trusted and true Maltese Cross and lamp arrangement. She proved a most amenable subject to hypnotism. In a very short time Jessica had reached a deep and comfortable state of trance. Hypnosis casts an entirely different light upon incidents and objects to memory alone. In the course of the regression I encountered several events, trivial in themselves, that took on an altered significance in trance: creeping from her bed on Christmas Eve to find the house filled with strangers standing around the Christmas tree; the thing that had stroked her hair in the ghost train at the amusements at Bray; a pair of hairbrushes, one backed with red for Grattan, the other green for Parnell;

a porcelain doll in a basement window; a horse that had collapsed and died on the North Circular Road being winched into a knacker's van; a dread of clowns; a long-remembered nightmare about the elevators in Switzer's. We worked backwards through the years, reeling them out behind us like twine in a labyrinth—age seven, age six, her fifth birthday, then, shockingly unexpected: "I can't go any farther."

"What do you mean, you can't go any farther?"

"I can't go any farther. It's like there's a wall right across my life, and I can't get past it. I'm stuck. I can't go any farther."

"What age are you?" I asked, making hasty notes on a foolscap legal pad.

"About four and a half, I think."

Remarkable, this state of consciousness we call hypnosis, as if our lives are some kind of picture gallery through which we tour in full adult consciousness. A wall. How very, very interesting. I decided that we had seen enough of the exhibits in this particular mental gallery, and counted Jessica back up to full consciousness. In those few moments, as she emerged from the trance into full cognizance, she seemed as pure and open as a Church Bible. Then, as she recalled where she was, what she was doing, guardedness and guile crossed her face like bad weather.

"Well, Mr. Rooke, did you get anything? Did you have your evil way with me?"

"It was very instructive. Do you remember anything?"

"I don't know. I'm not sure. Something about a wall? Does that make sense? I don't really know—it all seems so hazy. I hadn't thought it would be like this. I thought I'd remember everything. You could have had your evil way, and I wouldn't know a thing."

"I assure you, Miss Caldwell, your virtue is entirely intact."

"More's the pity."

"Tell me, what is your earliest memory? Think carefully."

"Let me see: I can remember being on a swing boat at the fun fair in Bray. I remember Daddy swinging the boat higher and higher and higher and Mummy telling him that

was high enough, it was frightening me, although it was her
that was frightened. I quite enjoyed it, I think."

"Anything before that?"

Concentration creased her brow momentarily.

"No. Should there be?"

"What age were you when you were on the swing boat in
Bray?"

"Oh, about five: Yes, just five. It was my fifth birthday,
I think. Yes, it was, definitely, my fifth birthday."

"And you can't remember anything before your fifth
birthday?"

"No. Should I? Is that odd?"

I did not answer her question. Rather, I said, "Well, that,
I think, will suffice for today. If you see Miss Fanshawe,
she will make you an appointment for next week. Thank
you, Jessica, it's been most stimulating."

The study door closed, followed a few moments later by
the glassy rattle of the office door. I could detect Miss
Fanshawe huffing and puffing and grumbling, grumpily,
and needlessly rearranging papers.

Little frigger, indeed!

4

Tribulation and persecution. Morning light saw the vicar
striding Protestantly across his glebe meadows with dogs,
gumboots, and his demand that the two unequivocally
undesirable *tramps* remove themselves forthwith, *tout de
suite*, chop-chop from his property. Failure to comply
would result in the summoning, without one second's
further delay, of an officer of the constabulary. Seemingly a
conclave of fresh-faced young evangelicals would be descending upon his vicarage that very afternoon for a
weekend of good, sound, *factual* Scripture teaching and
happy-clappy chorus singing about the Pearls of Great Price
to be found between the leather-bound covers of the
B.I.—B.I.—B.I.—B.L.E. and he had no intention of their
apple-cheeked washed-in-the-blood zeal being diminished

by close proximity to two gentlemen of the road, read tinkers, read vagabonds, read *tramps*.

" 'Religious persecution may shield itself under the guise of a mistaken and overzealous piety,' " declared Gonzaga as they picked their way over dew-wet hedgerows to the main road. The shift from Nagmara to *In Quotationem* generally presaged the heightening of sensitivity before a bout of gyrus building.

Where the main road crossed the river by a picture-postcard, ivy-covered stone bridge, Gonzaga paused to lounge against the wall of the Irish National Foresters Club while Tiresias surveyed the mythlines.

" 'Where the Mountains of Mourne sweep down to the sea,' " sang Gonzaga, disconsolately, then, galvanized into unexpected action like a pointer coming onto a scent, he plunged into a public litter bin on a lamppost and emerged with an empty Morton's Red Heart Guinness bottle.

Camp was established on a long sloping strip of land overlooking the lough known in the locality, so Tiresias informed his partner, drawing on the information stored in the mythlines, as Fiddler's Green.

"Legend has it the great Turlough O'Carolan himself, doyen of the blind harpers of Ireland, attended a *fleadh* in the village for which he composed a specially slip-jig, named 'Fiddler's Green.' " He hummed a few bars. Gonzaga lay back among the seed-laden grasses and looked out across the blue water to the Carlingford Mountains.

Gonzaga made flame with his firebox and brewed tea in his black iron pot suspended from a stick. The two tramps had long ago stopped being surprised by the fact they could survive, and even thrive, on the scraps and orts human society discarded. Both, however, shared a partiality to connoisseurs' teas they could not quite explain. Tiresias sipped the brew from a jam jar and contemplated the clouds.

"Galleasses, triremes, and feluccas asail upon the stream of consciousness," he whispered. Gonzaga had already slipped into his dream place; Tiresias's musings were for his own edification. "Two bastard nations," he said, sprawling on the sun-warmed hillside of one country, looking across the water at the hills of another. "And I fear the inevitable price of compromise will eventually be paid by every man, woman, and child of the pair of them. The tragedy of founding two nations upon nothing more solid than mythology. Myths, my dear Gogo. You cannot build a nation on myths, you cannot feed its children with myths, you cannot grind them out of its mills and factories. They will not shelter you from the rain; you cannot burn them to drive the cold winter away. They will not comfort you when you are old, when you are lonely, when you are afraid or in need. Yet they feed their children with them from their mother's breasts—Good King Billy on his white charger, remember 1690, the Battle of the Boyne, No Surrender!; A Nation Once Again, the Harp that Once through Tara's Halls, Cuchulain chained to the standing stone, his enemies all around him, the martyrs of 1916, the Soldier Boy to the Wars has Gone . . ."

" 'Hypocrisy is the homage paid by vice to virtue,' " Gonzaga murmured.

"Ah, Monsieur Le Duc de la Rochefoucault had it right, Gogo."

When the night had advanced onto the mountains and into the forest, they left their camp and climbed the sheep path to the stone. This close to the nexus, Gonzaga's more intimate senses came into their element. His nose led them up the hillside through grasses and twilight butterflies and Ministry of Agriculture, Fisheries and Forestry conifers. On the flat summit of the hill stood a massive perched boulder, a glacial erratic, Tiresias postulated, deposited on this mountaintop when the ice sheets retreated across Ireland.

"*An Clachan Mor.*" Tiresias picked the name from the mythlines. "The Great Stone, Anglicised to *Cloughmore*." Gonzaga scurried around the stone, touching, smelling, lifting pebbles, dirt, and leaves to taste them. Two late-evening walkers, plus a Sealyham terrier, paused at the stile on the tree line and, seeing the tramps, reconsidered their twilight constitutional.

Gonzaga emptied his haversack on the ground and picked through the malassortment of odds and sods—a brass button with an anchor crest; a chatter of gulls' feathers bound together with twine; pine cones; sea-smoothed stones; a packet of Navy Cut cigarettes ("It is a less commonly known fact than it should be that the sailor in the front is actually Charles Stewart Parnell."); snail shells; a piece of old car tyre; a lenseless pair of spectacles; seemingly far too many things for one small knapsack to hold. He weighed each item in his hand and either returned it to the sack or laid it carefully on the grass. The assemblage complete, he pressed an ear against the stone and worked his way around, tapping it with a silver thimble on the end of his right forefinger. Tiresias polished his glasses in the light of the rising rebel moon and listened to the voice of the wind in the wood. He could feel the phaguses close, gathering, present, massing on the borderlands between Mygmus and Earth.

Using a ball of string as a triangulation tool, Gonzaga began to mark a series of locations in relation to the stone. Some were underneath the overhanging bulk, some well below the tree line. Clouds rose from over the water to race across the face of the moon. Tiresias slipped on his newly cleaned glasses and the hilltop came alive with mythlines, the paths and patterns ten thousand years of legend had impressed upon the landscape. The mythlines flowed and eddied around the stone, numinous silver rivers filled with drowned faces, the phaguses, the differing manifestations of the basal archetypes of local story and song. Gonzaga moved through the river of faces, planting items from his collection at the junctions of the marker strings—four carefully piled pine cones among the trees, the Morton's Red Heart Guinness bottle by the stile at the entrance to the forest walk, a small dolmen of sea-polished slingstones here, a fossil belemnite there, a spiral of snail shells and cigarette ends there, here a feather, there a feather, everywhere a gull feather. Midnight approached, passed; dawn became an insistence on the edge of the warm early summer night. A pattern was emerging. Gonzaga was wrapping the balancing boulder in a complex of cycloids and endocycloids, a gyre of spirals and curves. Through the spectacles Tiresias observed how the mythlines were being frustrated, turned in on themselves, directed into fruitless whirlpools and eddies and woven into a cocoon of lights and faces.

An Clachan Mor stood in darkness unbroken at the centre of a shining wheel. Tiresias came to join Gonzaga at the heart of the gyrus. Gonzaga produced the Free State penny from his waistcoat pocket, held it up.

Tiresias removed his glasses, nodded.

Gonzaga inserted the penny into a crevice in the rock.

A sudden breeze stirred the trees, tugged greasy locks and clothing, rattled the barbs of the gull feathers. Flickers of nervous light, petty lightnings, ran fretfully along the curves and spirals of Gonzaga's weaving, lost themselves in the predawn darkness. Mist gathered around the perimeter of the maze, knotted into a face, many faces in one, features melting and reforming—old man young man wise man fool.

"Struggling for quotidian expression," muttered Tiresias. "Must be a more powerful local phagus, running through its incarnations in an attempt to find one relevant to the contemporary subconscious." The changing faces yelled and screamed silently within the wall of mist. Gonzaga pressed his face to the stone, stroked the Mourne granite with his fingers, his lips. Under his touch as tender as a priest's first experiment with love, the rock softened, melted. The Free State penny was absorbed into the substance of the stone. For one instant it glowed there, in the heart of the rock. By the light of a straggling, ragged dawn, the two men watched the signs and markers of the maze grow insubstantial and be absorbed into the soil; snail shell, gull feather, brass button, Guinness bottle.

" 'The boast of heraldry, the pomp of power,
And all that beams, all that wealth e'er gave,
Await alike the inevitable hour,
The path of glory leads beyond the grave,' "
Gonzaga dolefully consigned the sailor-suited Charles Stewart Parnell to the soil.

The bubble of mist and faces dissolved in the memory of a wail as the promise of dawn was fulfilled behind Slieve Martin. Tiresias sighed, expanded his birdlike chest, and breathed in the light.

"A grand and glorious day, my dear Gogo—a grand and glorious day altogether."

" 'He that hath light within his own clear breast, May sit in the centre and enjoy bright day, But he that hides a dark soul, and foul thought . . .' " Gonzaga left the quote half finished. Tiresias was standing, head cocked, nostrils flared, as if scenting something on the wind.

"Strange . . . strange. It feels like . . . No. Nothing.
Sorry to have troubled you, old friend. Felt for the briefest
quantum of time like . . . but no, tiredness, dog tiredness. We are not as young as we used to be. Come Gogo,
and let us partake of blessèd tea, if we can squeeze another
pot out of those leaves . . ."

5

*Scene: The GLASS TOWER rises out of a silver sea,
sheer-sided, smooth-shouldered, unscalable. The sea is
dark and storm-tossed—waves crash and break about its
base.*

The Dublin Bay Wave No.7: Hey me boys, ho me boys, up
and at 'em, up and at 'em, no resting no slacking no
slouching no skiving no sick days holidays holy days fair
days feast days, famine days, no Christmas Easter St.
Paddy's begorrah begob be-jaysus, it's up and at 'em, up
and at 'em, we've got to get all this ground down to sand
before the turn of the millennium, me boys!

The Sandman: Excuse me, but I would just like you to know
that I play no part in this dream sequence whatsoever, thank
you.
    *Sea gulls with a lot of swan in them, or swans with a lot
of sea gull, fly around the tower. They are chained together
at the neck by collars and links of red gold.*

Sea Swans/Swan Gulls: Squadron to tower, squadron to
tower, bandits ten o'clock high, ten o'clock high . . .
tally ho, chappies! NyyaaggHHRRRUuuummm. . . .
    *The GLASS TOWER hums in the wind, exactly as if you
had wet your finger in a wineglass and rubbed it around-
roundround the rim.*

The Wineglass: Ooohhhmmmmm. . . .
    *Fierce clouds crowd around the GLASS TOWER, like
supporters at the All-Ireland Football Final at Croke Park.*

•   •   •

The Football Fans: We're the boys from Tipperary, Up the Pope and the Virgin Mary!

Though the storm is all around and all about and the black clouds hang low about its sides, the summit of the GLASS TOWER is lit by a single shaft of pure sunlight.

The Carol Singers:

> While shepherds washed their socks by night,
> All seated round the tub,
> A bar of Sunlight Soap came down,
> And they began to scrub.

Upon closer inspection you see that the top of the GLASS TOWER is constructed in the fashion of a sundial. Upon the dial is a garden: fountains, mazes, pergolas, gazebos, Italian gardens, living statues, nymphs, fauns, satyrs, bambini, orreries, roses, wine, etc. In the centre of a small lawn stand two trees. One bears buds, blossom, ripe fruit, and leaves both green and brown. The other is divided root to crown, one half green with leaves, one aflame.

The First Tree:

> All seasons in one
> And one in all seasons,
> The green leaf, the brown,
> The blossom, the bud,
> The ripe golden fruit
> The bare winter
> branches
> The seasons of life
> All in one season
> All the days of one life
>
>   Life in a day.

This to the accompaniment of massed choirs of nymphs, fauns, satyrs, living statues, bambini, water organs, Aeolian harps, songs of birds, grunts of pigs, mechanical orreries performing the music of the spheres.

• • •

The Second Tree: Fire! Fire! Dingalingalingalingaling! 999! 999! Hello, what service do you require—Fire, Police, or Ambulance? Fire! Fire! Fire! Call for Moses! Call for the burning babe the burning bush the bush in the bulrushes the babe in the bush the burning bulrushes the burning baby help help help!

Enter FAERIE QUEENE dressed head to toe in ermine £3 3s 6d per mile from Arnott's sale second floor Haberdashery. Her crown is an oversized Carling Black Label bottle cap, inverted.

Faeric Queene: Jessica! Jessica! Jessica!
    Music tinkles, like ice clinking in whiskey glasses.

John Jameson, Old Bushmills, Paddy, Powers and Companie:

> Oi've been a wild rover,
> Fer manys a yearrrrr . . .
> And oi've spent all me money,
> On whiskey and beerrrrr. . . .

The FAERIE QUEENE smiles, revealing Dracula teeth . . .

(The Dublin Dentists:

> Twice a day, twice a day,
> Up and down, up and down,
> Till they're clean and sparkling.

. . . glistening with blood. She wipes her slavering mouth on her hand, notices the blood. Embarrassed, she wipes her hand on her ermine cloak (£3 3s 6d per mile, etc) which has by now grown to hang off the edge of the sundial garden and down the side of the GLASS TOWER.

The Arnott's Ermine: Those drops of blood, oh those drops of blood,
    Those drops of blood, upon the midnight snow . . .

• • •

Faerie Queene: Jessica, Jessica, please, Jessica, I love you, Jessica, I love you . . .

JESSICA awakens, head pounding, heart racing, soaked in sweat.

Voice of the Alarm: Ting a ling a ling! Ting a ling a ling! Half past eight on a bright and sunny Saturday, half past eight, time to be gay, be light, be shiny and bright, half past eight in the morning, oh!

Light streams through the window, a lattice of shadow on the counterpane. Without, the sounds of the streets— picking, clicking heels; the jingle of horse harnesses; the grumble of trams; the slam of letterboxes. From within, the thunderous gurgle of the plumbing and the joyful incense of bacon frying.

Jessica: Jaysus, what a dream I've had!

The definition of a Super Saturday (that is, of *Superness* as opposed to *Saturdayness*) was that it was one of those rare calendrical occurrences when the timetables of the Wesley Hospital, Dudgeon and Gowes, Ltd., Chartered Surveyors, and Mangan's Family Restaurant all meshed to give the three girls the same day off. Super Saturdays were events anticipated and grimly enjoyed with the determined enthusiasm of a family holiday: rain, hail, civic unrest, they would wring every last second of their Super Saturday dry.

One does not so much travel on a Dublin tram as *voyage*. All that brass and wood, that heady top deck exposure to the elements, that seaside ozone spritz from the overhead wires, you are reminded irresistibly of piers and steam packets; you expect bunting on every telegraph pole and lamp standard. In the backseats on the top deck, the conversation turned toward boys. Jessica was telling Em and Rozzie about the man she'd seen on the tram.

"So, what I told you at Rozzie's was a lie, but he wasn't; this is true."

"Like that time you swore on the Bible you saw Clark Gable getting out of a big car outside the Shelbourne Hotel?"

Jessica's father held the belief that to swear on the Bible was a vain thing, demeaning to the Holy Scriptures, which gave his daughter all the license she needed to abuse the Testaments for her own ends.

"Up your bums, repeatedly, with a sharp implement."

The tram deposited them outside the Bank of Ireland before crossing the Liffey into the cold and ill-spoken districts of North Dublin, where, according to Charlie Caldwell, they called the things you wear on the end of your feet *Bewits*, thus proving, if proof were needed, the superiority in every consideration of South Dublin over North Dublin. The girls lunched at a restaurant slightly more expensive than they could justify; being called *Madam* after a week of calling other women *Madam* was a gratifying luxury to Jessica. Then up Grafton Street, past the pricey glitz of Switzer's and Brown-Thomas's, to Gaiety Green.

Gaiety Green, me dearios, me cheerios, me fine and ducky queerios: to call it a flea market is to insult the fine and noble flea of which each and every one of the troglodytic stallholders is in copious possession. Call it a glass-roofed labyrinth, call it an Argosy with B. O. where the treasures of fabled King Solomon lie heaped and shimmering beneath blazing coloured light bulbs (for some reason, the blue ones are never working), where the air smells of hot fat and the urinous reek of shiny-trousered drunkards and the warm, oily stench of menopausal women, where cockatoos recite obscene limericks and within a dozen steps you can hear a dozen different musics, from the newest hep-hot waxings of Django Reinhardt and Louis Armstrong to the primal moanings of white-stubbled balladeers, eyes gas-blinded at Ypres but forever focused on the face of Fair Caitlin from Garykennedy, where pickpockets have their pockets picked and a policeman is as rare as an Orangeman in St. Peter's, and the voice of the stallholders and vendors do cry bargain bargain how do we do it how do we do it, five for a shilling, five for a shilling, unrepeatable offer, one hundred percent bona fide genuine bargain, money refunded if not totally satisfied, the large print giveth and the small print taketh away.

Gaiety Green: where else in God's Green Universe can

you buy a dozen gravy rings, the skull of Brian Boru when
he was a boy, a three-pound note, a first edition of the
Grimoire Verum, a portrait of the Sacred Heart with electric
eyes, a secondhand frock from last year's Castle Season, an
old Orange bowler, a brace of pigs' feet, a pair of magic
blue knickers sixpence a pair (never heard of magic blue
knickers? Part with sixpence and see if your dearest wish
doesn't come true), a holy medal of Pope Pius XII, a bottle
of holy Lourdes water, a sepia postcard of a woman
engaged in an act of oral outrage with a Tamworth pig, your
present, past, and future read by Madam Mysotis, Queen of
Little Egypt, with the aid of an inky palm print on an old
copy of the *Athlone Gazette* and a little cup of Cork Dry Gin
(to liberate the spirits, you understand); a spinning top, a
Claddagh ring, a tray of yellow-man pulled toffee that
would give a mule lockjaw, with a hammer to break pieces
off, a pair of boots that have walked to Tashkent and back,
a brass spaniel, a bag of bananas, a hand-coloured postcard
of Queen Victoria not engaged in an act of oral outrage with
anything, a pound of Davy Byrne's *prize-winning* sausages
for your Dublin coddle, a gallon of porter, a chest of Assam
tea, a jeroboam of champagne, a hogshead of sack, and still
have change from a shilling?

Jessica adored the place's vulgarity. Things found in dark
corners, under cobwebs and dust, were endlessly fascinating
to her. So rapt was she that she did not notice that somewhere
in the little hell of sweating lights and the blue haze of
deep-frying fat and grating brick-edged Dublin accents, she
had lost Em and Rozzie. On a secondhand bookstall that had
not seen the light of day in twenty years, she found a copy of
*The Scarlet Woman and The Many-headed Beast: The True
Teaching of Revelation*, by Dr. Edmund Zwingli Crowley,
published by The Firebrand Press, 1898, price three pence,
for her father. Calvinist theology was a hobby of Charlie
Caldwell's that had never, thankfully, spilled over into an
obsession. Having proved from diverse authorities that St.
Patrick had been the first Protestant, he was currently engaged in a massive reinterpretation of the Book of Revelation in the light of recent Ex-Cathedra utterances from the
Throne of St. Peter's and events in Stalinist Russia. She was

about to part with her three pennies when a voice picked her out of the general din.

"Here, lovie, over here." A small woman, wizened and wrinkled as the original apple in Eden, beckoned her from behind a mound of junk jewellery. Jessica looked around for someone else the woman could be referring to. "Yes, you, love. Come over here, I've something to show you." The crowd parted, and Jessica was drawn into the vacuum. The tiny woman leaned across the trestle table and opened her hand. In her palm was a wrist torque, scratched and tarnished with age, but the unmistakable glint of gold could not be disguised.

"Pretty, ain't it?" said the tiny woman. "Look, it's engraved, see?" The torque twinkled under ten thousand light bulbs. Jessica could barely make out a Celtic knotwork pattern like those in her father's book on which she practised her draughtsmanship. It seemed to be a cow or a bull; something bovine. "Would you like to have it?"

"I couldn't afford that."

"Who said anything about you being able to afford it? It's for you." With a sudden darting of fingers, the stallholder seized Jessica's wrist. She shivered with sudden gooseflesh. "You keep it."

"I can't. I couldn't possibly accept . . ."

"You've got to have it. You can't not." Her grip had tightened, a gin trap made of bone. Jessica swore, tried to tear herself free from the old woman's grasp. The old woman wheezed and giggled and tried to force the torque over Jessica's balled fingers. Then she saw him—a moment of clairvoyance, of the kind Madam Mysotis had spent her whole life seeking. That face, that brief glance over the shoulder of the dirty Army greatcoat, that flicker of recognition through the press and shove of Saturday afternoon people, that slight suggestion of a smile.

And somehow, the spell was broken. Jessica felt the old woman's skeleton grip fall away like withered leaves. Like a heroine in a Hollywood dream sequence, she fought her way through the crowd, but the press and shove of bodies only seemed to mount before her the more she exerted herself. Certainly, no Hollywood heroine ever swore as enthusiastically as she saw him slip away, with an almost mocking smile, beyond her reach.

She retraced her path through the crowd to give the old woman on the junk jewellery stall the benefit of the sharp edge of her tongue, but the stall was gone. A blowsy woman peddling cotton sheets stood between the religious curio kiosk and the tea booth. She possessed the utter solidity of one who has stood all day and not sold a thing.

"What you gawping at, you little gurrier?"

"Never seen a backside could dress itself and talk at the same time." Jessica noted some of the ensuing colourful oaths for future use.

Em and Rozzie were busily engaged in acts of oral outrage with ha'penny ice cream cones by the entrance.

"Where the hell were you?"

"This and that. My own business." Pointless even to try to explain. She saw them glancing at their watches—so many minutes until Colm and Patrick came and their Super Saturdays really began. As hers was ending.

To spare them the discomfort of having to dismiss her from their company, she made an excuse about having to be home for tea, which they accepted though they knew as well as she that it was untrue. As they walked away, she noticed how their pace quickened as they caught sight of their men shouldering their way through the homeward bound shoppers around the top of Grafton Street. She was astonished to find herself on the edge of tears. To be seventeen, going on eighteen, in Dublin, with nowhere to go and no one to go with, into the heart of Saturday night.

With typical vengeance she wished them all miserable—wished the girls pregnant, the boys smitten by green and seeping venereal diseases.

"Excuse me, could you give me a light?"

It was him. Him. She gulped audibly.

"Sure. Here . . ." Her hands were shaking. She thought her heart was going to stop.

"Waiting for the tram?"

She looked up at the pole with the destination board on it as if she had just seen it for the first time—as if there were some other possible purpose for it being there. He grinned. She liked that.

"I've seen you about a lot," he said. "Would you mind if I rode home with you, seeing as how we're headed in the same direction?"

She smiled offhandedly. Her tongue was somehow wedged in her vocal cords. The tram sailed in to the halt. Bells rang, latecomers leaped for the doors.

"Fine evening altogether," said the young man in the khaki greatcoat in the top-deck seat beside her. "You know, and I hope you'll pardon me for being so forward, but I find it hard to believe that a young lady with all your obvious charms doesn't have a boyfriend who would be taking her out on the town of a Saturday night. If you'll excuse me saying, it seems a proper shame."

The tram passed the front of the Shelbourne Hotel. A large and extremely shiny car drew up outside. Porters and bellhops fell over each other in their stumble down the steps to open doors, take luggage, tug forelocks, pocket tips. A tall, classically featured man with a pencil-line moustache stepped out.

"Look? Isn't that, isn't he, Clark Gable?"

The tram rounded the green, and Hollywood and hotel were lost in the traffic.

"I'm certain it was Clark Gable."

"This is Dublin, me darling—anything can happen here."

They sat exhaling plumes of pale blue Woodbine smoke and engaging in the desperate chitchat of people who can hear the clock running down inexorably to the time when they know they must part, but are still incapable of making that first, tentative move to communicate. Belgrave Road lurched nearer, stop by stop. Jessica was gripped by a helpless paralysis of desire. The tram crackled into its halt and she rose to her feet, stepped off.

She watched it continue on its journey with the feeling of guilty helplessness you get when, through your own reluctance to act, you see an altogether different and more wonderful life sailing away from you. A hundred yards up the road, the tram jolted to an abrupt stop, as if someone had pulled the communication cord. Which was exactly what someone had done. A figure appeared in the entrance—the young man in the army greatcoat.

"My God, that'll cost you five pounds!" Jessica shouted.

"Worth every penny," he shouted in reply. "Tomorrow, in Herbert Park, by the pond, at ten o'clock?"

And she said, yes, I will, yes. Then the tram resumed its interrupted meander through Victorian suburbia and she was running down Belgrave Road with her copy of *The Scarlet Woman and the Many-headed Beast: The True Teaching of Revelation* in her hand.

6

Walls. Clouds of Unknowing. Amnesias.

There are ways over walls, through clouds, lights that will illumine the deepest amnesias, known to the skilled practitioner of the hypnotic arts. Not so much ways over or ways through, but ways rather of moving from one side to the other without having to traverse the intervening space.

I did not know what might lie beyond the wall of forgetting, so I carefully prepared Jessica with a string of post-hypnotic commands to pull her out of the trance and erase any memories of the session should the experience prove too intense.

Then together we abolished the distance between remembering and unknowing.

"There are vans parked against the river wall. The vans have canvas sides. Green canvas, I think. Men are jumping out of them. They have things like bandages wrapped around their shins. The bandages are green, like the canvas. We are watching from the window, but when we see the men Daddy makes us get down on the floor and hide under the table. Why does he do that? Are the men bad men? They're shouting, the men; they have funny accents. Then we hear the shots. One of them comes through the window. Funny, it's not the sound of the shot that makes me jump, it's the crash of all the glass falling in. It makes quite a hole in the ceiling, too. It travels upward, you see.

"We hear them running about in the street, and there is the smell of paraffin everywhere. Mummy says, 'Oh, dear God, what's to become of us?' and starts to cry quietly. We hear the voices again. They sound ugly, pleased with themselves. I think they have voices like dogs. Then . . . whoomph! Fire! Fire! At either end of the quay, they've set fire to the houses! They've set fire to the houses! We all go downstairs to get out. We open the front door and there's a man in a black and brown uniform standing there. He's got a rifle. He says, 'Oh, no, not you, Paddy. You're not going anywhere, old son,' and he raises his rifle. We slam the door, run back up the stairs. There's the sound of shots. I can see the back of the door go into long, white splinters. Don't you see what they're doing? They're shooting at anyone who tries to run for it. They want us all to burn.

"The fire's racing along the roofs. There's melting lead dripping down into the gutters. Number three's already gone, number four's alight, number five's just caught, and numbers six and seven are smouldering. There are shots and cries and screams and the sound of people running. The room is filling with smoke. I can't see; I can't breathe! Can't breathe! It's getting so hot. Where's the Fire Brigade? Why don't they come? What's keeping them? Tans or no Tans, we've got to get out. We try for the front door, but the fire's got there first. The hall is full of smoke and flames. We can't get out. We can't get out—we're trapped!

"We're at the window. It's the only way out. There are people down in the street—our own people, not the Tans. They are getting back into their canvas-covered vans. The people are shouting, 'Don't jump. Don't jump, hold on, here comes the Fire Brigade.' They've come! They'll rescue us. The firemen have silver helmets. The helmets look gold in the light of the flames. They're getting sheet things. What do you call them?"

"Tarpaulins."

"Those, and they're unwinding their hoses. It's the Fire Brigade; they've come to save us. They're shouting for us to jump. I don't know, it looks an awfully long way down. The people down there are like ants, not people at all. They're looking at us. There's no one looking at the Tans. Look at the Tans, they're cutting the hoses, the firemen's hoses! We're going to have to jump now. But it's a long, long way down, hold on to me, Mummy don't let me slip."

She screamed.

"The roof's fallen in. The roof's fallen in. Mummy . . .

Daddy, I can't see them. There's fire everywhere . . . Mummy . . . Daddy . . . where are you? I can't see them, I can see a beam's fallen on them . . . I can see Daddy's face and hands, they're burning . . ."

"It's all right Jessica. It's all right. Look out the window. Don't look back at the room. Look out the window. Tell me, what do you see?"

"The people, they're shouting for me to jump, but I can't jump, it's too high. I can't jump. I want Mummy, but she's not there, she's burning. There's no one to help me now. I'm going to burn, too. No one to help me, except the Watchman and the Dreamspinner. I wish they were here to make everything all right, like the old woman said they would. She said they would watch over me and make sure no harm came to me."

I paused Jessica in her trance. From here, each step would have to be carefully chosen. We might literally be walking on the edge of a precipice. I had never dreamed that such terrors could lie within her unremembering.

"Tell me about these people, Jessica—the Watchman and the Dreamspinner, and the old woman. Who are they?"

Her expression changed from terror to beatific nostalgia.

"The Watchman and the Dreamspinner look after me when I'm asleep. The Watchman has magic glasses that can see to the end of the earth and he can see all the things that might harm me while they're still a long way off, and the Dreamspinner puts his hand in his sack where he keeps all the things that dreams are made of and he strings them together, like beads on a thread, and hangs them around my bed. The old woman told me about them—the man who sends the dreams and the man who watches over me when I sleep. I used to think I could see them, standing there in the shadows at the foot of my bed—two old men, one tall and thin, the other short and round, taking care of me."

"Thank you, Jessica. Please, go back to the night of the fire."

Amazing, how her expression reverted once again to the terror of a four-year-old trapped in the most appalling nightmare imaginable.

"I wanted them to come. I wanted them to help me, like the old woman said they would. She said they would take care of me, but where are they? Why don't they come? Why won't they help me?

"Fire . . . fire . . . Flames, everywhere. They're leaping up around me, they're reaching for me. Wherever I go, there are flames. There's nothing left, just flames. I can feel my face burning. My nightie—the one with the flowers on it—there's smoke coming from it. A flame touches the hem of my nightie. It's burning, I'm burning. I try to beat the flames out, but they burn my hands. I'm burning, burning!"

My heart was hammering. I could barely find the words to bid her continue.

"And then: the hand! It's a hand. It's sprinkling something on the flames—on my nightie, on me, something like dust. And the flames go out! Wherever the dust falls, the flames go out. It's them. They've come! At last! The old woman said they would look after me and not let me come to harm. One of them is picking me up—the tall one, the Watchman. He's not quite how I thought he would be, but people are like that—they're never just as you think they will be. The other one is the Dreamspinner. He goes in front sprinkling dream dust from his sack of dreams, and where the dream dust falls, the flames die down. They carry me out, set me down. There're people all around me. When I look, I can't see them. They're gone. I wonder where they went."

I sighed heavily. The emotional intensity had been overwhelming. There were moments in Jessica's testimony when I felt I had been there in person.

"That'll do for today, Jessica. Thank you, that was most illuminating. You can come back now." I counted her up through the levels of hypnotic suggestibility to full consciousness. She shook her head.

"I've got a fuc . . . fierce headache. Did you get anything?"

I rummaged in my desk drawer for aspirin and requested a pot of Miss Fanshawe's excellent tea.

"Quite a lot. Do you remember any of it?"

"Not a thing. Must have been someplace hot, though. I'm sweating like a pig. Oops, sorry. Is this the hell where people who tell lies and swear go?"

When Miss Fanshawe's Orange Pekoe and two aspirin

had done their work and Jessica was safely steered back into the Dublin traffic, I looked again at the session notes. Threatened in the extreme, her life in imminent danger, Jessica had called upon infant memories of mystic guardian figures and somehow, flesh and blood saviours, seemingly imbued with miraculous gifts, had come to her rescue.

And I reeled under an almost physical blow of *déjà vu*. It was as if a cloud of unknowing had covered my own understanding and suddenly dispersed in the heat of the sun. Connections were made between fragments of knowledge that had lain disused and forgotten, like museum pieces removed from public display: in a divine flash, I understood. By no means fully—not even one-tenth part, one hundredth part—but I began to understand. I *saw*.

7

Upon what subjects did Tiresias discourse during his and Gonzaga's pedestrian journey from Rostrevor Village to Newry town and thence, south by west, to Slieve Gullion's bonny braes, fabled in story and song?

The putative third and missing book of Aristotle; the art and science of goat husbandry; the doctrine of baptismal regeneration; the names and natures of ghosts; the nutritional and moral superiority of the vegetarian diet; the causes and consequences of the Wall Street Crash and its effect upon global commerce; the process of fermentation by which milk is converted to yogurt and its role in the lives of the great nomadic peoples of the Russian steppes; their Methuselan life spans; its role in the Imperial endeavours of Genghis Khan; the recent successes of Benito Mussolini in Italy and the potential threat of Adolf Hitler in the Weimar Republic; the virtue or otherwise of nutmeg in rice pudding; the genitive and subjunctive forms of the Irish language, with particular reference to the word *guirin* which, in its diverse inflections, means a dead crow; an excess of flatus; the act of persistently opening the bottom half of a half door; a slow puncture in a bicycle tyre; a bilious policeman; a carbuncle on the third toe; the quality of moonlight on

Kiltrasna Strand on the last weekend in June; the act of floating out to sea on an inflated pig bladder; the licentiousness of student teachers; the disappointment of finding a glass of brandy empty before expected; a hare's "twill"; a kind of Michaelmas pudding made from potatoes, pig's blood, and mashed eels; an unpleasant situation which every effort to improve only succeeds in making worse; a scatological priest.

For what reason did Tiresias interrupt said discourse at approximately twenty past nine in the morning at a point some two miles and three furlongs outside Newry town on the road to the village of Bessbrook?

It had come to his attention that his travelling companion was not attending to his monologues with customary concentration. Indeed, Gonzaga was standing on a bank by the side of the road looking over the hedge in a generally southward inclination. Also, Gonzaga's nostrils were somewhat flared and he seemed to be engaged in the general act of sniffing the air.

What was Tiresias's reaction to these actions?

He realised that Gonzaga was in a state of considerable perturbation, which caused him (Tiresias) to question the root of Gonzaga's disquiet.

What was Gonzaga's reply?

(In flawless iambic pentameter) That there seemed to be some untoward disturbance in the mythlines far to the south of them; that it seemed to him as if some titanic force were twisting and snapping the mythlines and reforging them into new disturbing alignments. This was particularly alarming, occurring in an area they had already pacified of phagus activity and sealed off.

Describe Tiresias's subsequent action.

The removal of his spectacles from his next-to-heart pocket; the placing of them over his eyes; the consequent sighting, after the customary moment's orientation, of a great dark mass, akin to a thunderstorm, on the horizon, shot through with purple lightning and encircled by severed mythlines whipping many tens of miles into the atmosphere and shedding phaguses.

What word best describes Tiresias's reaction to the revelation of his spectacles?

Consternation.

What, therefore, was their immediate and firm resolution of action with regard to this disturbing turn of events?

To abandon their current task in Slieve Gullion's bonny braes, to head south straightaway without hindrance with the purpose of investigating the gyruses they had surveyed and constructed for the express purpose of containing and controlling such an upheaval of Mygmus energy.

What was Tiresias's final comment upon the matter before setting off in the generally southward trend?

That he feared for the young lady.

8

The city had sweltered under the heat wave for twenty-one days now. Citizens checking their barometers first thing in the morning found the needle sitting stolidly on 1030 millibars and the thermometer heading for the upper eighties. Living memory had never seen the like. "Three weeks and still no relief in sight!" the newspapers bewailed. Lunchtime saw the city's green spaces populated with typists and shop assistants and legal secretaries and junior clerks rolling down stockings, removing jackets, loosening collars, eating sandwiches with hair oil dripping onto them. A warehouse fire in which the entire national stockpile of powdered ice cream mix was destroyed provoked citywide panic. The wireless reported scenes reminiscent of the Crash of 1929 as customers fought over tuppenny cones. An extreme Protestant sect prepared for the imminent end of the world by buying every last can of pork luncheon meat in the city. Fears of a wave of lawlessness as heat-crazed young hooligans ran amok never materialised, but that did not prevent the *Evening Echo* from reporting, with some glee, an outbreak of boot-polish-eating among sixteen-year-olds. There were daily reports on the level of the Blessington reservoirs. "To pot with the reservoirs," a well-known wag was reputed to have said. "The only water I ever drink is with me John Jameson's, and not much of that." Reliable sources reported that in the original, the words *to pot* had been somewhat more emphatically expressed. Assorted weather workers, rainmakers, prophets, and shanachies were consulted on when the drought would end. They promised rain next month next week tomorrow this afternoon but the anomalous lens of dense, hot air remained moored like a vast airship over metropolitan Dublin. It rained in Wicklow, it rained in Arklow, it rained in Naas, and there were reports of a spit or two in Balbriggan, but not a drop, not even a cloud, darkened the city's streets.

Twenty-one days. Exactly five days longer than Jessica Caldwell had been going out with Damian Gorman. It was as if Nature herself were bestowing a blessing on the relationship. Strolling in the stately cool of the National Museum's corridors, pottering about Sandycove Harbour in a hired rowboat with a gramophone in the stern playing "You're the Cream in My Coffee," evening promenades along Dun Laoghaire Pier, passing themselves off as gentry from Kingstown Yachting Club; bicycle expeditions to the wilds of Dalkey and Killiney Head with its view over the bay that the tourist brochures likened to the Bay of Naples but which bore no comparison; or into the Wicklow Hills; by charabanc to Glendalough with jaunting car ride and boat trip to the cave known at St. Kevin's Bed, all in for one-and-sixpence. In the sixteen days since that first tentative Sunday morning rendezvous by the pond in Herbert Park, she had been out with Damian twelve times.

She would have loved to have been able to tell someone about those sixteen days, but from the first meeting, secrecy had been an unspoken compact between them. She had told her parents she had been out with Em and Rozzie, but she already suspected that they suspected she was seeing a man and *questions* could not be long forestalled. Under no circumstances could they know that their daughter was seeing a unit commander of the Irish Republican Army.

She found some outlet for her confessional need in Jocasta. Her younger sister had always possessed this rocklike, near-ecclesiastical trustworthiness. When you told Jocasta it was you had painted the wash-hand basin black or poured molten lead smelted down from the seals of wine bottles down the plughole, you felt the double satisfaction of having confessed and the knowledge that Jocasta would take that confession to her grave rather than squeal. Jessica found herself regularly well after midnight on the end of Jocasta's bed enjoying the catharsis of feelings teased out like tangled wool. Dates, times, the exact anatomical location of each kiss and its rating on a scale from one brotherly peck on the cheek to ten impending suffocation; hopes, wild romantic dreams, fantasies. Jocasta sat through them all, silent, listening, lit with her own peculiar inner luminosity. At an early age Jocasta had decided to orient her life along a different axis from the rest of the planet. Jessica suspected that her confessions were as incomprehensible to Jocasta as propositions in analytical chemistry. When she crept back to her room, temporarily shriven, she was certain she could hear the click of a bedroom door shutting. She could never catch her in the act, but she knew The Shite was spying. *Let her listen,* Jessica thought savagely. *Little bitch is probably jealous.*

The one thing she did not confess to Jo-Jo was that her flights of fancy were causing her increasing alarm. The new vividness they had taken on since she had begun the sessions with Dr. Rooke had been initially enjoyable; a private reality she could summon and superimpose over the cabbage stench of Mangan's kitchen and the endless mastication of the Shopper's Special Luncheoners was a mental balm. But she was losing control of them. They came to her unbidden, in the kitchens, at the tables, on the tram, at dinner with her parents, listening to the wireless. They would descend, a cloud of unknowing, and carry her away. The tram seemed particularly attractive to visions. She regularly missed her stop because she was caught in a daydream that seemed more concrete than any reality. Once she had dreamed of a tiny woman dressed only in strips and scraps of red leather, which Jessica thought rather becoming in a vulgar sort of way, and a blind harper, a man blind from before birth, for blank skin covered the sockets where eyes should have been. Rags and snippets of cloth were tied to his hair, his blond beard, his fingers, the strings of his harp, so that he could feel the world about him in the slightest movement of the air about his body. He played upon the harp, and the small, almost naked woman danced a lewd jig.

That other, *ur*-Dublin, was growing closer to the true Dublin every day. So close now that pieces of that alien city were crossing over into familiar streets. After an inconclusive round in her internecine warfare with Fat Lettie, she had retired to the ladies' jax for a Woodbine and summoned a vision of herself seated on one side of the unbridgeable gulf the Bible teaches is fixed between heaven and hell, while on the other side, pinch-faced demons were basting Fat Lettie in her own lard on a giant iron griddle, a shrieking, naked mass of melting blubber.

The scream from the kitchens had frozen every forkful of Shopper's Special between plate and oblivion. Jessica burst from the toilets to find that an entire pan of boiling fat had somehow spilled itself over Fat Lettie. "All over her face and front," said a shocked Brendan. "Just fell off the stove. She never even touched it. It just fell off the stove."

9

There is (indeed, there must be) a certain amount of the sixpenny-thriller sleuth in every psychologist, and a certain amount of the psychologist in every detective. All those motives, all those hidden drives and desires, piled high, like so many Freudian peaches we cautiously examine in our search for truth, careful lest we pull the wrong one and the whole pile topples.

It was with not inconsiderable relish, therefore, that I donned the mantle of Holmes, Peter Wimsey, Poirot, and other such worthies and set off, metaphorical bloodhounds baying, on the trail of Jessica Caldwell.

Assuming from my transcripts of the interviews that Jessica had been adopted (I foresee a storm on the horizon when the time comes, as surely it must, when she learns that the people she has called *Mother* and *Father* all her remembered life never were her true parents), I made my first call at the Public Records Office in the Four Courts. I was not particularly hopeful of finding the identities of Jessica's true parents and was not overly disappointed when the clerk returned to inform me that no reference to a Jessica

Caldwell could be found. My frustration rather was reserved for those idiots who, in the all-mighty name of
Nationalism, wantonly destroy a nation's past: too much of
our racial memory was burned in the occupation of the Four
Courts in 1922 by republican forces, and their subsequent
siege and bombardment (with fragmentation shells, dear
God!) by Free State Troopers. I had at least one concrete
reference to lead me on: Jessica's harrowing account of the
burning to death of her parents in their own home by
soldiers could only refer to the burning of Cork City by the
Black and Tans during the War of Independence, in reprisal
for an ambush in which eleven of their men were killed.

Therefore to the rebel city I went, obtained a room for the
night in a rather overgrand (and, to my subsequent regret,
overpriced) hotel on Patrick Street and started on my
inquiries. They have long memories in Cork. Once I had
established the impeccability of my nationalist credentials,
the people I met in the hotel bar were only too keen (a
zealous light would come into their eyes) to recount the
events of that night.

From Jessica's descriptions and the local testimonies, I
narrowed the possible locations down to Merchant's Quay
on the north side of the Lee, in the shadow of Shandon
Steeple. Next morning, fortified on a true detective's
breakfast of bacon, tripe, and a local blood pudding called
drisheen, I crossed the river on foot to further my investigations.

Merchant's Quay was another of those periodic reminders
one comes across with too great a frequency of the grim
days from which our nation is only slowly emerging.
Elegant town houses built to the refined tastes of the
mercantile class of seventeenth-century Cork had been
reduced to blackened facades shored up against the final
collapse into the waters of the Lee by batteries of timbers
and props. In any other city they would have been long ago
demolished as an affront to civic pride; in rebel Cork,
always on the wrong side of any uprising, they were
maintained as a memorial to the Black and Tan's barbarity.
In the entire row only one house had survived. There is
always one that obdurately holds out when the fire passes,
when the people move out, when the developers move in.

This doughty survivor was a Mrs. MacCurtain, ninety-two, and bent treble with arthritis. She took it upon herself to invite me in for tea and fruit brack while she recollected that November night.

"There were only two deaths, though I don't know whether to be thankful that there were so few, or angry that they were any at all. From number eight, they were. The Mannions. Both of them died in the fire. They got cut off—the fourth floor, do you see? When the Fire Brigade came the Tans slashed their hoses, would you believe? They stretched out blankets, so, for them to jump, and everyone was out in the street, shouting jump, jump, for Christ's sake, jump! Never mind that their own homes were going up in flames before their very eyes, they were beyond saving, but there still might be hope for the man and the woman and the baby. Did I say they had a little girl? They did, so, no age at all, God love her, for such a terrible thing to be happening to her. The father, he was about to throw the little girl out, and his wife next, but suddenly there was a great whoosh of flame and the roof came down and, well, there was nothing we could do for them. But the little girl was still alive. The window bay had protected her, you see? We all shouted for her to jump, but she was afraid, she was so high up, and she no more than four.

"Then out of the crowd walked these two tinkermen. We didn't know who they were, where they came from, what they were doing there, but before anyone could say a word, they walked into the house; into the fire, would you believe? Straight in. Now, I was there, I will tell you what I saw, with my own eyes, and that was that the one who went in first, a small, swarthy man, like an Eyetalian, he was scattering what looked like dust from a bag over his shoulder, and when the dust fell, the flames died down. The next we saw of them, they were up in the window beside the girl. We all shouted, 'Throw her down, Throw her down!' but the other one, the tall, thin one, he picked her up in his arms and turned away, as if he meant to come back through the fire. They hadn't gone two steps when all of a sudden there was a tremendous boom! Must have been a gas main going up, or something, and this ball of fire blew the rest of the windows out. I tell you, the flames shot up one hundred feet, so they did, and it was a fireman himself told me that, so. Well, we all thought, there's another two poor brave idiots gone to their Maker, and the little girl with them, poor thing. Why hadn't they listened and done like we'd said and thrown her out? But then what did I see, but the flames in the hallway snuffed out like a candle and the two of them come walking out with the little girl like they were on a Sunday afternoon walk on Crosshaven Promenade. They set the little girl down and in all the rush and haste they had disappeared through the crowd before anyone thought to talk to them. Hadn't even stopped to be thanked, and we never knew who they were or where they had come from. They came and went without a single word. But for them there's not one would have survived in number eight. And I know what I saw with my own eyes, and other folk will tell you what they saw with theirs, and what happened is a miracle, a real Hand of God miracle.

"I tell you this one last thing: after the fire, the brigade checked their blankets and tarpaulins we'd wanted them to jump into, and they said they were so old and worn that anyone who jumped in would have gone straight through. Straight through. So that tall, thin one, he must have known, though don't ask me how, because we'll never know, none of us."

I asked what had happened to the little girl. Mrs. MacCurtain replied that she had been taken by a sister who lived in Dublin, and had later married a Protestant. It was not a mixed marriage; the woman in question had been confirmed into the Church of Ireland, a thing she regarded as an outrage to nature.

Satisfied, I was preparing to leave when Mrs. MacCurtain piped up like a little bird with a final reminiscence.

"Oh, yes, I quite forgot to tell you, Mr. Rooke. This was a strange thing. When the little girl was adopted by Mrs. Mannion's sister, it was the child's second adoption in almost as many years. You see, she had already once been adopted, so, by the Mannions. Poor old Mrs. Mannion was told by the doctors she could never have any children of her own, a dreadful curse to visit upon a woman," (she crossed herself devoutly) "so she adopted a little girl from the Sisters of Divine Visitation."

• • •

I was surprised to find that the nuns of Visitation Convent were not a foundling order. Presented with an orphan, I had automatically placed her in an orphanage. The Sisters of Divine Visitation were a brisk and bustling missionary order engaged in good works of supererogation across four continents. Their convent on the Mallow Road out of Cork was bright, clean, modern, and clearly very well-funded. The current Mother Superior was a fresh-faced, dynamic, almost aggressive woman in her early forties. Sister Agnes, her predecessor, had retired from supervision of the sisters five years before at the venerable age of seventy-four. A skipping teenage novice (too worldly by far ever to make a success of life in orders) took me to the cloister garden where Sister Agnes liked to spend clement afternoons in the sunlit recollection of the past. Sister Agnes was a tiny bone of a woman. Seeing her wheelchair among the buddleias and fuchsias, I made the error of mistaking serenity for senility: her recall was instant and total.

"Such a dear little thing—like a daughter to us all, a ray of sunshine in our close community. Women in close community can be such terrible old bitches. Sisters in Christ no exception. But little Bernadette-Mary brought out the good in us—all these maternal feelings that a vow of celibacy is supposed to dissolve away like smoke, which, of course, it doesn't. She was very tiny when she came to us, a mere babe in arms. I suppose we should have given her over to one of the foundling orders, but, one sight of her, well, could you? We had her baptised at once and hired a wet nurse from Grangegorman, a poor woman who'd just lost her fifth, and she looked after Bernadette-Mary until she was weaned. After that she stayed with us here in the convent, and she would probably still be here if the bishop hadn't heard about the child. There was a terrible to-do, we just managed to keep it out of the papers. The thought had never occurred to us, you see, but everyone would have thought the child was one of ours, and that would have been a terrible scandal, indeed. The bishop insisted we have the child adopted at once. We approached the woman who'd wet-nursed her, but she had her hands full with her second attempt at a fifth, so, after much searching—I was very particular about who would look after our Bernadette-Mary—she was put with a couple called Mannion. Nice people, they were. We were all very sad to see her go. Something went out of the convent the day she left to go to her new parents. She was almost three."

I asked if she recalled where the child had come from. It might have been yesterday to Sister Agnes.

"From my brother, in County Sligo." Seeing that despite myself, I had permitted a look of surprise to cross my face, she said genially, "Yes, even nuns have brothers. And mothers, too, and fathers. And families. A proud family it is that has a daughter a one-time Mother Superior of a convent; doubly proud if it has a daughter a nun and a son a priest."

"Your brother is a priest?"

"Was a priest. Called to the higher service of Our Lord these twelve years past. Not many of us left. A brother in America, of course, and a sister married to an Australian. My brother was the priest of a small parish just to the north of Sligo."

A sound like a slowly tolling, ponderous gong sounded in my head. The perfume of Sister Agnes's cloister garden was suddenly dizzying.

"Was the family name by any chance Halloran?"

"It was most certainly. Did you know my brother?"

"I knew some of his parishioners. Drumcliffe Parish, was it not?"

"Drumcliffe it was, under the shadow of Ben Bulben."

The extortionist who claimed to be a receptionist at my hotel in Cork charged me two shillings and threepence for a ten-minute long-distance telephone call to the Links Hotel at Rosses Point in Sligo to reserve a room for the following night.

Late spring was maturing along the hedgerows in sprays of blackthorn blossom and crisp dog parsley as I motored up from Sligo through Limerick, Galway, and Ballina. My spirits matched the season. After too long in Dublin, one feels one is turning to something of the consistency of waterlogged newspaper. I enthusiastically serenaded the locals with songs and snatches from Gilbert and Sullivan.

After an excellent dinner in the Links Hotel's renowned restaurant and a couple of whiskeys in the bar with its even more renowned view over the Atlantic, I felt ready for my visit to Father MacAlvennin, Father Halloran's successor. In Ireland, all detective work starts, and ends, with the parish priest.

Father MacAlvennin was a round-faced, cheery chap, doubtless destined for a premature coronary. From the number of detective novels hidden on his bookshelves between works of a more publicly pious stance, I judged he would be only too willing to assist me in my inquiries, as the police euphemistically put it. I sat in the amber buttoned-leather tranquility of his drawing room while he fetched the relevant parish records. He was very proud of his record keeping. His primary vocation was administrative. His ambition was to serve in the Vatican Civil Service. Eyes gleamed behind circles of glass at the thought of two thousand years of genealogies, histories, indexes, codices. He located the appropriate record in a shoe box of National Sweeps tickets and golfing scorecards—Father Halloran's gifts had lain in a different direction entirely.

"There you have it—Sisters of Divine Visitation, in Cork. The Mother was the sister of the Father." Only in Ireland can a sentence like the above have any logical meaning. "The child was a foundling, abandoned in a rush basket at the back door of a Mrs. Maire O'Carolan, widow of the parish. She worked for some time as a housekeeper at Craigdarragh House—the place achieved some notoriety, or perhaps fame, on account of it being the family home of the celebrated local eccentric, Dr. Edward Garret Desmond. You may recall that, in the early part of the century, he had a fanciful notion of communicating with creatures from another world by means of a giant illuminated telegraph in Sligo Bay, which consequently brought shame and ruin upon the whole family. If I remember rightly, was there not a scandal surrounding the daughter—a rape case, wasn't it? Now, what was her name?"

I declined to proffer a nomination. Craigdarragh. The Desmonds. How often in a lifetime do we follow a certain road so far, across changing and challenging terrain, to find that it leads to its own beginning? A sense of currents moving beneath a still surface, of unseen connections and associations, crossed over me like the shadow of a cloud.

"Emily, that was her name," the Father said, pleased at the efficacy of his memory. "There's a strange tale told about her in the parish—that she was taken away in a cloud of red mist into Faeryland; that her child was half faery and was therefore cast out and left as a changeling on Mrs. O'Carolan's doorstep. Idle nonsense, of course—you know how tongues wag in the country—and not the sort of thing that I would encourage in my parish, but there are many, too many, of my flock who believe the story."

In the morning I was given a little lesson in local history over brandies by the barman at the hotel, a veritable cornucopia of local knowledge. The incredible story of the lost girl and the cloud of red fog was well known to him—he even furnished me with a list of credible witnesses to the event. I declined to follow them up. I learned from him also that Craigdarragh had been sold to a Major Ronald Costelloe, ex-North West Rifles, ex-Pukkah Sahib, who, after becoming something of a local celebrity on account of his Indian housemaid and polo ponies, finally passed into popular history under a cloud of infamy for having aided and abetted the Black and Tans in the War for Independence. Such treachery had earned him an IRA bullet in the subsequent siege and gun battle in which Craigdarragh had been reduced to a charred shell. Equipped with a pair of bird-watching binoculars and a Swiss mountain-walking stick, I motored out to the house. I parked the car in the old gateway, slipped between the rusted gates, and walked up the drive. Even on as exhilarating a late spring morning as this, the melancholy was intense. The grounds had reverted to their natural state. Rhododendrons and shrubberies were riotous, the lawn a veritable jungle. The overwhelming sensation was of the encroaching woods reclaiming an old possession. The IRA had done an uncharacteristically thorough job on the house: it was roofless and windowless; plaster was peeling away in sheets from the scorched, blackened walls; chimney stacks made stark silhouettes against the sky; there were ashes, ruin, brambles, decay. Of the lives and circumstances that had moved within those walls, in those elegant gardens, there was not a trace—not so much as a scorched piece of trim from a silk parasol. It seemed to me a sad parable of the Ireland we have created.

From the sad remains of a great house, I crossed the stile at the end of the rhododendron walk into Bridestone Wood. Twenty years can span the life and death of even as great a house as Craigdarragh, but in the life of a wood they are as an evening gone, as the hymn says. There were a few halfhearted attempts at husbandry along the edge woods, a few sawn logs, damp cones of sawdust, an unruly stab at coppicing, but for the most part I walked in a woodland that had clearly never felt the hand of man. As with all wild, untouched places, a colossal, primitive sentience seemed to reside in every twig, every leaf, every uncoiling fern and spring flower. But there was a further uncanny sensation quite peculiar to Bridestone Wood: that of being *watched*. I could well believe the warnings of the barman at the Links Hotel when he had learned of my intentions for the afternoon. "Folks say it's haunted. Well, now, I wouldn't go so far as to say that myself, but I do know there's a mighty odd feel to the place." Indeed. Not quite haunted, but not quite not.

My general trend was upward, my chief goal the Bridestone. After a few hundred yards in what I felt was that general direction I found myself headed *downslope*. Reorienting myself, I followed a small stream upslope, made a small detour around a thick clump of brambles, and found myself once again disoriented. The stream which I had kept to my left sounded from my right. Presuming I had turned around inadvertently, I rectified the mistake, walked on, and found myself once again beside the dead oak I had used as my initial landmark.

By now thoroughly unnerved, I consulted the small compass built into the head of my walking stick. I followed the needle and kept my eyes on my feet. After a hundred or so paces I began to experience a mounting sense of dislocation—up, down, left, and right shifted alarmingly. I persevered, and as I pushed on I became aware of a growing sense of resistance, a kind of muscular inertia, as if the air had thickened against me. It took me twenty minutes to cover as many yards. Without warning, the pressure ceased.

I almost fell over in my exertion. By my estimates, I was less than a quarter of a mile from where I had parked the car; I felt like I had run ten miles. As I puffed and panted like an old man of seventy, the most baffling of the disorientations overcame me. I was still pressing uphill, but the slope of the ground seemed to increase until I felt as if I were climbing an almost vertical wall of vegetation. The evidence of my eyes had the wood sloping gently up to the foot of Ben Bulben; the evidence of my body had me on the face of a veritable Matterhorn!

Clinging there for dear life to every available hand- and toehold, I became aware of the birds—starlings, magpies, crows, ravens, eponymous rooks, all birds of ill omen. The trees were black with them. I clung to my rootholds and watched them come flocking in. As if by command, they rose as one and came at me.

I can remember very little—thudding wings, flashing yellow beaks, scaly legs, and clawed feet. I do remember hanging from my perch with one hand and lashing out with my Swiss mountain stick in the other, smashing hollow bones, snapping beating wings; the shrieks and cries and the whirring, flapping wings all around me. Beaks lunged for my hands, my eyes, my cheeks. I was engulfed in a storm of black feathers. I lunged and parried with my stick—too far! The grass tore in my fingers and I tumbled downslope. Trees, rocks, stumps, briars, loomed before me. Miraculously, I escaped being smashed and broken upon them. I came to an eventual rest in a clump of furze not ten feet from the dead oak, bruised, scratched, mud-smeared and covered with leaf mould; otherwise, considerably more intact than I should have been after a vertical fall of a quarter of a mile.

Bridestone Wood, or the spirit that controlled it, would not permit penetration by such as I. Trembling with delayed shock, I followed the rabbit path through the edge of the woods to the Drumcliffe Road.

A brace of Napoleon brandies in the hotel bar helped the recuperation process. From my table by the window, I could see the birds still circling above Bridestone Wood across the bay.

10

A felicitous succession of lifts and stowings-away brought
them to the Boyne Valley, and the tombs, by early evening.
Six millennia of legend and story had woven around the
megalithic cemeteries of Knowth, Dowth, and Newgrange a
nexus of mythlines too powerful to block at the source. Five
years before, Tiresias and Gonzaga had fought for a season
weaving a complex double spiral of gyruses about the minor
nodes and octave points, isolating the tombs' Mygmus
energy from the countryside mythline pattern. The Boyne
Valley remained a key strategic site. If the Adversary were
to regain control of the phagus-generating energies focused
there by six thousand years of human imagination, the
entire process of containment could be threatened. Proto-
phagus forms were abroad, boiling out of the earth like heat
haze; every hedge and thicket seemed to harbour a leering
Firbolg or Jack-in-the-Green. The sense of flow along the
mythlines toward the focus at the tombs was so overpowering that Tiresias was forced to dispense with his spectacles. Gonzaga was not so blessed; he could not turn off his
senses so easily. He walked as if bothered by a bad
conscience, pausing every so often to twitch and shake the
voices out of his head.

The dark was drawing down by the time they reached the
first gyrus. It had been sited on a minor chordal node on a
wooded knoll known as Townley Wood by the riverward
entrance to an old country seat abandoned in the War of
Independence. They groped in the twilight through the
debris left by early season picnickers. Gonzaga stuck his
finger into a partly decomposed condom.

"It has, since long, been this one's understanding, that
Mother Ireland eschewed the use of these," he complained.

They found the gyrus by the last glow of the sun between
the trees. Utter destruction. The buried elements had been
sniffed out and grubbed from the earth, as if by tusks, then
stamped into nothingness. As a final act of destruction, the

centre of the small clearing had been scorched. Gonzaga
sniffed the air.

"Pookah."

In its contemporary form, the pookah had been demy-
thologised by the centuries into another member of the
pantheon of faeries major and minor—a rural Puck figure,
generally good-natured, if prone to occasional acts of minor
domestic mischief. In its ancient manifestations, the pookah
had been terrible and dangerous, the spirit of the forest
itself, with its roots in the racial memory of the woolly
mammoth of the periglacial fringelands, haunting with tusk
and claw and sinew the nights of the Mesolithic settlers.

"Good comrade, please, one moment's perfect hush:
This one suspects a presence in this place
Not of ourselves. This one must hear and sense."

Townley Wood was in complete darkness. Tiresias had
spent too many years following the mythlines to fear the
dark, yet as Gonzaga turned slowly, as elegantly as a
dancer, in the fire-blackened clearing, he felt cold hands
touch his spine.

Gonzaga let out a wordless cry and pointed. Tiresias had
his glasses on his nose in an instant. Townley Wood was
transformed into a place of pale mists and rivers of pastel
light. He looked where Gonzaga was indicating. A tangled
worm of luminescence was unravelling and dissolving in a
shallow dell a handful of yards distant. He glimpsed faces:
the horse-headed homunculus, the sea cat, the satyr, the
werewolf, the wild boar . . . and then they were gone,
absorbed back into the Mygmus.

They spent the night by the desecrated gyrus, watching,
listening, waiting. Gonzaga cut two hazel branches and
stripped them into long staves. While Tiresias muttered and
fretted across the borderlands of the Dreamplace, he emptied his sack onto the charred ground. His fingers, like
small, bright-eyed animals, moved over the strewn items,
touching, weighing, selecting, rejecting. Dried flowers,
shards of broken crockery, Boy's Club badges, bones, bird
feathers, scraps of cloth, holy medals, broken jewellery,
coins, bottle caps; those that passed his test he attached to
the staves with short lengths of twine and button thread.

Motorists and other users of the Dublin Road were so

surprised by the sight of two tramps waving what looked like portable maypoles at them that, needless to say, they did not even slow down, let alone offer them a lift.

11

Despite clamorous reviews and long lines to book tickets, Damian had not been impressed by the film. Jessica had been annoyed with him because he had not enjoyed something she had anticipated so long. She had been excruciatingly embarrassed when he had laughed out loud at cutlass-wielding Errol Flynn springing from concealed trampolines in a tropical Panama (emphasis on the last syllable) that looked more like the Palm House in the Botanical Gardens than the Spanish Main—the only one in the entire audience who had laughed.

"Look at them," he said when the final credits had rolled and the audience was cramming the exits before the National Anthem froze them in their seats. "Is this the country our fathers fought for? Is this the Caitlin Ni Houlihan Pearce and Conolly and MacDonagh died for—a cinema full of Irishmen watching an American film of an English pirate played by a Tasmanian queer?"

Jessica sprang, as nimbly as Captain Blood himself, to the idol's defence, but Damian in this mood was inaccessible to her, walking alone through the pure landscape of the Gael—the blood-washed mountainsides where everyone wore kilts and spoke grammatically perfect Irish and played hurling and lived by the grim sea in a grim cottage with two grim wolfhounds; a land where no one had ever heard of the BBC Light Service, or F. W. Woolworth's, or Alexander's Ragtime Band, or the rise of Fascism in Italy, or Errol Flynn in *Captain Blood*. "We finally throw off eight hundred years of British cultural imperialism and stand alone, the last Gaelic nation, and what do we do? Spend half our bloody lives in the dark watching Clark Gable and Douglas Fairbanks and Errol Bloody Flynn. Jaysus!"

The sultry evenings had made St. Stephen's Green a natural magnet for strolling couples. That night there was the added attraction of a band concert.

"Can we go and listen to them?" Jessica sometimes felt isolated in Damian's company—she loved his uniqueness, that he was not just another Hoover salesman or conductor on the Howth electric tram—but she also loved the company of other people. Damian listened to the brassy notes softened by the warm, amber air. "Jaysus. *The British Grenadiers*. I despair for this country. Why the hell am I bothering trying to save you all?" Jessica stared at him in open hatred as he walked away. She caught up with him at the Leeson Street gate. He stood with his hands in his pockets watching a street entertainer grinding the handle of an old hurdy-gurdy. At his feet a monkey skipped and grimaced to the droning slip-jig and held out a sequin-stubbed bag for alms.

"Paddy-on-a-bloody-string," Damian said. He dropped a penny into the monkey's bag. It doffed its cap but its eyes were turned inward to purely animal concerns.

"Thank you kindly, sir." The hurdy-gurdy man tugged a cap peak. Jessica gasped. He had no eyes. Blank skin covered the sockets where eyes should have been.

The monkey screamed and chattered and threw itself at Jessica, straining at the extent of its tether. Pointed teeth snapped and clashed. Swearing at the monkey while apologising to Jessica, the hurdy-gurdy man brought the thrashing animal under control. Jessica was shaken. For one moment it had not seemed a monkey at all, but a very small, very old, very wizened, naked woman.

The hurdy-gurdy man was on his pitch by the Leeson Street gate, grinding out his doleful tunes when she passed on Monday evening after work. His archaic instrument gave a peculiar, almost lamenting air to even the most familiar of tunes; there was a spirit in those drones and strings that drew Jessica, while at the same time repelling her. The hurdy-gurdy man remained on St. Stephen's Green until Wednesday, when she saw him on a new stand by the canal locks. As she passed in the tram, the blind hurdy-gurdy man looked up and, with some sense other than sight, fixed his empty sockets on her. Thursday he had moved on to a new location in front of the big church on the Lower Rathmines Road. From her seat in the third row on the top deck,

Jessica's eyes met his eyelessness. The monkey thing skipped and gibbered. She remembered what it was about it that made her shudder when she had seen it outside St. Stephen's Green: for a moment, she had thought it was the tiny woman in Gaiety Green who had tried to give her the golden torque. The next day she took a different tram home, by a different route. A creeping sentience of being followed, through the streets and avenues, over the bridges and tram lines, to the brass welcome of number twenty, haunted her. She could not rid herself of the sensation that the hurdy-gurdy man's blindness in this world was vision in the other; that, in the alien perspectives of that shadow-Dublin, she shone in his sight as bright as an angel.

Friday the hurdy-gurdy man and his homunculus had crawled their blind way to residence in Belgrave Square, the next street down from Belgrave Road. She could hear his melancholy drone on the warm, yellow air as she sat at her mirror and made herself glamorous for Damian Gorman.

A scratch at the door was The Shite, leering malevolently.

"What do want, you little frigger?"

The Shite's leer deepened.

"I know where you're going, and what you're going to do, and who you're going to do it with."

"Oh, do you, now? And how the hell would you know?"

"The man told me."

Jessica seized The Shite by the lace collar of her sundress and dragged her into eye-intimidation range.

"What man?"

"The man in the park. He's ever so nice. It's such a pity he's blind, the poor man. He says he's a friend of yours, he knows all about you. He told me all about your boyfriend—Damian, isn't he? He told me he was in the IRA. He says he has something very important he has to give you. You can call down with him any time. He's got a nice monkey—he let me play with it."

"You stay away from him, you hear me? You go near him or his monkey again and I swear to God I'll break every one of your fingers in the door."

"You touch me and I'll tell about Damian, the IRA murderer, and what you do with him in the alley behind Hannah's Sweet Shop."

"You little frigger."

They glared at each other in mutual impasse, The Shite not the least intimidated.

"Get out," Jessica ordered. "You're a spying little bitch. Get out."

"God's very angry with you for being a Protestant associating with someone who's a rebel against His Law. God's going to punish you; God's going to make you have a baby."

"Up your bum till it comes right out your mouth, Shite."

12

"Yes! Oh, yes! There, look, don't you see it? So far away you'd almost think there was nothing there at all . . . there, I've glimpsed it again—something bright, like a silver needle, shining in the heart of the storm. I'm getting closer. I can see it more clearly now. It's not a needle at all, it's a tower, a tower of glass, so clear it's as if it isn't there at all, but at the same time shining with a light of its own. It seemed tiny because it was so far away, but now, as I fly closer, I can see that it's miles and miles and miles tall, it goes up forever and ever, straight and sheer and smooth, pure and perfect crystal. Closer still, and I can see there are no doors, no windows. Silly! What would a glass tower need windows for? It's all solid glass—pure, perfect shining crystal, rising out of the sea. The sea is so black it's like ink, and the clouds are black, too. It's hard to tell where the clouds end and the sea begins; it's hard to be certain of anything. Everything is so fluid and changeable, except the glass tower."

Despite the heat in the room, I felt icicles along my spine.

"Oh! The clouds have parted. I can see the top of the tower. It's opening up like a flower in bloom, like a rose with hundreds of petals and each petal is a different land, with hills and forests and rivers and seas. All different, so different, some with red skies and purple clouds; some where mountains float in the air; some where there is no grass, only many-coloured waving tentacles woven into patterns like a Persian carpet; some where everything is crystal, bright, brilliant sharp, diamonds and rubies and emeralds; and others that are made out of poems and music and time and hate. Here is a place where everything is made from dreams so that nothing is the same from one moment to the next, and here a place of wheels, all running around and around the outsides and insides of each other. All of them are different, lying folded next to each other like the petals of a rosebud unfolding to the light."

We had arrived; the place of Jessica's primal memories, the nonquantifiable domain from which all human symbology and mythic power is derived, a place where our notions of discrete time and space are without meaning, our Lost Edens, our Gardens of Earthly Delight. I shivered. A sudden, inexplicable chill had entered the study. Outside the window Merrion Square shimmered under the heat haze. Within, my breath hung in steaming clouds. My fingers were so cold I could barely scribble down my pencil notes.

"I can feel myself being drawn down, toward the petals of many lands. Like a sycamore seed I am spiralling down. I am being pulled toward one of the world petals. Why I am attracted to this one I don't know. It's strange—not like any of the others. Its hills and valleys and plains look as if they are made of *skin*. I'm settling toward it, into a little valley—not so much a valley, more like a pit, with steep, wrinkled sides. It's soft and warm, though, and I can feel deep underground the sound of throbbing. But I can't keep a hold. It's too smooth—I'm slipping, I can't hold myself, I'm sliding down into the pit, down, down. It's dark down here, and the sound of the throbbing is growing louder. What's happening, where am I going?"

The cold, it must be her doing. Is she drawing on the latent heat of the atmosphere, channelling it through her preconscious self? But to what end?

Manifestation?

"I'm inside now. This is strange. It's a bit like being in a cathedral—all pillars and arches and vaults—except, when you look closely, you see that the pillars and arches and vaults are made up of twisted ropes, and everything's red. It's more like hell than a church, but why do I feel so safe here? Why do I feel that this place welcomes me, that I'm returning home after a long time away? I can't understand this, that everything is so strange, and yet I feel so safe, so welcomed, so protected. Everything swells and contracts in time to the booming, beating noise. It shakes me to my very centre, but even that is comforting. Do you understand? How can something so overpowering and terrible be so comforting?"

The cold had grown so intense that every breath crackled like needles in my lungs. Delicate filigrees of ice coated the windows. The water vapour in the study was condensing out into a band of mist at dado-rail height. Knots and whirlpools in the mist layer fleetingly called to mind human faces.

"I'm walking through the cavern. I've been walking for what seems like miles but there's still no sight of an end to it. I can see things now I couldn't before—things pulsing behind thin translucent walls; things that look like bunches of grapes, except each one is the size of my head; tubes and pipes that throb and pump in time to the beat. I can hear something: a voice. I can hear it even over the pounding heartbeat; a woman's voice. She's saying she doesn't know what to do. She sounds very upset. She says part of her wants to keep the child here with her for always, but another part of her knows it must leave and enter the world. It sounds like the kind of talk you talk when you are talking to yourself—the kind of talk people aren't meant to hear. Wait, I can see something! I can see something."

Those phantom faces in the eddying mist, they were not the product of imagination.

"It's a woman. She's kneeling. She looks as if she's crying. She's naked. I come closer but she doesn't hear me. She just keeps talking to herself."

No mist now, but a circling choir of faces: fools, kings, priestesses, pretenders. Thick lobes of ice covered the windows and spilled onto the radiators. Ice; cold, ghostly faces. To Jessica it might have been an afternoon in a summer meadow.

"I'm beside her now. I'm bending down to touch her. What's the matter? Why are you crying? Can I help? She looks up at me. I see her . . ."

And her expression was no longer one of supernatural serenity. Her face was an inhumanly blank porcelain mask.

"It's her. She's here. She's come for me again."

I reached through the whirlwind of faces to take her hands. The shock was almost electric. I have never felt anything so cold, so dead.

"Who, Jessica? Who?"

"My mother," she said with devastating simplicity.

And all was still.

The manifestations were gone. Gone, too, the unnatural iciness. The sudden return of summer afternoon temperatures made the study seem tropical.

Some power other than I had decreed the session ended. Jessica shook her head, breathed deeply through flared nostrils. Her eyelids flickered. In a moment they would open and she would behold what she had wreaked upon my study. Questions, of a kind I did not much desire to properly answer, and would probably not be able to, would be asked.

Quickly, I asked her the level of her hypnotic trance. It is one of the features of my style of hypnosis that the subject remains conscious at all times of the depth of his state of consciousness, in ten-point levels, subdivided into integers for finer discrimination.

"Level thirteen," Jessica replied. "Level twelve, level eleven." She was surfacing rapidly, but still amenable to suggestion. Less than level ten and I would have been lost.

"Go to level thirty," I ordered. It was a level of deep hypnotic suggestibility, the one at which posthypnotic commands are best introduced. "At once. Your state?"

"Twenty-five. Twenty-eight . . . thirty."

"Good girl. Good. Excellent."

And, loath though I am to resort to such music hall tricks, I inserted a posthypnotic command that on my instruction she would get up, leave the study, make the usual appointment with Miss Fanshawe, and go straight home. At the tram stop, she would emerge from the hypnotic state and remember only that the study had been pleasantly cooled by a small breeze from the park through an open window. It grieves my professional ethics to play so light and free with the human psyche, but the alternatives would have been even more grievous.

A reality-shaping adolescent possessed of the full knowledge that her dreams and desires could become physical reality: the shiver that ran down my spine was not entirely due to the arctic state of my study.

After Jessica had left, seeming in every way no different from her normal self (well, I will admit, a little less uncouth), I sent Miss Fanshawe home early, and with the aid of tea, a week's supply of Huntley and Palmer's biscuits, and a pleasing Mozart piano sonata on the wireless, sat down in the reception area to think.

It is only in the historic period that the institution of priesthood has become an almost exclusively male preserve. In prehistoric societies, the role of guardian of the mysteries has largely been female. While man-magic in primitive societies is directed toward the exigencies of the hunt, women, as guardians of the fire and the home, and of the deep mysteries of reproduction and fertility, have developed a magic, a system of belief, that goes beyond practicalities into philosophical and symbolic conjecture. At some time in our racial history, did evolution bestow upon some guardians of the mysteries the ability to reach to that grey place where mind impinges upon reality, and through their shared-subconscious domain of symbol and myths, shape it into living, material expressions? And did those walking, breathing manifestations impress themselves into the subconscious domain again so that future manifestations would come to resemble them? It seems entirely possible that a few scattered mythoconscious individuals passing down through history could have been responsible for our entire mythic landscape, from primal bogeymen to Faeryland to Roman Catholicism. What is Blessed Mary, Ever-Virgin, in effect, but a mother-goddess figure, female gateway to the symbols and mysteries; was the Mother of Christ, of the Church, no different from foul-mouthed, lying Jessica Caldwell?

13

A city is as much a state of mind as a place—a set of perceptions of place.

On the last train home to Mullaghbrack or Gortyfarnham or half a hundred other BallyBogMans, two farmers fall to reviewing their experiences of the big city. One has walked the streets and avenues and come away with memories of glistening steeples and dreaming spires, monuments to men of bearing and import, Palladian porticos and grand civic cupolas, pillars, piers, and palisades, and the air full of singing birds.

The other has walked the same streets, yet his memories are of grey brick tenements shouldering against each other like nervous thugs; cracked fanlights, windows boarded over with card, baby carriages full of coal or potatoes, tramps in doorways, cabbage leaves underfoot, the perfume of urine and porter, pressing people with voices like flatirons.

They might have visited cities continents apart, but it is the same city.

And through the streets of that city flies one of the singing birds, and the city it perceives is an avian metropolis of ledges and perches and nesting sites connected by great canyons of air at the bottom of which shapes move, by day and by night, among whom endless food may be found.

And the eye of the bird passing through the highways and byways of the air spies a cat creeping in an alley, and to the cat the city is a cubist jungle of pheromones and territories and runways, some great, some small, some abutting each other, some sharing common ground, some occupying the same space on different levels, demarcated by oil, glandular secretions, and urine, mapped by nose and eye and whisker, defended by tooth and claw and hiss.

And the cat weaving along the boundaries where territories and pheromones touch passes a tramp lying in a gaslit doorway, and to the tramp the city is a place of doorways and archways, of dry places out of the wind and shelters from the rain and corners where the cold does not penetrate, of railway arches and wooden park benches, of public toilets by harbour walls, back alleys and abandoned houses, where life is cold, damp, and short, where sleep is hard and food harder, acquaintances few, friends fewer, love not at all, save for a dog, or a cat, or a singing bird.

Three cities, many cities, all different and inaccessible to each other, all continuous with each other.

By the signposts and Baedekers of the hidden city they came, by half-legible chalk marks, scratching on stones, careful defacings of street names, by the freight sidings on Abercorn Road, by gas lamps and laundry-festooned windows (flags of triumph, or surrender?), by tenement steps and cracked fanlights, by the low-rent streets of the bread-and-tea people, the six-to-a-room people, the child-a-year-till-we're-forty-thank-you-Your-Holiness people, the Junos and the Paycocks, the captains and the kings, under the shadow of the gunman and the Starry Plough blessed and cursed by priests and rebels, saints and martyrs, by the smoke-stained gods of the four rivers of Hibernia on the Custom House and the cabbies' shelter under the Butt Bridge with its tins of carcinogenic tea sickly with condensed milk and bacon sandwiches thick as a doorstep. Thence, with the lamplighter on his evening rounds, across Dame Anna Liffey to the shadow of the gasholders at Ringsend.

A fire was burning on the domed concrete inside the skeleton of the dismantled gasholder. It lit Tiresias and Gonzaga across the broken glass and rusted barbed wire and poisoned earth to the circle of tramps who had gathered there to pass around a bottle of milk through which they had bubbled gas from a street lamp. One of their company, an old woman named Sweet Molly Malone, had already succumbed and lay slumped in a heap of tattered woolens and shawls. The firelight glinted from the string of thick drool that leaked from her mouth. Tiresias and Gonzaga joined the circle and shared the sacramental bottle, though they were immune to inebriation, be it whiskey, methylated spirits, petrol sniffed from a red jerry can, or milk fortified with municipal gas. A vast blue evening opened itself like the wings of an angel over the city. Beneath the first tentative twinklings of stars, the tramps sat sharing their communion. Around goes the bottle, around and around the camp fire, to the widdershins, the witching side, the lefthand side, the sinister. Others were drawn from their particular cities into the circle, and one by one they too fell over where they sat, wits blasted by Dublin Corporation Gas. The bottle slipped from a hand and the milk ran out in an uncertain pool on the chipped concrete.

Gonzaga circled the ring of inebriates clicking fingers in ears, lifting eyelids. Satisfied there would be no witnesses, he moved to the edge of the firelight and began to set his watches and wards. The pookah phagus had gathered strength and definition with every mile they had drawn closer to the chaos of mythlines around the city. They had passed through the palisades of flailing, fractured mythlines with the sure and certain knowledge that they were being hunted.

"Our problem, in the proverbial nutshell," mused Tiresias, "is that we created our pattern of gyruses with the sole purpose of protecting our ward from attack from without. It is to our eternal chagrin that we never gave thought to the possibility of our charge breaking through to mythoconsciousness herself, breaking the pattern from within and thus leaving us exposed and vulnerable to the fury of our Adversary. We have been negligent in our duties, my dear Gogo—inexcusably negligent."

Gonzaga could feel the phagus, moving out there in the hot night like low, cold mist over the broken glass and barbed wire. He clutched his staff to his chest and set his watches and wards, a Guinness bottle here, the end of a roll of tram tickets there. Sounds carried for immense distances beneath the great lens of stifling, stale air that hung over Dublin: the clang and shunt of engines in the sidings at Fairview; a ship's siren, disconsolate as a lost soul, in the offing beyond the bar mouth: the oaths of drunks; the whistles of policemen; the crash of breaking glass; the peal of the great bell of St. Patrick's chiming one. The down-and-outs stirred and grumbled in their sleep. Gonzaga completed his task and sat across the fire from Tiresias. They watched each other's backs. Things that might have been rats or cats or dogs, and might as easily not have been, moved fitfully beyond the watches and wards. Tiresias felt the Dreamplace beckoning; hypnagogic illusions fluttered in the corners of his vision, crowded like insects around a beggar's eyes. Old Molly Malone—she who had succumbed first to the seductions of the bottle—called out in her sleep and started, as one deliberately waking himself from a nightmare. Her eyes flicked open.

Black vapour poured from her open eyes.

Tiresias and Gonzaga were on their feet in an instant.

The woman shrieked and tried to beat the smoke away from her eyes, but it was beyond her stopping. Within seconds it had mounted into an inverted pyramid of darkness that filled the interior of the gasholder. The woman's hysterical screaming and pleading was waking the other tramps.

"If you value life and sanity, remove yourselves forthwith!" Tiresias commanded, transformed by firelight and gas-befuddled wits into a shining Merlin wielding a magic wand. The tramps fled, ragged coattails flapping, clapping greasy hats to greasy heads. A tattered size ten came down on a packet of Senior Service cigarettes. Gonzaga let out a cry, but the errant foot had sent the empty pack spinning into the night. The circle was broken. The smoke-thing immediately condensed and solidified. Tiresias uttered a stream of early Mesopotamian oaths. With the phagus drawing only on the subconscious desires and fears of old Molly Malone, whose very unconscious power had sent her out from mainstream society into the company of the tramps, their staffs would have prevailed. Against a phagus shaped by the old alcoholic's imagination but powered by the almost limitless power the Adversary could summon through the rent it had torn in the Mygmus, all the pieces of power in Gonzaga's knapsack might not be enough.

The cloud of darkness swirled and knotted into the pookah phagus, dressed in the fears and longings of the howling woman. A thing of matted hair and shadows, it uncurled from its crouch to stand the height of three men. Accustomed as Tiresias and Gonzaga were to the powerful perfume of tramps, its stench still made them gag. It had no eyes. Black bare skin covered the sockets of orbs. It sniffed the air, caught the scent of woman. Its penis unfolded from the tangle of hair between its legs—six feet of rigid black muscle rimmed with spikes and rear-curved horns. Pleading with God, with Mary, with any deity that had not washed its hands of her, Sweet Molly Malone scrambled away, but too slowly, far too slowly. Claw hands scooped her up, opened her legs. The barbed penis juddered and smoked; twin blades of bone extended from the sides of the glans. It thrust one, two, three times, split the woman like a wishbone. The pookah tore the remains in two and smashed them against the girders while it ejaculated gouts of green semen. The stench was overpowering. Chittering and bubbling in its throat, it sensed other presences and reached for Tiresias. The old man's staff met the reaching paw. There was a cascade of sparks and a small crack of thunder. The phagus howled. Tiresias pressed home his advantage, swinging his staff above his head. Realizing it was more shocked than hurt, the phagus rallied. Its penis trembled against its belly and dribbled goo. Its attack was halted in a storm of thunder flashes, then a well-timed swipe separated Tiresias from his staff. Gonzaga had been slower to recover from the old woman's appalling death. Tiresias's plight snapped him to sensibility. His staff drew a line of blue fire across the pookah's back. Burning hair momentarily overcame the fishy, sexual reek of the phagus.

The two old men stood at opposite sides of the circle with the pookah, wary and burbling softly to itself, at the centre.

"It seems to me that we are in something of an impasse," Tiresias wheezed. "It can hold us here until it gathers enough power to finish us off."

"Have you forgotten all your phagus lore?" asked Gonzaga.

"Cold iron is the bane of faerykind,
Since the ancient blacksmiths of the Celtic race,
Did, with sword and spear of cold hard iron,
Drive their bronze-using elders from this land,
And all their goods and gods and mysteries."

"And, pray tell, where are we going to find enough iron to magic away this faery?"

Sensing an opportunity, the phagus lunged and was driven back in a blur of staff-play. Dawn was beginning to colour the east. Should day and the police find them here,

with a pookah and a dismembered alcoholic . . . Gonzaga
suddenly darted for the wasteland beyond. No longer
needful to mind its back, the pookah came down on
Tiresias, drove him back behind his swinging stick.

"Is needful you should buy this one some time!" Gonzaga yelled. Tiresias could spare him no more than a glance.
He saw hands busy and bloody with barbed wire.

"Good friend, please to direct the beast this way."

Tiresias stole another glance. Claws whistled across his
face. Gonzaga seemed to have connected one end of a
length of barbed wire to his staff, the other to the gasholder.
He gave ground, drew the pookah step by step over the
broken glass and crumbled brick. Trickles of black blood
ran from its ears, its nostrils, the skin over its eyes, its
penis, expressed by the force of its sexual fury.

"Down, friend, down and let my aim be honest!" Tiresias
threw himself to the ground. Gonzaga hefted his staff and
speared it with all his might at the pookah. The sharpened
tip penetrated the left shoulder. Ringsend shook to a
tremendous explosion. Tiresias squinted through his fingers
into the glare. The girderwork of the disused gasholder
blazed with blue lightning. Forks of lightning crackled from
girder to girder; drips of electricity fell to the concrete, blue
as burning brandy. The two old men danced do-si-do on the
broken bottles and broken brick as the phagus energy
dwindled to flickers, to a St. Elmo's fire glow, to nothing.

Gonzaga went to pick up his staff, and dropped it with a
howl. The heat of the blast had seared away everything
combustible—bottle caps, pieces of glass, crockery, cutlery, and miscellaneous metals had been fused to a cancer-
ous slag. The barbed wire had been vapourised. The
gasholder was festooned with viscous glops of blue mucus.
In the far distance, rapidly approaching middle distance,
were ringing fire engine bells.

"With watch and ward we sought to thwart her power,
But all along the power was in our midst.
In our company she found one like herself
Of latent gift, a rose that bloomed unseen
To waste its fragrance in self-dissolution,
The beast was here among us all along."

Then, as if scenting a change in the wind, Gonzaga added,

"Ereh fo tuo teg ew fi aedi doog a eb dluow ti kniht i."

14

It had taken days of psychological warfare, but she had persuaded Damian to take her to the Arcadia Ballroom. To hand your coat to the cloakroom attendant and buy cigarettes from girls with trays around their necks and step out under the glitterball was to undergo a rite of passage into Grown Up Stuff. Rozzie and Em went to the Arcadia Ballroom with their respectives, and their plush descriptions of that soft-shoe pleasure dome had made her prickle with envy. She would never have gone on her own—people would have thought she was *that* sort of girl. But as a couple, it was more than respectable, it was a social necessity. Jocasta aided and abetted in the deception. Caldwell *mere* and *pere* must never suspect if difficult questions and more difficult answers were to be avoided.

The band played "Moonlight Serenade" as she hoped they would: cat-sensuous, purring clarinets and muted saxes. The Harry Hall Orchestra sat in white tuxes and Brylcreem behind sequin-studded frontals. H. H. himself conducted flaccidly and shot twenty-four-carat smiles at the dancers moving in crowded orbits, dappled with glitterball freckles. Jessica pressed close to Damian. She was shocked and delighted to feel a hard lump in his number one best pants.

"Oh, you naughty bugger, what's that I feel?"

"It's, shall we say, my professional credentials?"

Jessica was considerably more shocked than she would have been if what she had felt had been mere erectile tissue.

"You mean to say that you are in here carrying a . . ."

He put his hand over her mouth.

"You never can tell . . ."

The dancers wove through a fog of mentholated cigarette smoke. A crooner crooned something into a squat microphone. Couples applauded. The night and the music played on. A cord of sexual tension wound tighter between Jessica and Damian. She looked at him and felt something in her chest struggle to tear free. The power of her emotion frightened her, and that edge of fear made her hunger sharper. They left the dance before the last waltz to make the last tram. They sat on the open top deck in the heat of the night, smoking, communicating at a level beyond speech. Jessica rested her arms on a railing and looked out at her city, purpled, mellowed, by the hot summer night.

"You think you have your life all set, that nothing's ever going to change, and then it changes, all at once. All of a sudden, things happen and life becomes very complex."

"What do you mean?"

She did not answer immediately, but rested her cheek on the brass railing and watched the city roll past. "Complex. Like you see all the things you've ever wanted for your life falling through your fingers and you can't keep a hold of them anymore."

"You come away with me, and you can be anything you want to be."

"Don't piss me about, Gorman."

"I'm not. I'm serious. Come with me."

"Oh? You keep saying that—come away with me, to the waters and wild, to Sligo and a new life, just us, together, forever. Daydreams, Damian, daydreams. Life is not like this."

She returned to a number twenty asleep, the house all dark save one sliver of light under Jasmine's door. The sliver expanded into a wedge. The Shite stood, arms folded, faintly intimidating in flannelette nightie.

"Go to bed, you spying little frigger."

The Shite was defiant, unassailable.

"No, I won't go to bed, I won't. You won't make me."

Jessica made to push her sister back into her roomful of teddy bears and toy horses and Girls' Brigade pennants.

"No one likes you, Jessica. No one likes you, don't you know that? You tell lies and swear and no one likes you because you have to be different from everyone else. You can't be the same, you have to be different, better. The boys don't like you; they all talk about you and laugh. Bullshit Caldwell, they call you, did you know that? None of them will go out with you. The only boy you can get is a murdering IRA man."

"Shut up!" Jessica hissed, fearful of lightly sleeping parents, but The Shite was speaking with a voice and inspiration of her own. She had discovered she could hurt her sister and was wielding her newfound power with vindictive abandon, twisting the knife.

"No one likes you. I don't like you—I don't like you at all."

"Well, you just have to like me, because we're sisters."

"No, we're not," gasped The Shite. "You're not really my sister. That's what the nice hurdy-gurdy man with the monkey told me. You're not my sister at all—not a real sister, like Jo-Jo is, and Mummy isn't your Mummy and Daddy is not your Daddy and you're not really their daughter." The Shite froze, hands to mouth, conscious that she had crossed the line between righteous indignation and calculated cruelty; moved into a region where cause and effect no longer behaved in strict ratio to each other—a state of minute action and colossal reactions.

Jessica's face was pale, as if drained of life by a vampire. Her lips moved faintly.

"What? What? What are you saying? What are you *saying?*"

Hearing the swelling strain of hysteria, The Shite slammed her bedroom door with a sob of fear. The sound of key turning in lock was uncannily loud.

The telephone rang.

Numb to everything but the demand of the ringing telephone, Jessica went downstairs to answer.

"Hello? Caldwell residence." Her mother insisted she call it that. It lent an air of gentility.

"Hello?" A woman's voice, incredibly far away. "Is that Jessica?"

"Who is this?"

"Is that Jessica?"

"Who is this?"

"Is that you, Jessica?"

"Yes, this is Jessica. Who is this?"

"This is your mother, Jessica. Your mother."

"Hello? Hello? Hello . . ."

"Your mother, Jessica. Your mother."

The heat in the hall was stifling.

"What is it?"

"Remember, Jessica. *Remember.*"

The line went dead.

"Hello? Hello! Hello . . ."

Seated on the threadbare carpet, worn by the passage of many lives, she *remembered*.

It had been as if her life were a broken bridge and she had stood on the edge of remembering, looking across the gap too wide to leap at the part of her life that was unremembered. Then the words were spoken and they were the keystone that completed the broken arch, and she was free to cross over into the unremembered and remember it. One foot after another, she had made the crossing and all the lies that had made up her life rose before her like startled birds. She saw, she heard, she touched, she remembered.

She had loved them with a child's intuitive, uncritical love, and all the time they had known it had not been their right. They had not deserved Mother-love, Father-love. Mother. Father. Sisters. She ripped away their names, their titles, and left them pure identityless faces, bundles of formalised relationship without substance. One short, clean stroke had cleaved the threads that bind individuals into a family.

Adopted. *Adopted.* The great whirling machinations of betrayal. The fanlight above the door cast a brightening rose of light across her; short summer's night at its end.

15

When she woke in the morning they were there. She struggled out from under the Army greatcoat, picked the straw from her hair and clothes, opened the shuttered hay barn window, and they were waiting for her. The birds. The field before the barn was white with massive, malevolent, yellow-eyed gulls; the hedges and telegraph wires were heavy with starlings. Rooks rattled their wings in the branches of the trees; on the telegraph poles, ravens fluffed their feathers and clacked their beaks. Every eye was fixed on her. She watched more glide in through the low dawn mist to join the vigil. She heard Damian moving in the still-dark recesses of the hay barn, preparing for this day's journey.

"Damian, come and look at this."

He looked up, saw her silhouetted against a rectangle of morning sky.

"Jesus God, would you get away from that window! You want everyone in the county to see you?"

"I was right. They are following me."

"For God's sake, girl!" In one blink of movement, he crossed to the window and pulled Jessica away. She sat down heavily on a hay bale.

"You bastard, you hurt my arm!"

He closed the window.

"I thought we had an understanding; we can't compromise on security. You want to get away, you follow orders. My orders."

"I'm not so sure I want to get away so bad with you issuing your orders orders orders all the time."

"You seemed sure enough yesterday."

"Yesterday was yesterday. Today I am tired and cold and hungry and I feel filthy and this is no fun at all, Damian."

"It was never part of the agreement that it had to be fun."

"God, I must look awful. I need to do something with my face. Go away. Just go away. Leave me alone, all right?"

Damian shrugged and went to hacking off hunks of crusty bread with a clasp knife. Jessica rooted out a hand mirror and sat examining her countenance. Realising the ridiculousness of what she was doing, she snapped the compact shut. Like her anger, it had been a mask for her apprehension. She had thought that in escaping she had hauled herself from an increasingly inexorable stream of events moments before it crashed over the falls into panic and chaos. She had thought that in running away she was taking control of her life. She had merely extricated herself from the torrent of events to find herself carried along by another.

Perils of Pauline. Tied to the tracks, with the express approaching.

She was gone before the milkman's cart came clinking on its rounds, taking only as much of her as she could indisputably call her own, stuffed into a carpetbag. No note; traitors did not deserve notes. With the milkmen and the breadmen and the postmen and the newspaper boys, she walked the Victorian red-brick avenue of Ranelagh and Rathmines until Hannah's Sweet Shop put up its shutters and she could pencil a message for Damian. He would not call there until half past four. She would find some way to pass the time. The aged Miss Hannah passed comment about her being up early this morning. Jessica did not hear. Her head was full of the rushing, pounding wings of betrayal. She spent the day in Pearse Station, dividing the hours between having protracted cups of tea in the station buffet and watching the infinitesimally slow progress of the hour hand around the face of the station clock from a bench on the platform. The sun moved in concert across the glass roof. Pigeons lived up there, under the roof, in the girders and pillars. Every passing train set the ones new to life in the station flapping and beating at the grimy glass in panic, steam billowing about them.

Damian arrived with the weary end of the commuter rush southward for Booterstown, Blackrock, Dun Laoghaire, and points south to Bray. He saw the carpetbag, the stony fixity of her face. They embraced under the clock. Over bacon and egg sandwiches she told him about the lies, the years filled with lies and pretense and falsehood.

"I had to get away, Damian. What's true, what's false, who I can trust, who I can't trust, who is lying, who is telling the truth; I don't know anymore. I don't know . . .

"Take me with you. You said you would, you said you wanted to, more than anything. Take me away with you to the hills and the mountains—somewhere where it will all stop hurting. You said all I had to do was say the word; I'm saying it now. Wherever you're going, whatever you're doing, I want to come with you. Damian . . . you're all I've got."

He was not looking at her. His attention, the attention of

every southbound commuter, was fixed on the roof. It was covered, every last inch, with the round, feathered bodies of birds.

"Now, Damian. Now. We've got to go . . ."

She led him by the hand down the station steps into Westland Row, heels clattering on the cast-iron stairs. Above them, the birds rose from their roost in a rush and clash of wings.

It was full dark before a car would stop. Jessica was footsore and half delirious with hunger and fatigue from twelve hitchless miles along the Mullingar Road. Damian had ruled out public transport; the police were certain to have a description of Jessica, and bus and train stations were the first places they would check. Hitching lifts carried a degree of danger. With twelve miles gone and the night close and cold upon her, Jessica had sat down on her carpetbag and refused to take another step. Twenty minutes later the headlamps of Mr. Peter Toohey, travelling salesman of Tomelty & Malloy agricultural implements, Multyfarnham, had swept across the fugitive couple. While Mr. Peter Toohey, travelling salesman of Multyfarnham, made lewd innuendos about what a young couple might be up to on the Mullingar Road at half past eleven, Jessica surreptitiously tore at the railway buffet sandwiches she had stashed in her carpetbag and guzzled red lemonade liberated in the name of Irish republicanism from a parked door-to-door delivery van in Chapelizod. Damian instructed Mr. Peter Toohey to drop them at a featureless farm gateway just beyond Kinnegad crossroads, which Mr. Peter Toohey did, though not without questions, none of which were graced with an answer.

Only when Mr. Peter Toohey's red taillights had vanished in the direction of Multyfarnham did Damian feel it was secure enough to mention the safe farm. "We'll spend the night here, then go on tomorrow." He helped Jessica over the gate.

"Where to?" They picked a careful course across a weed-infested cow pasture. The cows ruminated and farted with bovine gentleness.

"Sligo. I have friends there. They can shelter us while we decide what to do." The barn lay across a second gate and

field. From the farmhouse came the sound of the wireless
and the yelping grizzle of suspicious dogs. Jessica stopped
by the stagnant drinking trough.

"Listen."

"What?"

"Listen . . . I can hear them. I can't see them, but
they're here."

"What?"

"The birds. They've followed us. They're here."

"Nonsense. Birds don't fly at night."

"These birds do."

"Come on, will you, and stop standing there gawking
like an eejit. You want the farmer to catch us?"

"I thought you said this was a safe farm."

"It was; back in twenty-one, twenty-two."

"You're trying to tell me they allowed eight-year-olds in
the IRA?"

"Things don't change much in the country."

"Just how safe is this safe house?"

She could just discern a facial expression in the dim
sky-glow.

"Safe-ish."

Safe-ish. It had been a mindless impulse, to put space
between herself and the hurt of a betrayal that was still too
tender to fully admit, but that was what she wanted, to be
driven by impulse—her own impulse, for once, not the
endless whirring machinations of others. Damian came,
cautiously, with bread and a map.

"No toast?"

"No butter, no marmalade, no fire."

She ripped at the bread with her small white teeth.
Damian measured off distances on his map with his fingers.

"Will we get to Sligo today, do you think?"

"Maybe. With luck. Have you thought about what you
want to do when you get there?"

"Don't know. Don't care. Might just turn right around
and go straight home. I need time to think, to sort out what
I feel, who I am."

The sun was low and brassy in the mist as they stole away
from the hay barn through the gathered birds. Every click,

every clack, every rustle of feathers and flap of wing, sent Jessica's pulse racing. They passed down a boreen that led to the main road. The hedgerows were sharp and brilliant with beaks and eyes. As they turned into the road, they heard, all at once, the storm of wings rising. They did not look behind them. For half an hour after, a river of birds passed overhead into the northwest.

16

Damn Caldwell! What mad notion had possessed the man to try on the glasses? We had been within minutes of them. Even now they could be approaching Sligo while we remain sequestered in the Mullingar County Hotel waiting for Caldwell to regain normal vision, if he ever does. Every half hour we remove the heavy bandages from his eyes, but even the darkened hotel room is agony to him. Tiresias cannot predict how long it will be before he is sufficiently recovered to move. Damn the man!

Obviously, we cannot leave him in the room and continue the pursuit ourselves. Neither can I carry it on alone, as we will have need of Tiresias and Gonzaga's arcane abilities. They cannot go ahead without me as they cannot drive. Indeed, they seem loath to use any mode of transport more sophisticated than their own two feet. So we remain stuck in this down-at-heel country hotel like some Marx Brothers comedy. I was a fool to have let Caldwell accompany us.

"Guilt" is not a word with which psychologists have any truck, yet I feel guilty. She had left no note, but I was certain our sessions together were the direct cause of her flight. I had been so careful, plugging and caulking every chink and crevice, yet those constrained memories had seeped out. Memories not merely of her forgotten childhood and its traumas, but, more perilously, of the inheritance she has from her true mother. Responsibility, guilt: psychologist, heal thyself.

Jessica had been late for her appointment. My anticipation had been high, almost feverish, of being able to induce, at will, the state of primal consciousness in which the human mind interacts with matter and energy. I can only describe the sensation as the intellectual vertigo of standing upon a cliff edge overlooking a new landscape, vast and exhilarating, awaiting one's tentative explorations.

And, of course, she was late.

Twenty minutes became forty, became an hour and a half. I was sufficiently agitated to call Mangan's Restaurant, where she worked, and was informed that she had not been present for work that day. I called the Caldwell house—perhaps she had been taken ill and had neglected to tell Miss Fanshawe. Forboding began to grow in me when I learned that she had left the house before any of them had been awake, though it was not an unusual thing in itself. I told Mr. Caldwell of my call to the restaurant, and, voice suddenly filled with concern, he asked if I could call around as soon as possible. Having no further appointments that evening, I told him I would be present forthwith. Just as I was replacing the receiver, there was a loud knock at the door. I rushed to admit the visitor.

"Jessica," I said, "what kept you? Where have you been? Come in."

"I beg your pardon?"

In the corridor were two old men, two tramps. One was short and squat, like a toad, with a dishevelled mop of oily black ringlets; the other was tall and thin, almost a bird, wearing the most extraordinary pair of spectacles I have ever seen.

They introduced themselves as Tiresias and Gonzaga. Tiresias, the taller one, explained that they were searching for a Miss Jessica Caldwell—"the young lady" he called her, in a curiously archaic Anglo-Irish accent, like a seventeenth-century beau—and had traced a minor node of Mygmus energy to this place. Could I assist them in their search? They had information of the gravest import to impart to her.

It was as the tall, thin one was speaking that awareness dawned on me: here, standing outside my office door, were two actual mythic manifestations. These were no fleeting elfin shadows in Bridestone Wood, no half-real, half-wishful images captured on a photographic plate. Though their appearance and demeanour allied them more closely to the Lords of Little Egypt and the Counts of Con-Dom than the Ever-Living Ones and the Queen of Air and Darkness, these were *faeries*—the incarnations of the Watchman and the Spinner of Dreams.

I replied that Jessica had been undergoing a course of hypnotic therapy—obviously, this "node of Mygmus energy" to which they had alluded—and that she was long overdue for today's appointment. Indeed, and I could not say why I felt the sudden compulsion to say what I did, she had been absent from work and missing from home all day. From the way they looked at each other, the smaller one saying something in a language that sounded like Russian, to which the taller one nodded gravely, I knew that they suspected something untoward was afoot.

We drove at once to Belgrave Road.

The family awaited me in the living room, arranged as if in a Victorian family snapshot. The sullen tautness of the atmosphere indicated to me that some altercation had taken place minutes before my arrival. The younger daughters seemed on the verge of tears. Mrs. Caldwell was the very picture of the weary and distraught Hollywood vamp, down to the cigarette clenched nervously between two fingers; Mr. Caldwell's expression one of grim resolution in the face of withering revelation, like a member of the Russian royal family on the night of the Revolution.

I had taken the precaution of leaving Tiresias and Gonzaga in the car—they did not seem much to mind. Gonzaga busied himself down the back of the seats while Tiresias, outrageous spectacles on nose, surveyed minutely the front of the Caldwell residence. Their presence would only have provoked questions I did not desire to answer at that time.

"Go on, tell Dr. Rooke what you told us," Caldwell said. The barely restrained tears flowed as first the older daughter, a dark-haired, just-blooming beauty called Jocasta, and the younger, a child of almost inspirational plainness, like contemporary Catholic saints, named Jasmine, told their tales.

When they had concluded, I could well appreciate

Caldwell *mere* and *pere*'s expressions of numb bewilderment.

That there had been a man friend Jessica had been meeting clandestinely while her mother thought her visiting friends, or *me*, even more astoundingly, for over a month was shocking; that this male friend (if Jocasta's testimony was to be trusted, and it seemed reasonable to me that Jessica had had at least one confidante with whom she could be wholly truthful) should have been a member of an IRA Active Service Unit was amazing. But what most staggered, and I will admit, alarmed me, was the younger daughter's disclosure that she had been approached by the bizarre figure of a blind hurdy-gurdy man who seemed to be in possession of every detail of Jessica's life, including the secret of her adoption. It was Jasmine who had broken this lifelong secret—she and Jessica had never liked each other, and their mutual antagonism had erupted in the devastating revelation of Jessica's adoption on her return from an evening in the company of her IRA lover. Chastened, young, plain Jasmine fled the room in tears.

"Well, now we know why she's gone," Caldwell said. "If only we knew where. If only we could find her, bring her to her senses."

"She could be any bloody place by now," Mrs. Caldwell said curtly. "And if she's gone with that IRA thug, my God, they could be dragging her from a lake, or she could be lying dead in a ditch with a bullet in the back of her head. At the very least, at this very moment, my God, he could be . . . with her . . ." The vamp composure broke. Sobbing uncontrollably, Mrs. Caldwell also left the room. Jocasta Caldwell now spoke.

"I think I know where she might have gone." No premass hush beneath the dome of St. Peter's was ever so profound as the silence that awaited her words: "She said that Damian, that's her boyfriend, had been on at her to go away with him to his country, his own people, to Sligo . . ."

Caldwell did not even stop to ask if he might accompany me; I certainly would not have refused him. He scooped up coat, hat, and wallet, and we piled into my car. He did hesitate for a moment on seeing Tiresias and Gonzaga.

"Who are they?" he asked, not unreasonably. Tiresias quizzed him with his spectacles.

"It's rather a long story. Suffice it to say that there are aspects to this case that I felt I could not reveal in front of your wife and children." (I did explain them as we drove to our first port of call, Hannah's Sweet Shop, which, according to Jocasta, the lovers had used as a kind of jungle telegraph. The aged Miss Hannah was pulling down her blinds for the night but, sensing our urgency, she was only too happy to oblige, provided the two tramps did not come into the shop.)

As we drove to Pearse Station and Caldwell tried to digest the unpalatable hypotheses I had served him, I recounted all I had been told to Tiresias and Gonzaga. The presence of the hurdy-gurdy man caused them considerable agitation. Gonzaga said, tersely, words that sounded like, "Sugayff erprahh dnaillb uht eeeb tssum tt'y."

Tiresias announced gravely: "Gentlemen, the situation is worse than we had feared. Jessica is being harried by forces that are inimical to her, though for the moment, she is ignorant of the exact power and threat of these forces."

"You mean, her mother—Emily."

"Precisely, Dr. Rooke."

"What are you talking about?" Caldwell demanded.

At this hour, Pearse Station was the province of drunks and topers waiting on the last train home. Caldwell and I checked every bench, every kiosk, but none of the passengers could—indeed, were able to—remember seeing the girl in the photograph Caldwell kept in his wallet. One porter recalled having seen a girl eating sandwiches on a bench by the gents' toilet during the seven o'clock lull, but had no memory of a tall, dark-haired, pale-skinned young man in a British Army greatcoat, which was all the description of Damian that Jocasta had given us.

In Westland Row, where we had had to leave Tiresias and Gonzaga because the station staff would not allow them on the premises, a policeman was about to arrest them on a charge of sitting in the back of an expensive motor car.

"They're with us, Officer," I said. The policeman nonetheless took a note of our number as we drove off. As we passed the entrance to Phoenix Park on Parkgate Street, thunder growled somewhere behind us in the east and fat drops of rain burst on the windshield. By the time we reached Maynooth, the wipers could hardly keep up with the deluge. The car, a Morgan tourer, was never designed for four passengers, least of all with the hood up. What with Tiresias and Gonzaga virtually perched on our shoulders like Long John Silver's parrot, the thick stench rising from their damp clothing, and Caldwell starting for the hand-brake at every bush and shrub and muttering, "Surely we should have passed them by now," I may have had less pleasant driving experiences, but I am hard pressed to think of them. The tension in that car matched the grand electrical mayhem breaking behind us over Dublin. By the time we reached Kinnegad crossroads it had almost smouldered into flame. Caldwell and I exchanged heated words, burning looks, and the suggestion of blows to come in our disagreement over which road the fugitives might have chosen. It might well have come to fisticuffs, but for the intervention of our ill-smelling companions. Gonzaga thrust himself between us to keep us apart while Tiresias once more unfolded those arcane spectacles of his from their vellum wrapping, patiently cleaned off any trace of grease, put them on, and gestured for me to let him out of the car. He stood beneath the signpost, coattails flapping in the warm, wet wind, slowly describing one complete revolution before removing the glasses, polishing away the raindrops, and consigning them to the care of his waistcoat pocket. He pointed up the rain-swept Mullingar Road.

When he was wedged once more into the backseat and we were on our way toward Mullingar, Caldwell asked, seemingly innocently, "How do you know they went that way?"

"Disturbances in the mythlines, sir. As a gifted one herself, the young lady cannot cross mythlines without creating a flux—like the wake of a ship, you might say. The closer we come to her, the greater the disturbance of her passage."

"And are we close to her? To them?"

"I would say, sir, that we are about an hour, an hour and a half behind her."

"This wake, how do you see it? With those glasses?"

"Indeed, sir. My spectacles make the network of the mythlines that covers this country visible to the eye."

"To any eye?"

"To any eye, though there is a certain knack to the interpretation of what one sees."

"Would I, for example, be capable of using them? Could I use them to see where my daughter is?"

"I can see no intrinsic objection, but I would be loath for you . . ."

"Would you look again, just to be certain she hasn't set off cross-country?"

"I am fairly confident, sir, that she has followed the road."

"It would bring me great peace of mind if you were to just check . . ."

"Very well, sir." Caldwell turned around in his seat to watch Tiresias unfold the spectacles. The old man breathed on the lenses, burnished them with the soft vellum wrapping. Glancing into my rearview mirror I glimpsed ribbons and streamers of light shining deep within the glass.

And Caldwell struck. Quick as a snake! He had the glasses out of Tiresias's hand and onto his face before the old tramp could react.

With a wordless roar, Gonzaga lunged across the back of the seat and seized Caldwell by the lapels of his coat. Caldwell emitted a long, peculiar wail and fell forward, head hitting the wooden trim of the glove compartment with a fearsome knock. As he fell forward, Gonzaga was pulled in almost on top of me. The steering wheel spun out of my hands. I groped for the wheel, the hand brake, anything, as the car slewed across the road. I saw hedgerows loom before me in the twin beams of the headlights, and then somehow, the car was at a standstill across the middle of the road, front wheels mere inches from the ditch.

All this happened more or less simultaneously.

Tiresias ripped the glasses from Caldwell and replaced them, muttering furiously, "He shouldn't have, he shouldn't have—stupid, foolish human. He wasn't trained, didn't know, didn't have the gift . . ."

I keep a small bottle of brandy in the glove compartment.

Thinking it might be of some help, I rolled Caldwell back;
even in the dark I could see the bruise purpling on his
forehead. His mouth and eyes were ominously open. When
I shone the map-reading torch in his face he gave ululating
cry that froze me to the pith of my being.

"Too bright! Too bright!" he moaned. "The light, the
light!"

Gonzaga spoke hurriedly, hushedly, with Tiresias.

"We must get him to a safe place, quickly," Tiresias
translated. I ventured a hospital. "No, not a hospital. They
cannot treat his affliction."

"What is his affliction?"

"Seeing too much."

"Of what?"

"The mythlines, sir. He saw them all, all at once, and it
was too much for him to comprehend. He should be taken
to a safe place at once."

Caldwell was moved to the backseat where Tiresias
bandaged his eyes with a questionable handkerchief. In the
front seat, Gonzaga passed untranslatable comments on my
driving.

"When will he recover? Will he recover?"

"I cannot say, sir. This is unprecedented. In theory, he
should readjust to the vision of this world, but I am at a loss
to say how long it might take."

"Hours? Days?"

"As I said, sir, I am at a loss."

We arrived in Mullinger and beat on the door of the
County Hotel until an understandably ill-tempered manager
came down to admit us. He was not at all happy at the
presence of two ostensible tramps sullying the period decor
of his establishment, but after monetary inducement of a
proportion that even the piratical proprietor of the Munster
Arms Hotel would have baulked at, he conceded us a room
on the front overlooking the street. I ordered tea, and while
we waited rebandaged Caldwell's eyes with more appropriate material from the car first-aid kit. Even the slightest leak
of light through his tightly closed eyes seemed to cause him
agony. When the tea came, Gonzaga tasted it, squawked in
disgust, and emptied the lot down the wash-hand basin.
Producing a small canister from the military-style bandolier

slung around his shoulders, he proceeded to prepare a new batch from the hot water the hotel had provided.

Lapsang souchong. Like drinking a cup of liquid smoke. Never tasted finer.

17

An almost operatically flamboyant sunset was drawing toward its finale over the Atlantic Ocean as they reached the top of the long glide down into Sligo. They had stolen the two black sit-up-and-beg bicycles from outside a pub in County Roscommon that morning; now, beneath swathes of crimson, ochre, and Imperial purple, they freewheeled down into the darkening town. The day's exertions had left Jessica exhausted but exultant. They pedalled through the street as one by one the lights came on. From the bars came the yellow shine of the fellowship of pint and voices joined in amiable argument; the more restrained, intimate glow of fire and wireless came from the houses. Above them, flocks of small birds—starlings, sparrows, finches—stormed and swooped. Jessica felt no guiding intelligence from them— they merely obeyed the laws of the masses. That other flock she had not seen or sensed since it had risen up before them when they had left the hay barn.

Damian announced it would be pointless to press on any farther that day. He would find them a place to spend the night in the town, and in the morning they would go up into the hills to join his friends. He forced the lock of a small Church of Ireland chapel skulking in the shadow of the grandiose Catholic basilica. The rusted metal gave easily, and they were inside. Jessica was still breathless from the blasphemy of it.

"Can you think of a safer place to kip?" Damian asked.

They walked up the aisle between the rows of pews. The streetlights shining through the stained glass windows cast a hue that might have been mistaken for divine blessing over them. Damian opened a box pew, lifted carpet seating and hassock.

"You Prods like your creature comforts." He made

Jessica a bed from kneelers scavenged from before the altar rails.

"You have a sleep here and I'll go out and see what I can find to eat."

"You think I'm going to sleep on my own in this place? Damian? Damian?" He had already slipped away through the vestry door. Jessica squatted on her heels and pulled her knees close to her chest. A stray draft of wind stirred the dried petals of last year's poppy wreath beneath the war memorial. She counted the names of the war dead, the number of organ pipes, the number of tiles in the chancel, the number of cherubs on the stained glass windows. Changeless and incorruptible in their wall tombs, the Anglican dead of Sligo slept profoundly encased within Connemara marble while Jessica Caldwell made up rebuses and magic squares from the numbers on the hymn boards.

Damian returned with a pile of sandwiches wrapped in grease-proof paper and a bottle of communion wine.

"'Alto Vino.'" He peered at the label under the wan streetlight. "'Prinknash 1932.'" He took a slug from the bottle. "Rough, but it does the job."

"That's blasphemy. That's communion wine you're swigging."

"It's not the blood of Christ until it's consecrated. Even then, it isn't—not Prod communion wine. It's just fermented grape juice." Jessica peeled back the bread from her sandwiches and grimaced.

"Cucumber. God, I hate cucumber." Damian passed the Alto Vino Prinknash 1932. When they had finished, she lay on her impromptu bed under the Army greatcoat smoking a Woodbine and watching the occasional swing and play of car headlights through the north transept window.

"Damian, why do you never tell me about yourself?"

"It wouldn't be safe for you to know."

A silence.

"Frig you, Damian Gorman."

A silence. When Damian spoke, his voice was as hushed and intimate as a devotion.

"I was fourteen when my brother Michael was captured by the Free Staters. He had been set up, no doubt about it; someone had informed on him. They were waiting for him as he came out of the Beaten Docket Bar on D'Olier Street. February 1923. In one pocket he had a German automatic and three clips of ammunition; in the other, a British Mills bomb. Unlawful possession of a firearm was enough to get you hanged, in those days. Cosgrave and his *Clann na Poblacht* bully boys had no mercy. Under the British, we expected no better, but these were our own countrymen— men who had fought side by side with us in the G.P.O. and Stephen's Green and in the roads and lanes of West Cork and Tipperary. There was a trial, if you could call it that—the judge had the rope weighed and measured the moment Michael came into the dock. We appealed. It dragged on for two years; two years waiting to hear if the Justice Minister had granted clemency.

"Then we got a note in the post one morning, just a postcard, saying that Michael had been hanged by the neck until dead at dawn that morning in Mountjoy Prison. Just a postcard. 'The Ministry of Justice informs you . . .' Jesus!

"The same day, I joined up. I knew all the contacts through Michael. The Brigade Commander said I was young, but motivated. My mother disowned me; my father, I knew, was proud—proud that I was continuing the fight, that Michael had not died in vain. But he couldn't say anything, not against my mother.

"They gave me a gun—this same gun I still carry with me." Metal clicked where he tapped the black Webley. "It wasn't long before I was assigned to an Active Service Unit. I was thrilled. It was a chance for me to strike back at the traitors who had sold the martyrs of 1916 short." He broke into song, voice high and uncertain, to the tune of "The Red River Valley":

> Take it down from the mast, Irish traitors,
> The flag of Republicans claim,
> It can never belong to Free Staters,
> You've brought on it nothing but shame.

"You know that song?"
Jessica shook her head, then remembered Damian could

not see her. But the *no* was communicated. The red coal of his Woodbine weaved in the dark.

"My mission was Statues and Symbols. We couldn't carry the fight to the British, but we could carry it to the symbols of British Imperialism—crowns, lions, and unicorns, Queen Victorias, Good King Billys. My first assignment was painting out the initials of the British monarchs on the Free State postboxes. E VII R, G V R. We covered every postbox in Dublin with good green paint. Because the unit commander was pleased with the way I did that, he graduated me to statues. Two pounds of dynamite up Queen Victoria's ass sure made the old bitch come like she'd never done with Prince Albert. She certainly was not amused at that. Remember when Good King Billy outside Trinity College got blown up? It was me did that."

"Now I do know a song about that," Jessica said,

> Good King Billy had a ten-foot willy,
> And he showed it to the lady next door.
> She thought it was a snake and hit it with a rake,
> And now it's only five foot four.

"It was a lot shorter than that when I'd finished with him," Damian said. Jessica would have guffawed, but that Damian regarded his work with such seriousness.

"At seventeen I was promoted to the Enforcement Division—the youngest ever. The Republican movement's greatest enemy has always been the whispered word and the tinkling purse. That they trained me to deal with—a bomb through the window, a barn burning, a body left by the side of the road with a note pinned to the chest, *Informers Beware*. But then the IRA started to become its own worst enemy, and all the things I had grown up believing were as true as the Earth was round and there was a God in heaven were all thrown up into the air. Instead of Irish Republic One Two Three, suddenly there's one lot wanting to carry the war into England and fight the ancestral enemy on its own soil, and another wants to force the Free State into invading the six counties of British Occupied Ireland and there's a third lot want to reorganise the whole shebang into some Socialist Communist fifth column and turn Ireland into a revolutionary Bolshevist State. What happened, says I, to Mother Ireland, Sweet Caitlin Ni Houlihan and her Four Green Fields, what about the old-fashioned, pure-and-simple Republicanism they died for in 1916?

"Then, in the midst of the confusion, it was as if I had seen a great light, like the Apostle Paul on the Damascus Road, and I knew that I had been called to keep republicanism pure and holy, without taint or alloy. Me and those few flame-keepers, grail-searchers—a holy few.

"We used the old ways because the old ways have always been the best ways—the ways that drive terror like a spike into the heart of a man. You hear a knock on your door in the wee, wee hours. You come downstairs to find your baby daughter's dress nailed to the gate. You find a pot of stew simmering on the stove and when you peek inside, you see your dog's head. Terror. Terror. The holy fear of God. The only way to keep a man pure and right."

Jessica looked at his profile against the saint-light of the glass windows, saw the glowing coal of the cigarette tip trace its hieroglyphs, saw the smoke breath from his lips.

"There was a lad, from Clones town in County Monaghan. He'd been out in 1921 but he'd gone soft, taken up Socialist notions, Communist ideas. We'd had a good organisation up there in the border counties. Once. He ran a dance hall up in Clones, free admission, as long as you were prepared to listen to a bit of Socialist epilogue before the last waltz and sing the *Internationale*. We'd warned him about corrupting the minds of the young people. It was his own damn fault, he brought it on himself. He should have listened. We torched the place one Sunday night; mighty fine blaze it made, too. How were we to know he was inside unpacking a new consignment of pamphlets from the international Socialist movement? It wasn't our fault; he'd been warned. He should have listened. He should have."

The Anglican dead of Sligo looked down from their marble mausoleums without judgement or rancour, white and hard and passionless as angels. A moon rose behind the east window, filling the glass with ghosts. The cigarette, burned down almost to a nub, fell from Damian's fingers to the tiled floor. Trapped in a web of insomnia, Jessica raged at whatever justice decreed that those with the conscience of a killer should sleep like alabaster saints while she tossed and turned, dancing with the moonlit knight.

A clock struck one. All of Sligo was asleep save her. The clock struck the half hour; two. She could hear the visions, wings beating against the roof and walls of the church like chimeras, calling her out. The clock struck a quarter to three. An idle corner of her mind wondered if the clocks chime when there is no one awake to hear them, and the tappings and scratchings of the visions were gathered up into *music*.

The Unending Song, begun with the first syllable of the first human cry of "I Am" that went out across the savannahs of proto-Africa and carried on across all the world, along its tangled mythlines and over its legendary landscapes, to its cities and its wild places, its palaces and prisons, its towers and tenements, its basilicas and brothels; a trickle, a stream, a torrent of voices carrying the past forever forward into the future, forcing its way out of the cracks and crevices of rational confinement: the drone and slur of a hand-cranked hurdy-gurdy, rising, falling, near and far. The music struck assonances and dissonances that summoned Jessica from her pew, across the tiled floor to the vestry, and out the vestry door into the churchyard, where the music was vast and muscular under the stars, as if the strictly Calvinist geometries of the church had created a bubble of harmonic silence. Jessica heard it as a tearing elation, a pagan joy. The music was a living thing, a torrent of silver notes tangled together by their staves into the shape of the dancer. One sure foot after another, Jessica followed in the steps of the dance along the empty streets and laneways, past shuttered shops and parked cars and houses closed up till morning woke them—step-a-jig whirligig arabesque pavane. No illusion now, she could see the music that was leading her in the dance. Silver tendrils, like summer fog flowing low and fast over the cobbles, swirled and eddied around her ankles and the tyres of the parked cars and the street lamps and the telegraph poles. She could not resist the flow had she wanted to. The music drew her to its centre, to a small cobbled court between warehouses close by the cool and mist of the river. There, in the pool of limpid silver, the hurdy-gurdy man waited with his monkey, his arm turning the crank of his instrument for all eternity. Jessica fell to her knees, plunged her wrists into the silver light. The hurdy-gurdy man's fingers moved over the frets. The music boomed and rang from the stone warehouses that encircled the courtyard. A waterfall of luminescence poured from the sound holes of the instrument, and, with the silver light, came images: silver salmon, golden trout, leaping stags with crowned antlers, centaurs, fauns, satyrs, swans, and golden-bristled boars; winged horses, flying carpets, genies like Greek fire in bottles; warriors, thieves, queens, and lovers; minotaurs, dog-headed men, the Anthropophagi whose heads do lie in their chests; mermaids, mandrakes, brass colossi, and elephant-headed gods; bodhisattvahs and bodhidharmas, many-headed and many-armed; the Great White Whale, the Golden Apples of the Sun, the Wild Hunt; virgins and gypsies and fools, knights and dragons, medusae and andromedae; silver swords and singing swords and swords in stones; vampyres and succubi; incubi riding deer, goats, and pike; Venuses in cockleshells. Frankensteins, werewolves, Sherlock Holmeses and Dr. Watsons; Jack the Ripper's bloody knife and giant apes on skyscrapers swatting at biplanes; Quasimodo and the Phantom of the Opera, Flash Gordon in a phallus-shaped rocket ship; Caped Crusaders and Men of Steel; shining silver saucers and man-eating sharks; lurking space monsters and murder-stalked motels: Jessica watched, spellbound, as the Great and Shining Show spilled from the ancient hurdy-gurdy, all the dreams that men have ever dreamed could be—swan-drawn chariots ascending to the moon, gun-metal submersibles powered by the secret energy of the atom. Something inside her was singing—a voice she had never heard before was raised in counterpoint. Beneath her fingers the silver music-stuff assumed substance and texture, became fibrous, dense, for her to mould and shape and weave. The hurdy-gurdy man advanced toward her, eyeless eyes smiling. Jessica felt her fingers, her hands, her entire body, woven into a fabric of imagination that encompassed not merely Sligo but the whole land from East to West, North to South, past to future, beginning to end. The song within her was an agony of unrequited expression as from the hurdy-gurdy handle came new shapes, new imaginings: a plank decorated with human hands, a wheel made of flesh, the rim studded with eyes, a thing shaped like a human lung with a bone beak, a pair of skin-coloured bagpipes walking on legs cut off at the knee, a boat with insect legs and a windmill on its deck. The hurdy-gurdy man loomed over Jessica, let go his music-making to take her face in his hands, turn it upward to gaze into his gazelessness; teeth parted, a smile, a word.

The bullet took him on an upward trajectory half an inch below the orbit of the left eye. One seven-hundredth of a second later the entire anterior quadrant of his skull exploded in a gout of bone, blood, and hair.

As he spun up and away from Jessica, trailing ropes of blood and brain, hands windmilling, spastic, mindless, the second dumdum impacting one-tenth of a second later shattered the hurdy-gurdy into splinters of lacquered marquetry, smashing drones, snapping wires, before entering the body in the region of the lower sternum, passing through trachea and glottis and tearing away cervical vertebrae, spinal cord, and brain stem in a spray of shivered bone and windpipe.

The impact of the two bullets flung the hurdy-gurdy man the length of the small cobbled court, fetching him up against a barrel in a half sprawl that next morning, from the distance of the warehouse offices, would be mistaken for dead drunkenness.

Wreathed in blue smoke, Damian put his gun up. Wary, cautious, he advanced across the blood-spattered cobbles. There was a sudden, darting shriek, a sudden huge shadow thrown across the wall in yellow gaslight. Damian levelled the Webley at the monkey and it was gone, escaped into one of the thousands of ratways of the old warehousing district. Damian reholstered the revolver, snapped the leather flap shut, drew his greatcoat around the black Webley.

The clocks of Sligo struck three fifteen.

Jessica looked up at him from where she knelt with the deep, dark accusation of a mirror. Damian pushed her shoulder.

"Come on. We've got to go. Can't stay here—not now. Come on."

He was halfway to the wooden gates when she said, "Why did you do it?"

"He was dangerous."

"Why did you do it? Why did you . . . kill him? He had music, nothing but music."

"He was dangerous. He wanted to hurt you. I saw him, bending over you. He would have destroyed you, if I had not destroyed him."

"What are you talking about?" Then: "You heard the music, too, didn't you? Didn't you?"

"I woke in the church and you were gone and then, in the distance, I heard the sound of the hurdy-gurdy and I knew that you were in danger. Come on, we have to go."

"You heard the music, didn't you? The real music, the true music, the music you could see, like water, like a river. You heard it, didn't you? Didn't you?"

"No! Yes! No . . . Does it matter? Maybe I did hear something—does it matter? We have to go. Come on . . ."

Jessica rose and joined him by the gate.

"You heard. Why did you kill him?"

"Because he was a danger to you. Because, for all his music, whatever it was I heard, it came from a dark heart. I had to kill him. This isn't the time, the place, for explanations. Later, when we're safe, up in the mountains, in a cabin with a fire and bottle of John Jameson's, that's the time and the place for explanations. Not here. Not now."

They stepped through the doorway in the wooden gate and slipped away along by the river which seemed deep and full and silver and swarming with distant images.

The house was a blackened ruin; gable ends and eyeless windows, ferns cartwheeling from exposed brickwork, purple loosestrife and rosebay willow herb rampant on the mounds of rotted carpet and plasterwork that had once graced gracious rooms. Despite the smell of mould and ashes, Jessica felt a sense of welcome as she stepped cautiously over the charred timbers and smashed slates. A sense of *return*. A sense of *home*.

Damian had coaxed a fire to life in the old marble fireplace and was looping strings of Haffner's sausages—God alone knew where he had stolen them—onto sticks to grill over hot coals.

Birds dashed and darted above the roofless house.

"Last night," Jessica said, squatting down beside him on her carpetbag to warm her hands by the fire, "you heard something. What did you hear?"

"What did you hear?"

"Music. More than music. Music that had grown so great that it had stopped being music and become something else—images, legends, gods, heroes, every dream and vision we have ever held precious, poured out into the streets like spilled communion wine. What did you hear?"

"Something."

"That?"

"Not that. Something like that."

"Do you hear it often?"

"Not often. Sometimes. Hearing, and seeing, too. It's like . . . sometimes, it's like I open my eyes and for a blink, a moment, no more, I am in another place. It's like, for a moment, it is so intense I feel I am on the edge of something tremendous; and then it is gone again. The streets are dirty, the clouds are rolling in again, and it looks like it's going to rain. The angels have departed."

"How long has this been happening to you?"

"Off and on, for years. Sometimes months pass, sometimes three or four times a week. Since I was about fifteen, sixteen. I can't even begin to understand it, just that when it comes, I feel as if I am very close to something enormous and incredibly powerful, something ancient and untrustworthy."

"Is that why you killed the hurdy-gurdy man?"

"I don't want to talk about it anymore. You understand? Enough. Yes, I was frightened; because for one moment, I saw through doors that had always been closed to me before. Now, I don't want to talk about it anymore. Eat your sausages. We've got a lot to do."

They tore apart their Haffner's sausages with greasy, scalded fingers, and after eating, left the ruins of the great house through a memory of french windows, crossed the terrace, and entered the gardens. The sunken garden was a fulsome bog of dank, faintly luminous marsh flowers, the rhododendron walk a shadowy tangle of interlocked branches and leathery leaves. An overwhelming sense of someone having called her name caused Jessica to pause by the rotted turret of an old summerhouse.

"This must have been a beautiful place once."

"It was," Damian said.

They crossed the stile into the encircling wood. At once Jessica was aware of the birds. The dense summer canopy of leaves hid them from her sight, but she could hear them; wings flapping, beating, beaks clacking. The only sounds in the wood were wind sounds; stirred leaves, stirred feathers, the voices of birds. Damian's course took them uphill, a testing climb through bracken and bramble, nettle, and bare, weathered tree roots. Jessica became conscious of a strange disorientation—though her eyes told her they were on a steep hillside, her body senses insisted that she was walking on level ground. When she closed her eyes the conviction was so overwhelming that, on reopening them, the resulting dizziness almost overbalanced her. The higher they climbed, the stronger the disorientation became until, as the trees thinned where the upper edge of the wood joined the base of the mountain, Jessica felt as if she were running lightly downhill. The effect vanished abruptly as they emerged from the trees. Jessica wobbled. Damian sat down on the springy turf and admired the view over the treetops of a curving crescent of fields and farms and woods; the silver by the gold of dunes and bay; beyond, the heather-grey mass of Knocknarea; and beyond it, the deeper, holier blues of ocean and sky. Jessica settled beside him. The shadowy introspection of the woodlands had evaporated in the light and air of the spirit of the mountains.

"Is this where we're to meet your friends?"

Damian lay back, stripped seed from a grass stalk.

"Not quite. See up there?" He pointed a little way off to his left, to a stone that stood in a shallow depression in the hillside. "That's the exact spot. The Bridestone. But they'll see us here."

Jessica could see that the stone slab had a hole pierced through it.

"Would you mind if I went and had a little look at the stone?"

"Please yourself. They won't be here for a while yet."

The small declivity in which it stood made the Bridestone

deceiving from a distance. Close to, it looked taller than
Jessica, taller than any man. The hole was at a height that
demanded she stand tiptoe to peer through it. Coarse grass,
bracken, rabbit droppings. The stone felt cold and damp. It
smelled almost of sweat. She squinted through the hole
again; then, for no reason she could explain to herself, put
her hand through it. Bone grated against stone, and it was
through. Flint-chipped stone encircled her wrist. She wig-
gled her fingers, one two three.

And something grabbed hold of her hand.

Jessica screamed, tried to pull her hand from the hole.
The grip tightened. She battered and grazed her wrist
against the raw stone until blood flowed. She screamed,
swore, but could not pull free. A shadow fell across the
sun—darkness, coldness, a sudden fog, a cloud of unknowing, lay across the slopes of Ben Bulben. In one instant the
world was reduced to a sphere of grey—wet grass, a stone,
an unbreakable grip.

A disturbance in the fog became a darkness, and the
darkness a man walking toward her. He wore a pair of rough
hide trousers tied at the waist and bound around the calves
with thonging. Torso, arms, shoulders, neck, were a solid
mass of tattoos, blue scarified whorls and spirals. The
tattoos seemed to bleed away from his body into the whorls
and spirals of the fog, the whorls and spirals of the
unremembered past. Across his back was slung a copper
shield; in his left hand he held a quiver of javelins as lightly
as if they were straws. His hair was a mud-stiffened shock
of mats and locks into which the skulls of birds had been
worked, like beads. His face was as hollow and luminous as
a consumptive poet's, but his eyes were dark with old, old
rage.

For all the fury that had set like old, dried blood, she
knew the face. It was Damian's.

The Damian-thing squatted on his hams, resting his
weight on his clutch of javelins. The stench of urine was
overpowering.

"Let her go," he said. In English. The grip upon Jessica's
hand released. She pulled her aching arm free from the hole
and fled into the mist. A darting darkness on the grey,
something polymorphous, changing shape and form and

direction, rushed in upon her, a thrum of wings, a chittering of beaks—the birds, packed into a flock so close, so tight, it was almost a single organism. Claws raked, beady eyes flashed. Jessica was driven back to the stone and the waiting, watching Damian-thing.

"You were so vain," said the Damian-thing in a voice like the wind along the edge of a stone knife. "Did you think that you had created me out of your dreams? I know that you must have thought that; and it is true. I am the stuff that dreams are made of, and nightmares, too, but it was not you dreamed me into being. She is subtle; she rewards with love and hate. She drove you from herself, toward me, knowing you would come to trust me and be led by me away from your protectors to her."

"I. Did. Trust. You." Jessica shouted. Her words struck the fog and were absorbed like rain into the ocean.

"You were meant to. I was made for you to trust me. Who can resist the incarnation of his desires?"

"You killed the hurdy-gurdy man."

"He was made for me to kill, so that you might trust me more. You were wavering—to follow me, to go back to the city. But when you learned there was another who shared the one thing you felt made you alone and unique, you were decided. It was only a phagus—it could not really die because it never really lived. It was just a figment of your dreams plucked from the Mygmus and granted a temporary manifestation. As am I. Throughout history I have existed— the young warrior-hero, the defender and liberator of his people who dies in the glorious flower of youth.

"Before any remembering, I existed. I was Scriathach the Wolf Runner, and the Flame of the Forest. I have been Cuchulain the Hound and Diarmuid the Lover, who met his end upon this very mountain. I have fought against Vikings and battled Normans. I have been woodkernes and reivers. I have led the last futile charge at the Battle of Yellow Ford and swung from the gibbets of Cromwell and Good King Billy. The dogs have lapped my blood and guts from the cobbles of Dublin. I have been the Croppy Boy taking up his father's pike and Barry Linden the bold highwayman. I have been Kevin Barry and the Wild Colonial Boy. I have been the United Irishman and the Fenian Lad. I was there

when the French surrendered at the Battle of the Black Pig
and the English came on, muskets blazing. I went down in
the ruins of the G.P.O. in the Easter Rising and my mothers
sisters and lovers wept for me. And I was Damian Gorman
the Republican rebel, the young warrior hero of a new
nation—an old, old ideal. They say this century has no
room for heroes, no place for myths and legends, but the
nature of mankind does not change." He looked up, as if
scenting prey, or a predator. "She is here. My work is
done."

A second shadow approached through the fog, human
shaped but not human-sized: the hurdy-gurdy man's monkey, stumbling through the shifting mist on its hind legs in
a ghastly parody of walking. It grimaced at Jessica, canines
bared, mouth gaping. A shape darted forth—a head, a tiny
woman's head, shining gold. It heaved itself forward, and
the monkey's mouth split at the shoulders. Arms, breasts,
body heaved out. Golden arms peeled the monkey's mouth
down over hips, curving thighs, like a snake rolling off an
old skin. The woman was twice the size she had been when
she had forced her way out of the monkey's mouth, and was
growing visibly. The empty skin clung to her foot and she
shook it away, flung it behind her. In the mist, the birds
dived and gobbled for the carrion. Grown to full size, the
woman stepped forward. She was naked, but shone with
golden light. She gathered handfuls of the mist and from it
wove a vestment for herself—a cream silk wedding dress
decorated with embroidered roses. She reached out a perfect
hand to Jessica.

"My darling," she said. The voice of the bells of cities
beneath the sea; drowned carillons. "My daughter."

18

I have little difficulty in accommodating Tiresias's concept
of the mythlines as pathways of psychic energy superim-
posed on the physical landscape by generations of human
imagination and storytelling. The notion of an unseen
geography conterminous with the mundane is a familiar one

in folk anthropology: the alignment of stones and local landmarks, the placement of religious sites along "ley lines" in southern England, the Chinese "Lung Mei" or "dragon lines," the songlines drawn across primeval Australia by the Ancestors waking from the Dreamtime. No, what I found uncomfortable was this thing they called *the Mygmus*. From Tiresias's expositions, as we motored along through the predawn murk, one psychiatrist, one tableware designer still beset by occasional blinding reprises of distorted vision, and two tramps who were, to all intents and purposes, angels in disguise, I garnered an impression of a universe, quite small, quite close to our own, in which all human memory and imagination were stored—a pliable matrix we unconsciously imprint by the very process of thinking; an independent domain accessible only to certain individuals in rare moments of transcendence.

I could grasp, albeit dimly, the Mygmus as a psychic sink of human thought and symbol out of which a certain kind of consciousness could create phaguses. What utterly baffled me was the nature and logical working of Gonzaga's brand of pocket magic. Teapot spouts, tin Legion of Mary badges, bird feathers, bottle tops, cigarette packets, pebbles, vials of multicoloured sand and tin foil chocolate wrappers: with these he claimed to have defended Jessica from Emily Desmond's Otherworldly power for over twelve years and now proposed to challenge her directly at the heart of her command and control.

The first time Tiresias had translated his partner's gobbledygook into a request to stop the car by a charmless country crossroads some three miles outside Colooney, I had refused and found Gonzaga lunging forward from the backseat to yank on the hand brake with both hands. God's wounds! It could have been the end of us all. While he grubbed about in the roadside ditch, Tiresias endeavoured to explain the nature of their magic—*gyromancy*, as they called it. All I could make from his words was that form was more important than substance; it was the pattern in which the objects in the sack were laid across the mythlines that gave them power, though, conversely, there had to be a certain quality inherent in the objects themselves to render the pattern effective. What the quality might be that distinguished the tuft of sheep's wool Gonzaga plucked, grinning triumphantly, from the barbed wire fence, was quite beyond my fathoming. That was to be the first of fifteen such sudden interruptions of our journey to Sligo. With each halt and subsequent foray along the hedgerows, Caldwell's patience frayed visibly.

The whole of the previous day had been divided between the clock and the bandages over Caldwell's eyes. It had come as a terrible blow to find in the morning that he still could not tolerate the light of day. When, by nightfall, there was still no improvement, we had almost despaired. We had spent the day constructing and revising endless tables of distances, times, and speeds; that we might already have been too late was a possibility, fast approaching a probability, neither of us dared mention. In the depth of that long night, Caldwell told me that if he did not regain normal vision by dawn, to go on ahead and leave him. Fate, or perhaps persistent, heartfelt prayer, had it that when we removed his bandages for the three o'clock check he claimed that the rivers and floods of light were fading, and by four he could see normally, if a little blurred, by the electric light in the room. Without breakfast, almost without paying the bill—five pounds, three and fourpence, ye gods!—we were into the car and away before the first cock woke Mullingar.

Sligo was stirring itself as we passed through, interrupted only to allow Gonzaga to root about in an especially magical corporation rubbish bin for a broken briar pipe and a discarded Ogden's Nut Gone Flake tobacco tin. We drove straight out the Drumcliffe Road and I parked the car for the second time that month in the gateway of Craigdarragh House.

Space may be a stronger dimension than time—there are certain places that on revisiting you know that no time has passed since you were last there. Some great cities possess this quality. Indeed, it is an inherent factor of their greatness. But so may certain street corners, preserved intact by a trick of the lighting. From the blackened walls of Craigdarragh I could still recall the laughter of woman poets, the clink of sherry glasses, the rustle of taffeta, the whisper of old books taken from their places on library shelves.

Snuffling around in the pile of mouldering plaster and rotting carpet, Gonzaga's fingers lighted upon fragments of charred photographs—messages from that other age: a woman in a high-collared Edwardian dress, fingers tightly clasping a parrot's-head-handled parasol. I moved to stay Gonzaga—it seemed like a descecration. He looked at me from beneath his thatch of hair, mumbled an unintelligible mantra, and slipped the fragment into his knapsack.

Caldwell called me into the drawing room. Still-smoking ashes in the fireplace had excited him. Tiresias discovered a piece of blackened sausage in the hearth. Gonzaga hurried to look, took it between thumb and forefingers, studied it minutely before popping it into his mouth. Tiresias estimated the embers were no more than an hour old. Caldwell was all for racing off pell-mell, ram-stam, there and then. Gonzaga barked an order that needed no translation by Tiresias.

"There are a number of, shall we say, precautions it would be advisable to take," Tiresias said as Gonzaga measured us with his fingers, like a Gardiner Street Jewish tailor. "One would not wander out of the trenches into No Man's Land unprotected. While the dangers awaiting us are not of so direct a nature, they are still perilous." Gonzaga was sniffing up the lapels and down the shoulder seam of my Harris tweed sports jacket. From his sack he produced needle and cotton and a square, pierced Chinese coin which he sewed to my left elbow. Then from his sack he conjured an entire cornucopia of junk: buttons, feathers, cigarette cards, horsehairs, scraps of leather and wood, and lemonade bottle labels, with which he decorated the lapels, collar, and cuffs of my jacket. He then turned to my hat, pushing slips of green willow into the band, pinning an assortment of Boys' Brigade Service badges to the brim, and finishing it off with a length of butter muslin tied to the back like an explorer's mosquito veil. While Caldwell's jacket received similar treatment as mine, I became aware of the heavy sense of nostalgia I felt from the ruins of Craigdarragh lifting—the walls were walls, not boundaries of compressed memory; the old antique voices tailed off in their ceaseless reminiscing. I fingered the pattern of shells and jewellery that weighed down my jacket: power in the form, not the substance?

An intimate, junk-shop magic, indeed.

Gonzaga's final task was to cut two straight green sticks slightly taller than himself from the gardens and fix to them more of the same items with which he had adorned us. He gave one to Tiresias, and then the signal for the off.

I could feel the twentieth century disappearing behind me like the coast of a great continent as we advanced into Bridestone Wood. That first occasion, when I had been defeated by the wood, I had sensed a vague, numinous presence inimical to my intrusion. Now I sensed that presence doubled and redoubled into an active and malign sentience. Every branch, every twig, blade of grass, clump of moss, spray of bracken, seemed to protest my passage. I do not exaggerate when I say that I felt a tremendous, hostile pressure turned against me, barely restrained by the patterns of gyromancy Gonzaga had worked on my clothing. But for those scraps and sorts of junk, I would have fled, gibbering like a madman in a Gothic novel, from Bridestone Wood. Looking upward through the rare breaks in the leaf canopy for a glimpse of sun, I saw birds. Nothing but birds, gliding and wheeling. Noting my concerned upward glances, Tiresias commented, "I do rather fear she may have created the Bird Storm."

I took little comfort from his words. I was familiar with the allusion: the Norse myth of the Crow of Battle, the birds that flew from the mouth of Ragnarok, the Abyss that is the end of everything.

Caldwell let out a cry, stopped in his tracks, reached blindly out with his hands.

"Silver by gold, gold by bronze, silver, everything silver by bronze," he whispered. Gonzaga waved his stubby, grubby fingers in front of his face, muttered to himself.

"The mythline nexi here are so powerful that they are superimposing themselves onto his normal vision," Tiresias said. "The disturbance should clear in a minute or so, but be prepared for more of the same." As Tiresias had promised, Caldwell's vision did clear, but in the next ten minutes he was dazzled five times. Gonzaga offered to lead him by the hand, and guided Caldwell, eyes firmly closed, over roots and boulders. I was becoming increasingly convinced of a large, hostile presence stalking heavily behind us. When I mentioned this to Tiresias, the old tramp called a halt and slipped on his glasses.

"Rather as I feared, comrade. The pookah phagus seems to have reintegrated itself into a later manifestation. Phaguses, I had expected, but not so large, so close to the house." I told Tiresias about the disorientation I had experienced on my recent attempt to penetrate the secrets of Bridestone Wood. Observing the passage of birds across the sky through his spectacles, he said, "You were moving across mythlines, contrary to the flow. It was only natural that the wood would resist you. We are moving with the mythlines, along the grain, following the local microflow. She will not resist us, that way."

Gonzaga took us back and forth across the hillside in a zigzag. As we crossed the stream for the fifth time I reckoned we must be covering one hundred yards horizontally for every ten we gained vertically. My worry was that our return passes across the slope would bring us rather too near to the dark presence Tiresias had called the pookah phagus. I doubted the efficacy of Boys' Brigade badges and bird feathers against the claw and fang of the mythical shaggy beast of the forests. Tiresias directed my attention to a hollow tree stump a few yards off our course to the left. Perched just above the pool of stagnant water that had collected in the stump was a classically perfect faery, complete with diaphanous wings, decorous white shift, and flapper hairdo.

"As the Adversary draws herself further and further out of the Mygmus into this world, so the manifestations will increase."

In the space of a few dozen paces Bridestone Wood became a Celtic bestiary unleashed. Every leaf and fern concealed watching, liquid eyes. In every hollow and dell one could see the gleam of gold and the rainbow sheen of beating faery wings. The woodland rang with the sound of faery bells no larger than appleseeds. Faces streaked and striped with outlandish tattoos fled at our approach; I caught brief glimpses of leather-clad elves and woodkernes crashing away from us through the underbrush. Farther removed among the trees were glints of shield and spear. From farther yet came the distant baying of warhounds and the thrashing of pursued deer. In one moment of clarity I saw a pair of giant elk horns upraised in the light of a far clearing.

Caldwell stumbled on, oblivious—or was the nature of his affliction that he was unable to see anything but the phagus manifestations?—but even he paused when all Bridestone Wood throbbed like a harp string to a colossal pulse of power and over the treetops passed an immense aerial vehicle in the shape of a dish studded with glowing portholes. It hung for a moment over the hillside, then was gone the next, as if it had flown away at unimaginable velocity. Shortly after I had a clear view of a large manshaped metal automaton striding purposefully through the undergrowth. He granted me a parting glance. His eyes were red electric light bulbs, his cranium a transparent dome beneath which luminous glass tubes flashed off and on. As we prepared to recross the stream for the ninth time we found it defended by a fellow dressed only in mottled green pants and a red scarf tied around his forehead. This overmuscled chap was armed with a rifle so powerful it was virtually a one-man arsenal. We hid among the bushes with the faeries and pixies while he sniffed the air and moved off downstream. Before we had gone twenty paces a volley of gunshots in rapid succession and the scream of some unknown large animal in death agony sent the birds flapping and cawing.

No catalogue of faeries ever contained creatures like these. My conclusion, unpalatable as it was, was that these phaguses were the manifestations of future mythologies— the elves, pixies, and Wild Hunt of generations yet unborn.

Close to the upper boundary of Bridestone Wood, an inexplicable and unseasonable mist started to infiltrate between the thinning trees. It was visible even to Caldwell. He pulled up abruptly, reached out before him.

"Nothing," he muttered. "Nothing at all."

Tiresias and Gonzaga conferred. The mist alarmed them in a way the ghostly manifestations of the wood had not. I shivered—the temperature was dropping by the second. I recalled the time in my study that Jessica had drawn out the latent heat energy in the atmosphere to create pseudophaguses. We resumed our march. Gonzaga led, staff held before him in both hands. I followed. Caldwell and Tiresias, similarly prepared, took up the rear. We looked to my mind rather like a procession of minor clerics in some obscure High Church ritual. Within a few dozen more paces the mist had thickened to virtual opacity. Only by the change of texture beneath my feet did I know that we had emerged from the woodland onto the sheep turf of the hillside. The cold was outrageous. I became aware that I was cringing from an unseen presence; within the mist I could hear a muted rushing. Gonzaga screamed an order; instantly both he and Tiresias snapped their staves into position above their heads, arms outstretched.

And in the same instant, the birds broke upon us. Thousand of birds, tens of thousands of birds, close packed into a single flock-being, tunnelling toward us unseen through the mist. They hurled themselves upon us, and broke around the power of Gonzaga's pocket magic. Wings, claws, screaming beaks, glaring eyes, beat past me in an almost solid wall . . . and were gone. Caldwell's voice could barely be heard over the cries of the birds: "What's happening! What's happening!"

Tiresias and Gonzaga lowered their staves. The march resumed.

Twice more the birds attacked; twice more they broke around our protective barrier woven from bottle caps, beads, and cigarette coupons. But for the speed of the old men's reactions, I shuddered to contemplate our fate under those myriad slashing, pecking beaks.

As I was becoming convinced that we must walk forever through fog, I saw an area of darker greyness within grey fog. I knew in an instant what it had to be.

The Bridestone.

19

The mist swirled in close around the Bridestone and swallowed her. The changeless grey of death: bird wings fluttered, darted at her. Feathers brushed her face, her fingers. She grasped at them, but she was falling, falling forward through the mist, an infinite plummet. Feathers and wings beat about her in the mist and she saw that what she had thought of as grey mist was the grainy texture of an infinite number of objects filling the infinite dimensions of a perfectly transparent medium.

Birds. She was falling through a space filled with hovering birds, wings outstretched, touching each other at wingtip, tail, and beak. As she approached the uppermost of them she saw that the birds were immense, each the size of a continent. Their backs and spread wings were feathered with forests and mountain ranges, oceans and plains: each bird was a land unto itself. She fell past land after land after land, possible worlds cast in the shapes of hovering birds— worlds of ice and worlds of fire, worlds of chivalry and worlds of cruelty, worlds of cities in the shapes of great towers, or pyramids, or mountains, where cities sailed upon the sea driven by a thousand sails, or cruised the skies, held aloft by balloons or rotating blades or millions upon millions of swans; cities in the shapes of clouds, or forests, or icebergs; cities in the shapes of leaves, or smoke, or dreams; cities that corresponded to psychological and emotional states; New Jerusalems, Infernal Dises. As she fell between the unfurled feathers of a world that was one endless city from which the smoke of a great burning went up and up, she saw far below her the gleam of gold in the greyness. It arced up toward her through the spaces between the touching wingtips. She fell between a dark, blasted birdland lit by the flare of eternal trench warfare and a pastoral Arcadia of chateaux, formal gardens, minor members of the Greek pantheon, and dairy maids on swings. The shining form drew parallel to her infinite plummet.

"See, Jessica, every dream and vision that lies within the mind of man."

Mother and daughter, they grazed past a world composed entirely of chained naked bodies piled on top of each other, one million high, one billion wide, glowing with the heat of their own combustion, close enough to gag on the stench of searing, putrefying flesh. Jessica looked within the golden light and saw not the mythic figure that had revealed itself to her on the mountainside by the Bridestone, but a girl of fourteen or fifteen, bright, eager—a girl she could have imagined for her own younger sister. To their right was a world entirely of steel, all tubes and pipes and ducts and rectangular protrusions, and a billion lit windows. In place of a tail were two engine parts, blue-hot, each large enough to swallow a moon.

"Otherworld, Jessica. The Mygmus—the domain of infinite potential symbolism. My world, my domain; your heritage, Jessica."

The fall continued. A land of plump, contented cumulus clouds grazed by paisley-pattern living blimps, each a mile long. A two-dimensional world of cartoon creatures, a Technicolor celebration of noise, mayhem, and mindless, impotent violence.

"Infinite worlds, Jessica. Faeryland. My faeryland was just the start, the access to all the others. See how they touch wingtip to wingtip, beak to tail? You can cross from one to another; eternity itself will not be long enough to explore all the worlds of the Mygmus. No limits here, Jessica; anything, anyone, you want, you can have."

A moon-blue landscape of bare, rounded hills was littered with dismembered statuary. A stone head half a mile across followed their descent with its eyes. Its lips moved, silent syllables.

"Everything that has ever been, everything that ever will be. We are outside time, Jessica, in eternity, where everything exists forever at once. All this I promise you; all this I will share with you."

They fell on through the unending greyness. From the ramparts of a cloud-piercing tower, a sentry blew an alarum on a great golden horn as he spied the falling women beyond the edge of his world. Pennants emblazoned with eagles and swords snapped in the wind from beyond.

"Mother and daughter, together forever. What could be more natural, more perfect than that?"

But Jessica had seen the deeper darkness embedded in the grain of the Mygmus: four patches of shadow that seemed to enlarge by absorbing the bird flecks into themselves. They grew with astounding speed—black stars in the greyness; rough star shapes, like crude sketches of people.

People.

They were people.

Four people.

The infinite grey space dissolved into mist. The close-touching bird lands broke apart and fell away from each other in a storm of wings. She felt the Bridestone cold and slick against her back. Four figures approached through the mist. Without waiting for the command from his queen, the Damian phagus tore his javelins from the earth and ran to meet them. He crouched low, readied a javelin. Jessica recognised her father's tall, vacant silhouette against the mist, and that of Dr. Hannibal Rooke. She shouted a warning but the javelin was aflight, an unseen song in the mist.

Gonzaga moved with dazzling speed. Hands swung, spear cracked against staff and went singing away, end for end, through the mist.

The Damian thing rose from its battle stance and withdrew circumspectly. The four entered the small amphitheatre around the Bridestone. Hannibal Rooke's expression was one of disbelief unwillingly suspended. Jessica's father turned his head from side to side, searching, unable to find.

"Jessica?"

All her rage, all her betrayal, all her hurt, all her hatred: her heart tore in two.

"Dad. Daddy."

The Damian thing had its sword from its scabbard and at her throat in a whisper. In the same breath the two old tramps, who seemed so uncommonly *familiar* to Jessica, had the long staves they carried hefted and ready. The Damian thing drew back a fraction. Was that fear Jessica saw, like a dull glitter, in the corner of his eyes? Wrapped in her cowl of light, indistinct, indefinite, caught in a state of dissolution and redefinition between old woman, goddess, and child, the Adversary was disdainful.

"These held me in check these years? I'd expected better of a daughter of mine."

"I don't know what's going on here!" Jessica had wanted to scream to exorcise herself but the nightmare endured, frozen in tableau against a backdrop of everchanging changelessness. "What are you talking about? What's happening to me?"

Tiresias and Gonzaga approached. The Damian thing growled gutturals from the Indo-Aryan dawn, but stepped

back with a glitter of sword and eye. The sun hung like a
drop of red red blood in the mist. The two old men laid
down their staffs, knelt arthritically. Tiresias's rheumy gaze
looked up to meet Jessica's.

"Truly, you do not recognize us."

Gonzaga moaned in his throat. His hands, like little
creatures, busied themselves on the turf. Nothing to find.
Nothing to be done.

"But you do remember!" The voice was Hannibal Rooke's.
"You do remember. The fire, Jessica! The fire. Remember
the fire."

"I. Remember. The . . . fire . . . I remember the fire!"
She screamed at him as she had screamed at the Mother
thing, as she had screamed at the flames a lifetime before.
"I remember . . . everything!" She looked into Tiresias's
face—skin like mildewed leather, teeth stained yellow by
tea, swathes of sweaty white bristles. Tears filled the old
man's eyes.

"Madam, you called on us to protect you, and we came,
and for thirteen years now we have been faithful to our
calling. It was never our intent to fail you; never our desire
that you should be brought to this sorry pass; forgive us the
things we have left undone that we ought to have done."

"All they could ever hope to do was contain me for a little
while," the Mother thing said. "As her power was awakened, so theirs began to ebb because, don't you see, all you
vain and foolish creatures, when she created them, she gave
all her power to them. They grow weaker and weaker, and
she still does not properly understand her power. I stand
with all the glory of the Mygmus behind me and who would
deny me now?"

The birds, the red drop of sun, the wind, the breath in the
lungs, hung motionless, a moment frozen in time.

And a voice spoke. An almost voice; syllables trapped in
a throat. Gonzaga's face was the concentration-contorted
mask of a dumb man trying to speak.

"I . . . do . . ."

He rose to his feet unsteadily, took his staff in both hands,
and thrust the whittled end into the turf. Thunder growled
around the heights of Ben Bulben. A sudden wind whipped
across the hillside, clutched at clothing, rattled the Damian

thing's brasses and bronzes, jingled bottle caps and B. B.
badges, and was gone.

The Emily thing's scorn was devastating. Her laughter
flayed like a whip.

"You dare me, who can summon whole legions of faery
warriors at a whim, more angels than there are in heaven,
stars in the sky?"

Tiresias rose painfully. He lifted his staff, swung the tip
to almost touch Gonzaga's. A bar of solid blue arc light
burned between them. Fat drops, blue as brandy on a
Christmas log, fell sputtering to the turf. The lightning froze
the Emily thing's face in the mask of a petulant thirteen-
year-old. Gonzaga once again wrestled with words.

"She . . . can . . . too."

"Your powers are balanced." The fusion light lent
Tiresias's face a hawkishness, a lean evangelical zeal. "She
can match you, army for army, host for host, legion for
legion, creation for creation, dream for dream, whim for
whim."

The Emily thing looked about to stamp its foot. Tiresias
continued, "Your powers equal each other in every way but
one—they are differently distributed. Yours is contained
within you except for that small part that maintains your
faery lover phagus. Hers is more fully subsumed into us; as
you so rightly deduced, our web of gyruses only began to
unravel when the good Dr. Rooke unwittingly awakened her
nascent abilities. The only thing that prevents her from
assuming the full mantle of her might and majesty is us. In
our absence, that power will revert to its mistress and she
will be free to decide as she wills." He swept his staff up in
an arc, away from Gonzaga's. The faery light was extinguished; eyes blinked away yellow afterimages. Tiresias
plunged the sharpened tip of his staff into the soil beside his
partner's.

"Come, brother." He rested a hand on Gonzaga's shoulders. The small tramp lowered his head, mumbled a few
tongue-tied words, then looked with affection into his taller
partner's eyes.

"Yes, it really is the time."

Gonzaga muttered again, the words incomprehensible,
but the tone unmistakable: *at last.*

They helped each other to undress, stripping off layers of torn tweed and holey woolens, frayed shirts and wads of newspaper. Gonzaga laid his knapsack and bandolier of tea caddies in a reverential heap. Tiresias placed his spectacles in their vellum pouch gently on top. The Emily thing hooted in derision; the Damian thing spat at them. In the end they were two naked old men, gooseflesh and wattles, slack breasts and translucent hair, shivering in the cold mist. They lay down side by side on the saturated turf curled into fetuses, recapitulating at the last the birth they had never known, and closed their eyes. Dew settled on their bodies, trickled down flanks cold, white, and hard as porcelain. Flesh colour ebbed into colourlessness, then into a granite grey. The turf grew up about their sides, their contours slackened and slumped, and at the end, there was no memory of Tiresias and Gonzaga, but only two more round grey boulders embedded in moss on the side of Ben Bulben that might have fallen a thousand years ago from the face of the mountain, watched over by the stark verticals of their totems.

"No," whispered Jessica. "You didn't have to do that. Why did you have to do that?" It was only in their fading, their failing, that the full realisation of the years they had held watch over her life fell upon her—the greatness of their humility, the unstinting loyalty of their endless journeying through the mythlines. She saw what manner of love they had lavished upon her and was deeply unworthy. She would have paid any asking for them not to have faded, failed, ebbed, and dissolved back into the landscape from which she had created them so many years before. "No!" But then she heard a whisper, the memory of a whisper, in the greyness of the mists that enveloped her. *Not gone, not gone, merely changed, transformed from one glory into another. Only for a time, and a time, and a little time. As long as you have need of us, we will never desert you.* A whisper that only she could hear. A promise that only she could redeem.

She would try to be worthy of the power they had released in her.

A cry. The cry of a fox run down, the cry of the boar trapped in the forest thicket.

The Damian thing held up its hands in anguish. The bronze, leaf-shaped sword fell to the ground and was turned to rust in an instant. His fingers stiffened, hardened, turned to wood. His leather and bronze sandals split open; white rootlets quested forth and buried themselves in the ground. His arms, his legs, were sheathed in bark; his outstretched fingers elongated into twigs and sprouted leaves. Within the duration of one cry, he had turned into a wind-blasted mountain ash. With the fading of the cry into the mist, a branch broke from the knothole that had been his mouth.

Then Jessica felt the visions that had waited so long, so patiently, at the corners and junctions of her life, rise up in a flock and break free. A terrible, exultant joy burned up in her. She gathered the flocking, swarming visions in the grip of her imagination and stretched them into robes and wings of fire. Anything. Anything at all she desired, she could have. The visions came to her call and settled on her hands and arms, and she saw that they were shaped like birds, like the endless possible worlds of the Mygmus.

She stepped away from the stone, toward the Emily thing, spread her phoenix wings wide.

"Yes," she said. "Oh yes, yes yes . . ."

She saw her father and mother—the woman who had pretended to be her mother, the man who had pretended to be her father, the girls who had pretended to be her sisters; she saw Dr. Hannibal Rooke and Miss Fanshawe and tiny yapping Cromlyn; she saw Fat Lettie and Mr. Mangan and the Reverend Perrot and Em and Rozzie and their Colms and Patricks and all the ones who had ever betrayed her or hurt her or ignored her or disbelieved her or pretended they had liked her when all along they had despised her, had laughed at the girl who had had to make up such outrageous lies as the price of their friendship. She saw them all, and the things and places she could wish upon them if she but touched them with the tiniest edge of her desire. And she saw the Emily thing, the Mother thing, and saw in her the sister she should have had, and their faces, looking upon each other, were like an image and its mirror reflection. And she saw the hillside open behind her mother, her sister, and within, a gulf of light unending.

"Yes," said the Emily thing. "Yes, yes . . . yes."

The voice was that of a very small child, leading her new friend to the ferris wheels and coconut shies and dodgem cars of the fairground of the heart.

"No," said a voice, a voice full of amazement at its own sound, as if in possession of something it still did not fully comprehend. Hannibal Rooke's voice. "No, Jessica. Don't you see? She doesn't care for you. She's never cared for you. Never, Jessica, never."

Jessica turned her light full upon Hannibal Rooke, but he stood small and anonymous and shadowy and uncowed as a Covenanting preacher. Her father stared blinded and striving into the light.

"No, she doesn't care, she never cared." Hannibal Rooke's words came spilling out like water from the singing fountains of Rome, tumbling over each other in their haste to express themselves. "The only reason she wants you back is because she can no longer bear the loneliness of the Mygmus. Endless worlds, endless possibilities—oh, yes, I don't deny it—but never to have anything, anyone, that you have not created yourself with whom to share it. She wants you because she can not bear to be totally and irrevocably alone forever. All for her, Jessica, all for her. Never a thought of you, of your life, your needs and dreams, your hopes and ambitions."

The Emily thing shrieked, "You're lying, you're lying, you're lying. I've loved her, I've always loved her, she was my child."

Hannibal Rooke stabbed his finger through the veils of glory: the accusation.

"Then why did you send her away from you? Why did you send her into a world without a mother, father, a family; alone, a child of three mothers, dear God!"

"Because I wanted what was best for her!"

The accusation did not waver.

"That is a lie, I submit. You did not want to share what you had found with another, even with your own daughter. No, it was your own world, the private world you had always dreamed of where you could escape from all responsibilities, and you could not tolerate the responsibility of a child in your own personal wonderland, could you? You could not bear the thought that something might spoil

your enjoyment of the paradise you had created for yourself, I would submit."

The Emily thing raged, and her rage shook the very hills.

"You're a horrid, horrid man, Hannibal Rooke, horrid."

"And I would further submit that your so-called love for
your daughter only began when you realised that what you
had thought of as eternal heaven showed itself to be a very
subtle kind of hell. Yes, Miss Desmond, hell. Hell is not
other people. Heaven is other people. Hell is oneself.
Forever and always, oneself. Self. Self. That has been the
entire motive of your . . . I hesitate to call it *life*. *Existence*, since you gained the ability to be and do exactly what
you liked."

"I hate you I hate you I hate you I hate you," the Emily
thing screamed over and over and over and over, and her
voice was the voice of a five-year-old's tantrum.

"Is it true? Mother, is it true?" The birds that had swirled
and swooped within the mist now felt to Jessica to be
beating and flailing inside her stomach. "Is this true?"

"Lies. Lies, all lies, every word of it, lies!" the Emily
thing shrieked.

"It is the truth," said Hannibal Rooke, and it was he who
had grown to the dimensions of a god—a stern, Bible-black
Calvinist patriarch—and the Emily thing reduced to a
spanked four-year-old sent to snivel in the corner.

Then the one voice that had yet gone unheard on the
hillside spoke.

"Jessica, only you can decide that," Charlie Caldwell
said. "No constraints, no obligations; this time the choices
are all yours."

"I'm going to turn you all into something so horrible you
won't even dare to look at yourselves," shouted the Emily
thing. "I'm going to send you all to hell forever and ever
and ever and ever. Amen."

"No," Jessica said, "I'm not going to let you do that."

The light intensified to a point where it became more than
light—a sound, a dull roar, a hot, flaying wind. Hannibal
Rooke clapped hand over eyes.

"For God's sake, close your eyes, man!"

"I can't, don't you see. The light is always there!"

The rocks beneath their feet groaned and stirred. The air

hissed and seethed. The two men felt the skin on their faces, their hands, scorch and blister. They braced themselves against the burning wind. In their mutual blindness they felt unclean winged things brush past them, snatches of goblin laughter whisper in their ears. The earth heaved and moaned; the sky tore itself apart in lightning and thunder. Caldwell's ecstatic cry was barely audible over the battle song of Otherworlds grinding past each other: "I can't see! No light, nothing, I can't see!"

And it ended.

The two men uncovered their eyes. The backs of their hands were seared raw red. Their faces itched; there was a smell of singed cloth and hair.

"What do you see?" Hannibal Rooke asked, carefully.

"Mist," Caldwell replied. "And birds."

The turf was littered with the bodies of dead birds. Hannibal Rooke knelt to inspect one. It was frozen solid, a tight, glazed bullet of flesh and feather.

"Jessica," Caldwell asked. "Emily?"

Rooke shook his head. The solitary mountain ash close by the foot of the Bridestone was dead also, shivered to the pith by fire. Its blackened trunk smoked; red lozenges of ember glowed and flaked away. Fire had passed over the two totem staffs. Hannibal Rooke picked up a metal tea canister lying on the turf, dropped it with a start. It was colder than ice. But the rocks remained—the Bridestone; the two low, glacier-worn granite boulders, were unchanged.

"God, are we dead?" Caldwell asked suddenly.

The mist moved across the hillside, changeless in its everchangingness. And, in the changing changelessness, an area of stability, certainty; a dark shape. A dark shape approaching. Terror seized the two men's souls. The dark approaching shape loomed huge in the distorted perspective of the mist, and became human.

The human broke into a run.

Jessica hurled herself upon her father and he swallowed her up in his arms. And at that most intimate range too close for words, tears and touching and the deep, wordless expression of the soul were all the communication they needed. A wind sprang up, whipped the reluctant mist like

a sow dawdling to market. Rents of blue appeared above;
the sun seemingly raced across the clearing sky. The mist
tore on the jagged tips of the trees, minute by minute the
world made itself more visible.

Father to daughter: *What happened?*

Daughter to father: *Don't ask. I can never say.*

Father: *Can't say, won't say?*

Daughter: *Can't say. I decided. That's all.*

He: *You decided for me? For us?*

She: *I decided for me. I decided for life.*

The mist was gone, the sky early high-summer-afternoon
blue. Memories of *heat,* of *warmth,* of *summer* began to
steal across the hillside. Across the bay, Knocknarea rose
green and purple and beyond it, the hills of County Mayo.
And beyond them, the ocean; and beyond the great ocean,
a new land, a new world, where summer was also come.
And beyond that, other oceans, other lands, other summers,
and seasons; the great sea, the wide world. Enough for any
life. Down there, where the ribbons of road laced between
the fields, it all began.

With one footstep.

They walked down among the bodies of the birds, to the
trees where it all would begin to happen.

PART III

CODA
LATE SUMMER

They had cycled so far, through the old Victorian suburbs and the new municipal housing developments spilling like salt across the lower slopes of the mountains, out of Dublin, up into the mountains, along the old military road, and where the road could no longer take them they had abandoned the bicycles by the side of an old stone bridge and walked on, up into the heath and the heather, two figures on a hillside, wading thigh-deep through bee-busy purple heather, she with the rug and the thermos, he with the picnic basket he'd carried balanced so carefully on the back of his bicycle all those miles climbing up up up away from the city into the mountains of County Wicklow, and the bees were humming, and high above a lark was diving up through the clear air, up up up, the sun was so hot and the scent of the moorland flowers so powerful she felt she must swoon and fall among the bracken and springy purple heather, was he not done yet, not he; forging on tireless as an ox, up up up over the boulders and crumbling black peat, up up up into the land of the lark and the myrtle, the high places where sheep with patches of red or blue on their rumps looked up from their coarse grazing and cantered skittishly away, shit-clogged tails swinging heavily; she looked at him, his shadow against the sun, strong, tireless as an ox this Owen MacColl, son of builders, red-brick, utility-built with sure and solid foundations, no major structural defects and all internal and external timbers guaranteed free from rot for ten years; she could watch him forever, toiling up the sheep paths through the bog-myrtle, she loved to watch the way his body moved, solidly, certainly, she wished he would take his shirt off, she would have loved to have seen the play of light on his sweat, loved to have caught the perfume of that sweat, honey-sweet, salt-sour, on the light airs of the hills; even though she knew he stripped to the waist in summer like the rest of squad she knew he would never do it alone with her; it is one thing with a gang of mates; it is quite another with a woman beneath God's blue sky with the lark ascending; oh, he was daring enough—he'd kissed her, mouth open, like they do in France, that first time, in the Atheneum Ballroom, she hadn't expected it, he had taken her by surprise, for a moment she hadn't been sure she liked the quick, hard dart of his tongue into her mouth, but she knew Em and Rozzie were watching (Colm the apprentice tiler was long history, once again Em was coursing the spangled dance floor like a shark, five months' gone and Rozzie's baby still didn't show, her Hoover salesman had found Liverpool the better part of valour, but her father knew a surgeon on Harcourt Street) and she was damned if she was going to look like a clumsy fifteen-year-old in front of two girls who claimed to have actually *done* it, though proof positive of having departed the blessed state of virginhood was only conclusive in one instance, so she had pressed her tongue into his mouth and felt his teeth close gently on it and she'd felt something not quite like anything she'd ever felt before ignite a smooth, slow burn, like the engine of a limousine, down below her belly button, and she'd known then that he could do what he liked, whatever he liked, whatever he asked, and she wouldn't mind, not one bit; hello, what was he at now? he'd found a place for them to eat, where the bank of the stream they had been following had been cut away in a small cliff by the torrents of winter, a quiet place, a secret place, with moss and heather for a bed and rover-smoothed boulders for a table, a table in the wilder-

ness, where was that from? the Bible, was it? she spread the
rug on the moss, thinking, *This would be a grand place to
do it, where only the sky and the lark can see us,* and as he
unpacked plates cups knives forks spoons sugar salt sandwiches cold chicken cold ham cold tongue Scotch eggs from
Dlugash the Butchers fruit brack faery cakes tins of Bournville chocolate, she stood on the stream-polished boulders
and looked down the little valley the stream had cut to the
greater valley below where two threads, many threads, of
silver were spun into a single cord and the cars moved like
sluggish black beetles, furious with the heat, through the
haze and shimmer bouncing from the Military Road, he
called her and everything was ready and laid out for her
pleasure, with the sole exception of himself, and as she ate
the sandwiches and the chicken and the ham and the tongue
and the Scotch eggs from Dlugash the Butchers and the fruit
brack and the faery cake and the Bournville chocolate and
drank the tea from the thermos, she watched the way his lips
closed upon the food, could not tear her eyes away from the
way his lips closed upon those morsels of food, and she
knew one word and only one word kept what they wanted to
happen from happening, and neither of them dared to ask
the other what that word might be for fear that they might
speak it, so that her hand shook when she held up her cup
to ask for more tea and his hand shook as he poured it from
the thermos, and hot tea with milk and *two* sugars spilled
over his shirt, his suspenders, his flannels, soaked and
burning in the same instant, and he leaped up with a cry and
she leaped up with a cry and said "Take it off, your shirt,
off, get it off," and he took his shirt off, and then she said,
"Take them off, your pants, off, get them off," and he took
them off and she said, "Take them off, all your clothes, off,
take them off," and he did, and she looked at him standing
there under the river cliff, cut by many winters, in the
beauty of his nakedness, and the word neither of them had
dared speak was spoken and she came to him and he to her
and they went down together on the bed of heather and
bracken, on the rug she had carried up from the city on the
back of her bicycle, like lovers from old old legends, and
under the hot sun with the bees swimming lazily about
them, heavy with nectar, she opened to him and he entered

her and pushed pushed pushed and she went oh oh oh afraid
that she was going to die afraid that she was not going to die
from something wonderful and terrible at the same time,
like God, she thought on the heather and bracken bed with
her knees up and he pumping pumping pumping away and
up up up she was going to explode, a rain of Jessica
Caldwell age seventeen and three-quarters coming down in
red rags and scraps all over the heather and the stray sheep,
oh oh oh and then he came half in and half out and as he did
she felt something go *click!* in her head and with that click
the visions that had been crowding in around the edge of her
field of view for so long she could never remember a time
when they were not there disappeared; gone, vanished, and
she cried a little and he died a little and that was all the
poetry that was in it; then she looked over his shoulders and
through the tears, the unexpected tears, she saw two
boulders and two trees and two birds in the clear air and two
figures tiny tiny walking away far far out across the summer
hillsides.

PART IV

SHEKINAH

Arise, shine, for your light has come,
and the glory of the Lord has risen:
Isaiah 60:1

It is not much of a party. But then advertising parties never are. The music is too ideologically correct to be really danceable; the people are trying too hard to have fun to be really enjoying themselves. Someone will probably be arrested before dawn, everyone hopes. Only then can the party to celebrate winning the Green Isle Freezer Foods account be judged a success. Junior copywriters and assistant financial managers are lining up to take turns singing to a karaoke machine, heavy on Elvis and the Beatles. Says a lot about the vintage of QHPSL's junior copywriters and assistant financial managers. The Blessèd Phaedra, the boss, despite her name, Enye does not like, is thundering out "River Deep, Mountain High" in a skirt far too short for her seniority. Oscar the Bastard, the boss, whom Enye does like, despite his name, is doing a passable, if balding, Ike on the Mike.

Warping social orbits, she finds Jaypee Kinsella, her creative partner, confidante, mentor, and, yes, Best Friend, sitting under a shelf bearing a lamp in the shape of a brass Buddha seated on the back of a cow. She slips onto the arm of the chair beside him. Grossly drunk, he demonstrates how he can make the brass Buddha go on off on off on off on off like a karmic lighthouse, calling souls across the rocky Sea of Enlightenment. He seems to find the exercise hysterically funny.

In the room with the karaoke machine, Judi-Angel from Traffic, whose house this bash has appropriated, is singing about the Careless Whisper of a Good Friend as if it is something she knows a lot about.

Enye begs leave to be excused. Between the end of one note and the beginning of another, between the end of one chronal quantum and the beginning of the next, she has felt them. Distant yet, like the dim thunder of the jets that bank in over the city, but drawing closer, growing in definition and clarity.

On the street, the presence is sharper, clearer. She shivers. Her breath hangs in thin clouds, faintly luminous under the acid yellow street lamps. In the car she pops the first tab of Shekinah and clicks Mahler's Sixth into the stereo. As the passionate tide of strings and winds surges between the speakers, she lies back in the seat and waits for the stuff to take effect.

It is never long coming, but she has never been able to give a precise moment to when it begins. She can never say when they move from something felt to something perceived. A police patrol car prowls past the end of the street. She hopes none of the neighbours have complained about the ideologically correct dance music. Keep moving, Fascists.

She starts the car, moves off down the street. Drizzle-wet, the October faces of the red-brick town houses seem black in the standardised European yellow streetlight. At this hour the avenues are empty but for taxis, police, and ghosts. Led by the twine of the sky signs, like the polarized stress patterns in car windows, she drives to a damp northern suburb of aluminum-clad boxes where every street has a name like Padraig Pearse Gardens, where every tin-town house has a portrait of the Pope in front of the net jardiniere living-room curtains and a ten-meter whip of an aerial to hook down the airwaves of the TV stations across the water from their higher ether. At some indeterminate point, the drizzle has passed into sour yellow rain.

The sky signs draw her to a small suburban supermarket. Fluorescent pink and orange posters proclaiming This

Week's Special Offers sag from their tape fastenings behind the metal security grilles. The interior of the supermarket is lit horror-movie blue by the refrigerated displays. The red eye of the burglar alarm system winks at her. The rush and flow from beyond buffets her like a mighty wind as she steps out of the Citroen 2CV. She kicks off her party shoes, fetches a pair of Reeboks from the back. Bright red. They clash with her party clothes. She wishes she could change those, too, but if shoes are all she is to be allowed, that is all she needs.

Check.

In her handbag, the computer is winking green to the burglar alarm's red. Graph lines twine black on grey on the readout. She slips the computer onto her belt, untangles a coiled lead terminating in a multiway connector.

Check.

Still wrapped in old newspapers on the floor in front of the back seat: the swords. *Katana* and *tachi*. Long sword and companion sword. She slips them from their sheathes. *Kenjitsu*, the Way of the Drawn Sword. *Philosophic and moral considerations pay homage to victory in combat.*

The spirits rise within her: spirit of expectancy, spirit of trepidation, spirit of fire, spirit of void, spirit of small suburban supermarket at twenty past one on a Saturday morning with veils of drizzle blowing in off a chill, radioactive sea.

Spirit of *crossing at a ford,* of taking your capabilities to meet your enemy's in the place and time of your choosing.

Never let your enemy see your spirit. Be neither over- nor underspirited. Both are weak.

She advances through the driving rain down the entry leading to the rear-of-store car park. By the roll-down delivery door, she plugs the computer into the socket mounted on the handle of her long sword. Words, symbols, forms too fleeting for human comprehension fill the small display: the words DISRUPTOR LOADED flash, silver on grey. Grey on silver, glyphs swarm from the *habaki*, the sword hilt, along the blade, an ideographic miscegenation of Chinese and Mayan. Within one second, the blade is sheathed in a shifting patina of silver glyphs.

She advances across the rain-wet concrete toward a lager

hoarding. She can feel them as an electric tautness in the skin across her forehead.

A sound, a scuffle in the warm shadows around the gently sighing heating ducts.

Action/no-action. Conception/no-conception. The swords whip into *Gedan No Kame, tachi* above head, *katana* held downward at forty-five degrees.

Hi-tech trainers scuff gravel. Betrayed, the syringe glitters in stray suburb-glow. Something-teen, greasy black hair, Day-Glo Wyldechylde T-shirt, severed heads, pentagrams, and bondage.

Caught crouching in the warmth of the ducts, the boy throws back his head and opens wide his mouth, as if to swallow down the raining sky.

And it spears from the open mouth: a long worm of intestinal darkness, lashing and writhing in the driving diagonals of rain that slash across the car park. Head, arms, legs bifurcate and tear free from the flexing body. In an instant, one instant, it steps out of the pile of rain-sodden clothing, the translucent, luminous husk of the boy's body.

It towers over her, tall, thin as a willow. Its thin willow fingers are thirty centimetres of razor-blue steel. Its mouth is fused shut in a plate of whalebone; its naked skull sweeps up into an arabesque of raw cranium. It is dressed only in its own leather hide and a few scraps of clinging, pale human skin.

She strikes in *one timing:* the skill of striking the enemy while he is still undecided, spirit and body unsettled from the transformation. Steel rings on steel. It catches her cutting edge on its claws. Steel shrieks on steel as blade rakes along blade. Glyphs shower from the edge and burst about them like dying fireworks.

It heaves her back across the car park, follows closely, but she is on her feet in a thought, red Reeboks firm on the wet concrete. She flicks rain-slick hair from her eyes. The Shekinah is a burning song inside her. *Nihon Me:* the long sword flashes upward, sideways, into the *Jodan*, the middle position, to cut through the chest. *Ippon Me*, the companion sword, turns, catches the light, high to cleave the crest of bone. They clash in a flicker of steel and rain. *All strategy is to cut the enemy. Hitting, striking, touching the enemy, is not cutting*. Its blades gleam with stolen light; the long sword slips up to *Jodan* to block their downstrike. The blow almost tears the sword from her grasp. *Thought and action, one unity*. The short sword in the left hand cuts across from *Waki* through *Chudan*.

"*Tō!*"

The great *kiai* explodes from her lips. The right arm, severed just below the elbow, spins away. Steel claws scrape sparks from the concrete.

Pale ichor fountains from the stump. It reels and in that instant begins to regenerate itself. Spraying dream-juice from the horrifying wound, it drives her before its singing steel claws across the car park. Lightning screams and flies from the clashing, parrying blades. It drives her hard, hard enough to momentarily take the breath from her, hard against the lager hoarding. Five times thirty centimetres of razor-blue steel shred the blue and piss-yellow of the lager poster and draw back for the killing thrust through the throat.

And in that quantum of indecision, the long sword moves with the deceptive slowness of the flowing water cut.

It all happens in one timing. The look of disbelief that momentarily crosses its face as its head topples toward the damp concrete, which is never reached as, in one timing, body and severed head erupt in a silent detonation of thistledown sparks. The outline of her adversary burns briefly through the glow, then all that remains is a fading nimbus and a handful of errant, luminous puffballs bouncing across the car park.

She bows properly, formally, to an honourable enemy, kneels to unplug the long sword. The glyphs fade and fail. The rain drives in hard, hard across the concrete. She is shaking, dripping with sweat. And weary, so weary. Bone weary. Spirit weary. It is always like this, after the Shekinah. She picks up her swords, returns to the car. She leans, one-handed, head down, against the door, the classic three A.M. pose, wracked with nausea, saturated, shivering in her party clothes. She knows it is dangerous to drive in her condition, but she has no other choice. Twenty past two. She gets into the car and finds that someone has got in before her and stolen her cassette player and all her tapes.

• • •

The radio alarm wakes her with a cry, and a start, and a shudder. The duvet is a sodden, scrunched huddle in the corner of the bed. Grinding dreams. Sweat dreams. It is always bad, the morning after. It can take all day for her hands to stop shaking. Radio KRTP-FM news, headlines on the hour, every hour: ethnic unrest in the Soviet provinces, resignations in the British cabinet, Hurricane Hugo blows the roof off a church and kills everyone inside. Weather: cold front moving in across the country from the northwest; high of 12 Celsius, 52 Fahrenheit; wind slight to moderate; rain by midafternoon. Good morning! And today's Radio KRTP-FM Listener File is sent in by Kevin McLoughlin from out there in Dundrum. Hi, Kevin, hope you're listening. Star sign: Capricorn; favourite drink: Harp Lager; favourite food: ham and pineapple pizza; favourite band: Dire Straits; favourite film: *Dirty Dancing*; favourite actor: Sly Stallone; favourite actress: Cher; favourite car: white Austin Metro GTI.

For these disclosures, Kevin McLoughlin from out there in Dundrum wins a Radio KRTP-FM sunstrip for his white Austin Metro GTI and would they play "Money For Nothing" for his girlfriend Anne-Marie. Surely will, Kevin McLoughlin from out there in Dundrum.

Guitars pick and strum and she makes tea, Chinese tea, scalding hot, almost flavourless. Muscles she did not know she had are dully furious with her. Must be getting out of condition. She should get back into training—cycle some, swim, work out, practice down at the dojo.

Enye MacColl. Twenty-wise. Five foot-wise. One twenty-wise pounds. Pure black hair—the sort that makes you want to bury your face in it and breathe deeply, imagining that you will smell the freshness of your first adolescent love again. Smooth olive skin; a genetic throwback to ancestors swept ashore with the Armada, hints of even elder stock, the Firbolg, the dark mesolithics swept away by the red-haired, freckle-faced Celts, the First Come. The black olive eyes of an elder race; devastating in casual glances, cat-unpredictable, cat-playful in intimacy. Like all women of character, she can be both beautiful and ugly in successive instants. If you saw her on the street, you would look again and think, *What an* interesting *woman*. Enye MacColl.

The light of her answering machine is glowing. Three calls.

Call one: Jaypee Kinsella (fated to pass through the world reduced to his initials; even Enye does not know what the Jay and the Pee stand for), perilously post-party: we've got to do something, darling, about those station idents: the Blessèd Phaedra is rumbling.

Call two: Saul, inquiring about her enjoyment of the party last night (she had not passed on the invitation to him; she knows he despises advertising parties) and her availability for dinner that night, dress formal, pick up eight sharp, ring back if not convenient.

Call three: her brother. Ewan. He needs to talk to her. Can she meet him for lunch at one o'clock?

If she hits the shower running, she can just about make it.

The place they have arranged to meet is a wrought-iron and glass snackery on the top level of the glass and wrought-iron mall they built on top of the old flea market. People slide up and down on escalators. They look nervous, like atheists in a cathedral. Everything is open plan, plate glass and delicate filigree, transparent. That is why the people look nervous—they fear that, unbeknownst, their bodies and souls may have become as transparent as glass. Enye thinks of a megalithic Ministry of Shopping in some Capitalist Totalitarian Dystopia. She picks at her green salad, toys with her Perrier. Her hands are still trembling from the psychic and physical strain. Her brother thinks she is hung over. She wills her hands to be still. *Make your everyday stance the combat stance; make the combat stance your everyday stance.*

Neither wants to say the first word, but a first word must be spoken. And a second. And a third.

"She asks about you."

"That's nice of her."

"She worries about you."

"She has nothing to worry about."

"She's not well, you know."

Her fingers are steady on the glass, as if they were holding a sword.

"What is it this time? Shadow in the brain, palpitation of the heart, dreadful lumps in the breast? Nothing trivial, I'm sure."

"What do you mean?"

"You know what I mean."

"She is our mother, for God's sake. Your mother."

"And he is our father. Your father."

Heads are turning at the closer tables. Their hopes of sibling strife will be disappointed. They are like two entrenched armies. They long ago ceased to be able to seriously damage each other. They long ago ceased to have anything they could say to each other. Enye catches a gum-chewing waitress's eye and pays the bill. Ewan leaves. At the edge of earshot, he turns.

"She really is ill, you know."

The escalators carry him down into the throng of glass people.

The masters of strategy, in their books and teachings, mention that it is possible to defeat an opponent and still lose the war.

She last saw her mother the year before, at the funeral. They had almost spoken, afterward, when the people were walking back from the graveside along the neatly tailored stone avenues to their cars. She had seen her mother clutch her brother's arm for support and, seeing her suddenly weak, no longer ageless, *mortal*, would have spoken, had there been anything she could have said. The moment tarried, stretched beyond the elastic limit of time, and passed, unspoken. She had turned away and Ewan was leading her mother away through the aisles of precise cypresses and the headless pillars of young Victorians felled before Eminence.

The death had been sudden, but not without her grandmother's customary grace. In the summer months the old woman had Consuela, the semiresident, semilegal Spanish home help move the wicker chair in which she did all her

illustrating down beyond the Stone Gardens to the shade of
the trees. It was there, in that chair, that she crossed the bar
between life and death with a half drunk cup of lemon tea on
the grass beside her and her favourite calico cat on her knee.
Consuela had gone to call her in when the shadows began to
grow long and the evening cool and had introduced the sole
note of gracelessness into the dying by waking Ballybrack
from its teatime drowsiness with operatic Hispanic shrieking and keening.

The calico cat had jumped down and run off through the
Stone Gardens and was never seen again.

The service had possessed the dignified festivity of a
bouquet of dried flowers. The day of the funeral was a final
celebration of summer before a damp and dowdy autumn.
The church was packed with the wonderful people the old
woman (no, not old—to die at seventy-three is to die having
barely sipped the pleasures of old age) had known in her
terrible, terrible years as an illustrator: artists and poets and
writers and critics and publishers and dancing teachers and
bass saxophonists and retired missionaries and pensioned
off chorus-line girls and faded madams. Enye had mean-
dered from conversation to conversation, listening to the
unself-conscious eulogising. She was sure Ballybrack Parish Church had never seen so many sinners under its roof at
once. One pass of the collection plate would have restored
the rafters, renovated the organ, and paid for a new hassock
in every pew.

After the interment (none of the claustrophobic dread of
spadefuls of earth thumping on the coffin; rather, a sense of
eager return to an elemental state of mineral existence) and
the inspection of the floral tributes, which were many and
glorious—one, from the publishers, was in the shape of
Miss Miniver Mouse, her most enduring creation—Enye
had noticed two figures standing some way apart from the
throng. They were dressed in tattered mourning of an
archaic design—frock coats, top hats held respectfully,
heads bowed. They looked like undertakers fallen on hard
times. One was short and squat, the other tall and thin—
relics from the Golden Age of Screen Comedy, incarnations
of celluloid. She would have spoken with them, for they
struck a hemichord of recognition, but then the artists poets

writers critics publishers bass saxophonists retired missionaries chorus-line girls faded madams had parted, leaving her
mother reaching for her brother's arm, and the moment was
sacrificed.

When next she had looked, they were gone. But her
half-recognition resolved into a memory.

As far as she can trace the line of memory, the house in
Ballybrack is there. Inextricably connected to it are memories of sea gulls calling in the morning; the smell of sea;
endless days of endless summer when summers were
summers; the dusty, tan, earth-sweat smell of hot days; the
taste of cherryade and the sting of sunburn on the backs of
the legs; the vinyl smell of the inflatable paddling pool; the
lurk of a calico cat in the rhododendrons on star-filled
evenings. It was a house that suggested associations with
eminent people. It could have been a judge's house, or a
surgeon's, or a rural dean's—white walls, black paintwork,
tall privet hedges that screened it from the road, and a
swathe of crunching gravel. Martins nested every summer
in the eaves of the double garage that smelled of stale oil
and lawn mowers. In her vaguest memories, Grandfather
Owen sequestered himself in the conservatory to smoke and
read the racing papers. Behind the house, the garden,
guarded from without by great ashes and beeches, maintained its own small secrets in shrub-enclosed bays and
coves, a wellspring of endless fascination for the young
Enye. After her grandfather's death, her grandmother had
embarked upon her transformations and constructions. Behind a screen of rhododendrons, in an intimate corner, a
spiral maze had been built from pieces of broken crockery.
Fragments of willow pattern, pieces of Meissen dairymaids
and blue delft windmills, shards of Coronation mugs, the
upper half of Edward VII's face, a headless Queen Eliza-
beth II dandling an infant Bonnie Prince Charlie on her
knee, the grimly righteous cow-features of Queen Victoria,
inviting the curious to follow its convolutions inward. From
the china maze you passed behind the bed of asters and
ageratums grown for the purposes of floromancy to a
crazy-pathed atrium from which rose a small Babel of stone
towers—hand-sized flat slabs of slate piled without cement
into pillars the highest of which was slightly taller than

eight-year-old Enye and the shortest barely reached her ankle. From thence you passed by way of hollyhocks and purple heliotrope to a specimen copper beech, its branches hung with old watches, broken carriage clocks, dials, escapements, hairsprings; shards and orts of broken time. And thence onward, into other gardens within the garden.

The only justification Grandmother MacColl ever gave for her constructions was the one Enye instinctively comprehended—that their purpose lay in their arrangement, not their elements. She knew that in those gardens within gardens one became aware of things one had not been aware of before. The china maze rewarded the one who followed it correctly to its centre with the ability to see the wind. Or what she thought was the wind—streams and rivers in the air not quite visible, not quite not. In the bottle garden, where green, white, brown, blue, yellow glass was planted in the earth like flowers, the spirit was one of stillness—the essential quiet that lay at the root of all dynamism reflected and magnified by the optics of the embedded bottles. Copper wind chimes fashioned from lengths of plumbing pipe suspended from the branches of an old, dried, magic apple tree called up a sense of simultaneously expanding to sky-dwarfing proportions and dwindling to a size so infinitesimal you were in danger of falling between the crumbs of soil, while among the stone towers Enye felt certain that if she turned around quickly enough she would see that the stone pillars were the towers and skyscrapers of another city in another world, its crazy-pathed boulevards bustling with golden chariots and the ox-drawn pantechnicons of strolling mummers.

But she knew she could never turn around fast enough so she created that city in her imagination, the capital of the imaginary land of Stone Gardania. On those long summer stays, when Something At Home that was never named brought Enye and five-year-old Ewan on indefinite visit, Stone Gardania slowly emerged from the wholly imaginary into the substantial: a nation state, with geography, history, economy, and politics. She created a citizenry out of novelty erasers in the shape of cute dragons or koalas; pencil-top rubber monsters with popping eyes, lolling tongues, fangs, and waggling tentacles, and plastic models of diverse breeds of dog from cereal packets. Overnight, new housing mush-roomed in the streets between the stone towers. By constitu-tion every citizen was allocated a yoghurt carton with a door cut in it as a highly desirable weatherproof residence. A pebble on top of the carton kept the home from blowing away in the wind. Stone Gardania's more prominent citizens, the members of the Hegemonic Council, lived in bijou maisonettes made from carefully piled stones atop the pillars. Access to street level was by toy helicopter. The highest level of all was reserved for the Sargon Raymondo I of Stone Gardania, a genial three-centimetre yellow dragon—that is, until over-rough handling of his Sargonic Majesty caused his head to fall off, whereupon the greatest surgeon in the land—a rubber bat called Black Swoop—performed a lifesaving operation known as a *pinography*, involving securing the Sargonic head to neck by a sewing pin from Grandmother MacColl's sewing basket. Later refinements to the operation utilised laser power—a beam of light focused through a hand-lens, capable of fusing rubber or plastic. The operation was only ever used experi-mentally on prisoners: Enye provided the agonised screams herself.

In those periods of time away from the white house in Ballybrack, between Something Happening at Home, and Something Happening Again, Enye plotted out the future history of Stone Gardania in exacting detail. A terrorist group calling itself the Nying Nyong Guerrillas, led by one Percy Perinov, a pencil-top anthropomorphised pear she had never liked, wearing a modelling-clay sombrero and mous-tache, attempted a coup in the streets of Stone Gardania. Only the valiant intervention of the ISF, the dread and exceedingly secret Internal Security Force, in their painted-on black uniforms, rescued the Sargon from a fate beyond even the power of a pinography to redeem and the grateful populace of Stone Gardania from the tyranny of an organisation whose party anthem was: "We will prevail in the end, 'cause we are so much better than you."

And when next Something Happened, with the shouting voices from the room downstairs that sounded like animals biting at each other, the Battle of Stone Gardania was fought on a chilly October morning with Enye partisan to both

sides (slightly biased toward the Sargonese forces) hurling
matches tipped with flaming chunks of fire lighter through
the air. The official Stone Gardanian newspaper *Die Draken*
("The Dragons": rubber dragon erasers formed a powerful
oligarchy in Stone Gardanian society) reported in depth the
trial of Percy Perinov, in his suave hat and moustache, and
in rather gratuitous detail, his subsequent execution: sealed
in a Curiously Strong Peppermints tin and smelted to death
by her late grandfather's gas blowtorch.

The game grew more elaborate—though she would have
been highly affronted to hear her unfolding history called a
game: Stone Gardania was more solid and real to her than
what passed for a world beyond the privet hedges and
screening beeches. From their yoghurt cartons and maisonettes, Stone Gardanians went roving out on the tops of
toy cars to colonise her Grandmother's other constructions
and transformations and weld the hegemony of individual-
istic provinces into the Stone Gardanian Empire. As the
process of Empire-building unfolded, she noticed that the
character of the provinces, and the colonists who settled
there, reflected the character of the gardens they occupied.
The citizens of the bottle garden, which she called Glasso-
nia, tended toward philosophic introspection and lived in
old beer glasses half buried on their sides in the soil. The
Glassonians were an honest and angelic race, peace-loving
and unwarlike. Not so the colonists of the magic apple tree:
Tubular-Bell-Land, Enye christened it. Their city was a
place of little platforms and tables, helicopters and para-
chutes. A bellicose breed the Tubular Bellians, given to
displays of martial might and shouting. They were the most
rebellious of the Stone Gardanian provinces. When ultimately faced with the ISF in black, matches ready to fire
from the muzzles of toy howitzers, they broke ranks and
fled. Big on the outside, little on the inside. Yet when the
stream that marked the outermost edge of Grandmother
MacColl's domain burst its banks in the Great Flood of '72,
it was the Tubular Bellians who came to the aid of stricken
Stone Gardania, swooping down in their helicopters and jet
packs made from empty ink cartridges and rubber bands to
effect the daring rescue of Stone Gardanians swept to almost
certain doom in their desirable yoghurt-carton residences.

"It's like the Stone Gardens suggest the stories," she said to her grandmother. It was a wet Wednesday in the Christmas holidays; nearly seven Ewan was banging on a piano three rooms away. Undeterred, possessed of an almost beatific tranquility, Grandmother MacColl was at her drawing desk working on roughs for a cover for Sibelius's Fifth Symphony. Since those rude, raw, beautiful drawings for the leather-bound collector's edition of *Ulysses*, she had gloried in the title of Enfant Terrible of Irish Illustration—one critic had called her rendition of Molly Bloom's sexual solioquy a "Brutal, obscene raspberry to ten centuries of book illustration, from the *Book of Kells* onward"—though she was best known for her Miss Miniver Mouse series of children's books, which she produced under the name of French. When word had broken that the Laurel French of the children's section was the Jessica MacColl of *that book*, not a few libraries had withdrawn Miniver Mouse from their shelves.

"I don't have to think up anything, it's already there, written somewhere else, and I just act it out. Does this make sense?"

Grandmother Jessica turned from the pool of light the swan-necked brass drawing lamp spilled over her board to pour tea for two, and a Viennese fancy.

"It's like everything that can happen has happened, and that everything that has happened has happened only because it is going to happen."

Nearly twelve, she sipped her tea, fingers sticky with yellow fondant.

"Do you know what I like about it? It's that I feel safe. Looked after. Like someone is watching me who understands and approves and wants to join in, but can't for some reason."

Grandmother Jessica crossed to the french window to pull the curtain. She paused, hand on sash cord, to look at her gardens, where the short December day was rapidly diminishing.

"I know why you make them. Because it's real there. The things in your head are real there. You can *see*."

A finger and a smile, both slightly crooked, called Enye to the window. In the gathering shadows beneath the

screening trees stood two figures, almost shadows themselves: one short, square, one tall, stretched. They stood
like scarecrows on a wooden cross and Enye knew that
theirs were the watching eyes, the safeguard kept on her
enactment of the story of Stone Gardania. Grandmother and
granddaughter stood behind the latticed window watching
until the shadows rose up out of the ground and covered the
two figures and drew them into themselves. A tremendous
sense of having touched the very edge of something
mystical and enormous stole out of the garden over the
house.

"Who are they?"

She saw tear tracks on her grandmother's cheeks.

The Stone Gardanian Empire, that might have endured a
thousand years, moving from glory to glory, was swept
aside in less than a week by the tidal wave of puberty.

Saul is tall, but you cannot tell that because he is sitting
down. Saul is strong, but you would only know that if you
had seen him naked. Saul has a face like a geomorphological feature. Saul has long black hair with just the least tinge
of grey. He wears it gelled back from his face and, when he
is not on official business, ties it into a pigtail. Saul is a
solicitor—that branch of the legal profession that does all
the work and garners none of the glory. That is reserved for
the other branch of the profession—the gowned and peri-
wigged barristers. As they wait in the ludicrously overpriced, underportioned restaurant for the *doppios* to come,
he tells Enye about a ward of court case that hinges upon the
mother's conviction that she is not Mrs. Marion Hoey of
Kincora Road, Clontarf, but Mrs. Elvis Presley, seduced,
impregnated, and secretly married in a Wesleyan chapel at
which the rhinestone legend, on bended knee, sang "Love
Me Tender." All this allegedly happened during a clandestine shopping trip by The King to the Clontarf branch of
PriceRite stores two years after his (putative) death. The
justice calls for Mrs. Marion Hoey of Kincora Road,
Clontarf. Mrs. Marion Hoey of Kincora Road, Clontarf, is
conspicuous by her absence. Again he calls, and a third

time, whereupon an usher is dispatched to return red-faced, and stage-whispers into His Honour's ear: "She says she isn't going to come unless she is called Mrs. Elvis Presley."

Case closed.

She watches Saul's hands as he recounts the story. They are not the hands of a lawyer. They are the hands of a mountaineer, a geologist, or, she thinks, an assassin. She watches him, animated and smiling, and he notices her watching him and sees that behind her smile she is far, far away.

"You don't seem quite yourself tonight," he says. "Are you having your period?"

She wants, suddenly, to throw her tiny cup of espresso in his animated, smiling face, and she is afraid of herself. Is this how it ends, she asks, the trivial irritations becoming minor annoyances becoming simmering resentments? Do we fall out of tolerance with each other? Do we collapse into a vague nebula of angers and rages? She has been wondering whether to end it for some time now. She is not certain if she loves him. She never was. She is not certain he loves her, would love her, if she told him all the secret things about herself she has never spoken aloud.

She cannot conceive speaking aloud the truths about herself. Who would believe her? And, believing her, who could love her? Strange, the one she has come closest to telling those truths is Mr. Antrobus, downstairs.

At the next table in the overpriced, underportioned restaurant, two men are wrapped in a very serious discussion about Batman. They are saying that he is an archetype of the modern mass psyche, a classically twentieth-century urban existentialist antihero. Saul is doubled up with laughter, softly ramming his serviette into his mouth to stop the loud laughter from spilling out.

"This is a middle-aged man who dresses up in black tights and his mother's old curtains, with an unhealthy relationship with a prepubescent boy in scaley knickers, who swans around dark alleyways at dead of night, and these guys are talking about him like he was Marcel Proust."

"They're looking at us," she hisses.

As she follows him in her car through the neon and diesel to his apartment in a tree-lined avenue of neo-Georgian town houses, she can feel the distance between them. It is as if all the many separate points that came between them have been gathered up and laid end to end.

Afterward, when he is lying like a great slab of stone across the bed, she finds a place to wait for morning inside the curve of his shoulder and gazes at the slats of shadow and yellow streetlight cast across the plaster mouldings of the ceiling. Early morning jets scream in low over the city. She is tired, tired, but she cannot sleep. Not yet. She has battles to fight, endless battles.

Tired, tired, so tired. But they never tire.

Saul stirs in his monolithic dreams, cries out, an incoherent child's voice, Saul-that-was, tumbling back through the years. Enye listens to the traffic, the shriek of distant police sirens, and waits for morning in the hollow of his shoulder.

How much confidence can one be reasonably expected to have in a solicitor called Swindell?

Not expecting to have been remembered in her grandmother's will, she had not attended the formal reading. It came as a surprise to be interrupted in the middle of the DairyCrest Creameries account by Mr. Swindell's Dickensian lisp inviting her to call upon him in his chambers at her earliest convenience to take possession of an item that had been bequeathed to her.

Said item being a bulky brown paper parcel tied with string, like a fat woman in a too-small bikini. Corners of paper peeped tantalisingly from tears in the wrapping; the package rustled and smelled faintly of must and flowers. The bindings cut with a faint, elastic twang—the brown paper had been folded, not taped. Within was an untidy heap of notes written in black ballpoint, pencilled sketches, jottings, photocopies of press snippets, and eighty-four watercolour studies of flowers. There was no explanatory note. At the very bottom was a hand-lettered frontispiece bearing the words: *The Secret Language of Flowers*.

It had grown dark without Enye's realising. She took the piled papers to the table in her pine kitchenette, switched on the overhead pull-down lamp, and addressed herself to the task of ordering the jumbled pages. Hector Berlioz's *Symphonie Fantastique* played from the midi-system in her living room.

It seemed to be a book, or a notion of a book—a book of the kind that is wholly conceived as a labour of love and thus can never be satisfactorily completed. Grandmother Jessica had made veiled references to a project she regarded as "her life's chief work," but as proof of it was never forthcoming, the magnum opus had been dismissed as an old woman's bargaining with mortality. What Enye had spread in heaps across her pine table was clearly the work of years, if not decades, of stolen moments—midnight jottings, notings after tea or before breakfast, afternoon sketchings and scribblings; entire winter nights in her studio. The work was fragmentary, disorganised: next to a series of studies of bog-irises might be some hurriedly pencilled note on the symbolic meanings of jonquil ("I desire a return of affection."), canterbury bell (acknowledgment), dock (patience), valerian (an accommodating disposition), and turnip (charity). Paper-clipped to these might be photocopied snippings from obscure herbalist magazines of a cure for diseases of sheep prepared in the Caucasus from agrimony, feverfew, and beech bark. Enye divided the work under two major headings. Sketches and Drawings, and Jottings and Scribblings. These groups she later subdivided into Botany; Herbal and Remedial Effects (Medicinal); Herbal and Remedial Effects (Environmental) (the effect of the presence of differing species of flowers in a room); Symbolic Meanings (Tokens); and Symbolic Meanings (Floromancy).

The many and diverse flower beds at the house in Ballybrack (sold, she had learned from Mr. Swindell, to a property developer with outline planning permission to convert into a development of six *luxury* apartments to be known as Ironbridge Mews) were a result of her grandmother's fascination with floromancy. She had developed the art from the Victorian lovers' language of tokens given and tokens received into a method of divination and oracle.

An early memory, so early she could not be certain that it was not imaginary, fleshed out from things she had been told, was of being sent into the garden to pick a posy of ten flowers (no more, no less). Any flower she wanted, as long as there were no more than ten. Her grandmother laid the gathered posy on the table, studied each flower diligently, and noted her conclusions in a pocket-sized loose-leaf notebook, the first such Enye had ever seen.

"Lupin for imagination, acanthus for fine art, chamomile for energy in adversity, magnolia for persistence, night convolvulus for deeds done in darkness; monkshood: knight-errantry, bravery, valiant-for-truth. White oak for independence, walnut leaves for strategy. Rhododendron: Danger, beware. Not close, danger far off, too far to be seen. That's only nine. One more. What have you got in your hand, Enye? May I see it?"

She had opened her hand, shown the leaf that lay pressed within. A breath, sharply intaken. "Mandrake."

When in need of oracular wisdom, her grandmother would select a distinctive butterfly and follow its path through the gardens, noting the plants upon which it settled in her ring-bound pocket book, until it flitted across the boundary brook into less meaningful topographies. Late in life, she claimed to have made all her investment decisions by floromancy. Enye wondered how it worked in the winter in the absence of butterflies and blooms. Birds and evergreens, perhaps? The records of meanings and conjunctions of oracles given, futures divined, gave no indication.

The deeper she delved into floromancy, the more she became aware of a concealed subgroup which she hesitantly designated "Spirits and Elementals." A small corpus of work this, chiefly from the latter years of the old woman's life—an apologia for the principles of floromancy argued from an arcana of elemental characters, spirits, that inhabited, visited, inspired the various flowers. Flower faeries? Hobgoblins? Enye worked back through the pile of prints and drawings and picked out a series she had on first viewing thought whimsical juvenilia: daffodil warriors, tiger-lily Jezebels, snapdragons breathing puffballs of floral fire, red-hot–poker guardsmen, erection-stiff. She placed them with the growing pile of material tagged "Spirits and Elementals."

She looked up and saw her face reflected in the night-

mirrored window. The clock on the freezer blinked 1:21 at
her. Hector Berlioz had long since come to his appointed
end and clicked off like an unremarkable life ending. She
scrubbed at her temples with her knuckles. Somewhen in
the evening she had developed a terrible headache.

"What about a green cow? Like that Swiss chocolate
that's actually Belgian that has a lilac cow: with a green cow
we kill three symbolic birds with one iconic stone: you've
got the good green grass, health and fitness, the let's-all-
get-exercise-bikes-and-pedal-our-way-into-the-coronary-care-
unit lobby. You've got the green environmental aspect—no
additives no preservatives no artificial colours no E numbers a hundred percent organic and fully biodegradable in
less than three days. And you've got the good oul' Wearing
of the Green Twang on the Nationalistic Heartstrings aspect,
all wrapped up in one chartreuse bovine: brilliant Jaypee, a
genius Jaypee, Advertising Campaign of the Year Decade
Millennium Jaypee, why don't you retire and go live out your
days on a tropic isle with twenty firm-breasted Filipino
masseuses and live on just coconuts and fish from out the
sea?"

"Mmmm?"

"Mmmm? The first idea we've had in weeks and all you
can greet its advent with is 'Mmmm'?"

"Sorry, Jaypee. I've got this mother of a headache and I
can't seem to shift it."

"You tried aspirin codeine paracetamol morphine heroin
cocaine?"

Enye nodded, careful not to send any loose plaster
tumbling from the cracked basilica of her skull. Mrs.
O'Verall trundled her tea trolley past their glass-walled
strip-lit workstation on her rounds of what its inmates called
the Glass Menagerie. Jaypee obtained a pot of her hot water
and a cup and produced from the darkest recesses of his
darkest drawer a tea bag which he treated with the reverential awe of half a kilo of Colombian White.

"Three Harmonies Pink Tingler," he announced dunking
the tea bag with precisely timed dunks into the hot water.

"It's from California, so it's got to be good for something."

It wasn't.

In the women's room, she tried not to throw up into the washbasin from the pain beating beating beating behind her eyes. Pastel waves of nausea washed across her vision. The Blessèd Phaedra, the Boss She Did Not Like, and Who Did Not Like Her, emerged from a cubicle, pulling at the knees of her paisley-pattern tights.

"Anything wrong, MacColl?"

"No. Nothing, I'm all right." Though she knew that at any second high-pressure brain matter might come squeezing from the suture lines of her skull.

"You don't look too good to me. I think maybe you should go home and look after that."

"No, dammit, I am all right."

Well, it's your life, dearie . . .

She did not know how the thing with Phaedra had started. Perhaps at the party at which Oscar the Bastard had introduced the new Accounts Manager to the inmates of the Glass Menagerie. She had always suspected that her whispered comment to Jaypee that a mother must hate her kid a lot to have christened her Phaedra had been a little more public than she had intended. Overheards notwithstanding, they were enemies because they recognised each other. One Master of the Way will always recognise another, be that the Way of the Sword, or the Way of the Corporate Hierarchy. And as there can only ever be one Master, they both knew that someday, they would meet to decide who that Master was to be.

At least the need to empty her stomach into the avocado-coloured porcelain seemed less urgent.

Jaypee was uncharacteristically testy when she returned to the glass and plastic work space.

"Well Words?"

"Well Pictures?"

"Green Cow?"

She squinted at the hand-drawn rough, grimaced.

"Leave it with me. I'll stay late tonight and see if I can generate some suitable words for your pictures. Sorry, Jaypee, but the hemispheres of my brain feel like two distant tribes communicating by talking drum."

She made sure both the Blessèd Phaedra and Oscar the Bastard saw her stay after the rest had gone back to their timber-frame Tudorette dwellings in corporate ghettos with names like Elmwood Heights and Manor Grange. The Little League of Decency and Purity came around with their vacuum cleaners and environmentally friendly spray polishes. Enye sat in a box defined by dribbling white aerosol and polishing yellow dusters, the victim of a troupe of geriatric French mime artistes.

"Make sure you switch off and lock up when you go, now."

She waved to the Little Leaguers through her gleaming glass walls and presently hers was the only illuminated glass box in the Glass Menagerie. She scribbled things on pieces of paper. She stared at Jaypee's Early Plastics Connoisseur calendar. She pushed the pieces of paper with things scribbled on them around her desk. She cut out the drawing of the Green Cow with scissors and blue-gunked it to the wall. She threw crumpled pieces of paper with things scribbled on them at the miniature waste bin basketball net Jaypee had bought her to welcome her to QHPSL. She found her Walkperson and listened to the stringent, ascetic counterpoints of the Brandenberg Concertos. She wrote *I hate DairyCrest Creameries. I hope you all catch Bovine Spongiform Encephalopathy* in large fat letters on a sheet of A2, taking a minute for each large, fat letter.

Nothing would *come*.

The Garfield wall clock informed her it was twenty past ten (*ten!*) and in panic she scribbled down the first five things that came into her head.

And yes, she remembered to put off the lights and lock up.

In the elevator it struck like a physical assault. She gasped, pressed her forehead against the dimpled metal walls, praying for cool, for release. The door opened. She stumbled into the stale-exhaust atmosphere of the underground car park. Bulkhead lights in wire cages threw uneasy shadows over the oil-stained concrete and squat pillars decorated with black and yellow warning chevrons; the exit ramp curved up into darkness. She fumbled in her handbag for the pass card. Her green and white Citroen with the bamboo and wicker pattern was the only car. It seemed a tremendous distance away across the ulcerous concrete. Each footstep set nuclear fireworks exploding through her frontal lobes. Safely behind the wheel, she closed her eyes and waited for the throbbing to ebb away. She opened her eyes.

The air was boiling.

Soft motes of black light fell from infinite height to detonate on her retinas.

She reversed the Citroen 2CV around in a reckless arc, pointed its de Gaulle nose at the ramp.

The boiling air coalesced, solidified. At the foot of the ramp hovered what looked like nothing more than a transparent vagina.

Enye pressed her fingers to her temples, pressed, pressed, as if she could press them through into her brain to tear out the pain.

The vagina-mouth puckered and opened.

Out of the mouth in the air emerged something that looked like a pepper pot made of elephant flesh that crept upon thousands of red millipede feet.

It advanced into the car park. Its top, which, had it been a pepper pot and not something altogether other, would have turned to grind pepper, revolved slowly. It was studded with eyes. From each eye shone a beam of poisonous lilac light.

Behind it, within the vagina-mouth, Enye saw others struggling to push through, pushing at each other, pushing at the invisible muscles of the gateway. Others: like a spinning black-and-white-striped something that went from being like an upturned grand piano to being thinner than a razor's edge. Others: like a dog with the head of nun, like a crimson tree with its branches covered in mouths, like leprosy that has devoured its victim and still walks erect, like something that could not be clearly seen but which sounded like oiled steel being bandsawn.

The pepper pot's eye beams glanced across Enye; she heard bells and rocks being crushed, tasted brass, felt elation, disgust, vertigo, and acute ennui.

She jammed the Citroen into reverse. The engine wailed as she slewed back across the car park. The pepper-pot thing sent its eyelights flashing and darting off pillars, roofs, warning signs, bulkhead lights. Half blinded by the pain, Enye slammed the car into forward gear, gunned the engine, popped the clutch. Tyres screeched and smoked. The left fender of the Citroen caught the pepper-pot thing and flipped it up and over the roof. It lay on its side, millipede feet waving frantically, eyes rotating from side to side.

Tyres screeched again. Enye put the car into reverse, lined up the weaving eye lights in her rearview mirror, and put her foot down.

The Citroen jolted.

The pepper-pot thing split and burst, spilling a watery blue ichor across the concrete.

Something like a headless wolf dipped in luminous oil with a grinding lamprey maw tore free from the pressing labia of the gateway in the air. Screaming hysterically, Enye rammed the car into first again and floored the accelerator. The Citroen juddered and slewed. It caught the lamprey-wolf squarely, shattered its thin bones beneath its wheels. Enye threw up her arms to protect her from the impact as the Citroen's Gallic nose wedged and stuck in the vagina mouth.

The pain inside her head went up in a searing detonation, as if lightning had struck inside her skull.

The smell of ionisation woke her; the sharp tang of electricity and smoking rubber. Every electrical circuit in the car was burned out, every fuse blown. Thin smoke trickled from the cassette player. The tip of the radio aerial had melted and run into chromium droplets.

She had no idea of the time—her watch had stopped. The metal casing was slightly warm to the touch.

She stepped out of the car. What had been might never have been. That patch of blue dampness on the concrete might have been glycol from a leaking radiator, that shrivelled, decomposed thing behind the pillar a black plastic garbage sack left by the Little League of Decency and Purity for pickup. She pushed the dead car back into her parking space.

Her head was clear.

Her head was *clear*.

Shivering by night in her day clothes, she walked by the university palings to the taxi rank. A pair of hopeful buskers held a pitch in a shop doorway, hunting down the small change of the pub-and-club crowd. A boy played electric guitar through an amp/speaker assembly mounted on a backpack; his colleague, a punky girl in holey fishnets and leotard, danced with startling gymnasticism to the stalking, rhythmic guitar. Driving home in the taxi, Enye thought it strange that the boy should have been wearing shades after midnight, well after midnight; the little plastic digital clock on the driver's dashboard, between the little plastic Garfield and the little plastic BVM, read twenty past one.

The shakes hit her on the third stair. She sat on the worn carpet and willed her hands to be still. When finally she could open her front door, there was an envelope waiting for her on the mat. The envelope had a distinctive smell she could not quite place. Taped to the creamy white envelope was a note from Mr. Antrobus: the letter had been delivered at noon by a bicycle courier and in her absence he had signed for it. He hoped she did not mind his using his passkey to leave it for her.

The creamy white envelope contained an invitation for her to call at the offices of Mr. Martland of Messrs. Ludlow, Allison, MacNab, Solicitors, at her earliest convenience.

She could place that distinctive smell now.

Lawyer.

Mr. Antrobus has lived since the end of the last world war in three downstairs rooms of the house on L'Esperanza Street with his posters of Greek temples by Ionian sunsets, his twelve (at the last census) cats, and his television. In those forty-four years he has never opened his front door any wider than necessary to collect his morning milk. The people of L'Esperanza Street, he maintains, have always been suspicious of him, partly because of the foreign sound of his name, mostly because of his Proclivities. He was conceived in a misfortunate decade, he says. One generation later and he could have taken his Proclivities and waved them over his head and no one would have batted an eye. Anywhere but L'Esperanza Street, that is. Enye tells him he should try again—it is never too late, you are never too old—but he dismisses her suggestions with a wave and a scowl.

"Changed too much," he says. "Too aggressive, too violent these days. They terrify me, all that barely contained aggression. For a time, it was a beautiful thing. Not anymore. Anyway, there's always the chance of . . . you know."

The truth is that for the last forty-six years he has mourned an unrequited love for a fiacre driver on the island of Kos where he landed with the Allied Forces in 1943. On the first night out of Alexandria, he had dreamed that a youth of Homeric beauty beckoned him across the wine-dark sea to an island of sun-bleached white houses and olives older than the topless towers of Ilium. And there, standing on the quay with his duffel bag on the sun-bleached limestone, he had glimpsed among the rowdy fiacre drivers, sham-fighting each other for the privilege of driving the Liberators to their accommodations, the face he had dreamed of in the belly of the troopship. It was love at first sight. He stood paralysed by the drugged arrows of Eros.

He never rode in that fiacre, never spoke to its driver, never came closer than a street table at a café across the square from the stand where the drivers gathered under the shade of the trees outside the Church of Aghios Nicolaos. But he has carried in his heart like an icon these forty-six years the image of the young men of Kos diving naked at sunset for sponges and his young fiacre driver standing like Apollo newly sprung from the brow of Zeus, silhouetted against the sinking red sun.

It is a story Enye never tires of hearing, as Mr. Antrobus never tires of telling, for they both understand that unrequited love is the most enduring love of all.

After the war Mr. Antrobus came into possession of the house on L'Esperanza Street through a succession of bequests and, having hived off sufficient living space for himself, rented the upper floor as a self-contained apartment under the stipulation that any tenant must undertake to do his weekly shopping for him. Enye enjoys shopping for him—she sees it as her duty to introduce him to a new and interesting culinary experiences. Proclivities notwithstanding, she knows that Mr. Antrobus is not a complete prisoner of his three rooms. High summer has been known to lure him into his back garden in Panama hat, singlet, and aged, aged Army shorts with aged, aged deck chair to join her on her sun lounger, and in the dawn and dusk hours she has seen the beam from the lamp on his aged, aged black Phoenix bicycle weaving unsteadily down the alleyway at the back of the row of houses. She knows better than to ask. They have their closenesses, and they have their spaces. Sunday afternoons she visits him for tea and individual apple pies.

Sunday mornings are for the dojo. Her *sensei* has noticed a tendency toward open aggression in her sword style, contrary to the spirit of *Ai Uchi*, of cutting the enemy in the same instant as he cuts you, the spirit of dispassion, of treating one's enemy as an honoured guest.

"My enemies are not honoured guests," Enye says darkly.

"You will lose the Way," her *sensei* admonishes.

Enye does not say that she fears she lost the Way long ago. Master and pupil, they kneel in *seiza*, swords on the right-hand side, and bow to each other.

Now she sits on Mr. Antrobus's overstuffed old chesterfield, curled like one of his contented cats in a pair of old jeans so soft from washing they spontaneously go into holes and a loose rag top she knitted herself. Mr. Antrobus passes a willow-pattern teacup with an individual apple pie still in its foil cup perched on the side of the saucer.

"Have you ever thought what hell is like?" In the four years Enye has been visiting him the emphasis of his conversation has moved with stellar slowness from love remembered to death anticipated. "I think about it a lot. At night, when I cannot sleep, I feel the oldness and tiredness of my flesh and a dreadful chill comes over me, as if a cold hand has closed on my heart. I am going to die. Some day, and that day is drawing closer with every tick of the clock, I will die. No escaping it. No exceptions, no exemptions. My heart will stop, my blood will go cold, my thoughts will freeze in my brain, and this consciousness, this self that is all I know, will gutter out like a candle. Do you think about death?"

"Like Picasso said, a little every day."

"But then I think, what if it is not the end? What if there is something beyond death? What if there is a heaven and a hell?"

"The smart money bets on there being a God. If there is no God, and you bet there is, you lose nothing. If there is a God, and you bet there isn't, you lose. In spades."

"Yes, but have you placed your bets?"

"No, not yet."

"Ah. And neither have I. But either of us could have to face that question at any moment, and if we are wrong, it will be hell for all eternity. Hell." He licks his lips. "Can you image it; torment without end? Can you imagine the moment when you are dismissed from the presence of God? Can you imagine the fall that is supposed to last nine days and nine nights? Can you imagine the demons that carry you through the walls of hell that are four thousand miles thick? Can you imagine the moment when the chains lock around your body and you know that you will never move again? And then you pass through the brass gates of Pandemonium that bear the legend 'Abandon Hope All Ye Who Enter Here,' and you hear the screaming—a million, a billion, a trillion voices, all screaming, screaming for a million, a billion, a trillion years—and the demons that have borne you thus far set you down at the edge of the pit and you see the bodies: as far as you can see, bodies, piled on top of one another, the bodies of the damned, screaming and roaring and blaspheming at each other. Then the demons of the pit itself lift you to take you down to the place they have chosen for you, and as they set you on top of a pile of bodies and fly away you know that eternity begins now, that from now on nothing will ever change, nothing will ever happen. You will never be free, you will remain in the same place forever and ever and ever, the same people beside you, the same people in front of you and behind you, the same people below you and heaped on top of you. You will never see anything else but their bodies; you will never hear anything other than their screaming and roaring. A hundred years will pass, a thousand years will pass, and a hundred thousand, and a hundred million, and still . . ." He lowers his voice to a thin whisper: "And still: *not one instant of eternity will have passed.* It never ends. It never ends, on and on and on and on and on, forever and ever and ever, never changing, forever."

"We create our own heavens and hells," Enye says. "Each of us, each second during our lives, build those heavens or hells. If our lives are built generously, caringly, spiritually, in the pursuit of beauty, goodness, and harmony, then that is what we will receive. If our lives are spent selfishly, greedily, uglily, in the pursuit of wealth and self-aggrandisement, than that is what we will receive. Those who seek holiness will have holiness, forever. Those who seek themselves will have themselves, forever."

"Not much room for a just God in your heaven and hell."

"A just God would give each person what he wants most in the world. If that is God, he shall have God; if that is himself, then that is exactly what he shall receive. A sinner wouldn't want what heaven has to offer."

"Too iffy, too butty for me," says Mr. Antrobus. "And I'm too old for philosophic casuistry. I need to know on which side to place my wager."

"As I said, the wise money chooses God."

"Yes, but will God choose me? Or will he say, at the very last, *Away from me, you old and vile sinner, into the place I have prepared for such as you?* After all those years I wasted, fearing Him, trying to live to please Him?"

The lamps have gone on in L'Esperanza Street. The yellow light is shattered by Mr. Antrobus's blinds into narrow bands falling across the sleeping forms of the cats. The bottom half of Mr. Antrobus is illuminated, hands resting on chair arms, long shins, shoes; the upper half remains in shadow. In the room Enye feels the Mygmus shift, like magnetic particles reversing polarity to lie along new orientations.

"I brought you the Delius tape you asked about. Would you like to hear it?"

They sit and drink the tea and listen to the piano music coming from the radio-cassette recorder, each wrapped in their private heaven or hell. Night descends on L'Esperanza Street. The only light in the room comes from the yellow street lamps, the occasional flarings of collapsing coals on

the fire, and the tiny glow of red and green LEDs on the
radio-cassette. But Enye can smell Mr. Antrobus's death.

The man from the garage had been almost awestruck.
"How did you manage to burn out every electrical circuit?"
he had asked, walking around the green bamboo and wicker
pattern Citroen with the reverence of a pilgrim at the tomb
of a saint. "You get hit by lightning?"

"Something like."

"This is going to cost, you know."

"Doesn't it always?"

She had taken a taxi to Messrs. Ludlow, Allison, Mac-
Nab, whose junior partner, Mr. Saul Martland, was explain-
ing his letter of the previous day.

As is the perennial lot of junior, junior partners, the more
idiosyncratic cases tended to fall into his In tray, none more
idiosyncratic than the Rooke bequest.

The late Dr. Hannibal Rooke had enjoyed a certain
notoriety in the early decades of the century as a pioneer
paranormal investigator, but in his later years had retired to
a near-hermetic existence in his house on a headland
overlooking the sea. He had died in unusual circumstances,
which Mr. Saul Martland was not willing to disclose despite
Mizz Enye MacColl's interest, some three years before. The
will had only recently been settled, due to a large number of
expectant beneficiaries disappointed by their exclusion
contesting the legality of a final testament on magnetic tape.

Enye envisioned a Danse Macabre Game Show with
scantily clad hostesses stepping out of neon-lit, mink-lined
coffins, and a gold-lamée-suited deceased cantering down a
flight of silver steps from dry-ice-shrouded pearly gates to
leap from prize item to prize item. "Mrs. Mary Kernohan of
Sunnyside Villas, tonight is your lucky night; you have just
won two hundred pounds' worth of Marks and Spencers
shares, a case of sterling silver dessert forks, and a
foul-mouthed cockatiel in a Moorish bird cage on: Open!
The! Box!"

"We established that you can write a will on the side of
a buffalo in its own dung and it will be perfectly legal,

provided it is witnessed and signed. Preferably not by the buffalo."

She liked the way he said that. Solicitors do not talk about dung.

She liked a lot about Saul Martland—his generously cut double-breasted blue microstripe of the kind particular to just one shop in London. His jazz-coloured tie, fastened with a pin in the shape of a B-52 bomber. His hands: their jewellery-freeness. His desk: its executive affectation-in-the-shape-of-paperweights-brass-staplers-leather-bound-blotters-Newton's-cradles-freeness. His name: its sonorous Biblicality, like tablets of stone. His reproduction *Views of Edo* prints which decorated the otherwise corporate starkness of his blacque-tech office. His eyes: how they could only hold hers for a moment before flicking away to his jewellery-free hands, his affectation-free desk, his *Views of Edo*.

She smiled.

He liked the way she smiled.

She liked the way he smiled when he saw her smile.

This is how it develops—by small smiles.

"There were a few—ah—unorthodox codicils to the will," said Mr. Saul Martland. "One of which was that a package be delivered by the executor of the will—that is, myself—to the eldest female descendant of Mrs. Jessica MacColl. That is yourself."

"What is this . . . ah . . . package?"

"This is."

A padded yellow envelope, stapled shut, addressed to Ludlow, Allison, MacNab, Solicitors. Contours suggested something the size and shape of a B-format paperback book. Or a videotape. It did rattle videotapishly when she shook it.

"Do you know what this is?"

"It could be half a kilo of Colombian White for all I know."

She liked that, too.

"Why me?"

"All I know is that I was instructed to deliver the package to the eldest female descendant of Jessica MacColl. Who, I discovered after some poking in the public records office, to be you."

And that, it seemed, was all the time the junior, junior partner of Ludlow, Allison, MacNab had assigned to her.

Not even an invitation to dinner.

In her apartment above L'Esperanza Street, Enye tore open the stapled yellow envelope.

As she had supposed, a videotape, unmarked, unlabelled, anonymous in every way, fell onto her welcome mat with the geese with bows around their necks. She brewed coffee as strong and black as witch's piss and sipped it while the VCR clicked and whirred and flashed liquid crystal digits to itself.

The screen lit.

In a glass conservatory overlooking a blue, blue sea was an aged, aged man in a wheelchair. He was dressed in a white linen suit of the type that look so well on aged, aged men and so poorly on any others. In his buttonhole was a carnation. His brown-blotched hands rested lightly on a straw hat in his lap. His tie was fastened with a pin in the shape of a golden salamander.

The camera closed up on him, advancing silently through the climbing figs and geraniums in their terra-cotta pots.

The aged, aged man smiled.

"Good day to you, whoever you are, whatever your name is. My solicitors, the worthy Messrs. Ludlow, Allison, and MacNab, will have delivered this to you as per my instructions. I have my reasons for doing what I have done in the way I have done. Pray Jesus you will never need to understand why.

"Forgive me, though forgiveness is for the living and if you are viewing this, I am long past any human forgiveness. I was grossly remiss in not introducing myself. My name is Dr. Hannibal Rooke." The aged, aged man leaned forward in his chair and beckoned the camera to close up. Enye felt drawn against her will into an intimacy of unfolding conspiracy. "My dear Mizz, forgive the use of the generic honorific, I am afraid I know very little about you, except that you are a MacColl, and, more significantly, a Desmond by blood. I am compelled to give you a warning. The female offspring of your bloodline possess, to a greater or lesser degree, a talent—yes, let us call it that; a talent it is, a gift, an *art* of a kind—that threatens to place you in very grave danger.

"It may have already done so."

Dry ice crystals formed in the pith of her spirit. She knelt before the television, reached out to touch the screen. Prophecies from a dead man.

"If so, then I pray that there is still someone to watch this tape. I do not know, I cannot say. What I am doing is a stab in the dark, a bottle cast into the sea of time."

The camera closed right in on the aged, aged face.

"You are in danger, mortal danger. From your own talent, and the talent of another. Until you are better informed, it would be wiser for me not to say more on the subject. Knowledge will arm you, and unarmed, you may not survive.

"I am the possessor of that knowledge, perhaps the sole possessor. I have made the purpose of this last half century of my life the accumulating of that knowledge. I know the value of that knowledge, and, as with any thing of value, there is danger. There are others, not amicably inclined toward my possessing this knowledge, or you. Therefore, I have been forced to take steps to safeguard this knowledge, and have arranged after my death for it to be removed to a place of safekeeping. My solicitors have instructions to reveal only this much to you upon proof your identity—please, do not tell them, or anyone, the nature of this knowledge. To involve others is to endanger them as well as yourself. Don't worry, the rest will be revealed to you at the proper time."

The camera had zoomed out to take in the beautiful, beautiful conservatory with the view over the incredible blue sea.

"Thank you for having listened so attentively. Please be assured, everything will be explained to you shortly, and please, do heed my warnings. They are not the ravings of a crazy old man. They are truth. You have enemies; they are cruel and powerful. But you have allies, also, where you last expect them."

The next morning, while the frenetic corporate life of QHPSL gyred madly about the four glass walls of her workstation, she called Mr. Saul Martland of Ludlow, Allison, MacNab.

"Was that all there was?"

"That all what was?"

"The tape."

"The tape?"

"There weren't any files, or boxes, or documents?"

"I'm afraid you have me at a disadvantage . . ."

"Would it be possible to see the house?"

"Whose house?"

"His house."

"Oh, that house. Yes, I could arrange that. You would have to be accompanied by the keyholder, though."

"And where can I get in touch with the keyholder?"

"I am the keyholder. I'll pick you up after work."

It was almost an invitation to dinner.

Mr. Saul Martland drove an anonymous German something car with Catcon. Enye ran her fingertips along the acrylic spines of his car cassette collection, slipped the Amsterdam Concertgebouw recording of the Mozart Flute and Harp Concerto into the stereo—several models up from hers, she noted—and immediately found herself worrying that she might be thought overly populist and insufficiently contemporary. Or, horror, *rockist*.

They drove south in the German-something car, beside the catenary wires of the rapid transit system. The red and white striped twin stacks of the city's main power station could be seen across the bay. They could be seen from just about anywhere in the city. If any feature could be said to typify the city, it was those red and white striped stacks. They drove past the terminal where the ferries to England took on French and Dutch articulated trucks, and past the Martello Tower where plump, stately Buck Mulligan shaved himself in the sacramental bowl. They drove to a district where white villas clung to the side of a wooded hill behind white walls and remote-control wrought-iron gates and monitored each other's comings and goings through long-red video eyes.

Fire had utterly razed the house. The white walls were scarred with scorch marks that looked like human figures leaping in a furnace. The roofless rooms were clogged with a litter of charred wooden beams, rotting plaster, and rain-soaked carpet. Weeds had taken root in the mouldering rubble.

The beautiful beautiful conservatory had survived untouched by the flames, though some of the wooden floorboards had been pulled up and discarded under the shelves that held the dead plants in their terra-cotta pots. The wicker furniture was covered in singed dust sheets.

"How did it happen?"

"The house burned three days after the death. Arson, without a doubt. They tried to pin it on the housekeeper, but it wouldn't fit. Neighbours reported seeing figures escaping down the road just before the place burned."

Enye looked through the filmy panes down the wooded hillside, with its secretive villas and narrow, winding avenues tumbling down to the long crescent of sand that swept up into a rock head as bare as the one from which she viewed was populated, and the incredibly blue sea.

"I thought there would be something here."

"Something like?"

"I don't know. The tape hinted at information. Files, notebooks, something. Knowledge, he said. Knowledge."

"There's nothing here, unless you want to rip up the remainder of those floorboards."

She traced a finger track in the old dust. A man's dust—the disintegrated fragments of his outer integument—remains after him. Windsurfers in macaw-bright rubber suits cut chords and arcs across the crescent bay.

"How did he die?"

"His housekeeper found him. He was in his wheelchair, just here, in this conservatory. He had been hacked to ribbons. In the night, someone had entered the house and murdered him. The police said it looked as if it had been done with a sharp blade of some kind—a sword, perhaps. There were signs of a break-in. Despite the evidence pointing to the fact that the old man knew who his killer was, they never got anyone for the killing."

"Most murder victims know their murderers."

"Strange thing—he didn't put up a fight. Not that he could have done much, but he didn't even make token

resistance. Just sat in his chair as if he was expecting it.
Pathologist said he'd never seen an expression quite like
his. Like a saint, he said. Utter serenity."

"He said in the tape he had enemies. Powerful and cruel
enemies. I rather fear I may have made them my enemies,
too." Enye looked at the bright sails of the windsurfers on
the incredible blue sea. "Can we go now? I've seen
enough."

As they drove back toward the red and white striped
smokestacks in the German-something car, he asked her if
she would have dinner with him, some time. If that was all
right, if she hadn't anything planned, would she?

She said she would.

If that was how it began, this is how it ends.

She has given him all she can. Her time, her emotions,
her love, her desire, her body. He wants more. He wants her
soul, he wants her life. He wants all her days and all her
darkest nights; he wants to shine the light of his love into
her every shadowy corner. And she cannot let him do that.
He wants permanency, he wants commitment. And she
cannot give that. When a man is come thirty-wise, he needs
more than days apart and nights together, days together and
nights apart. He is too old for boys' games; he needs a
firmer definition of what *relationship* means: he *needs to
know where he stands*.

Enye despises that expression. *Knows where he stands*.
Hypocrisy. What he really needs to know is where he lies,
where he sleeps, and with whom, and for how long.

He wants them to live together. He is a liberated man. He
would not mind moving in with her if that is what she
wants, though her apartment is half the size of his and less
well equipped, and in not such a highly sought-after area. It
does not matter. He wants to live with her, be with her,
share her days and her nights.

And she will not let him do that.

He gets angry. Worse than his anger is his suspicion. She
knows he imagines a thousand vile and agonising betrayals,
suspects treachery behind her every secret and in every

word she leaves unspoken. He has accused her of ten thousand lies in concealing the truth from him. It never ceases to confound her how one who loves her so much can hate her so much.

"Your goddamn precious independence." On his lips the word becomes a weapon, an arrow. It wounds her to the quick, time after time after time. "You can be so damn immature, so adolescent. This quest for independence, for living your own life, for finding yourself—it's something most people grow out of when they grow hairs they can sit on."

The arrow wounds her every time because she would love to give Saul all her days and her nights. *Independence* she discovered long ago to be fool's gold. She *needs* as much as he. She *wants* as much as he. But she cannot come any closer to him. She fears that the secrets of her darkest nights would destroy them both.

Sometimes she wishes he would be unfaithful (though fidelity was never an agreed clause of their contract). Or just take himself out of mind and memory; then it would not be her fault. She gets so angry when he tries to talk about it, and he becomes angry because he thinks she is angry at him, but she is angry at them, her enemies—the ones who have damned her, one way or another, to lose the love of Saul Martland.

In another, secret life, the war continues. Beneath a winter sky crazy with air signs, she cruises past the pitch once, twice, three times, to be sure her talent has not misled her, to be sure *this* is the one. Contact trembles on the edge of her web of Shekinah sense: not a strong contact; she will have to watch and wait. She parks the Citroen 2CV down an entry out of the sodium-yellow street glow, settles back into the seat, clicks the Schoenberg quartet into the new stereo she bought to replace the one she lost last time out hunting.

The sleek, metallic cars of the executive castes come and go, cruising, crawling, streamlined contours catching highlights from the street lamps, tyres shurring softly, slowly, on the wet blacktop. The prostitutes bend low to the open power windows, dull bovine faces the colour of cancer by the dashboard light. Breath hangs in steaming clouds. Even in her car Enye is cold—fingers, toes, nose, numb. How must it be for these creatures in their hot pants, Grand Canyon cleavages, and fishnets? They do not look like humans. Perhaps they do not feel the cold, like the inhuman things they resemble. Aliens. From her dark entry, Enye extends her senses. She has it narrowed down to two or three of them now.

Doors open, doors close—fat, satisfied *clunks*. In the sleek metallic cars, the prostitutes come and go, for quickies in car parks, fellatio in dark side streets. Enye waits. Schoenberg ends. She searches the airwaves for traffic. Between a Christian station beaming Aryan gospel out of Monaco and Radio Moscow she finds late-night news and weather. Fear of interest rate rises. Lines of East German cars at the Hungarian border. Boatloads of refugees interned in Hong Kong. French farm labourer charged with murder of three-week bride. Dow-Jones up. FTSE down. Hang Seng hanging ten despite uncertainty over colony's future in '97. Rain spreading from west to all parts wind variable gusting gale force six gale warnings in force all shipping.

There is only one left—the young one. Face thin, like the face consumption would have, if it had a face, bleach-blonde hair cropped gamine fashion. The men like that—they like them to look like boys. She stands in a Georgian doorway, hands thrust into the pockets of her quilted bomber jacket. Sixteen, fifteen, fourteen?

Touch.

Contact.

She pulls out of the entry, across the street, in beside the kerb. Folds down the passenger-side window. Her mouth is dry. She does not know how she is to do what she has to do.

Spirit of void, spirit of potentiality and expectancy, fill me now.

The girl bends from the waist. Black lace doily dress sticks up in the air like a piece of gingerbread architecture, making the most of her long, Lycra-clad legs.

"Hey, you can forget it. I don't do women."

"It's not for me. It's for a friend."

"Bull. Shit. I know what they look like and they look nothing like you. I don't do women."

"Fifty."

"I said . . ."

"Hundred."

"Jeez, you deaf or something?"

"Two hundred."

"Oh, go on, then. Nothing funny, mind. You got a place?"

"A what?"

"Never mind. Use mine."

Enye hears the hammering, hammering, of her heart as she drives through the streets with the girl beside her crossing and uncrossing and recrossing her long, Lycra-clad legs.

It is not as if she will be killing anything. Anyone. It is only a phagus, a bubble of information, an eddy of Mygmus energy shaped and channelled by mythoconsciousness.

It only thinks that it lives.

No, it will not be as if she will be killing anything. Anyone.

Place is the word. A long tenement attic, partitioned by stud walls that do not reach the steeply pitched roof. Festoons of wet laundry. Condensation trickles down the skylights. A boom-box, a black and white portable, a half-eaten pack of chocolate sweetmeal biscuits, a mattress on the floor. The prostitute mistakes Enye's tension for sexual nervousness. She notices the sports bag Enye is carrying.

"What you got there? No funny stuff, I said. Funny gear'll cost you double."

In the sports bag are *tachi*, *katana*, and computer. Enye sets the bag on the floor, settles on the mattress. The girl is already undressing, back to her.

"Do you mind no lights?"

"Why?"

"I've got like this birthmark, all over my body. It puts some people off. Some people like it, mind."

"Leave the lights."

As the girl wiggles out of her net skirt and silver tights,

Enye unpacks the swords, unsheathes then, uncoils the lead from her computer.

"Jeez, lights: I think maybe I should charge you treble."

"I'm ready now," Enye whispers. The entire tenement seems to be beating time to the hammer of her heart.

The girl (sixteen, fifteen, fourteen) turns, naked, sees the naked blade of the *katana* in Enye's lap, screams.

Enye once saw a cat run down at midnight on a fast road. It had screamed like that.

"I know what you are."

"Oh my God oh my God oh my God oh my God oh my God oh my God oh my God . . ."

"Please, don't."

The girl squats in a naked, vulnerable huddle on the filthy rug, knees hugged to breasts.

"What are you going to do?"

"I should think that is obvious."

Do you have to?"

"I have to."

Two silent tears rest on the girl's cheekbones. She sniffs. "You know," she says. "You know, I think I always hoped that you, someone like you, would come, so I could get back there. I hated her for sending me here, but I hate her more for never letting me forget where I come from." She stands, opens herself to Enye's eyes. A green-brown birth-mark covers her from right shoulder to waist—breasts, belly, upper arm, neck. "She left me with it to always remind me where I am from."

"I don't understand."

"Look close," the prostitute says. And in the cold attic room with the condensation trickling down the cracked skylights, Enye inspects the girl's body and the stain seems to be suggestive of gulfs and peninsulas, great sweeping hinterlands studded with landlocked seas of pale, unblem-ished skin, of outlying archipelagoes scattered across belly, hips, thighs. A map.

"Look closer," the prostitute says.

Enye touches her fingers to the girl's dreadful mark.

"No," she whispers, "not a map at all, a land-scape . . ."

She sees with her mythoconsciousness that the fractal

geometries of coastlines and rivers are more than tricks of pigmentation. The mark on the body is not a map, but an actual Otherworld imprinted on the teenage prostitute's skin. Enye feels that if she could but focus closely enough, she would see the green-brown texture of the skin resolve into forests and plains, mountains and valleys, cities and castles and fair Caer Paravels, where palladins and palfrey-women hunt the stag through forests deep as forever with their red-eared hounds. In the silence of the attic room, she hears the horns of Elfland calling through the microforests of Otherworld.

"Ripples. That is all we are. Ripples. You drop a stone into a pond and ripples spread out until they reach the edge, where they cast something up. She came into my world, like something falling from heaven, breaking the skin between our worlds, and sent ripples of our world slopping over into yours. Cast up upon the shore. What's the word?"

"Flotsam."

"You know, when you get to a certain age you understand that *why* questions are useless. Why this? Why that? Because. That's all. Because. I used to stare at myself in the mirror for hours, peering at my reflection with a magnifying glass in the hope that I might see myself one day, down there in those valleys, in the woods, the me that was before she flung me through the skin into this world."

"Did you kill them?"

"We're not all your enemies, lady. And we're not all your allies either. Some of us just . . . are. Some of us make the best of this world. Me, I look around, I see the streets, I see the men, I see the big cars, I see this world of yours . . . jeez.

"Send me back. It's in your power to do it. It's what you would have done if you thought I'd killed them. Don't wimp out on me."

Enye's resolution flutters. She sees her sword lying naked on the bed, sees the uncompromising sharpness of its blades.

"It's what you came to do. Come on, do it."

She lifts the computer in her hands, holds it out wonderingly.

"If you didn't, then who did?"

"There are a lot of us, lady. All different. We don't all know each other. There's one who does . . . only one who does."

"Who?"

"Argus. That's what he calls himself. I've never met him, but I've felt him watching. That's what he does. He would know."

"How can I find him?"

"Same way you found me, lady. Now. Do it."

Grey lines mesh and twine on the small screen. The naked girl takes the multiway connector. Opens her mouth. Smiles.

Puts the connector into her mouth.

Enye does not look as she presses *Enter*.

And the sour, cold attic room is empty.

(Shortly after the fall of the Stone Gardanian Empire, Shane the aged aged liver and cream springer spaniel (run over by Enye on her tricycle while in his doggy prime and cursed ever after with a Richard-the-Thirdian hobble) had embarked on his last journey to the rubber-topped table. His sudden, unexpected squattings and fruitless strainings had been amusing, if puzzling, in the garden or on walks; in front of guests in the middle of the living room carpet, not once, not twice, but seven times, it had been a case for Curt Morrow MRCVS's evening surgery.

"It's his heart," Curt Morrow MRCVS had said. Heart conditions show up as symptoms of trying to pass a bowling ball? They did. And suddenly Curt Morrow MRCVS was asking her mother would she like to stay while he put the poor old thing out of its misery and her mother sat too God-struck even for tears and she heard herself say yes, she would. Someone ought to be there with it. Would that be all right? She sat by the rubber-topped table and held Shane's paw while Curt Morrow MRCVS filled the syringe and she could not tell when the paw changed from living paw to dead.

It is like that, but not exactly. No, she looks at that dead dog on the table, and herself holding its paw because someone had to do it, and it is not really like that all.)

(One blue and yellow January afternoon when she was quite young, before Somethings had started Happening at

Home and the visits to Ballybrack, she had seen two boys on the beach, dense silhouettes on the hard, shining sand ripples, beating at something with sticks. She went to see what they were beating and saw it was a beached jellyfish. They split open its dome of translucent jelly, smashed the delicate indigo and violet internal organs, scattered quivering chunks of flesh, beat them into the damp January sand. Filled with righteous indignation at their joyful cruelty, she had shouted at them, "Don't kill it. That's cruel. Don't hurt it!"

They had paused in their beating, beating, beating, to laugh at her.

"Stupid, don't you know, it's dead already!"

That is how it is. Dead already. But the unspeakable cruelty.)

She can imagine what Saul will see when he answers the door. Drained, dark, shadow-ridden, hag-ridden: she looks as if she has been to hell and back in one night, he says once he has gotten over the initial incomprehension at finding her on his doorstep on the wrong side of midnight. He is not far wrong there, she thinks.

She asks can she come in.

Come in, come in, please, come in, he says. My God, you look terrible.

She knows she looks terrible. She feels worse. Deep down, in her spirit, her *Chi* she feels filthied. The last few micrograms of Shekinah circling in her bloodstream feel like ash. She knows it is dangerous to have come here. She knows that her swords and computer and Shekinah capsules are in her car, knows that he is bound to ask questions, but she needs him, needs his presence, his life, his light, his warmth and energy, to rekindle her embers. She puts her arms around him and pulls him to her and buries herself in his geological mass. For the first time in a long time, it is a healing for her.

She vacuumed the apartment for his coming, put little individual shell-shaped soaps in the bathroom, polished the brass, agonised for half an hour about what to be wearing when she so casually answered the door. The little black number. It had never failed before. With the Berber silver earrings.

He came precisely at the appointed hour.

She added that to the list of things she liked about Saul Martland. *Punctuality*. Later, it was to become just another of the thousand thousand irritations that drove them apart. But not yet.

He was wearing jeans going going gone at the knee, battered Doc Marten's boots, and a plaid shirt soft as a kiss from washing. His hair was swept back from his face like the bow wave of a destroyer.

He looked, Enye thought, *fantastic*. (Realising that this is how it progresses.) But not especially like someone on a dinner date.

He drove her in the German-something car through the darkening streets (while she began to worry if maybe the little black number with the Berber earrings was too much—she did not want to be thought of as *tarty*), out of the city to a country lane that ran by the threshold lights of the airport. In the yellow glide path lights Saul unloaded coolbox coolpak coolsac. They sat together on the hood of the German-something car and drank supermarket Spumante from snap-together plastic champagne flutes and Enye in her black number and Berber earrings would have remarked that a picnic at the end of runway one was not what she had had in mind when she accepted Mr. Saul Martland's dinner invitation but for the shattering scream of a Boeing back-throttling in toward the countdown markers. She had never heard anything so loud. The roar consumed everything, filled the entire universe. The scream of the turbofans drew out all her dark and hidden emotions, all her frustrations and quiet desperations in one long, cathartic yell, screaming back at the engines. The aircraft's belly lights swept over them; the undercarriage hung perilously close to them . . . And it was gone, thumping down on the tyre-streaked concrete beyond the threshold lights.

"God!" she shouted. "God God God God. That was amazing!"

"Here comes another one," said Saul, and as it passed over them, huge as a falling moon, they both yelled and surrendered all their frustrations at being humans in a city, in a society, among other, frustrating humans, to the thunder of the engines. Beneath the belly lights of the low-flying aircraft they laughed and toasted to nothing and smashed their empty plastic champagne glasses down.

She offered Saul coffee back at her apartment, of course. Of course, Saul accepted.

She busied herself with the Mr. Coffee (a present from Jaypee's last trip to New York—the most American thing he could find), and out of the corner of her eye watched Saul explore her apartment: squatting down to run a finger along the hard acrylic spines of her CDs, cocking head on one side to read the titles of her books, picking up her Chinese pots and Satsumaware to check the authenticity of the chops on their bases.

The aroma of Mr. Coffee doing his business drifted from the dining area into the living room.

"This is yours?"

He held the *katana* out before him in both hands. The companion sword rested in its wooden cradle. He made to draw the sword.

"No. Don't . . ." In two steps she was beside him, taking the sword from his hands. "There's a right way to draw a sword, and a wrong way. *Saya*—that is, the part of the sheath that covers the *yakiba*, the cutting edge, upper-most. Cup the *saya* with the left hand, so, with the *tsuba*, the guard, at the centre of the body, the *Tan Tien*. Thumb of the left hand secure on the *tsuba*. Now, as you take breath . . . draw, with dignity and respect."

She brought the sword down to her right side in the position called *Waki Kamae*.

"Where did you learn all this?" Saul asked.

"University. I'd always been interested in Japan and Japanese culture."

"A yen for Japan?"

"Ha ha. As soon as I got the chance, I studied *kendo*; there's a good dojo at the university. I'm in a private dojo now. Bamboo sword first, then, only if the *sensei* thinks you are good enough, do you progress to the *katana*. The skill is in stopping the blade just before it cuts your enemy. So. *Nihon Me. Sanbon Me. Yonhon Me. Gohon Me.*

Roppon Me. Nanahon Me." The sword was a song of steel about Saul's head, chest, arms, torso, dancing from position to position, never quite touching. The point finally came to rest on his breastbone, just touching the second button of his soft plaid shirt.

"*Chudan No Kamae*," she whispered, and the sword was a channel between them, a conductor of sexual electricity. Her breast heaved, but her sword arm was miraculously steady. She looked at his eyes and she felt she would destroy herself in a white noiseless blast of sexual tension.

"I think your coffee's ready," he said. Enye bowed, resheathed the sword, and returned it to the company of the *tachi*.

He did not try to sleep with her. He drove off through the drizzle and the cones of damp yellow streetlight in his anonymous Teutonic car. She watched him drive away through chinked blinds. She lay on the bed with a whiskey and Sibelius's Fifth in the machine, feeling vast, attenuated; flickering across a borderline between incredible presence and ecstatic self-loss, where the LEDs of her midi system became the riding lights of colossal, imaginary starships. Her childhood memories contained many such sacred moments of numinosity: watching from her bedroom window the silver rain of the Orionids, on the beach at sunset with Shane the dog and Paddy the dog; grey Saturday mornings, dark November afternoons, the smell of pine, Vaughn Williams's orchestration of "The First Noel." Her mother had had a wonderful expression for it: "Cloud-gathering."

He had looked *fantastic*.

And so had she.

The sexual symbolism of the swords was a dark crimson throb behind her navel she thought invisible to all others, but which in truth could have been no less visible had it been stamped on her forehead in letters of fire.

Enye. In. Love.

She denied it. Of course.

But Jaypee read the signs. Judi-Angel from Traffic read the signs and wanted to know, under the conspiratorial roar of the hot-air hand dryer in the Ladies' Room, Just Who He Was. The Blessèd Phaedra, while congratulating her on a particularly successful campaign for DairyCrest Creameries, saw the signs. Oscar the Bastard, too. Even Mrs. O'Verall.

Her *sensei* at the dojo saw it.

"The sword may be a phallic symbol, but it doesn't mean you have to wield it like a dick," he said. Enye, exuberant and sweating from the fight, knelt, bowed in *seiza* to her partner, tried not to blush. "The Way of the Sword lies in the control of energy, not spraying it around all over the place like a fire hose." The farthest east Enye's *sensei* had ever been was a European Championship in Belgium. His Zen proverbs tended to the homely.

She was last out of the dojo. The city was dark as she drove under the yellow streetlights to L'Esperanza Street. She took the car around the back to the service alley; there had been a spate of window-smashings and stereo-stealings. Mr. Antrobus's tumbledown lockup where the black Phoenix bicycle resided between enigmatic early-morning excursions provided a small measure of security. She checked the padlock, rattled the rusted hasp, went to pick up her bag and swords. Paused. Troubled by a sense of presence she could not attribute to dogs, cats, rats, bats, or any other legitimate night-farer.

"Hello?"

The shadows around the gate into Mr. Antrobus's garden seemed arranged differently.

"Hello?" A wait. For . . . nothing.

"I-ma-ma-ma-ma-ma ma-magination," she sang, shouldered the equipment, fumbled for the rattly gate catch. "I-ma-ma-ma-ma-ma-ma . . ."

The shadows around the gate stirred.

Teeth—each the length of her own fingers—opened and snapped shut like a gin trap in her face. Fangs, claws, flaring nostrils, hair, burning eyes. Pure shock sprawled her back across the laneway among rusted sweet corn cans and crushed paper milk cartons.

Something uncoiled to its full height and stepped with dreadful ease over Mr. Antrobus's back gate into the laneway.

Something with three heads.

Three *heads*. Dog heads. Rottweiler, Doberman, pit bull terrier. But it walked erect like a man: a hybrid of Cerberus and Minotaur. She scrabbled away from it in the litter and detritus and acid-rain-blighted private hedge. The fingers of her right hand closed on the leather bound *habaki* of the long sword.

The Cerbertaur took a step forward, dog heads gobbling and snapping.

The fingers of her left hand touched the sheath of the short sword.

She would have liked to have cast herself in the role of Righteous Avenger (Emma Peel in black leather cat suits a formative childhood media memory), but what action she took was the pure application of years of submission to the Way of the Sword. Crouching in the shadow of the mythological abomination, she flicked the sheaths from the blades. No time, no thought for the niceties of propriety and respect. The Rottweiler head lunged for the killing bite through the throat. Enye met it with a desperate cut of the *katana*. Neatly severed, the Rottweiler head tumbled across the rutted mud trailing gobbets of blue ichor.

Purest of spirits: spirit of instinct. The purest form of combat—that which is without conception or strategy, the strategy of strategylessness. Stunned by the unexpected resistance, the Cerbertaur hesitated. Enye cut again. It reeled barely in time—the tip of the *katana* shaved whiskers from the pit bull head. Composure recovered, it advanced again. The hedge-lined laneway was filled with its growlings and slobberings and Enye's panicky swearing. She retreated behind a wall of swordplay toward the street entrance, and light, and movement, and traffic. It was never an equal contest. Mere flesh and fang, however enchanted, were no match for Murasama steel. Within metres of the street her flowing-water cut sent the last head, the pit bull one, into the darkness. Headless, the thing reached its arms helplessly toward the streetlights, toppled like a felled skyscraper. Enye waited, panting, trembling with shock and exertion, swords ready in the attitude of "open on all eight sides" Waited. Waited.

Waited.

Stepped forward to slip past, down the alleyway, into the garden (thinking: *God, what do I do with this—call the police or what? Someone's going to find it sooner or later*).

The fingers of the dead left hand twitched. Flexed. The headless body heaved itself up from the ground, crawled toward her on its elbows.

Enye ran.

A white Italian hatchback pulled up at the end of the entry. The passenger door opened. The driver, a faceless figure in a grubby white hooded sweat top with a Tibetan mandala on the front, shouted, "Get in!"

The voice was a man's, though she could not make out his features beneath the pulled-up hood.

"Get the hell in, right now! It's starting to regenerate itself."

Unable to think of anything wiser to do, she swung into the white Italian hatchback. Before the door was even closed the driver was burning away in a melodrama of smoking radials.

"Nice work with the swords. They weren't expecting resistance. It'll be ready next time, though. Get a bloody move on!" The driver slammed the horn at an aged aged Ford scabbed with grey spray primer pulling slowly away from traffic lights; swung out, overtook, horn pumping. "They regenerate. It'll take more than swords to stop them. Thankfully, you did enough damage that it will take it quite a while to regenerate a new manifestation, but it'll be back. Bank on it. We just hope we can teach you enough so you'll be ready for it next time."

"Look, friend . . ."

"A Nimrod. Or rather, *the* Nimrod. As in Nimrod, the hunter. And you, the hunted."

The white Italian hatchback stopped dead at a red light. Enye bounced her forehead painfully on the sun visor.

"Should wear a belt," said the driver, tapping his fingers on the steering wheel. "Come on come on come on. . . ."

Impaled by a fateful spike of curiosity, Enye took the moment of opportunity the lights presented to reach across and pull down the grubby white sweatshirt hood.

The face, the entire head of her rescuer, was deformed into a curve of flesh and bone, a crescent moon, a moon face. She reached for the door handle, pulled futilely. Moonface had his finger on the centralised locking button.

He pulled the hood back around his features while traffic queued behind him hooted in frustration.

"Sorry sorry sorry sorry," Enye whispered as the moon-faced man jammed the white Fiat savagely into gear and jumped the lights as they changed back to red.

"No matter. No matter. Better you'd found out when you were ready, but you had to find out eventually. I'm on your side, I promise. An ally." The car drove away from the lights and neons and faery-light-spangled trees of the main thoroughfares into a dismal district of recession-hit video libraries, peeling posters for gigs by bands long broken up, and municipal housing. "He did mention to you about enemies and allies."

"We're talking about Dr. Rooke."

"Yes. Him. I—rather, we—are the allies."

"And that was, that is, if I take you right, the enemy?"

"Got it in one. A phagus. A few are good, some indifferent, most are bad. Well, maybe not bad. Let's say, their concerns are not human concerns."

"And would you count yourself one of the good ones?"

"Shit, no. We're not phaguses. We're humans. Most of the time. If you cut us, do we not bleed?"

"*Merchant of Venice*?"

"Very good. Very good. You can get out now. This is as far as we go." The white Fiat slewed into a narrow cobbled laneway that opened into a small court half-filled with massive industrial galvanised steel garbage bins. It stank of rotting cabbage and garlic. The moon-faced man carefully dropped the keys down a drain grating.

"Wouldn't want anyone else stealing it."

"I have been risking life and limb in a stolen car?"

"Borrowed. Liberated. All property is theft, and that kind of shit. I can get into most cars in under ten seconds. Come on, get a move on. It'll be getting light in a few hours."

They were six—Moonface, Lami, Sumobaby, Fingers, Cello, and Wolfwere. Collectively they were the Midnight Children, after a celebrated magic-realist novel. Fingers, it was alleged, would read anything. Their habitat was a huddle of cardboard boxes that had once held washing machines and tumble dryers roofed with plastic refuse sacks under the last arch in a brick-vaulted rail viaduct. Night freights across the border clunked ponderously overhead, shook teardrops of drip water from the little calcite stalactites that had leached from the joints in the brickwork. Their fire was a low smudge; they claimed it was a precaution against sparks igniting their flammable city of cardboard crawlways and plastic padded nests. Rather, Enye suspected, it was to conceal their presence and appearances from any other citizens of the night.

Moonface was the leader, the spokesperson, the car thief, the one by dint of his deformities freest to venture abroad in the night city.

Lami was a beautiful, beautiful girl of about twenty. Enye could not understand the nature of her deformity until the shadows among the cardboard hovels stirred and she saw that from the twelfth rib down she wore the form of a flesh-coloured snake. Chattering inanely, she busied herself making coffee over a small camping gas stove. She wore a cut-off T-shirt bearing the legend "SunMed Capo Blanco" and a short denim jacket laden with costume jewellery. Silver bangles jingled softly on her wrists as she busied herself with coffee.

Sumobaby might once have been a man. Once. Now he was a massive wedge of blubber, taller squatting naked and sweating by the fire than Enye was standing. Tiny, Thalidomidesque arms waved uselessly; he did indeed resemble some fat-farm hybrid of sumo wrestler and blue-eyed baby.

Fingers had the body of a woman. In place of her head was a giant hand. When Enye was introduced, the fingers of that hand uncurled from the fist into which they had been clenched to reveal two round blue eyes in the centre of the palm. Two eyes, long eyelashed, blinking. Nothing more. Fingers breathed through a flapping tracheotomy lesion in her throat.

"Lami was a med student," Moonface explained, which was no explanation at all.

Of the six, Cello's deformities were the most horrifying. Whatever transforming power had touched the others had changed him (or her—gender had been swept away in the wave of transformation) into something that, as the name suggested, was nothing other than a cello shaped from human flesh, with a single arm for a fingerboard, a hand for a tuning head, and strung with its own vocal cords. Breath soughed from the F-holes; the strings hummed and whispered, shaping the still air beneath the viaduct into a memory of human speech.

Of the six, Wolfwere seemed the least affected by the changes: a moon-pale, green-eyed girl crouching by the fire in a blanket, never speaking, never looking up, moving only from time to time to lick at her belly and armpits. Then Moonface explained that before the Transforming, she had been his dog. Now she was an inverted were-creature—dog by day, by night a human, with the mind and intellect of a dog. Indeed, all the Midnight Children's terrible deformities were a type of lycanthropy—by day they were young men and women, and dogs, grubbing what living they could from the fringes of society, cars, shoplifting, petty burglary, dope dealing. When the sun set behind the shunting sheds, they reverted to their midnight incarnations.

"Don't confuse the woman," the one called Sumobaby said, jelly-blubber jowls quivering. "None of this will make sense without the archive." Lami nodded. Fingers hissed through her breath hole. Cello's strings seemed to sob in agreement. From a place of safekeeping behind loose bricks in the viaduct wall, Moonface handed a blue Ziploc document folder over the embers to Enye. Manila files, envelopes, loose papers paper-clipped together. The Midnight Children sat drinking their coffee from their black-cat mugs while Enye riffled through the papers. Fingers lifted up the mug to armless Sumobaby's lips.

"This was what Dr. Rooke referred to in his videotape."

"We were the place of safekeeping," said Moonface. "After the murder, we removed the material, according to his instructions."

"So you torched the house."

"No. They did. They hoped to destroy the archive, and so keep themselves safe."

"The phaguses?"

"Some of them."

"Let her read," said Sumobaby. "It will not make sense until she does."

Lami passed joints around the fire. Sumobaby and Fingers shared one, between lips and trach hole.

Pick at random. Inspiration of the Holy Spirit. Enye pulled a manila envelope from the plastic file, began reading. In the background, all-night radio played, wired into a car battery, all the oldies, all the favourites, the ones that make your day when Mistah DeeJay plays them on the radio.

The Mygmus may be viewed not so much as a place, a spatio-temporal relationship, a quasi-Euclidean geometrical domain, but as a state. *The concept is a familiar one in modern quantum physics, in which time is not considered a dynamic process, but a succession of recurring states eternally coexistent. Such thinking liberates us from our essentially linear concepts of time, with past, present, and future abacus beads sliding along an infinitely long rail. It enables us to see past and future as states, and our concept of "present" the zone of transition between these two states. The analogy here is the constriction of an hourglass, with the disordered potential events of the future being given order and apparent sequence by the constriction before they pass once again into disorder and timelessness. In both future and past, all events exist together, eternally and atemporally. Everything that is past is past, be it a thousand millennia or a millisecond ago. It is all equally inaccessible—everything that is to come is in the future, whether that be the next minute or the next millennium.*

But how then is it that we perceive an ordered flow of events from future state to past state? Why, to be flippant, is Tuesday October 8, 1958 not followed by Friday, November 9, 1989, or Monday, July 10, 663? The answer, I feel, lies in the word perceive. *Certainly both future and past, as states, potential domains, are contained within the present: all possible events await selection, and are mathematically equally likely. What selects these events and parades them before us in the temporal order we understand of future to present to past, in a continuous and ordered flow, must be nothing other than human consciousness. Consciousness itself may be nothing more than a veil that filters future from present from past, that shuts out the inconceivable anarchy of all possible events and reduces it to our familiar linear time sense.*

If, then, the present is a function of our consciousness,

therefore the past must also, in a sense, be a figment of our imaginations. By selecting an order for events, we select therefore also the order in which they pass from present state to past state.

Common to every people is this concept of a timeless time: the Dreamtime, the Age of Gold, the Ginnungagap—a state of timelessness and changelessness which endures (if endure *is a valid word to use in the context of something essentially nontimebound) eternally, or would have endured eternally save that some event, usually, the creation of humanity, and human consciousness, caused change in the changelessness and unleashed the concept of directed time.*

(Pencilled underneath in faint 3H) *. . . could be that mythoconsciousness predates chronoconsciousness, that our distant ancestors were not what we would define as* sentient. *They perceived their universe with naked understanding, in a time when the gods, their future selves, what they would one day become, waiting in the potential state of future events, literally walked the earth.*

"What does this mean?"

"Read on, sister."

Being subconscious creations, phaguses are beyond, or rather, beneath such upper-brain distinctions as ethical or moral discrimination. This makes them, as faerykind has ever been, both delightful and dangerous, beyond good and evil, and utterly unpredictable. Their sole ethic is that they be true to the subconscious desire (or dread) that created them and shaped their character. They can be both one's stoutest ally and most deadly enemy.

The concept of the Mygmus as a state in which all past events are equidistant and simultaneous strips a little of the mystique from the process of phagus creation.

The symbol-store of the Mygmus is constantly being imprinted with information from the human imagination. What the mytho-creative individual does is remove the "past-tense" tag from an event or person or concept or imagining in the Mygmus, thus making it present-state, and actual.

"Certain individuals have a genetically determined ability to interact with this Mygmus state, and manipulate it according to the terrain of their subconscious mind. Dr. Rooke called this ability *mythoconsciousness*."

A coldness had seeped from the brick, the concrete, the subdawn chill, deep into the fibre of her *chi*, her spirit.

"And I am one such individual."

Or was it the cold of the un-place, the timeless state of the Mygmus?

The one called Cello emitted a sudden, strident discord. The Midnight Children looked in alarm to the sky.

"Soon, Moonface."

"You will have to leave, lady."

"I've hardly even begun . . ."

"Please. We are placing ourselves in considerable danger by allying ourselves openly with you. There is a very real danger that in associating with you, we may attract the attentions of the Nimrod, or worse. It was able to pick out the glow of your emergent mythoconsciousness, as were we—that was how I was able to find you, and in the nick of time, too. It may now be able to discern our presence within the network of mythlines. Our day selves are invisible to the Adversary, unless, that is, you make them known to her. That is why we decided we must hide them from you. Please understand."

"Can I at least take the file?"

Eyes conferred. Fingers closed her hand-head twice, three times.

"I think that would be all right. We'll be here, every night, after darkness has fallen. Please, don't try to look for us by daylight. We will teach you what you need to know to master your ability. Go. Now. Please . . ."

She looked back, of course—as people caught up in legends always do—but there was not one soul to be seen in the cardboard city as the first vagrant light of the cold cold day stole into the shadows under the railroad arch.

A green bus with an advertisement for the Prudential Savings Society she had designed herself came along the road between the shunting yards and the echoing fastnesses of the port authority. There was no stop here but the driver stopped anyway. She had just enough money in the patch-pocket of her Reeboks for the fare. The only other passenger, an all-night drunk, stared and stared and stared at her naked swords.

Of the many, many things she likes about Jaypee Kinsella, the thing that goes to Number One in her Personal Top Ten is that he can invite her to a party, for a drink, for dinner, to the movies, to the opera, to view his collection of early twentieth century plastics, without there ever being a Question of Anything Between Them. They are friends— best friends in a way she can never be best friends with Saul. She tells Jaypee things about Saul she would never never tell Saul about Jaypee. You think it is odd for a man and a woman to be friends like that. You think, there must be *something*; you cannot see how creatures as alien as a man and a woman can be so close without sexual attraction, and when you see that there is Never Any Question of Anything Like That, then you begin to think it is a strange and unnatural relationship. There must be something wrong if they don't feel something for each other. Maybe he is gay, maybe she is, you know, a lesbian. You think it is improper because these people enjoy a closeness and intimacy of relationship without the need for sexual attraction that is missing from your relationships where sex is the only closeness and intimacy you understand. And you are jealous.

But even in the heart of this intimacy lies a shadow.

"Most days you look serious," says Jaypee, vapourizing Mrs. O'Verall with a meson blast from the hyperphazosonic plasmobuster pistol, batteries not included, Enye brought him from a day she had at the seaside with Saul. "Today you are looking exceptionally serious. Crucially serious. Is that man of yours giving you trouble again?" He blows imaginary smoke from the LED nozzle. Mrs. O'Verall, reduced by the beam of coruscating force to an indescribable sphere of radiance suffusing all circumambient space with incandescence, continues on her rounds with her pots of hot water and sachets of assorted herbals and decafs.

"My life is kind of . . . complex," Enye pleads.

And he knows she is hiding the truth within the shadows of her heart, and she knows that he knows, and he knows that she knows that he knows, but the truth stays hidden, in the shadows of her heart.

Putting station idents and pixels and quantels and fractals and all the televisual bestiary of the Computer Aided Design Unit behind them, Jaypee takes Enye for a prime-time pint in an advertising bar close by where people with names like Natasha and Jeremy hold conversation totally in CAPITALS or Initials, or A.C.R.O.N.Y.M.S. and junior copywriters whisper furtively about the Great National Novels they have tucked away in the bottom drawers of their desks.

Jaypee sets two cream-capped jars of the Great National Beverage on the mock Art Deco table.

"To quote the immortal Flann O'Brien, 'A pint of plain is your only man!'" he says by way of toast and invitation to pour it out let it run and plume and splash onto the floor, run out the door and into the streets, fill them with its torrential onrushing, down to the sea, the sea, and forget-fulness. And suddenly she wants more than anything to say it, say it out, say it now. Be free of it; her albatross.

"Jaypee?"

"What?"

"Jaypee, I have something I have to tell you."

"Please remember that you are in licensed premises and may not legally, much less morally and ethically, be responsible for anything you might say."

"No, Jaypee, I have to tell you this. You're my oldest, dearest friend; nobody else knows this, not even Saul."

"I tremble in anticipation."

The words come. In a rush. In a storm. Like many, many birds. They come to the edge of her lips, the tip of her tongue.

And will not go any farther.

"My life is kind of . . . complex."

The shadow.

He knows it. She knows he knows it. He knows she knows he knows it. And as if it is the sign and seal of her isolation, it comes to her: the wrongness, like a throbbing pressure, like a sore about to burst and spew black pus. She excuses herself, makes for the mock Art Deco Ladies' Room, where she cries aloud from the pressure in her head

and heart. She excuses herself, apologises: a migraine.
Jaypee comments that she has been getting a lot of those
lately. Pressure of work, she tells him. He looks at her in a
way that says many things at once, none of them capable of
being spoken aloud. She goes home to wait for night. The
city is dark. In the darkness of her apartment she pops a tab
of Shekinah. She pulls on her black zip-up one-piece. She
ties her hair back from her face. She laces her red shoes
onto her feet. She pulls on a short brocaded jacket and an
embroidered Moroccan hat Jaypee brought her from one of
his many and wide-ranging travels. She goes to the rack in
her living room, bows respectfully, lifts the swords, and
puts them in the back of the car.

She is afraid. Every time, she is afraid. As she drives, the
fear is so intense it is almost sexual. This time she may not
be able to defeat whatever is waiting for her. This time
whatever waits for her may destroy her. Impelled by the
vertiginous swoop of Mygmus energies on the edge of her
perceptions, Enye MacColl drives out of the two A.M. city
to the corrugated steel hulks of a recession-struck industrial
estate close by the threshold lights of the airport. The
location does not surprise her. They tend to be attracted to
places with which she has associations. She stops at a
closed-down factory unit. A hoarding inside the perimeter
wire directs interested parties to a city centre real estate
company. The light in the small glass and plywood booth is
the security guard. He is reading a horror novel by an
American author. A car at this hour does not concern him.
It is a popular area for couples. Enye should know. Under
the scream of back-throttling Boeings she cuts the wire with
a pair of bolt cutters she keeps in the back of the car. She
has quite a respectable little house-breaking kit in there. She
gains entry to the vacant unit and there does battle with an
Iron Age warrior armed with a spear that unfolds into a
rosette of barbs. They battle across the concrete floor,
striking sparks from the steel pillars, while the big jets come
and go in thunder and light. The warrior goes down before
her fire-and-stones cut. She slips out the way she came in,
under the wire, into her car; drives off. The night watchman
is listening to his radio now.

A police car stops her on the way home. She tells the

incredibly young policeman she is coming from a party. The incredibly young policeman shines his torch over her; looks into her face for signs of drink, drugs; checks her license; and salutes as he wishes her a good night, remember to drive carefully. During the entire encounter the incredibly young policeman's overweight, middle-aged partner sat chewing at the edges of a hamburger while the prowl car radio crackled and spat night-static.

When she is sure they are not behind her, she stops the car and shivers spastically for the best part of half an hour from nervous tension.

She opens the door of number twenty-seven L'Esperanza Street to find Ewan watching the late news and drinking her coffee. There have been mass resignations in Eastern Europe, apparently, and bomb warnings to American airlines. A delegation of twelve European Muslims has failed to lift the death sentence for blasphemy imposed upon a prize-winning author. The star of an Australian soap opera is to appear in a pornographic movie.

She is furious. And afraid. There are things he should not see all around him.

"What the hell are you doing here?"

"Your landlord let me in. Said you wouldn't be long. What time do you call this?"

"Is my brother my keeper? Just what do you want?"

"What do you think?"

"Our mother. Our sacred, virginal mother."

"She's been to the doctors. They say there's nothing wrong with her—nothing medical, that is. They say she's as fit as a flea, but she's going downhill, Enye. Downhill. You should see her—she's lost pounds, she's listless, she has no energy, no enthusiasm, won't eat, won't talk, won't go out. She's sick. She's a sick woman. She's a woman who has made herself sick. She's a woman who is being eaten from within because her own daughter will not forgive her for what she did to her father."

"Well, let me tell you why this daughter will not forgive her mother. Because her mother lied to her. Not once, not twice, not three times, or ten times, but repeatedly, constantly, for fourteen years. She lied to me, to us, to both of us, Ewan, never forget that, about why our father left. She has never told us the truth, she never will. I know she lied. I was here, at the time of the Christmas tree."

Names have power. To name a memory, to say it out, is to live it again.

She cannot remember why she is decorating the Christmas tree on her own; that has been edited out, cut and recut like life in an Australian soap opera. She is draping tinsel garlands over the branches of the fir by the glow of the faery lights. She loves that glow—it is the light of Christmas, the Christ light captured in a hundred tiny glowings. The doorbell rings, she goes to answer it. It is a man her father worked with. She knows him vaguely; he obviously knows her better than she knows him. Can he come in? Yes. Can he sit down? Yes. She continues decorating the tree. They are both uncomfortable.

Is her mother in? No.

It's about her dad. Just to say, when he comes back, if he comes back, his job's open. Any time, he can have it, we'll always find a place for him.

And he goes.

And she knows . . .

(Slipping the rubber band around Li'l Lilli Langtree the faery's wasp waist onto the top of the tree)

. . . that this is the first of too many moments she will never be able to share.

"She said they'd fired him because he had been embezzling money. She said it wasn't the first time it had happened, but it was the last—she couldn't live with someone she couldn't trust."

"And?"

"I am too much like my mother."

"For God's sake, because of a little white lie, you won't forgive her?"

"Won't. Can't. As I said, I am too much like my mother."

"She's willing to forgive you."

"Very magnanimous."

"She needs your forgiveness."

"I don't know. Maybe. Just drink your coffee and go away, Ewan. I don't know anything anymore."

When he has gone, long gone, she goes to the telephone.

There are a number of messages on her answering machine, all of them from Saul. He is angry, a sound to be pondered over, savoured. It is a rare vintage, Saul's anger. Where the hell is she, what is she doing, and with whom? This is the way it ends, staking claims around other's lives, with demands, and suspicions, and message after message on answering machines.

She cuts the machine off.

"Saul, my life is kind of complex," she whispers. On the pale blue screen tomorrow's weather unfurls across the country in neatly positioned symbols. She punches a number she has never quite managed to forget.

It is ringing. Two, three, four times. It is late. There will be wondering, who can be phoning at this time of the night? Maybe there will be alarm, maybe fear. Maybe she should hang up and call again another night, another week. Six times. Eight times.

"Hello? Who is this?"

She cannot say it.

"Hello? Hello? Who is this? Who's calling?"

She cannot say it. Not one word of it.

"What's going on here? Who's calling? Look, you had better tell me who you are or I'm putting the phone down, right now."

"Hello?"

"Hello?"

"It's me."

Even those words are too many. She presses the hangup button. Prrrrrrr. After a time that seems like no time but is longer than she has realised, a computer-generated voice says, "Please replace the handset and try again. Please replace the handset and try again. Please replace the handset and try again. Please replace the handset and try again. Please replace the handset and try again. Please replace the handset and try again. Please replace the handset and try again. . . ."

He who does not have the spirit of discipleship will never become a Master of the Way. The spirit of discipleship is the

*Way of the teachable spirit. The Way of the teachable spirit
is the spirit of the open hand; which is the spirit that brings
nothing with it, that lays claim to no thing, no value, no
knowledge; the spirit that is open and receptive.*

Her *sensei*, in his homespun Zen *koans*, often chided
Enye that the only thing that stood between her and true
mastery of the Way of the Sword was the want of a
teachable spirit. "Your hands are too full," he would say,
striking the knuckles of them gently with the sheath of his
katana. "Your head is too full—full of strategies and tactics
and cluttering thoughts. That may be the Way of Advertising, but sure as shit it isn't the Way of the Sword. Let go,
woman. For the love of God, just for once, let go. What the
hell is it you're holding onto so tightly?"

She was never sure.

Only when she came to kneel at the feet of new Masters
did she begin to understand what he meant. With the fall of
the early autumn nights she would return, and return again
to the place beneath the railroad arch where the Midnight
Children in their exquisite deformity waited to lead her in
the new Way.

She learned the names and natures of her enemies, the
phaguses, the Nimrod—both names uncomfortable and
unwieldy, though in time they would become as familiar as
old gloves—and why, despite the appalling wounds she had
inflicted upon it, the Nimrod had refused to die, was even
now regenerating itself into a new form. Not being any kind
of living creature, but a manufacture of the subconscious
mind, it, all phaguses, would continue to manifest themselves as different aspects of that same subconscious mind-
set. Until either the anomaly in the reality/Mygmus inter-
face that permitted their existence was restored to harmony.
Or the subconscious mind-set was erased.

She learned the name and nature of her own power: *mythoconsciousness*. The word tasted bitter at first, like her first sip
of ceremonial Japanese tea, but as she drank deeper of it, so its
sacramental nature filled her being. Mythoconscious—she
was mythoconscious; of that rarest sisterhood that throughout
human history had channelled and shaped humanity's deepest
fears and hopes into the gods, demons, and heroes of its
darkest nights. *Mythoconscious:* she wielded the name, the

title, like a sword; like a sword, it cut reality and left it bleeding.

"Unlike your Adversary, you don't have the gift of the great dream-shaping," Sumobaby told her, with the ember light raising dull highlights on his sweating flesh and the boom box wired to the car battery beating it out into the night hip-hop rhythm. "The genes were diluted by recessives. Skipped a generation. You have only recently developed the ability to interact with the Mygmus. The talent must be consciously developed if you are to bring the healing."

And, pressed up close to the afterglow warmth of Saul's sleeping body in her bed, she read from the Rooke archive by the light from the yellow streetlights:

I have this dread that afflicts me in the dead of night: it is that somehow, we have lost the power to generate new mythologies for a technological age. We are withdrawing into another age's mythotypes, an age when the issues were so much simpler, clearly defined, and could be solved with one stroke of a sword called something like Durththane. We have created a comfortable, sanitised pseudofeudal world of trolls and orcs and mages and swords and sorcery, big-breasted women in scanty armour and dungeonmasters; a world where evil is a host of angry goblins threatening to take over Hobbitland and not starvation in the Horn of Africa, child slavery in Filipino sweatshops, Colombian drug squirarchs, unbridled free market forces, secret police, the destruction of the ozone layer, child pornography, snuff videos, the death of the whales, and the desecration of the rain forests.

Where is the mythic archetype who will save us from ecological catastrophe, or credit card debt? Where are the Sagas and Eddas of the Great Cities? Where are our Cuchulains and Rolands and Arthurs? Why do we turn back to these simplistic heroes of simplistic days, when black was black and white biological washing-powder white?

Where are the Translators who can shape our dreams and dreads, our hopes and fears, into the heroes and villains of the Oil Age?

And again, with the rain cutting in sheer and cold across

the grey industrial sloblands, she muffled up in her fleecy hooded sweat top:

"You keep telling me telling me telling me I'm to bring healing. I don't know what you mean, how, even why."

Raindrops drummed on the black plastic roof to their small council chamber. Lami had coiled herself tight, hugging thin arms about her body for warmth. The joints passed around the circle, to the left-hand side, to the widdershins, the witching side. Moonface spoke.

"The deeper your Adversary pushs her roots into the Mygmus, the more powerful she becomes, the more the boundary between present-state and Mygmus-state become uncertain. It may not be tomorrow, it may not be next year, next decade, but a time is coming when the distinctions between reality and Mygmus become so tenuous they vanish altogether."

Lami took up the thread. Fingers exhaled a pale tree of aromatic smoke from her scar.

"We're talking the collapse of consensus reality, of our comprehension of a universe of space and directed time. Cause and effect would cease to exist; present time, past time, and future time would cease to be discrete entities; everything would exist simultaneously and eternally. Things would happen, events occur, objects be created and decreated without any causation or reason."

"Chaos," Sumobaby said. "Utter chaos."

"But how?" Enye shouted. "How how how? You never tell me how. My God, I'm supposed to save the universe, and you won't even tell me how I can get through next week."

"Help from beyond comprehension," said Moonface, grinding out the roach on the cardboard floor with the heel of his Doc Marten's. "Your own mythoconscious talent is the only thing that can help you. Somehow, somewhen, it will provide you with a weapon."

"And Shekinah," said Lami.

"Shekinah," Sumobaby whispered, and Cello moaned a minor chord, and Fingers folded her hand-head tight, into a gesture that spoke more eloquently the word *danger* than any words ever could.

The name of Shekinah was one the Midnight Children

mentioned often; one which, when questioned, they hid from Enye's light in some deep dark casket of sorrows. But there were hints and allusions in the Rooke archive.

If we accept mythoconsciousness as an altered state akin to hypnosis, dreaming, drug hallucination, may it not be possible to artifically induce it, as these other states may be artifically induced? In the past I had success in inducing a mythoconscious state through hypnosis; admittedly, in a naturally highly mythoconscious individual. Might it not, through artificial means, be possible to stimulate the mythoconscious talent we all possess, even in subjects as singularly insensitive as myself?

I think the answer may lie in the use of drugs. The sacramental use of narcotics has a central role in many religions—not in the least Christianity. After all, alcohol is the most abused narcotic. The mystical experience seems common to all religions, and depends largely on the use of disorienting media (in Hinduism, repeated mantras: in Zen, the psychic assault of repeated questions; in Sufism, the physical act of whirling; in Christian hermeticism, extreme physical sensation through the mortification of the flesh) to induce altered states of consciousness.

They mythoconscious state is closely allied to the mystical state. It might be possible, using some form of psychedelic drug, to break down the walls between consciousness and mythoconsciousness, between present, aware state and Mygmus.

It is a very gentle kind of psychedelia methinks; certainly contemporary synthetics are too powerful and too crude. I rather favour older, more natural drugs, from fungi and the leaves of certain plants. Fungi seem to hold out particular promise—there are a number of specimens that can induce psychotropic hallucinations.

Saul stirred in his massive sleep. Umble-grumble: *Whajja readin'?*

"Nothing. Nothing, Go back to sleep. Little lawyer's got himself a busy day in court tomorrow."

Mr. Antrobus knocked on her door before the shower-and-muesli hour next morning, wondering if she knew of anything untoward going on in the rear laneway.

No, should she have? (*Liar*. And to dear Mr. A.)

Only that he had heard funny noises last night as he was putting the cats out. Like dogs. But not exactly.

The nihilistic November rain was still raining raining raining down as she walked across the scablands toward the smudge fire of the Midnight Children.

"It's a drug, isn't it? Hannibal Rooke's mythoconsciousness enhancing drug."

"Mythoconsciousness *creating* . . ." Moonface's correction was cut short by the touch of Lami's hand on his sleeve.

"We've got to tell her." Those of the Midnight Children capable of assent agreed. Wolfwere scratched under her blanket at her crotch. Lami pulled her human torso close to the fire, zipped shut the leather biker's jacket over a raggedly cut-off cerise leotard. "What the Rooke archive doesn't tell you is that Hannibal Rooke needed assistants in his experiment to find his mythoconsciousness drug. Five of them. One was a psych post-grad, one was a doctor of chemistry, one was an undergrad pharmacist, one was an anthropologist researching sacramental narcotics among Orinoco Amerindians. And one was a med student."

"You."

"It's a long and fairly uninteresting story. The research finally culminated in a combination of drugs that stimulated those areas of the hippocampus that seemed connected with human chronoconsciousness. Rooke tried it himself, of course. We took notes, shot a video. There's nothing to see on the tape but an old man in a wheelchair raving on, but he claimed that under the drug he was capable of perceiving the mythlines, the lines of human psychic energy that generations of faith and belief have laid down across the physical landscape—more, that he had generated some ill-defined proto-phagus. The official experiments ended there—he may have tried it again himself, privately. It wouldn't surprise me. He was murdered soon afterward."

"You think he may have created his own murderers?"

"We think his breaking through to partial mythoconsciousness signalled his presence across the mythlines to the phaguses. And to the Adversary. He knew her personally, you see."

"Shone out like a bloody great lighthouse," Sumobaby swore, almost religiously.

"Why kill him?"

"Because a mythoconscious individual—any mythoconscious individual—is a threat to them. Some of them hold the pseudolife they've been given very dear indeed."

Suddenly Enye knew what question she must ask: a question she had known she must ask from the first time she had been brought to this dismal huddle of shacks, a question she had always known was never appropriate, never right. Until now.

"Lami, *why are you as you are?*"

Fingers expelled a great shuddering sigh from her tracheotomy wound.

Even as she asked, Enye knew the answer Lami would make.

"We took Shekinah."

"Why?"

"After Rooke's murder, we took it upon ourselves to try and heal the damage the Adversary had done."

"And you broke through . . ."

"A massive overdose . . ."

"And touched her reality-shaping power."

"Drew it down into us. And were reshaped, according to our subconscious hopes, and fears, and whims, and fantasies."

"Dear sweet God."

"We thought at first . . . I don't know, God knows what we thought: we thought we'd all died and gone to hell, that's what we thought. We thought we were going to be this way for always, that's what we thought. We didn't know the change only endured during darkness. Even so, it was enough to make sure that we couldn't live in society any longer; not people who are men, and women, and God, even *dogs* by day, and things like you wouldn't even dream in your worst nightmares by night. God, men used to think I was beautiful."

She wept. Moonface drew her to him. Small solace. Her tears ran down the curve of his crescent face.

"You know you can bring us back," he said. "You know that. You have the reality-shaping power. You have the ability to heal and restore to harmony. You can change us."

"I would. Don't you think I would, this instant, if I knew how?"

Fingers held out a small transparent plastic sachet in the palm of her left hand. Inside was what looked like a year's supply of toenail clippings and bleached pubic hair.

Shekinah, she breathed through the hole in her throat.

Shekinah: the Radiant Presence of God.

"No, I can't. What if, what if . . ."

"You have to. Yours is not the great gift. Yours is the lesser gift, and it must be tuned, and amplified, and trained," said Sumobaby.

She ran from the cardboard shelter, through the long grey rain of November, away from the railroad viaduct and the heavy night freights shunting and clunking over the points. The plastic envelope remained where she had dropped it, on the roach-scorched cardboard floor.

She found Mr. Antrobus sitting on the stairs. He had been crying. When she asked him what was the matter, he began to burble and blubber again. He had never been ashamed of his tears, Mr. Antrobus. One of his cats had not come home with the others when he had banged his fork on the side of the cat food tin. Unheard of. Something amiss. He had gone out to look, calling *Tigger Tigger here puss puss puss* and rattling a favourite little jingly toy. He had found the body in front of Mrs. Blennerhasset at number three's garage.

"Horrible, horrible, horrible," he said. "All torn and smashed and ripped apart. It looked as if something had tried to eat him. Poor poor little Tigger. What kind of thing could do that to a poor little cat?"

Enye did not like to answer.

Omry will tell you Lycra is *the* fabric of the decade. Omry wears black stretch one-pieces with boots and ridiculous quilted micro-bomber jackets. Omry looks like a testimonial to the joys of totalitarianism.

Omry works as a dispatcher with a bicycle courier company. Omry will tell you the bicycle courier is the street-level ground-zero hero of the decade. Jimmy Dean in chamois padded shorts. Life in the bus lane—live fast, die under the wheels of an anonymous German-something car with Catcon. Omry would be in the coronary care unit if she cycled more than two blocks.

Omry insists people call her Om. Omry will tell you that it has significance for the new decade which will be an age of transcendence and peace and general niceness to all living creatures. Omry's real name is Anne-Marie. She comes from the north lands, where the accents can make good morning sound like a declaration of war. It is the only place outside China where it is possible to have a conversation entirely in monosyllables. Everyone still calls her Omry.

Omry is a Purveyor of Organic Holistic Naturopathic Compounds. Omry will tell you all her merchandise is guaranteed One Hundred Percent Natural and Organic No Synthetics No Additives no colourants no preservatives no added sugar sodium-free high in fibre low in cholesterol fully biodegradable. Omry is a pusher. A vendor. A peddler. A dealer. Omry does it for the money. Omry specialises in odd fungi and unusual highs. Some of the wrinkled scrotumlike things in her antique apothecary's chest are so abstruse the police aren't even certain if they are bustable.

Omry is Enye's supplier. Enye learned about Omry from the Midnight Children. Omry is possibly the only person to have seen them in their light-of-day manifestations. Or then again, maybe not. Omry takes orders on the office fax machine. For a Purveyor of Organic Holistic Natural Compounds, Omry is surprisingly technophilic. Enye expects to hear that she takes all major credit cards. She calls 0800 BIKEBOY and is gratified to hear "A Short Trip in a Fast Machine" as background music, a pleasant change to the usual digi-beat and scratch-sample Omry purports to like.

"One hundred grams each, okay," Omry says in her flat, spadelike northern accent. "It'll be a day or so to get that much together. This stuff is hard to come by. Just what does it do, anyway, huh?"

"You wouldn't believe me if I told you, my little scrap of Lycra."

The bathroom-cabinet Shekinah factory is a lot more sophisticated than it was in the early days (*early days:* she finds it difficult to believe that it has been just over a year since her grandmother's funeral). Macerate in industrial alcohol, set to dry on silk screens in the airing cupboard, mix to a paste with crushed chalk and a binding medium and roll into nice little pill shapes on the wooden pharmacist's pill paddles she found in a Saturday antique market along the quays. They pass quite convincingly as Vitamin C in the right bottle.

Omry will tell you she places a high value on harmonious and mutually fulfilling customer-client relationships. Omry delivers on time, every time, exactly as ordered. In a day or so, Mr. Antrobus comes aknocking at Enye's door with a small padded envelope which he accepted, *in absentia*, from a punky but cute bicycle courier. Also, a bouquet of flowers from Enye's young man. He does hope there is nothing the matter. Would she care to discuss it sometime over tea and pikelets? Which, Enye realises, she would, very much. She would love to pour it all out in slops and spills over Mr. Antrobus's worn paisley carpet under the watchful eyes of his cats and Greek sunsets; would love to have half the burden of hurt and uncertainty borne by another's shoulders; but instead she stuffs the flowers into a vase and sets the two hundred gram packets of obscure fungi in a glass beaker of alcohol in the microwave low setting for half an hour or so.

She will need Shekinah, much much Shekinah, if she is to reach out with her mythoconsciousness to hunt her enemies through the twist and twine of the mythlines.

It is poor strategy to allow yourself to be led around by the enemy. This is the meaning of the term "to hold down a pillow"—not permitting your enemy to raise his head. To suppress the enemy's useful actions and permit only his useless actions. This is the way of strategy.

Is your enemy's spirit flourishing or waning? Observe his disposition and thus gain the position of advantage. This is what it means to "know the times." Once you know his metre and motivation, you may attack in an unsuspected manner.

All things collapse when their rhythm is disrupted.

Think of the robber trapped in a house. The world sees him as a fortified enemy, but we see with the eye of "becoming the enemy." He who is shut in is the pheasant. He who enters to arrest is the hawk.

You must appreciate this.

Consider this deeply.

Study this well.

Research this deeply.

Train diligently.

Apply yourself to this discipline.

When your spirit is unclouded, when the fog of confusion clears away, there is the true void.

Nihon Me.

Sanbon Me.

Yonhon Me.

Gohon Me.

Roppon Me.

Nanahon Me.

Nihon Me. Sanbon Me. Yonhon Me. Gohon Me. Roppon Me. Nanahon Me.

Nihon Me. Sanbon Me. Yonhon Me. Gohon Me. Roppon Me. Nanahon Me.

The swords flash and fly. She is dressed for the night. The Shekinah is a hymn inside her. Under the disciplines of the *Kamae,* body and spirit are approaching unity, the void. She is high like never before, high and vertiginous. She is running on burning soul.

nihonmesanbonme . . .

The telephone rings.

The singing silver blades freeze in their dance.

Ring ring, Ring ring, Ring ring; Ring ring, Ring ring, Ring ring; Ring ring, Ring ring, Ring ring . . .

"Yes."

It is him. He wants to know what is happening to her, to him, can he see her again he wants to see her again he must see her again he has to know what he means what she means. Any moment he is going to say it. He says it—*where he stands.*

"Not now, Saul."

"Enye . . . Enye . . ."

"No."

The telephone clicks down.

She is guided through the dripping, ringing levels of the old abandoned warehouse building by the information that all doors but the right ones are locked against her.

He is expecting her.

He has, he says, been waiting for her for a long, long time.

He is an aged, aged man, sitting, hands on thighs, on a tattered swivel chair. The vinyl upholstery has split; crumbling foam peers out. He is dressed in buckle sandals, gray slacks, and a grubby aran sweater. Face and hands are deeply eroded. He wears round, wire frame glasses like Samuel Beckett. The only light in the room is from the dozens and dozens of television sets. Wall to wall, floor to ceiling, stacked eight, nine, ten high, all designs from old mahogany veneer monochromes with fabric-covered speakers to flat-screen blacque-tech with full Dolby stereo. Televisions, dozens upon dozens; hundreds of images, all, Enye realises, different. Most of empty streets, the nova-glare of streetlights, puddles of neon and halogen, the cometary trail of red taillights. Punks roistering in a deserted rapid-transit station; street-cleaning trucks intimately connected with the city's gutters by pulsing umbilicals; delay-struck night-flyers bent, exhausted, over their suitcases in airport departure lounges; immigrant women skating vibrating polishing machines over the marble concourses of the capitals of industry; night watchmen, watched; prowl cars; waitresses in all-night coffee shops; the staff of pizza dens and burger stops packing up after another thankless night; drunks in doorways; road repair crews; taxi drivers; buskers. She stops at that one. The boy with the electric guitar and the punky, gymnastic girl in the ripped leotard—lovers; police, thieves.

The aged aged man on the rotting typist's chair notices her watching. "I wouldn't waste your time, if I were you. When you have been watching as long as I have, you'll come to realise there is nothing new under the sun. Every show is a repeat. We are condemned to play out the same trivial soap operas, the same tired and trite old clichés, the same clunking old plot mechanisms. You have no idea how glad I will be to see the final credits roll and the little white dot vanish in the middle of the screen. Come in, come

close, you have absolutely nothing to fear from me. I am
not an actor in this drama, I am the spectator in the gallery.
Argus of the Hundred Eyes." He turns back from her to his
flickering televisions. "I think it must be twenty years,
judging by the seasons, since I came here, since I found
myself in this room, with my televisions. Oh, not as many
then—the technology was not so sophisticated. No memories of any place other than this, a life other than this, than
watching the televisions. I concluded early that I was not as
those I saw on the screens—that these screens were, indeed,
no ordinary televisions. To this day I still do not understand
what powers them, or where they come from—and come
they do, I know the signs now, while my back is turned, and
only while my back is turned, I feel a prickling along my
hairline and I know that if I look back, there will be another
television added to my collection. Models constantly up-
dated, I'll say that. That one there—" he points, but they
are all blue video shine to Enye, "that's high definition.
Technology that's only just being made available. No off
switch, though. On any of them. Another of my early
realisations was that the channel I watch is the city, and the
programme life. In a sense, I am the memory of the city, old
Argus. I am the witness of its continued existence. You
must have heard the solipsistic riddle of the tree falling in
the forest. Does it make any noise if there is no one there to
witness it? The old Berkelian conundrum, when a thing is
unperceived, can it be said to exist? I like to think that
without my constant observation and witness, the city
would have disremembered itself and vanished into nothingness, for there must have been a time, even the briefest
moment, the merest fraction of a fraction of a second, when
I was the only one awake and aware of the whole teeming
population. A conceit, or perhaps, when I am gone back to
the state from which I came, one dark night the city will
indeed unremember itself and dissolve like a forgotten
dream. Oh, I have no illusions about myself—a man who
never sleeps, never eats, never excretes, never tires, is
never prodded by the goads of sexual longing; a man who
has never, in at least twenty years, been able to set foot
outside this building in which you find him because of the
crippling dread that makes it impossible for him to leave

this chair for more than a few minutes at a time. What else could such a man be but someone else's dream, someone else's nightmare?

"Oh, I have watched you on my televisions. I have seen what you have done, and I knew that in time you would come for me. Because of what I am, because there are questions you have that only I may answer. I am Argus of the Hundred Televisual Eyes. More than that, at my last count, which was some while ago, I must admit. Surely I must have seen who it was murdered Dr. Hannibal Rooke, who it was destroyed the Midnight Children? I would help you if I were able, but even with my slightly over one hundred eyes, changing channels every two seconds, it takes me over a year, a year, to look into the hearts of every soul in this city. There is so much that passes me by. I have no factual evidence to give you, all I can do is advise, and pray you continue with your own search. It is not the place at which you arrive that is important, but the way you come to it." The aged, aged man turned again to face Enye. The light from the televisions deeply engraved the lines in his face. "Understand realities: your swords, your computer, your drug. Do not think I am ignorant of them. I have been watching your progress through the nightlands of the city. They are no more real, or necessary, than I. Symbols. Your war is a war of symbologies, a battle between ghosts, spirits, mythologies, at once both the most real and the most unreal of entities. Any power they possess is from you, your own power, your own ability to cross the Earth/Mygmus membrane and shape its substance according to your own personal mythologies, your own hopes, and wishes, and fears. That is why the Way you go is more important than the place you arrive, because while you are on the way there is hope for change, and growth; to arrive is to enter changelessness and stasis.

"I advise you as some of us exist in this world knowing our nature and longing for our return to the Mygmus, so there are those that love the lives they have scraped out, and will hold tightly to them.

"Just because I am an old man, without defences, without strategy, who can therefore do nothing but welcome you, do not imagine that we will all be equally helpless. We know each other—how can we not?—for we are all of one substance with each other. By now they will know of you, and will be preparing themselves. I tell you this: beware the Lords of the Gateway.

"There. Now. I have warned you. Now, kindly deliver me from this impotent existence of watching and return me to my true domain."

He sits upright in his chair, palms flat on grey flannel trouser legs, sandalled feet flat on the floor. His head is held erect, his expression sublime, like a saint or windswept tree, or some other intensely present object. She has read that in the Middle Ages women were executed like this, seated in a chair.

"Ya!" The lesser *kiai*. *Chudan No Kame*, the middle attitude, culminating in the *Men* cut, the neck stroke, the perfect stroke, most difficult of all strokes to master.

For the first time, she understands what it is to treat one's enemy as an honoured guest.

The screens of the banked televisions are all swept by a sudden blizzard of video snow.

Even Jaypee asks, didn't you wear that outfit yesterday? People in QHPSL notice things like that.

He regards the transparent plastic bottle on his desk with the suspicion he normally reserves for government letters in brown envelopes.

"It's quite simple," says the Blessèd Phaedra on one of her rare progresses through the Glass Menagerie, bestowing grace and favour and transparent plastic bottles with firmly fitting screw tops. "Just fill it."

"What? From here?" Jaypee doubles up in music-hall laughter. Enye, tarnished and groggy and vaguely nauseated, leans back in her chair, rolls her plastic bottle around the desktop with her stocking feet—pedal self-massage.

"You get that, MacColl?"

"MacColl got that."

"Words is throwing a strunt this morning, Phaedra, darling. It's either a man or a period."

"It's always either a bloody man or a period to you men."

"Whoa whoa whoa, *pulcherina* . . ."

"Piss off, Kinsella."

"What a good idea."

The Blessèd Phaedra passes on her way. When Jaypee returns, he holds the bottle up to the light.

"Chateau Mouton Kinsella; an insouciant little number, but I think you'll be titlilated by its braggadocio. If I'd known this was scheduled for this morning, I'd never have had the cream of asparagus soup." Judi-Angel from Traffic cruises past, little plastic bottle in hand. "Oh, Judi-Angel," Jaypee sings, "do you know if you drink a glass of your own piss—no one else's, mind—you'll have a complexion like a baby's bottom?"

She mouths F. U.s at him. He swivels in his chair, sings out the open office door in fifties doo-wop style,

Judi-Angel, I love you, don't you see?
Judi-Angel, though you smell somewhat of pee.
For your skin, soft and lovely, I so much want to kiss,
Is so smooth, 'cause each morning, you drink a glass of
    piss.
Judi-Angel, doobie doo-wah, Judi Angel, dum dum dum
    dum . . ."

A thing like a hostess trolley with telescopic steel whiskers comes whining through the Glass Menagerie.

"Cup of chamomile, perchance?" Jaypee asks.

"What happened to Mrs. O'Verall?"

"The Blessèd Phaedra happened to Mrs. O'Verall. Advances in office automation, and all that."

"God help Mrs. O'Verall."

"God help us all, and you especially, Enye MacColl."

"Why?" asks Enye, dexterously turning the bottle upright with her toes.

"You been backpacking in Munchkinland, *pulcherina?* The Blessèd Phaedra's attempt to come clean with her conscience, or, I rather suspect, acting on the express instruction of Oscar the Bastard. QHPSL puts its hand to its heart to stand with Nancy Reagan and Babs Bush and Superman and Wonder Woman and Mandrake the Magician to declare itself drug-free. We're being dope-tested."

• • •

It's Christmastime. Cuttin' down trees. Puttin' up rein-
deer, singin' songs about feedin' the world, and Wishin' It
Could Be Christmas Every Day (can you imagine, all those
pairs of slippers and holly-leaf boxer shorts and perfume
you don't like, spending the rest of your life watching
reruns of *The Wizard of Oz* in a rising pall of silent hot
fermented turkey fart) and dreamin' of a "White Christmas"
and "Dashin' through the Snow on a One-Horse Open
Sleigh" and "Chestnuts Roasting on an Open Fire, Jack
Frost Nippin' at Your Toes" (Stays pretty green around
here, didn't snow last year, probably won't this. Warmest
winter since records began. Something to do with global
warming). Fattenin' up credit cards. Stunnin' turkeys with
five hundred volt shock probes before guillotinin' them with
automated shears; pullin' technically drunk corpses from
wrecked hot hatchbacks; January sales startin' on Christmas
Eve; Christmas trees up since the end of November;
Christmas Muzak in the hypermart since the end of October;
Santa Claus arrivin' at his Enchanted Ice Grotto in the
suburban malls since the end of September; and someone
sent a letter to the paper claimin' to have seen the first
Christmas card in the shops the end of August.

Saul gave Enye a present. He leaned, head cupped in his
hands against his pillow, and watched her, kneeling on the
end of his bed in a "Save the Rain Forests" T-shirt and
panties that were nothing more than a postage stamp stuck
to a piece of clastic, turn it over and over and feel its bumps
and listen to its rattles and rumbles and harmonics with her
ear and rub it against her cheek and taste it with her tongue,
lick its wrappings, its bitter adhesive tape, with oohs and
aahs and a childlike glee he found deeply erotic, tearing off
the wrapping and tearing open the box and tearing away the
transparent bubble wrap.

"It's an electronic personal organiser. Like a portable
computer. Address, telephone numbers, calendar, diary,
planner, appointments, memos, personal information,
watch, alarm, thesaurus, pocket calculator, currency ex-
changer. It's got add-on ROM packs, and there's a twenty-

pin adapter to connect it to a micro or a mainframe, and an interfacer so you can squirt numbers out of the memory straight into the telephone. There's even an add-on printer . . ." She was already lying on her back with it held over her face, pressing buttons.

"Oh, hey, here's yours."

While he tore off the Hokusai print wrapping paper and walked about in front of the mirror in his wardrobe, admiring himself in the real silk Japanese *yukata*, her fingers played the buttons.

"Saul, look." She held it out to him. "Merry Christmas, Saul" marched, Fascist black on grey, across the display. Elsewhere, the radio news reported that the search area for wreckage from the transatlantic jumbo that had crashed four days before Christmas had been widened to cover a fifty-mile-diameter circle across the Southern Uplands of Scotland.

Here is the rundown for the penultimate Christmas of the decade in L'Esperanza Street. Kids get skateboards and jackets with Australian soap stars on the back. Dads get camcorders, or, a lucky few, satellite dishes. Mums get sweet things, smelly things, and underwear they'll never quite have the courage to wear.

Enjoying her one night of self-company apart from the Cuba Libre limbo of advertising parties, lawyer parties, dojo parties, friends' parties, friends of friends' parties leading up to the grand bacchanalia of New Year, Enye was barefoot and cat-curled on the sofa listening, half hypnotised by the soft-focus highlights of her Christmas decorations, to *Madam Butterfly*.

There was a knock on the door, a small, hard musket ball of intrusion into her treasured privacy.

She let them knock again. She was not expecting anybody; anyone who would be knocking she did not want to see.

And again.

And again.

She surrendered on the fifth knock.

They were the kind of people her mother had told her not to open doors to. Two men, anonymous, forty-wise; something in accounts somewhere, or the marketing of uninteresting but essential components for machine tools. Dressed in matching black suits two sizes too small, over white polo-neck sweaters. All they needed to be apprentice Men from U.N.C.L.E. was to take pens from their pockets and whisper "Open Channel D." One carried a small briefcase, held high in front of his chest. They seemed uncomfortable, ill-fitted to themselves, like novice door-to-door evangelists.

"Mizz MacColl? We're from General and Far Eastern Electronics. We believe you recently became the owner of a Sony-Nihon Mark 19 Hakudachi Personal Organiser?" They peered around the door into her apartment. A card was proffered and accepted. Enyc studied the smeary black typeface.

"We've been receiving a number of complaints from owners of Sony-Nihon Mark 19 Hakudachi Personal Organisers about a number of faults and my company has decided to recall the last batch. If you could, would it be possible for us to see your Sony-Nihon Mark 19 Hakudachi Personal Organiser?"

"What sort of problems?"

"Oh, this and that—small, irritating things."

"I haven't had any problems with mine."

"They tend to take a while to show up. General and Far Eastern Electronics thought it simplest to recall the entire batch."

The second man, Mr. Accounts-something, was fiddling with the brass catches of his glintingly new briefcase as if he had never seen them before. Mr. Uninteresting but Essential Components continued, "Ah, the Sony-Nihon Mark 19 Hakudachi Personal Organizer?"

"I'll get it, but I don't really think . . ."

"Would it, ah, be possible for us to come inside? Just for a moment? There are a couple of tests we'd like to run."

"If you must." Though it was the last thing she wanted to do. Inside, they stood helplessly, apparently confused by the geography of her apartment.

"A seat? Sit down?"

"Oh no, thank you, we'd rather stand."

Mr. Accounts-Something had managed to open his brief-case. As she went to the bedroom to fetch the personal organiser, Enye observed how keen he was for her not to see what was inside. Mr. Uninteresting but Essential Components took the Sony-Nihon Mark 19 Hakudachi Personal Organiser, passed it without comment to his colleague, who set the briefcase on the carpet by the door and knelt in front of it. Mr. Uninteresting but Essential Components was very careful to keep himself between Enye and his colleague. Washes of coloured light lit the kneeling Mr. Accounts-Something's face. He closed the briefcase, having had some difficulty with the catches, and stood up.

"Um, my organiser?"

"Oh. Sorry. One of the defective units. Quite unmistak-able, once you know what to look for. General and Far Eastern Electronics will supply a suitable replacement as soon as new stocks arrive."

"I've got information and stuff in that. Personal stuff."

"I'm sorry, but General and Far Eastern Electronics will supply a suitable replacement as soon as new stocks arrive."

They backed out of the door, bowing, getting in each other's way. Mr. Accounts-Something had not spoken a word in the entire exchange. Mr. Uninteresting but Essen-tial Components had sounded—the simile came to Enye and struck her with its appositeness—like a ham actor delivering poorly learned lines.

Of course, the number on the smeary business card returned the data space white keen of Number Unobtain-able. Of course, directory inquiries could find no reference for a General and Far Eastern Electronics. Of course, the electronics shop that had sold Saul the Sony-Nihon Mark 19 Hakudachi Personal Organiser did not list General and Far Eastern Electronics as a supplier, had never heard of a General and Far Eastern Electronics.

"Sounds to me as if you've been conned out of one Sony-Nihon Mark 19 Hakudachi Personal Organiser," said Jaypee, more than a little frayed at the edges on his fifth straight night parrrrrtying.

"Sounds to me like a classic M.I.B. phenomenon," said the Bryghte Younge Thynge in the black net tutu who had been trying most of the evening to chat Jaypee into concupiscent intrigue. Saul was elsewhere, an innocent abroad among the danceables and drinkables, the smokables and sniffables and screwables; Enye discovered an ingrowing talon of mild jealousy to which she had never suspected a vulnerability. She did not know, no one knew, under whose auspices this End of Year Bash had been thrown, but the same old faces that graced every other in-between day function could be found in abundance, liberally salted with Bryghte Younge Thynges making their social debut.

"M.I.B.? A British Secret Service agent stealing a Russian fighter?" inquired Jaypee.

Black net tutu and legs that went all the way to her you know you know had a laugh like cars being crushed.

"No no no no no. Men in Black. M.I.B. Classic Youfoe events. Someone has a Youfoe experience and then these funny men come around, from the air ministry, or something like, and they ask like these really *gauche* questions. They always go in twos, and they usually either dress in black or drive a black car or carry black briefcases or something like. Never seem to know exactly what they're doing, sort of like confused, like people who've been brought in off the street and asked to play bit parts in a movie. Classic pattern. Your two sound like classic Men in Black events. You had any experiences of Youfoe consciousness lately?"

"Nothing classic."

"You mean flying saucers and all that?" asked Jaypee, who did not much want to enter into concupiscent intrigue with black net tutu legs, etc. "Atlantis and power crystals and out-of-body experiences and channellers, who take all major credit cards and claim to be in contact with thirty-thousand-year-old entities? One wonders what priceless pearls of wisdom one might get from a thirty-thousand-year-old entity when one crosses its palm with plastic? Watch out for sabre-tooths, and don't eat the plants with the blue flowers if you don't want to be shitting yourself for a week?"

"Jeez, like you're so *gauche*."

Bryghte Younge Thynge flurried off in high, rustling dudgeon to spend the remainder of the year being chatted up by a man who claimed to have had carnal knowledge of a Pointer Sister.

"*Gauche* being the opposite of *classic?*" Enye asked as the old year passed away and the new arrived.

That Ufology and all its attendant corpus of faith should be a facet of mythoconsciousness did not surprise her. Of greater concern was that two ostensible phaguses had found her, entered her house, and taken a piece of her property.

In the morning, with the statement from the credit card company, was a brown paper parcel laboriously wrapped in string in that way that looks so inviting but no one can be bothered to do anymore. Nestled in tissue paper in a green cardboard carton: a Sony-Nihon Mark 19 Hakudachi Personal Organiser with a compliment slip written in a large, loose, childish hand:

> *General and Far Eastern Electronics wishes you the compliments of the season and every happiness with your new Sony-Nihon Mark 19 Hakudachi Personal Organiser.*

She did not know whether to switch it on or hit it with a hammer.

She fetched the hammer from under the kitchen sink.

And switched it on.

Words and symbols too fleeting for human comprehension flickered across the liquid crystal display. Lines meshed and intermeshed, formed Op Art moiré patterns. The screen cleared, then flashed the words, silver on grey:

DISRUPTOR LOADED.

She was thumbing through the instruction manual when the screen cleared to proclaim a new message.

PRESS 8 TO CONTINUE.

As instructions not contained in any manual scrolled across the screen, she understood. Like seed crystals in supersaturated solution, her subconscious cry for help from beyond comprehension had precipitated into Men in Black.

She had created, and as ignorantly dissolved back into the unsubstance of the Mygmus, her first phaguses, bearing a gift of wonder and puissance.

A weapon.

Mr. Mooney of the antiques restoration firm who undertook the servicing and sharpening of Enye's swords had been horrified at what the small, sallow, black-haired woman had wanted him to do to a Murasama blade. But he had done it. The intensity of the small, sallow, black-haired woman compelled him.

That night she watched the silver disruptor glyphs swarm from the *habaki* and meld with her blade. She swung the *katana* through the Five Attitudes. It sang for her, a new song that no ear but hers could hear.

Two samurai stand on the side of a hill, swords drawn. Rain is pouring down. They are soaked through by the pouring rain. Neither makes a move. They have been standing since dawn in the pouring rain, neither moving. They are Masters, the greatest exponents of the Way, and yet they stand there, soaking wet, neither moving, for to move is to reveal your spirit to your enemy and give him advantage over you.

So neither moves. And neither will move.

Unless one possesses a weapon of overwhelming superiority.

Phaedra is too fine a strategist to let anything as unsubtle as a victorious glint shine in her eye, but from the moment she enters the glass office that from its superior level overlooks all the transparent lives of the Glass Menagerie, Enye knows that this is the hour when the irresistible weapon is unholstered.

The irresistible weapon is a sheet of dot-matrix computer flimsy. Columns, rows, tabulations, figures.

"Would you care to explain this to me, Enye?"

First names. So.

The results of the urine analysis. Without understanding a single decimal or percentage point, Enye knows what it says.

"It's off by several points, Enye."

Shekinah. The Radiant Presence of God.

"Look. Spare me any pious shit about company commitments to stand valiant and firm in the face of the greatest social menace of the century because, quite frankly, it just doesn't sound convincing coming from someone who has the Gross National Products of several South American countries stuffed up her corroded nostrils."

Phaedra smiles a Phaedra smile.

"Would you care to see my analysis? It's right here on the desk. I can point out the discrepancies."

"I'm sure it's as pure as the finest Colombian White, Phaedra."

And if the hillside upon which one of the samurai stands overlooks Hiroshima?

It was a moment that, in any other mood, in any other circumstance, she would have bronzed like her first pair of shoes: Jaypee Kinsella with frostbite of the witticisms. She knew he wanted to say something. Her look dared him to as she gathered up the disseminated fragments of her personality in three cardboard boxes. Two mugs three pencil sharpeners (one Garfield, one regulation aluminum, one in the shape of a Great Northern Diver) pens papers pads executive mercury mazes and roll-the-ball-into-the-hole games, a Rubik cube soft-soaped for speed-solving, a set of pornographic saké cups with marbles in the bottoms that, when filled with saké, magically revealed a couple engaged in an act of oral outrage, a ball of aluminum foil the size of a fist, one Walkperson, three sets of dead batteries leaking toxic orange pus, a tape of *Die Meistersinger* she had thought lost forever, a copy of the collected short stories of D. H. Lawrence, pairs of tights, packets of tampons and sanitary towels, candles, icons, pieces of quirky blue china, an Endangered Bat Species of the World mobile, a water pistol, desk tidy, pencil pots, assorted Schefflera, Hypoestes, and Ficus Pumilla, a solid gold swizzle stick, a half-eaten bar of chocolate (dark), several cardboard folders of diverse papers, an expired car-tax disc, a threatening letter from the Tax Department, a credit card company statement, a communiqué from the Reader's Digest informing her that she *may have already won* a totally ludicrous sum of money, a copy of *Cosi Fan Tutti* she had likewise thought gone forever, a pair of high heel shoes for special occasions, a packet of paracetamol, a packet of sinus decongestants, a packet of antihistamines, a packet of fructose tablets, a plastic dog turd, birthday cards Christmas cards get-well-soon cards congratulations-on-joining-us-in-your-new-job cards.

She extends a hand to Jaypee. She cannot look at him.

"Well, good-bye, Jaypee, it's been good knowing you, but this is it. Good-bye."

"Shit, Enye, she didn't have to fire you . . ."

"She didn't. I quit."

"Fine gesture, Enye, noble gesture, but what the hell are you going to do?"

"God knows, Jaypee. God knows. Not advertising. Phaedra'll have word out all over town. Hear these words, Kinsella: if you have ever entertained one creative thought in your head, if you have ever even for a minute considered originality, freshness, creativity, and genius to matter, if you have one iota of artistic integrity in your soul, you will quit, too, because this place is death to creativity. Death, Jaypee. Death."

Then she stalks out of the Glass Menagerie with the three piled cardboard boxes in her arms, and every head in every glass cubicle turns to follow her, and she does not acknowledge a single one of them.

The machine on the barrier of the QHPSL car park swallows her card and rewards her with the message CARD INVALIDATED.

She is too angry to settle in her home, too angry for any of the things that usually calm her—music, a bath with a whiskey, calisthenics, sword practice at the dojo, a walk in the garden, a talk with Mr. Antrobus. She wants to take her anger out into the city, pace it about in the streets like a panther on a leash. She wants people to see her anger, hear the air crackle as she passes by, feel its heat on their faces and hands.

She has not been to the city centre coffeehouse since her student days. Then it had been a place of dreams and plans and notions, of attempts at beginnings. That is why she is drawn again to its mahogany-panelled walls and whistling brass biggins and sooty stained-glass windows. A church for agnostics. The coffeehouse is busy; fragments of other lifelines carrying trays entangle briefly with her own. A small, birdlike lady with an English accent asks if she minds if she and her friends share her table. They're down from the north for the day, where the friends she is visiting live. She likes Enye's city very much. She thinks it is a magical place. Is she waiting for a friend? Enye says no, she hasn't any friends. The bright, birdlike lady cannot believe that she does not have any friends. Enye says friends are fragile things—illusions of atmosphere, environment and lighting; like that! (click of the fingers) she has just lost the person she thought of as her best friend.

There is more than one star in heaven, says the birdlike lady and she smiles and it is as if she and Enye have been caught up together in a dazzling, audacious conspiracy.

She almost calls him that afternoon. Almost. But then the thought of his voice brings back to her all the things her life is easier without: his needs, his weaknesses, his clinging, his irritations and obscurities. Instead she goes to get her hair cut. One inch, all over. She roots through her apartment, collects any item of clothing that might possibly be suspect of Power Dressing, stuffs them into plastic garbage sacks, and drives the lot of them down to the nearest charity shop. The break has to be total. Total. Only one thing stops it from totality.

Such confusion of emotions on Saul's face as he opens the door to her. Such confusion of emotions in her spirit as the door is opened to her; that, despite all those things her life is easier without, she is standing here in his tastefully decorated neo-Georgian hall with the early morning rain dripping onto his majolica floor tiles.

"My God," he says, staring at where the hair in which he had so loved to bury his face used to be. "What have you done?"

She answers all the questions he asks her; he blusters and blows threats of litigations against the people who would do this to his Enye.

"Saul," she says. "Do not be stupid. Understand that: I did it."

Pressed close to the great, vital heat of his body beside hers in the bed, she slips out of the Thunderbirds T-shirt Saul has lent her, presses her tense, taut self against his slumbering mass, calls him with her tense, taut desperation to love with her. Afterward, she lies watching the motes of darkness coming and going across the plasterwork of his ceiling, as she has so many times before, listening on headphones to nighthawk radio playing Album-Oriented Rock. The break is made. Now she can walk on. They are playing an old song she used to like from her student days. She whispers the words in time to the music: *Slip-slidin' away.*

She had a weapon now, but no enemy. Ostensibly in defence of Mr. Antrobus's cats, she patrolled, swords in sheaths, computer hooked to her belt, the laneway at the rear of the gardens, much to the surprise of other residents. (Who, of course, said nothing. What went on in *that* house was nobody's business.) The Nimrod, whatever its form, or stage of metamorphosis, was gone from the immediate environment. After a local radio reported the destruction of a number of hen coops and pigeon lofts by an unidentified but large animal, she expanded the perimeter of her search to include that neighbourhood also. Her breath steaming in the January air; she willed her mythoconsciousness out into the night. Nothing. *Rien. Nada.* Not even the migrainous neural drumbeat she had learned to recognise as the touch of the Mygmus. She returned to the car, wrapped the swords in an old copy of the *Irish Times,* drove away through streets broad and narrow.

She could smell it as she locked the Citroen in the safe parking place among the towering industrial refuse bins. As she approached across the broken bottles and shredded plastic bags, the sensation left the purely subjective to become objective, external, tangible. Not the nausea of mythoconscious contact. Something other. More intimate. The pheromone of dread.

The darkness under the brick arch had a different shape, a different mass, a different timbre. And a new perfume: the smell of burning. Of cardboard and wood. Of the oily black combustion of plastics. Of scorched meat. *Flesh*.

Reaching from the massed darkness into the light of the shunting yard floods was a pale shape. A hand.

She fled.

Twin headlights challenged her as she drove down the rutted grass laneway behind L'Esperanza Street. She shielded her eyes, stopped, stepped out of the Citroen. The twin beams dipped, extinguished. Through the blur of retinal afterimages she saw a blue Ford station wagon growl forward, softly, slowly, wheels crunching over the cinders and litter of the entry. It stopped, license plate touching Enye's shins. Moonface stepped out.

"They hit us."

"I know. I went there."

"You did what?"

"There was something I had to tell you."

"I suppose it was inevitable. Only we never expected . . . We never expected at all. Nothing we could do. Three of us got away—the ones who could move fast enough. I stole a car." The Ford's courtesy light clicked on; in the front seat was the Wolfwere, legs pulled up beneath her doggy-fashion, hands resting on the dash, doggy-fashion. In the back was Lami. Even with the backseat folded forward, there was barely enough room for her snake's body. She looked Enye the look of accusation of a dreadful crime.

"They? More than the one Nimrod?"

"The Nimrod, and two others. And things . . ." Moonface's face was scarred by sudden pain. By the yellow glow of the courtesy light Enye saw he was nursing a wound to his left arm. The grubby mandala-print sweat top was stained darkly, wetly.

"Things?"

"Things like you couldn't even begin to believe," Lami said.

"What are you going to do?" A heaviness fell upon Enye, the first exploratory testing of a burden of undeserved responsibility, unwarranted guilt that she knew would grow to the crushing mass of an entire world until it was discharged.

"Drive. Vanish." Moonface raised his eyes to the unseen hills to the south of the city. "There's a couple of hundred miles in the tank. That gives us a lot of country to lose ourselves in. It'll be harder in the country, but we'll work something. I'm sorry that your education should have ended before you were properly prepared."

"We should never have started. If we'd minded our own business, Paul, Liane and Marcus might still be with us," Lami hissed, and her voice was the voice of the snake within at last possessing the form of the snake without. Enye felt compelled to apologise.

"You'd rather we stayed this way forever?" Moonface said.

"You'd rather Paul, Liane, and Marcus were still alive?"

"We haven't the time for this. Look." Moonface held out his hand. In his palm was the transparent plastic envelope.

"I don't need it. That's what I wanted to tell you. I've found a weapon." Enye explained the events of Christmas past. The hand remained extended.

"You still need it. In this bag is the difference between fighting a rear guard action and taking it to the enemy. With this, you can be the hunter, not the hunted. With your swords, you can only destroy. With this, and your mythoconsciousness, you can heal. Take it. Take it!"

All the same, she hesitated. A thousand doubts, a thousand horrors, a thousand possible futures, radiated from the distance between their fingers.

"Take it."

She snatched the plastic bag, thrust it down down down into a hip pocket. Headlight beams swayed and darted, gear boxes whined as she reversed out of the alleyway to permit the Ford station wagon exit. In the back window was a KRTP-FM Number Wun-4-Fun sticker. The car stopped window to window.

"Will I see you again?"

"Don't look for us. You're too dangerous. Lami was right. If we hadn't involved ourselves with you, things might have been different. Or they might not. All I can promise you is that I hope someday a stranger will come up to you in the street. You'll not recognise him, but he'll recognise you. He'll greet you like an old, old friend, like someone who has done him the greatest favour anyone could do. He may have a pretty woman with him. You'll not recognise her, either. And they may have a dog."

The stolen Ford drove off. Its engine echoed and re-echoed down the red-brick streets until it was annihilated in the great night-voice of the city.

As she drove in to QHPSL the next morning, crawling through the city's choked vascular system, the radio news reported that the Social Services were expressing concern over the increasing numbers of young people living on the streets following the deaths of three in a fire in their shelter. The police were not ruling out the possibility of violence between rival groups of street-dwellers; though the fire appeared to have been started by a camping gas stove, the bodies showed signs of having been gashed and lacerated. The two young men and the young woman in question had not been identified.

Shekinah. The Radiant Presence of God.

It still looked like a year's supply of toenail clippings and bleached pubic hair. An adhesive label held dog-Latin taxonomies and a list of instructions: one five ml. spoon this, two five ml. spoon that, infuse for so long in so many mls. water . . . She prepared the brew in her bamboo-handled Japanese teapot, poured a cup, and let cup and pot go cold while she sat staring at it, more afraid than she had ever been in her life. She reboiled the kettle. Emptied the pot. Brewed fresh. Poured a cup. It smelled of concentrated woodland. It tasted of light bulbs. She drank the cup down in one swallow and panicked at the irrevocability of her recklessness. When the cold panic had passed, she went to sit in her most comfortable chair for whatever was to happen. The chair was not comfortable; she was not comfortable. She felt she should be sitting in a special place, in a special posture, listening to special music, wearing special clothes. She contented herself to kneel on the rug in front of her rack of swords.

The Radiant Presence of God did not so much overwhelm her like the trumpet blasts of Apocalypse as steal upon her like a thief in the night. She could not say at what point she became aware that what she had been brought up to believe in as concrete and immutable was unravelling, dissolving to reveal a more intimate reality hidden within like an unborn child. It was always to be so, when she took the Shekinah. There should have been fear as her hands, her arms, her kneeling thighs, her body, the floor upon which she knelt, the walls that surrounded her, the roof that sheltered her, grew insubstantial and translucent. But in the Radiant Presence of God there is no fear, only awe and reverent joy, and she gasped aloud in wonder to see the concealed revealed in the tongues of fire, like the Fractal dragons of Chaos Theory that were her hands, or the young tree half summer green half afire that was her body, or the currents of many-coloured light, like oil on water, that flowed about the contours of her body through the walls and floors of her apartment.

She crossed to the window and looking out, saw a city transformed. Light. Endless light. Primal light. With a cry, she turned away; too much, too soon. But she understood that what she saw no one else could see for the sight would have scorched their synapses and stamped the shape of that searing sight onto their molten, malleable bodies. She returned to the window, winced, gasped, tried to rub the ache of seeing too much out of her eyes, looked. Heard. Felt.

Out there, in the infinite degrees of complexity of spirals within spirals about spirals of the *ur*-city, was a malignancy, a darkness, an unfittedness that she felt as a nausea, as a tightness in her heart, a constriction in her breathing. She saw them like a cancer, heard their muttering voices like the voice of cancer if cancer were to have a voice; the voices of the fallen angels of the Mygmus.

Then she went out into the alleyways and industrial parks to hunt the hunter. The sky signs led her to a laneway that smelled of semen and grease between a convent school and a row of shops. The Nimrod was cramming garbage from ripped open plastic sacks into its maw. It looked up, startled. It had taken the semblance of a pig, some primeval myth memory from the very edge of human consciousness, some denizen of the psychic tundra below the breath of Ice Age glaciers. Curved tusks glinted skull-white in the neons of an all-night video shop. Yellow pig eyes shone with unalloyed hatred. She stood, back to the neon glow, swords held comfortably, easily in the attitude called "Open on All Eight Sides." LEDs glowed at her waist.

"Hi. I'm back."

The afterblast blinded her for several seconds. Scuzzballs of oily blue light caromed off the red brick walls and dented garbage bins. Voices from the flats above the shops were every-syllable clear, guttural, puzzled. Should they call the police, the gas board, the electricity board? What happened? Lights were coming on, windows opening.

Enye sheathed her swords and loped away through the web of intersecting alleys and back entries to the row of rusting corrugated iron garaging where she had left the Citroen.

She must be out of condition. She had not thought she could feel so bad after one day on the bike. Her thighs are so stiff and sore they can hardly carry her to the hot, deep, steaming, foaming bath and the glass of whiskey perched on the rim. Her inside leg feels like it measures at least three metres. She should have taken that guy with the long hair, what is he called? Elliot, yes, his advice and bought a proper pair of shorts with chamois gusset. She can kiss adieu to sex for at least the next six months. Even the thought of it makes her wince.

For all her street smarts, Omry had proved remarkably easy to blackmail. The very mention of the Narcotics Division had her call-you-back-in-five-minutes-yes-there's-a-vacancy-for-a-rider-if-you-think-you're-up-to-it.

Nothing better, Omry? Nothing with a little frisson of executive glitz?

This is a bicycle courier company, sister, not Saatchi & Saatchi. Do-me-no-favours.

At least it keeps her in credit (a checque every Friday. She's surprised to learn that she isn't making that much less than she did at QHPSL) and close to her source of supply. It will give her time and space to resupply and regroup and devise a strategy for her hunt for these Lords of the Gateway, whatever they are. Once she gets the chamois padded shorts and ditches her old saddle for a customised formfitter (£39.95 from MacConvey's Cycle Boutique but worth every centavo), once the legs get into rhythm and remember their old student day stamina when she thought nothing of cycling two hundred miles in a weekend, once she learns the ground rules of life in the bus lane, like which truck companies don't mind you hanging onto their under-rider bars for a free ride and which ones do, and which cops will give you a ticket if you leave your Peugeot eighteen-gear ATB in a no-parking zone, which companies tip, and which companies want you out of their black rubber and endangered wood lobbies before you've even entered (hardly surprising: QHPSL belongs to this latter flock), she finds she loves her job. She loves its immediacy, its presentness. She loves its lack of abstraction—just Enye MacColl and the traffic, a Day-Glo corpuscle weaving its course through the city's vascular system. A thousand challenges, a thousand threats; she faces death and serious injury a thousand times a day. She loves the art of living by her wits. True strategy, total immersion in the present, the happening moment.

The couriers are an affable, piratical mob, bound together by an us-and-themness, an *esprit de corps* common with Mujahaddin guerrillas and space shuttle crews. They know it is a jungle out there. They are an eclectic outfit: see the guy with the hand-customised flames on his frame, he's a trainee clergyman; see the girl with the Mandelbrot set pattern on her solid rear wheel, she's a resting actress; see that guy with the neat chevron tights, he's done time on an Alabama chain gang. Yes, sir, of course it was drugs, what else do you get put on a chain gang for these days, except being black. There's at least one doctor of atomic physics, a disaffected housewife who walked out on husband kiddies and Hi-Fibre Malt-Enriched Weetie-Bangs one morning; a psychopath; someone who may or may not be the next James Joyce; actors, patricides, fools, priests, pretenders. And Elliot.

Elliot thinks he may be the only Elliot in a country of males named after pale-faced plaster statuettes. Elliot may be right. Elliot has long hair he never wears gelled back or tied into a pigtail; just long, and blond, and smelling of frequent-wash herbal shampoo. Elliot gets There first, wherever There is a first to be, or to have. First to get the new Shinamo eighteen-speed gear-reduction system for his ATB, first to hit the streets in the hot-off-the-plane-from-Milan shirts, first with the belt pouch and the oversized rubber driver's chronometer on elasticated sweat band, first to introduce himself to the virgin recruits Hi I'm Elliot, the only Elliot in the country, probably; greetings.

Elliot has Noticed Enye.

Enye knows Elliot has Noticed her. Enye is not certain she wants to be noticed by Elliot. It is all the good things and all the bad things about Saul freshly laundered and ironed and laid out; his needs, her secrets, his hunger, her inability to satisfy that hunger. She wants and does not want to walk that valley again.

Elliot asks Enye, by means of conversation, what she is into.

"Music," she says.

"Like jazz? Folk? Four aran sweaters singing the 'Wild Rover,' God forfend? Rock? Heavy metal?"

"No," she says, "*Music*."

Elliot is into designer dance. Street music. Musi*que*. Maximal rhythm, minimal melody. Found sources, cut-ups, samples, ethno-beat: Ikombé drummers and wailing muezzins. He lives it with an intensity, an immediacy that draws Enye. She knows what it is to burn the flames of private obsession. She knows it is this that Elliot has noticed about her. When he talks about what he wants to do—make music, cut disks, session at clubs and warehouse parties, the energy crackles between them like summer lightning. Enye plays him Ives's Symphony Number Three on her Walkperson. She sees the intensity of his concentration, his keenness to comprehend something beyond his experience. She likes that. He asks can he borrow the tape. Next morning, as they gather the dispatches from Omry, it is as if he has had a religious experience.

"This is, wow, this is . . . cosmic. There's something going on in here I don't quite understand, but it's pretty cool." It must be a sign of Something, Enye thinks, that she refrains from sarcasm at his *wow* and *cosmic* and *cool*.

"You just watch yourself," Omry says to her as he launches himself on his eighteen-gear Shinamo system ATB into the great soul river. "That ass has my fingerprints on it."

That evening he invites her to his *place*. He is the kind of person, Enye thinks, who would have a *place*. She has shared her music with him; he wants to share his with her. Somewhere beneath the movie posters and racks of cassettes, the spools of reel tape and tangles of leads, the tape recorders and the microphones, the radio, tape, and CD decks, the graphic equalizers and mini-mixers, the QWERTY boards and green-screen monitors and synthesizers and touch-pad rhythm generators, must be the fundaments and furnishings of a quite nice little attic apartment. She calculates the number of pedal miles per metre of coax.

"When you got a passion, you got a passion," he says. "Try this." *This* being a mini-mike headset connected to a tape deck.

"I could get to like this!" she shouts, embedded in interlocking rhythms and driving bass lines. Then she realises, a little foolish, there is no need to shout. The loudness is all internal.

He cuts the play back, flips a switch on a mixing board. "Say that again?"

"I could get to like this?"

And he runs it through his processors and it comes back at her transmuted into a gospel-singer's soul-moan.

"I like to work with found sources. I'm puritanical that way. The remix is the dominant cultural form of the last two decades of the twentieth century—do you know that? It's a cultural form that has only been possible for the last twenty years—William Burroughs and Dada excepted—it's the only cultural form that is entirely in harmony with the technological ethos of the age. Remix is possible only because of technology.

"You think about it. You listen to the radio, you go to a club, you buy a disk, you see an advert on the tube, what do you hear? Remix music. You buy a book, see a movie, watch TV, what do you see? Old familiar plot lines, old familiar characters, old familiar motivations and relationships, endlessly remixed. You go to buy something to decorate your house, something to make it look pretty, look nice, yes? What do you get? Remix Victorian. Remix

Edwardian. Remix Art Deco. You tried to buy any clothes recently? What's this year's fashion? Five, ten, fifteen years ago's fashion, remixed."

"I always knew I should have held onto those flares," Enye says but Elliot is being ridden hard by his muse and people do not laugh when they are being ridden by their muse. They do not think of anything but the thing that is riding them, hard. It is a sight at once disturbing and deeply beautiful. As the sight of people being ridden tends to be.

"Even our nation, our history, our past, are subject to remix culture: see how we're transforming ourselves into a national theme park, see how we're changing our national identity into other nations' expectations of what that culture should be? Even in our schools our kids are being taught history remixed in accordance with our particular late twentieth century fixations. Green history, anyone? It happens in Russia every time they have a change of political climate. Remix. Everything is remix. Taken apart, analysed, sampled, put together again. That's what I want to do. Dub reality: the ultimate remix. I want to go out into the street and make music from what I find there. I've got buskers, Salvation Army bands, car backfires, police sirens, children being spanked; all kinds of street sounds digitalised in here. Ultimately, I'd like to create a complete sound map of the whole city. Can you imagine it mixed down onto one master tape? You would be able to experience the entire city at once. You seen the sound system system on my bike?" Enye has and has decided she wants one for herself; she likes the idea of bombarding pedestrians and traffic with *La Traviata* or Bach's St. Matthew Passion from her handlebar-mounted microspeakers, even if it means fitting a quick-release collar so she can take speakers, Walkperson, and all in with her when she makes deliveries. Street music, street crime. "Folks are always asking me, 'Hey, Elliot, why is there no beat coming out of your sound system?' and I say, that is because my system is for collecting sound, not throwing sound around. I map the city with my cassette recorder, define each street by its sounds and voices. I've caught some of my most valuable material purely as overheards. You like to hear the sound of your own city?"

Found Sources.

A street preacher proclaiming hate in the name of love: *You're all going to hell, every one of you. The wages of sin is death! The wages of sin is death! Ye must be born again! Ye must be born again!*

A lovers' argument: she accusing him, he defending himself, he moving from defence to offence, she thrown momentarily back, she rallying with a strong counterattack, he gaining strength for a countercounteroffensive.

A conversation between two thirteen-year-old girls, a complex, utterly banal exchange of agreed allusions, themes, and references quite opaque to anyone outside their social orbit.

A drunk's monologue, projected on the inside of his skull in full Technicolor by the *Cinema Nostalgique*, of an encounter with a ghostly policeman.

A business man's oaths and imprecations as he waits for a long overdue wife to return from shopping, gathering in vehemence; then, when she finally appears, the stunning hypocrisy of his glad-to-see-you-have-you-had-a-nice-time-darling greeting.

A madwoman from a mad land reciting memorised pages from the telephone directory in a voice of prophetic hysteria.

"This is just a start," Elliot says. "I have this grand dream of remixing reality: you have this computer program, see, that's constantly scanning worldwide television, radio, and telecommunications, stealing samples and then mixing them down to rhythm tracks generated by a subroutine. I use a lot of computer-generated rhythm tracks; most dance music is seventy, eighty percent computer-generated. What I want to do is to take the human element out entirely to make it more human, you understand what I mean? I want the abilities of a computer to contain and express the diversity of what it means to be human. Reality, the twelve-inch version. The Happening World, Club Mix. I get invited to a sound-system party and I just plug in the computer and give them this happening world at five hundred watts per speaker. The people who go to these parties, they just want dance music as a means of escape, something to stuff their heads full of Ecstasy to, or whatever, and let the dope and the music toast their neurons. Me, I want to use dance music to *explore*. I want it to be dangerous, radical. I want dancing to be political."

"The politics of dancing?" Enye asks.

Elliot looks at her as his muse rolls, sated, from him and withdraws into her divine cloud of unknowing.

"You what?"

She breaks into the dead amusement arcade through a skylight. The rotted, paint-blistered wood yields with only the faintest cry to her crowbar. It is not as great a drop as she has feared. Her red Reeboks hardly make any sound. She drags a retired one-armed-bandit across the pitted linoleum floor and stations it beneath the skylight. She may have to leave the way she entered. She cannot resist one pull, for the sake of all those fat copper pennies she slid down all those chromium gullets in all those childhood amusement arcades. The mechanism has jammed solid. Three lemons, the final payout.

It is a strange contact, the pulse of mythoconsciousness in this seaside town huddled behind its breakwaters and shingle beach against winter; a variable star in her neural constellation, at times so dim and wan as to be virtually imaginary, again, an actinic flare of nova light burning out from among the closed-down arcades and hot dog stalls and rain-washed promenades. Its variable nature and its distance from the mass of phagus activity ranked it low on the list of priorities. Now it had worked its way to the top by dint of Enye having removed all contacts more interesting than it.

She had not been surprised to find this closed-season arcade where she had rolled her pennies as a child the focus of the mythoconscious contact. As she sat in the Citroen listening to Nielsen symphonies and dripping gobbets of Thousand Island dressing onto the upholstery from the burger she bought from the sole late-night eatery on the storm-lashed seafront, she had found herself submerging into cotton-candy reverie. Days when the sun seemed brighter, hotter, cleaner than the sun that shines upon this dog-end decade; days when mothers wore slacks and fathers wore sandals and rolled up their trouser legs, and kiddies wore shorts and white knee socks and babies wore sun bonnets. Days when the souvenir shops unself-consciously gloried in their curious hybrid of naive vulgarity and patriotism. Dirty postcards cheek-to-cheek with pictures of Padre Pio bleeding all over the revolving display rack. Flags of all nations on little wooden sticks to deck the ramparts of your sand Versailles.

Rain had speckled the windshield, washing away the sand castles of other decades. Dead neon, peeling paint, swags of faery lights rattling in the wind driving the cold black breakers onto the shingle shore, graffiti felt-markered on green-painted seats and shelters. The entropy of the heart. When the teenage crew of the solitary late-night burger bar rolled down the shutters, leaving the memory of dirty grease in the morning air, she had made her move.

She slides open a lathe and glass door, enters the main body of the arcade, a long room filled with the discarded corpses of arcade games. There is enough light from the promenade for her to make out the names on the cabinets: Astroblaster, Shark Hunt, Penny Falls, Torpedo Run, Wheel of Fortune, Derby Day, The Drunkard's Dream—she remembers that one, ghosts appearing out of barrels, trapdoors, at windows while pink elephants wheeled across the background, all for a penny—Space Invaders I, Space Invaders II. Pinball machines; an art form in themselves, tail-fin pink Thunderbirds, Caesar's Palace hostesses winking lewdly, Space Bimbettes in bikinis and goldfish-bowl helmets wedged into the armpits of men in scarlet tights, silver boots, and improbably bulging crotches far more threatening to the marauding aliens than the mix/blend/whip/puree ray pistols in their hamlike fists. Her parents had never allowed her to play pinball. The prerogative of Bigger Boys. She pauses, turns, scans the room with her Shekinah sight. This is the heart of the enigmatic contact.

"Hello?" She unsheathes the swords slung across her back. Rain rattles on the windows.

A video game click-buzzes to itself.

"God, don't do that."

But the power is off. She remembers noticing that as she

came in. The games are all plugged into the ceiling sockets, but the master isolator is up. The power is off.

One by one the dead arcade games flash and hum into restored life. Old fluorescents flash and wink, the pinball machines chatter their counters down to zero and rattle their buffers. The video games awaken in a dawn chorus of buzzing, of buzzings, zarpings, beepings, and growlings. Somewhere, a sailor in a glass case shakes his shoulders and laughs maniacally. Sparks fly from the old "Electric Chair," smoke rises from the jerking mannequin's ears. Penny Falls shoves log jams of outmoded currency toward the brink.

Enye advances through the arcade, swords held in the stance of *Gedan No Kame*. Around her screens light with video explosions, glowing red torpedoes lurch toward their targets, wheels of fortune spin, plastic racehorses gallop.

Something.

Behind a cabinet. She turns to face it. Again—the briefest flash of something, low, scurrying, scuttling. A dart of motion. She cries out, rubs, her right ankle. Pain, like a whiplash or a cigarette burn. She sees it clearly for one instant on top of a game cabinet, a small, glowing gremlin shaped out of neon. It looks nothing more and nothing less than an archetypal Space Invader. She cuts with the *katana* but it is gone. She winces. Her neck stings. A second Invader crouches on top of a Teletennis cabinet. It spits a bolt of electricity at her. Enye barely parries with her *tachi* blade.

"*Tō!*" The creature leaps, too slow, too slow. The swinging blade of the *katana* smashes it into a puffball of bathroom pink fluorescence. Dozens now, on every vantage, spitting out their tiny shock bolts. Too many to parry; each hit is a sear and puff of scorching fabric and flesh. She retreats, they follow through, hopping from cabinet to cabinet. She sees one tearing itself free from a screen, annihilates it, but it is liking killing wasps. There are always too many of them. She takes refuge behind an Astro-tank 2000 cabinet. There is a smell of burning, of electricity, as the cabinet absorbs fire. The laughing sailor in its glass cabinet regards her with a malevolent eye. Ceases in midlaugh. Turns its head toward her.

"Bet you never met one like me before," it says. Mickey

Mouse gosh-golly-wow voice. An Invader leaps down from the top of Enye's cover, releases a bolt. Enye yelps, swears. The *tachi* flies from her hand, spins across the scabby linoleum. She sucks the burn on her left hand. The Invader leaps to attack again. The *katana* catches in it midair.

"How you like this arcade game, sunshine? This one shoots back. Adds a whole new dimension of excitement, wouldn't you say?" says the Mickey Mouse matelot. "Tell me, gorgeous, how's it feel to be on the receiving end for a change?"

"Spare me the clichés," Enye says, rolling to retrieve her sword. As she hoped, the thick fabric of her parka protects her from the hail of bolts. She takes fresh cover as a wave of neon Invaders overrun the Astro-tank 2000 game. The laughing sailor tracks her with his head.

"Shaped charges," it says. "Kind of cute, don't you think? My own little army of phaguses. Of course, they're not terribly robust, but they make up in numbers what they lack in individual durability."

Enye raises the *katana* to smash the glass cabinet and its occupant into nothingness.

"I wouldn't waste your time," says the sailor. "I'm Little Mr. Everywhere, aren't I? The Ghost in the Machine, I like to think of myself. The Faery of the VDU. Today, video games, tomorrow the banking networks, next week the defence systems. Well, you've got to dream, don't you?"

"I cannot believe," says Enye, breaking from cover behind a flickering dance of steel and electricity, "that the Mygmus ever stored a memory like you." She backs toward the wall, trying to make her way to the sliding doors. She has an idea. The sailor's face rezzes up on an Asteroid's screen.

"Oh, I wouldn't say that. Each generation generates its own mythologies, its own gods and demons, its own imps and sprites. I am merely a response to the collective unconscious of the times. But seriously, gorgeous, have you ever considered that these creatures of the Mygmus you are battling with such zeal and determination, I must admit, might not be the hopes and fears of your so-called adversary, but your own fears and hopes, reflected back at

you? Pluck out the beam from your own eye before you cast
out the mote from your brother's, and all that. It's worth
thinking about, you know."

"Ya!" Enye plunges the *katana* through the screen. The
tube detonates in dust and flying glass.

"Temper, temper," says the taunting Mickey Mouse
voice from a Wurlitzer jukebox. Invaders advance, formed
up into ranks and files, once over each other like tiny
musketeers. The death of a thousand cuts. Each tiny burn,
each tiny shock might be no more than an irritation, but
multiplied a hundred, five hundred, a thousand, ten thousand times . . . Seared, scarred, half-blinded. Enye cuts
her way toward the glass door. Shaped charges. Ghosts in
the machine. Bolt after bolt strikes home as she pulls tall
cabinets around her and the junction box.

"Where is it where is it where is it." She traces the power
main, down, along. There. The fuse box. She hammers at
the catch with the hilt of the *tachi* until the box falls open.
She rips out the ceramic fuses, casts them away behind her.
Disconnects the computer from the *katana*. A power bolt
strikes the back of her neck like a whip. Tiny neon ghosts
appear around the edge of her barricade, over the tops of the
cabinets, squeezing between the black fabric-covered
boxes. The air smells of sweat and ionisation. She jams the
multiway connector into the open contacts of the master
fuse.

The death cry of the phagus is terrible as silver lightning
blazes from cabinet to cabinet, through every wire and
microprocessor and neon of its silicon nervous system.
Glyphs flock and storm like birds. Where they intersect
Invaders, both are destroyed in a silent blossom of light.
Enye holds the connector to the fuse box until there is
silence and darkness absolute in the dead arcade. The dead
videos seem like tombstones, the Wheels of Fortune and
Penny Falls and pinball machines strange mausoleums. Winc-
ing, she heaves herself onto the old fruit machine and out
into the rain and the cold. Only the Lords of the Gateway
remain. Most cunning of phaguses, so deeply absorbed into
the life of the world she has not yet been able to pluck their
signature from the sky signs. But she will. Soon.

• • •

According to the instructions, you pass the little plastic wand through your stream, place it in the indicator unit, and wait four minutes.

Four minutes, that's two hundred forty seconds counting at one hippopotamus two hippopotamus that's a long time and an awful lot of hippopotami (a veritable stampede, do hippopotami stampede, are there ever anything like two hundred forty of them in one place at any time?) damn, cloud-gathering again, she's missed the four-minute mark, will that matter, will that make a difference; no, no matter, no difference; it's blue, bright blue. Blue as the most incredibly blue thing you can think of. Bluer.

She slumps onto the toilet seat in her street-riding clothes.

"Goddamn you, Saul Martland. You finally got what you wanted from me."

The woman who calls herself Marie, the one who was once a disaffected housewife for whom the daily barrage of Snap, Crackle, and Pop grew too much, hears her voice and looks into the cubicle. One glimpse is enough.

"Please, don't go telling everyone," Enye says. But they know already. Pheromones, hormones, ketones, esters; chemical semaphore. One by one they come into the women's room, fold themselves as best they can into the cramped space. All of them, even gum-ruminating, ethnic-hatted Omry.

"Jeez, Enye, sorry . . ."

"Have you told him yet?"

"Are you going to tell him?"

"Are you going to get married?"

"How long you going to keep working?"

"What you going to do with it?"

"Hey, like we're here, don't ever forget that . . ."

She'd skipped a period, like a faulty typewriter, hah hah, old joke, outmoded and outworn; it's word processors now and they don't miss a *thing*. And now everything is cast into the air to hang like dust. Her job with the courier company, her ability to maintain her apartment, her relationship with

Saul, and Elliot, and, most important, most devastatingly, the hunt for the Lords of the Gateway. All changed, changed utterly. Changed terribly. The biological clocks are running. She has a strictly limited amount of time to find and destroy the Lords. She imagines she can feel the cells of the thing inside her dividing and re-dividing and re-re-dividing.

That last time. It must have been. But she was on progesterone. Unless the progressive doses of Shekinah she had taken to heal the scarred membrane of mythlines between Earth and Mygmus had tampered with her hormone balance. Suppositions, probabilities, improbabilities. The undeniable reality is that she is pregnant.

Out on the bike that day she feels appallingly self-conscious, as if her womb is made of glass.

As she is signing out that evening (how early the dark is drawing, how short the days) there is a polite, solicitous clearing of a throat behind her, of the kind only made by someone who is shy of a task they have been given. Sumpta, the girl who is the resting actress, hands a fat brown envelope to Enye.

"We, all the girls, us all, we talked among ourselves, you know, and we thought, we thought, in case you want to . . . you know, we thought this might help."

The fat brown envelope contains a fat wad of soiled bank notes.

Until receiving the fat brown envelope from the hand of Sumpta, she had not thought of abortion.

She turns off the tape before it is one-third played through. Haydn's disciplined, measured harmonies are thin and trivial to her tonight, like so much tinsel. They have never sounded like that before. She snatches the cassette from the desk, rips out metre after metre of brown oxide tape; rips and rips in anger and frustration as she tries to break it and the tape just reels out endlessly through her fingers, yielding, infuriatingly.

At school it had always been the fat girls, the ugly girls, the stupid girls who got pregnant, the girls who knew they could not get a man any other way, who knew their only contribution to society was a few squirts of woman-juice in the gene pool, the ones with short short skirts and bare legs in *winter*, yet, in those few weeks before their mothers took them out of school, went around smirking and self-satisfied as if pregnancy had endowed them with some final and absolute authority over the thin girls, the pretty girls, the smart girls.

Smart girls pretty girls thin girls do not get caught. Smart girls pretty girls thin girls do not have stand-up quickies behind discos, or in the backseats of Fords. Smart girls pretty girls thin girls say no, and when the time does come to say yes, smart girls pretty girls thin girls know all about contraception.

Smart girls pretty girls thin girls have *futures*.

She had not loved him. She had only wanted his presence to prove how little she needed it.

She imagines what will happen if she calls him. His shock. The stunned stammer that he lapses into when in the past she has surprised him. The shock will turn into guilt, into concern, into responsibility. Now she can hear his voice enfolding her like a winter quilt; it's our responsibility now, let me take care of you, let me look after you, let me be a father to your child, a good father, a caring father, a loving father, let's be a family together, all together, locked away from harm in the protective circle of my arms, from anything and everything that would harm you or the baby.

Lord! No!

She lies on her bed, stares at the ceiling, listening for the perhaps real, perhaps imaginary synchronicity of heart-beats.

If not Saul, then who? She lists the men she cares about most in the world. Jaypee? As strange to her as an amputated limb would be. Elliot? Too unworldly; like seducing an angel. Mr. Antrobus? She would terrify him; a wedge of assertive female sexuality thrusting into his carefully ordered world of Greek temples and Ionian sun-sets.

If not these, then who?

The answer surprises her.

She lifts up the bedside telephone, punches digits.

"Hi. It's me. Yes. Listen, can I come and see you?"

• • •

Because it was the last summer day anyone expected ever
to see (global climatic change due to underarm antiperspi-
rant and soft toilet tissue were going to shift the climate to
approximately that of the Mosquito Coast), Mr. Antrobus
had dared to bless it with the bare skin of his legs and arms.
Enye was already too hot, iced coffee notwithstanding,
draped on her sun lounger, at the constantly-pushing-up-
the-shades-that-are-sliding-down-my-nose-on-account-of-
the-sweat-and-the-oil phase when Mr. Antrobus came
wading through the rampant hollyhocks with his deck chair
under his arm like a refugee from the Hope and Glory days.
Net curtains twitched at neighbouring windows; prurient
thoughts about what an old man, Proclivities notwithstanding, was doing with a girl like *her* in a swimsuit like *that*.
She peered over her shades at the watching windows,
slowly ran her tongue with unspeakable lewdness around
her lips.

It had been a heady, hallucinatory summer, an illusion of
heat haze and dazzle. Enye was no longer certain how much
of her life was diurnal and tangible, how much nocturnal
and illusory. Advertising copywriter by day; romancer of
Saul Martland by the long summer evenings; by the short
summer nights, street samurai, Knight of the Chromium
Lotus, battling on the edge of reality. Oh come *on* . . .
The bizarre parameters of her life had crept over her with
such stealth that she had not before thought to question
them. *City Terrorised As Drug-Crazed Swords-woman
Stalks Streets By Night*. In the heat of the last day anyone
expected ever to see of summer, it strained her disbelief
further than she was willing to suspend it.

As ever, Mr. Antrobus looked stuck with his crossword.
Normally she would have helped him; she had the gift of
instantaneously solving anagrams in her head, which Mr.
Antrobus did not always appreciate; he enjoyed stuckness as
a spiritual grace, in the manner of Buddhist monks. Today
she had a question she wanted to ask him that he could not
answer, for it was a trick question, meant for herself, a
question she could only truly answer herself.

She put down her copy of a magic-realist novel that had earned its author a death sentence for blasphemy.

"Mr. Antrobus. Do you think the world has gone mad?"

He answered immediately, as if it was a question he had been waiting all his life to be asked.

"The world has always seemed mad as people get older. Mad, and getting madder. Whether it actually is or not I don't know. It looks mad, but then it has always looked mad; any sanity it has ever seemed to have it had only because we were at the time equally mad. Why do you ask?"

"It just seems to me that people are acting as if they no longer understand the rules on which their lives, their society, their world is built; as if there are no longer any rules, no longer any foundations. Or, as if the rules have been twisted by an outside agency so that evil is strong and therefore good and good weak, and therefore evil. As if the world has been possessed, lost its soul."

"Now that is a different question altogether. Has the world lost its soul, is that what you are asking me? Has the world been possessed by a dark spirit? Is there a Satan? Is God dead, or merely gone away? My answer would be to say that if it seems that way it is because the world has lost its *present*. We don't enjoy the present moment anymore—we don't savour the pleasure of *being*. The present is just a tiresome intervention between where we were and where we want to be, a thing that comes between us and our desirable futures. What impatient creatures we have become, always wanting to be where we are not yet, to become what we are not yet. We are not content to be present where we are. Becoming is everything, being is nothing. We have forgotten the Sacrament of the Present.

"I first learned of the Sacrament of the Present from an old Greek Orthodox monk in the monastery near the town where I was stationed on Kos. I used to go up to the monastery a lot; we had bicycles. The people of the town gave us their bicycles as a token of thanks for their liberation. Such grand and generous people, the Greeks; now they are folk who know what it is to live in the present. They said the olive trees around the monastery were the oldest on the island, older than the monastery itself, they said, older than the coming of Christianity to the island. Certainly, the shade, the peace, was deeper under those olive trees than anywhere else I have ever known. Why did I go up there? I don't know. Perhaps I felt the need to be absolved of something. Perhaps I needed to know from God whether the love from which I suffered was right or wrong. Can you understand that? The monks came to recognise me; they let me walk in the cloisters and spend time in the chapel—the eyes of those Greek icons, like the eyes of God Himself. Beautiful, beautiful eyes. I used to sit for hours in the dark and the cool of the chapel, gazing on the frescoes.

"I think his name was Brother Anastasis, which means 'resurrection' in Greek. He was the only member of the community who spoke more than three words of English. I think he saw my spiritual welfare and guidance as his personal ministry. They had a wonderful spirituality in that place—silence and singing, stillness and dancing. A kind of languid grace that only comes from the deep deep practice of the presence of God.

"Presence, he said, was everything. Even then, in 1944, he said that man had forgotten the Sacrament of the Present. Too much, too high, too far, too loud. Not enough silence and stillness; too busy becoming to truly be. Not enough presence. I asked him what he meant by the Sacrament of the Present. He took me out into the olive groves that were as old as Christianity itself, made me look at those gnarled, ancient trees, and told me his answer. Those words he spoke to me I know I will never forget: *A tree, by being a tree, is, and so worships God.*"

The last sun of the last summer beat down like molten copper into the garden. When it set that night it took part of Mr. Antrobus down with it beyond the edge of the world. For the rest of that summer, endless days of grey overcast and damp drizzle, he became oppressed by premonitions of death and judgment, as if the door to God had stood ajar before him all his life and he had not recognised it. As Enye herself remembers that last bright day, before the darkness and disease of the winter and the war against the Adversary took firm hold of her life.

• • •

Mothers know, you know.

It amuses her to see that the process of subdivision goes on. Her mother's home—the long, low bungalow behind its high wall and green wooden gates—had been built in the garden of Enye's maternal grandmother's house. Now her mother has a tiny mock-Georgian house with a French hatchback parked outside it built in her garden. She wonders, can the process go on *ad infinitum*?

She has read that smell is the most powerful stimulator of memory. She strips scale-leaves from the cypress hedges, rubs them in her palms, inhales. Sea gulls crying. The mournful voice of the ferries down in the harbour, slipping away to sea. Sunsets. Sunrises. Starry, starry nights. Frost on the flagstones. The surprise of waking to find the garden white with snow, the peculiar earth-sweat smell of sun-burned ground returning its heat to the sky in the cool cool cool of the summer evenings. Trees. Herbaceous borders. The loom of her maternal grandmother's Victorian pile over her childhood. Cigarette smoke and steaming kitchens, forever associated with the theme tune of "The Magic Roundabout." Smells. Memories. The old house. The windows need repainting; there is a cracked panel in the glass door. The brass letter basket is new, but she knows she will have to press and press and press to get the doorbell to ring.

And the dogs will come leaping and barking and wagging their tails: Shane and Paddy's successors.

She is looking old. Small; desperately small, and vulnerable, pushing away the barking, wagging dogs. Gone the universal competence with which Enye and her brother had endowed her; perhaps it never was, and this old, terrible fallibility has always been her true complexion. She can imagine how Ewan would have thought it a sickness.

"Come in, oh come in, come in."

The house smells different, like an old woman's house. The smell puzzles Enye until she recognises that her own personal perfume, the smell of her life and presence, has leached out of the walls and the rooms and furnishings and dissolved away. There is no part of her here now, not even her smell.

Tea is prepared, homemade cakes and biscuits set on polite plates while Enye pats the dogs' heads and asks them their names and if they have been good boys, as people will ask dogs, and shakes their proffered paws and tells them what good boys they are, as people will tell dogs.

"So, tell me, how is advertising, then?"

"It isn't."

"What happened?"

"I quit. Personality clash with my Creative Director. Constructive dismissal. It would have happened sooner or later. Just happened to be sooner."

"And so, what are you doing with yourself now?"

"Would you believe, I'm working for a bicycle courier company? I've got one of their cards here. Here you are, see? Keeps body and soul together, and me pretty fit."

"You thought yet about what you want to go on to do?"

"No. I don't know. Hell, Mum . . . dammit . . . no, I said I wouldn't do this, sorry . . . I'll be all right in a minute."

The dogs lie on their sides in front of the fire and thump their tails against the carpet.

"When's it due?"

Mothers know, you know.

"Goddamn. July. Thereabouts. I haven't been to see the doctor yet. I don't know for sure . . ."

"What you're going to do with it?"

"Yes."

"Whether you want to keep it or not?"

"Yes."

"What about the father?"

"Saul." She smiles, the entropy of the heart. "Saul. You'd like him. He's a solicitor, very desirable. He doesn't know. I'm not seeing him anymore."

"Would you think of marrying him?"

"Saul?" She laughs, a deep, cleansing, painful laugh. "Oh, he'd love that. He would. He's a born husband and father. He'd be a much better father than I would a mother. No, I'm not going to marry him. I'm not going to tell him. He would have me in a mental institution in five years, or

up for manslaughter, pleading diminished responsibility.
The girls at work, would you believe, passed the hat for me,
in case I wanted to get rid of it and couldn't afford to."

"And will you?"

"I think so. I'm about seventy, eighty percent certain. I'll
give it until I'm ninety, ninety-five, before I make a
commitment."

"Oh, Enye . . ."

"Shit, Mum, everything is a mess. Everything is just
falling apart and running through my fingers and I can't stop
it." She crosses to the window, looks out through the blinds
at the neo Georgian house where the garden she had played
in as a child once grew. She runs a thumb along her
mother's record collection, selects a Mozart symphony, sets
it spinning on the turntable.

"Ewan says you're sick. The way he puts it, you were at
death's door."

"Ewan exaggerates. Ewan will say anything to get his
own way. I'm all right."

"You look different."

"Older."

"How long is it?"

"Ten years."

"I couldn't wait to get out of the house as soon as I got
that university scholarship."

"You look well."

"That's pregnancy. Every woman's supposed to look
radiant. Tell me that when I'm a walrus."

"You'll look good then. Oh, Enye."

A pause, a space for Mozart to have his say.

"Mum, do you think it would be all right for me to stay
here a day or so?"

She is given her old room back. All the posters, the
books, the tapes and toys and things are in place. She
cannot sleep. Who can sleep in the shrine to his memory?

They go to the big mall down by the ferry port. They pick
things out for each other they know they will detest. They
make shop-assistants' lives hell. They shop, they coffee and

Danish, but it is only when they are back home again and Enye's mother says that tonight she really ought to put up the tree does Enye realize that Christmas has stolen up on her unawares. Her mother asks Ewan if he wants to help; he scowls across the dinner table at the two women. He has used every available excuse to take himself out of the house since Enye has come back. He, the one who so much wanted this reunification.

"I worried about him when he was small," her mother says. "His imaginary friends, always happiest with his own company, not fitting in at school."

"You never worried about me and I was the one who invented entire imaginary countries populated by rubber monsters."

"The doctors never said that you displayed symptoms of incipient schizophrenia."

"What?" Enye says, but her mother will not speak again on the subject. Enye senses that she may have already spoken too much.

They plant the tree in its bucket of sand and earth and set it in its immutable position by the living room door. The tiny, individual Christ lights are taken from their box, tested, repaired where necessary, and spiralled around the branches. Enye's mother goes up on the kitchen step stool to drape the fat, furry tinsel garlands.

"Why did you lie to us about our father?"

She does not falter on her step stool as she drapes the fat, furry garlands over and under and over. She has had ten years to prepare for this question.

"Because I didn't want you to be hurt."

"But I was hurt."

"All I had was a choice of evils."

"It wasn't as if it was one lie, it was lie after lie, years of lies, a lifetime of lies. I still don't know if you've ever told me one true thing about my father."

"You think you are God that no one may lie to you? You never lied to me?"

Without the least flavour of malice, or rancour.

"It hurt me that you thought I would never be mature enough to handle it."

"I knew you would come back when you were mature enough."

"And what is the truth?"

"I have lied to you, I admit that; but Enye, just let me hold this one thing, keep it mine and not burden another with it. Just let me take it down with me into the earth and let it be dissolved away and forgotten."

"Why? For God's sake? Can it be so terrible, can it be any worse than what I have imagined all these years?"

"It can."

She dreams of her father that night, for the first time in many, many years. For the first time in many, many years, she can remember his face. He is walking toward her from a very great distance across a great flat plane. His hands are held out, but they, like this face, like everything about him, are indecipherable. Concealed intent. Hidden spirit. As soon as he draws close enough for her to be able to reach and touch, he dissolves and reappears, an eye-blink of dust in the great distance, far, far across the great flat plane, approaching step by step.

The breakfast radio news has reports of people breaking up the wall between the two Germanies with hammers and kitchen cutlery, and of unspeakable barbarism from a land whose kings had once impaled their enemies on long wooden spikes. Two spoonfuls of yoghurt on the muesli, tea from a china pot.

"I reached ninety-eight percent this morning."

Her mother continues pouring the tea.

"I'll be going today. I'll take the evening sailing."

"There are places here will do it."

"Back-street chop-shops. I want it done properly, and legally. I owe it that much. The girls have given me an address. It would seem I am not the first cycle courier to have needed an abortion. My God, I cannot believe I am talking like this . . ."

By correctly identifying the voice of a well-known country-and-western singer, Mrs. Marion Doyle of St. Brendan's Avenue, Coolock, has won herself a Radio One KRTP-FM sunstrip for her car.

Her mother comes with her as far as the ticket barrier. She presses an envelope into her daughter's hand. "If your mind's made up, your mind's made up." Then she turns and walks away and in a dozen steps is lost among the press of passengers surging into the boarding tunnel. In the brown envelope are one hundred bills of small denominations.

"God. Mum! Mum!"

The surge and press of passengers and suitcases and baby buggies and luggage trolleys sweeps Enye before it into the great white ship.

She wakes in the night, in her coffin-narrow berth. The other passengers with whom she shares the cabin sleep on, a topography of breathings. It is 2:33 on the little portable alarm clock. What? Not a change in the steady vibration of the engines, or the hum of the air-conditioning, not the dull thud of a mid-Channel floating something banging the hull, nor the change of attitude as the great white ship crosses a sea current. Not a presence of anything. No, an absence.

She has it now.

The glow at the base of her skull has gone dark and cold. The sense of *presence* which has for so long been an integral part of her Enye MacColl-ness, is gone. She has moved beyond the outermost edge of the web of mythlines of which her consciousness is a part, into new and unfamiliar geographies.

It strikes her with almost physical force. An end to the war, to the walls of secrecy that daily grow higher around her—the light long since shut out—an end to the schizophrenia of days riding the streets of the city on her eighteen-speed flame yellow ATB and nights stalking those same streets pursuing the spectre of unspeakable, unending violence. An end to fear, to a responsibility that is crushing the life from her like a great falling moon. To simply walk away, to be able to live and love and work and play and be human, to be the Enye MacColl Enye MacColl had always intended Enye MacColl to be. To have relationships in which she can afford to care, can afford to be spendthrift with her emotions. All by the simple act of walking away.

And she knows, in that berth in the belly of the great ship beating across the currents of the cold northern seas, that she cannot do it. She must see it ended. She must heal the sickness once and forever so that it will never again threaten her soul. She has responsibilities. She cannot walk away.

The late winter dawn finds her on the deck as the great white ship enters a wide estuary. Docks and piers, warehouses, lights, buoys and beacons, the monolithic flanks of bulk carriers with names like *Neptune Amethyst* and *Transglobal Challenger*. Kilometre after kilometre of cranes and piled cargo containers slide past her on the shore. White gulls hover over the white wake, raucous and greedy in the dawn light, hunting for morsels thrown to the surface by the twin screws. The air is cold and damp; it smells of sea and oil, it smells of morning. A middle-aged man in a blue track suit is jogging around the deck. Ten laps equals one kilometre. He nods to Enye each time he passes. His breath steams. They are the only two people on deck. The great white ship passes through a series of locks and moles and ties up. Police check the passengers as they disembark. Everyone from Enye's country is automatically under suspicion. They alight on a young man with a dark complexion who has not had time to shave this morning. He looks like their idea of a terrorist. A taxi takes Enye into the city. It is still too early for the clinic to be taking bookings. She finds a café open for breakfast, which, for the people of this city, seems to consist wholly of toast. Every two minutes a waitress with a whining voice shouts "Toast's ready!" and deposits a plate on a customer's table. Enye eats all the toast she is capable of looking at after a midwinter sea crossing and it is still not time for the clinic to open. The address is near one of the city's famous cathedrals. She thinks it would be silly to have been here and not seen the sights. As the first Beatles tour is not for another two hours, she opts for the cathedral.

Immersed in drowning in embedded in: light. Rainbow coloured like God's covenants. It might be heaven. Christ Triumphant enthroned in primal light receives the glorias of saints and seraphs casting their crowns upon the glassy sea while the dead summoned from their graves are caught up in rapture to receive beautification or damnation. *Christus Omnia Vincit;* the Last Trump sounds, in shafts and columns of light Michael stoops like a hawk upon the Great Worm; the pit of fire opens its maw to receive the Deceiver and those he has deceived. *Light*. Primal light overwhelms her. Cantos from Klopstock, the inspiration to Mahler for

the final movement of his Resurrection Symphony, resound
in her mind.

> *Ich bin von Gott und will weider zu Gott!*
> *Mit Flugeln, die ich mir errungen.*
> *In heissem Liebesstreben,*
> *Werd' ich entschweben*
> *Zum Licht, zu dem kein Aug' gedrungen!*

Classical Remix Kultur.

The trumpets of resurrection reverberate as she passes
from window to window: the Gates of Eden sealed and
guarded with a sword of flame, the Deluge thundering down
upon the unrighteous; the covenant going up at Carmel with
Abraham, coming down at Sinai with Moses. *Gaude te,
gaude te, Christus est natus, ex Maria Virgine, gaude te.*
Voices join with the primal light to fill the vault. She has
come at choir practice, doubly blessèd she. Signs and
wonders, bread and wine, loaves and fishes, lion ox man
eagle, alpha and omega, YHWH, I Am What I Am, INRI
XPI.

By the ancient lights God reveals Himself to Enye
MacColl contemplating abortion. Handel now: *And the
Glory of the Lord.* A sense of numinous awe she has not
known since childhood days of Cloud-gathering enfolds
her. She knows herself to have been touched by the finger
of God. *A tree, by being a tree, is . . .*

She walks from the cathedral through the wakening city
down to the waterside, takes a fat, bustling ferry across the
wide river, meanders with the expectant aimlessness of the
true explorer about the town on the other shore; discovers
delights and delicacies of Victoriana and Edwardiana;
wrought-iron and glass, pavilions and piers and esplanades
and boardwalks; the autumnal tranquility of a seaside resort
permanently out of season. She buys ice cream from a
pastel-pink clapboard booth, the sole booth open on a
promenade of windswept flapping Japanese paper lanterns.

The ferry takes her back to the city. She buys a pizza with
a little of the money her mother gave her, goes to see an
afternoon movie: a Polish film. The posters describe it as
"The Deeply Disturbing *My Bath and Hat.*" She is the only

member of the audience. They still run the film. Would they have run it for an audience of zero? Old Bishop Berkeley again—does The Deeply Disturbing *My Bath and Hat* play if there is no audience to see it?

The early night of year's ending falls across the city. She makes her way down to the ferry port. She cannot explain why she did what she did, why she did not do what she did not do. She had gone to the cathedral to kill time before having a foetus cut out of her with chrome-plated tools. She had not expected, much less wanted, to encounter God. She stands by the rail in the bitter cold and wind and watches the lights of the foreign city fall away behind her and become churned up with the waters of the estuary to white froth by the propellers.

She keeps herself awake until the great white ship crosses the borderline between geographies and returns her to her familiar mindscape of mythlines. The presence, the subliminal whispers in her spirit, are familiar friends, the dim glow at the base of her consciousness the comfort of a child's night-light that watches over sleep. She sails in with the dawn on the great white ship into the city that is her home and the bells are ringing out for Christmas Day.

And if the bells ring now, they ring for the soul of Mr. Antrobus. Heigh-ho. Heigh-ho. Slipped away in the grey in-between days, heigh-ho heigh-ho. Saw too much, did Mr. Antrobus of twenty-seven L'Esperanza Street; saw the shape of the coming decade while still a formlessness on time's horizon and knew that it would have no place in it for old, tired men with Proclivities.

Enye would like to think he died of unrequited love, heigh-ho heigh-ho.

Alas, poor Antrobus.

When she had knocked and received no answer she had first thought it an old, tired man with Proclivities's pique that she had not come on Christmas Day with her traditional gift—something warming and pourable that they could share over whatever new recording she had been given. She had spent Christmas in the house behind the green gates with her mother and her brother, to explain to them and to herself why she had done what she had done and why she had not done what she had not done. And to touch the city with her mythoconsciousness to draw out the oscillations and turbulence patterns of the Lords of the Gateway. In vain.

After dark she had come knocking again. In vain. The scratch and wail of cats confined against their will had alerted her. She had knelt down and sniffed at the underdoor gap—adequate draught-proofing had never been one of Mr. Antrobus's priorities. Cat shit and urine. She had called the police.

As they broke down the door, a wave of cats bolted out and ran into L'Esperanza Street.

One glimpse, and Enye fled upstairs.

He was seated in his favourite chair. He was wearing headphones. Red LED level meters danced on his radio-cassette; it was still tuned to the Final Station. The fire was dead clinker; in the hearth lay half-burned scraps of glossy poster paper. The topless towers of Ilium, burned.

Heigh-ho, heigh-ho.

On the day of the funeral, which is the penultimate day of the year, a lugubrious parade enters L'Esperanza Street. It is headed by a trio of musicians—three elderly, toothless gentlemen in crow-black suits and bowler hats making music upon accordion, sobbing clarinet, and arthritic fiddle. In time to their doleful music steps a motley bag of similarly dressed aged aged men, some adorned with black bowlers; some carrying tightly furled umbrellas, though the day has the electric blue clarity of bright winter days; some weighed down by medals they have won in a dozen campaigns in as many countries. Some wheel black bicycles as old and decrepit as themselves. One carries a Bible on a purple plush cushion trimmed with gold braid; another with white gloves and cuffs holds, upright, a naked sword. A third bears a flag; not the flag of any nation, more like the flag of a society or sodality. At the very rear, a man with his trouser legs rolled up (so much gooseflesh on such a cold, clear winter day) leads a goat on a piece of string. The parade processes with weighty dignity up L'Esperanza Street with the patient steps of aged aged men. Enye recognises the trio's music: a stripped-bare and mutilated variation of the second movement of Haydn's "Clock" Symphony.

The people of L'Esperanza Street are drawn from their windows and doors to watch the parade. The children leave their plastic fantasy figures and computer games to run from their gates and gardens and fall in alongside the marchers. Their feet cannot match the rhythm of aged aged men—they are too full of impatience and energy. The parade arrives at the palings in front of number twenty-seven and arranges itself, quite naturally, without any prerehearsed signal or instruction, into a semicircle. The trio falls silent, the accompanying children also. They can sense the sacredness of the moment. The talent has not yet been educated out of them.

Two old men in black bowler hats carry a large wreath of lilac and white flowers. Enye in the window wonders how she can have failed to see it; it is so large the two aged aged men can barely carry it, and it is not so very great a parade. Accordion, clarinet, and fiddle strike a chord. Hats are doffed, held over hearts. The wreath is laid by the side of the gate Mr. Antrobus only ever went out once, and that once horizontally. The man with the white gloves and cuffs raises his sword above his head, then brings it down smartly in front of his face. The flag is likewise raised high but the wind is too light to stir its heavy velvet folds so that its legend may be read by the people of L'Esperanza Street.

For one minute, there is stillness and silence.

Sword and flag are lowered, the trio resumes its abuse of Haydn, the parade reforms in the same reverent silence and, closed up by the man leading the white billy goat, proceeds on down L'Esperanza Street. A small cortege of delayed traffic has built up behind it. The expressions on the drivers' faces are hard to define. The expressions on the faces of the people of L'Esperanza Street are hard to define. The children run back to their parents and presents; the procession is gone, a momentary diversion from the grey limbo of in-between days. The parents take them indoors to watch the Disney channel on satellite TV.

Heigh-ho heigh-ho.

Poor Antrobus.

•   •   •

Question: Is it the last great party of the old decade, or the first great party of the new decade?

(Truth is, the new decade doesn't start until the Year One of any ten-year period, as one smart dick points out, only to get himself bounced by the gorillas on the door for being a pedant and party-pooper).

Answer: Both.

One of those magazines that likes to think it is indispensable to the street culture of the city has hired out an architecturally (and ideologically) sound warehouse down by the old docks and fitted out the entire second floor with five trucks' worth of sound and vision. And to breathe spirit into their five-trucksful, they have hired half a dozen of the acts they think will be germinal in the next decade.

Elliot, it would seem, is germinal.

He thinks this sounds kind of dirty. Then he realises that the offer is in deadly sincerity, panics, and needs the combined diplomatic efforts of his work mates to prevent him from throwing all his accumulated years of equipment out his window into the street.

All the city will be there, the magazine says.

"God, they better not be," says Elliot.

The organisers think it will be good for his karma if they bestow upon him a fistful of complimentary tickets so he can at least fill the dance floor with friendly feet. One pair of which belongs to Enye. Two hours to go and she has run out of human resources to settle his nerves. Certainly, the great acoustic barn is filling by the minute with the Bryghte and the Bootiful and the Mandarins of Fashion (who are predicting that This will be The Decade When Fashion Goes Out of Fashion) and the Socially Credible. "Could you lend me one of those swords of yours so I can quietly fall on it?"

The organisers have declared that this is to be a Theme party, though they have neglected to broadcast what the Theme is. The Theme seems to be Be Your Own Theme. Enye has come in a short hand-print *yukata* and a pair of black and gold shell-suit bottoms, slung her swords across her back, and rooted out a papier-mâché Kabuki mask which, at the moment, is pushed up onto her head. "Urban ninja," she says. "Knight of the Neon Lotus." Elliot is in combat pants, Jimi Hendrix "Are you Experienced?" T-shirt, Hawaiian shirt, and helicopter-pilot mirror shades. The *My Lai* look, he calls it. One forty to go and he checks and rechecks his equipment, checks and rechecks and re-rechecks. He has hired a Linn programmer and two black girls in the mandatory black leather microskirts to help him and he hasn't seen any of them in over an hour.

"'Next day on your dressing room they hang a star,'" says Enye. "Me go mingle. See what's happening out there. Back before long." She kisses him. He tastes surprisingly good.

She presses through the pressing bodies. The only dance possible under such degrees of overcrowding is a kind of shrug of alternate shoulders and side shuffle of alternate feet.

"Those swords real?" asks a sweating man dressed as an Islamic fundamentalist. He is too neurally napalmed to be worthy of a reply. Enye glares at him, slips her mask down. The heat is stifling but she has privacy.

The year ticks away.

She recognises a face from the Deep Sea Wave of faces. It is Jaypee. She flips up her mask. Jaypee recognises her. Exchanging directional hand signals, they work their ways to a rendezvous as far as possible from the band and the bass and the back seat. Jaypee looks like a dyspeptic owl. He tends to at parties. He is miffed that no one has recognised his costume: American televangelist. "Can't you tell from the trousers?" He shows her his handkerchief with the Four Spiritual Principles fabric-painted on it. "No one here has a sense of humour. You're looking good, Enye."

"My job keeps me active."

"The QHPSL rumour mill grinds exceeding fine, but word up is you're a bike girl."

"All stretch fabric and belt pouches, Jaypee; eighteen forward gears, no reverse, and quick release saddle."

"Reach out and touch the screen and be healed, sister."

"So."

"So."

"What are you doing here?"

"Always first on the scene at the epicentre of the social

seisms, Enye, honey. You know Jaypee. Happens the art
editor of that rag that purports to be a serious contributor to the
cultural health of our city and one did time together at art
college. Couldn't move for complimentaries, dear thing."

"And the . . . ah, the?"

"Glass Menagerie? Well, they've assigned one a new
partner. He's here somewhere. He felt it was meet right and
his bounden duty, but one managed to lose him, Amen and
Amen. He's young. He's dynamic, he's thrusting; he's not
you, angel."

"I'm touched, Jaypee."

"The Blessèd Phaedra's here somewhere, should you
want to run her through with one of those wicked little
swords of yours."

"She did me a favour."

"Having thigh muscles like California redwoods is a
favour?"

"Ask me that from a horizontal position."

"Enye, Enye, your exposure to the streets is turning you
into a vulgar little gurrier."

"My advice to you still stands, Jaypee."

"Alas, dear heart, one is too great a coward to heed it.
One likes one's creature comforts. Time has made Jaypee
Kinsella a great conservative. Lay hands on me, sister! I
need the power of Jesus to heal me of terminal conserva-
tism!"

Mistah DeeJay is playing hits from the past ten years
back-2-back. Sometimes you can almost weep with nostalgia.

All changed, changed utterly.

"See you about, Jaypee."

"Probably not, Enye."

And the conflicting currents that stir the party at the edge
of the decade move them apart again.

People and people and people cram into the second-floor
warehouse. Under the FX lights, it becomes more and more
like Mr. Antrobus's personal hell. Human gravitation:
through the orbiting bodies Enye is drawn to Omry, jigging
disconsolately at the foot of the stage. She is dressed as
ever, in the fabric of the decade. Enye wonders, is she going
to change at midnight, whirl around like Wonder Woman to

reveal the fabric of the next decade in all its wonder and glory? Omry's theme is Herself.

"Those swords real?"

"Second person to ask that. Third person gets one run through him. Or her."

"Great party idea. Could I borrow them sometime?"

"I think not. Too much spirit in these swords."

Omry understands this.

"Elliot asking for you. He's shitting blue bricks back there."

Elliot's is the final set of the year. The last half hour all to himself. Fifty-five minutes to launch: how time flies.

"I suppose I'd better go see him."

The great amoebic party animal stirs.

"Just to say . . ." Omry shouts across the heads and the EmCee announcing the next band, ". . . he's yours. I relinquish all claims. Wipe my fingerprints off his ass. I was no good for him. We didn't commune at all. You and he, you commune all right. You have great spirits."

Enye understands how much it has cost Omry to say those words. She shouts thanks and gratitude but they are shattered to dust by the first power chords ripping out from the new act. She slips down her mask again. She had glimpsed Phaedra, head tossed back in jewelled laughter behind an ermine domino mask on a stick. Buttons, beads, bows; Marie Antoinette. A liaison hunting for danger.

It takes the two black girls in the mandatory leather microskirts sitting on his arms and Enye sitting on his chest (Hey, what am I *doing*?) pouring antihistamines and cans of lager down his throat to convince Elliot that he is going to be, not fair, not average, not good, not great, but mega-great, superhyperterrabevagreat. Five minutes to showtime, the penultimate set of the year has ended, the hits of the past decade come right up-to-date, the faithful roadies have moved all his keyboards and rhythm generators and sampling computers onstage, the Linn programmer he has found from somewhere is posing about studying output levels and wave forms and harmonic profiles and the EmCee has the microphone in his hand and is trying to make himself heard over the general party clamour.

Elliot falls back to the floor. Enye draws the *tachi*.

"If you do not go up on that stage, I will kill you," she
says.

"That sword real?" asks one of the black girls.

"Laydees and gennelmen, nonsexist persons, let's dance
the old year out with . . ."

Strange. As she drew the sword, she felt, like quicksilver
along her spine, the old black magic tingle of mythoconscious contact.

Mask down, she goes front-of-house to hear the set. The
entire warehouse is dancing. Tight and righteous, one KW
per channel, beaming out on the adrenaline frequency.
Behind her mask, she smiles. He is good. She recognises
her own "I could get to like this" woven into the fabric of
rhythms and samples.

"Enye!" The voice shouting in her ear over the digi-beat
and processed orgasmic sobs of the black girls is like a
pistol shot. She whirls: eyehole to eye.

Him.

"I recognised the swords, Enye."

"Saul! Shit, Saul . . ."

"You look . . . you look . . . you look."

"What are you doing here?"

"Can't hear you. Let's go somewhere we can talk."

They go somewhere they can talk, out into the cold of the
end of the year, into the frost and moonshine on the fire
escape. The wrought-iron vibrates in sympathy with Elliot's
transcription of reality.

"Not quite the St. Matthew Passion," Saul says.

"If you give it enough time, you can get to like it."

"I'd heard you were slumming it," Saul says. "What,
bicycle courier company?"

Now she sees what has always been obvious: that he
wanted to possess her so badly only so that he might have
a mirror in which to see himself reflected. Enye wants to
hurt him with weapons duller and crueler than her swords.
She wants to punish him for his sins in a way that is
endlessly cruel and goes on forever and ever and ever.

"It has its compensations as a job," she says. "All those
tight little backsides. Spoiled for choice, really. I must
introduce you to Elliot. He's onstage right now; he comes

off at the end of the year. You should meet. You've absolutely nothing in common."

Saul stiffens. He is dressed as Rhett Butler. Stick-on moustache and suave hat. Like Percy Perinov. Look what happened to him. Should she tell him about the baby? Dandle it in front of him, then snatch it back inside her life forever?

"We're finished, Saul. We outgrew each other. Can't you understand that? You are so stupid. Stupid stupid stupid man. Go away, won't you? Let's consent to be pieces of each other's histories."

She can feel the old year straining at the boundaries of time, eager to be gone, heigh-ho heigh-ho. And something more: the distant, panicky nausea of mythlines gathering and gyring. A sudden wave of vertigo sends her reaching for the cold iron banister. She wants him gone. Gone now. Gone for good.

"Why did you come here? You hate things like this; you always did. You never came to any of the parties I invited you to because you hate people. You hate people because you are afraid of people. You fear the *other*, anything but yourself. You always did, Saul. Go away. I am *me*, understand. Me."

"Let me see your face. Take off the mask, please."

"Go away, Saul."

He goes. And she is alone on the fire escape. And she feels very much like crying. And she feels very much like running her sword through the first person she meets on the other side of the door. And while she feels these feelings, the old year dies and the new enters in.

She returns to the party. Balloons have cascaded from the ceiling. Bryghte Thynges and Bootifuls and the Mandarins of Fashion are shrieking and spraying polymer string and champagne over each other. Ritual ejaculation. Girls with gelled hair, blue mint lip gloss, and ludicrous skirts are jumping up and down screaming while the men they came with are kissing other women altogether. The EmCee has cleared the stage after Elliot's set; as Auld Acquaintance Is Forgot and Never Brought to Mind, he tries to make himself heard over the drunken singing.

"Citizens, comrades, people people people, let's wel-

come in the next decade" ("It doesn't start till next year!"
followed immediately by the meaty knock of fist on flesh)
"with an act that we know is going to be just enormous.
When we saw them first on the streets of our fair city, we
knew that they had to be the act to open the new decade."

A guitar power chord, long on the sustain, fading away in
a feedback howl. Pin spots wheels, searching for a target.
An urgent, insistent guitar riff, repeated as a theme through
a processor over which is laid layers of improvisation. The
spots swivel, snap, and focus. A girl with a starburst of
gelled hair and Morticia Adams makeup dives from the top
of a speaker stack into the lights as the guitar theme lifts in
resolution. And explodes. Floods up: the crowd roars and
applauds the boy with the mirror shades and the electric
guitar and the amp-pack on his back and the mad dancer
with the ripped leotard.

At the foot of the stage, a long silver needle of pain drives
through Enye MacColl's brain.

"Comrades, citizens," bellows the disembodied voice of
the EmCee, "please put various parts of yours and anyone
else's anatomy together to welcome The Lords of the
Gateway!"

In the same instant she knows them, they know her. The
guitar hesitates in the middle of a chord progression, the
dancer falters in her cascade of liquid movement for a
second, for an eigenblink.

The girl dancer dives to the front of the stage, lowers
herself to floor level. Kohled eyes make contact with Enye's
behind the Kabuki mask. Then she backflips dazzlingly to
the rear of the stage. The parrrrtyers roar. Behind the roar,
Enye hears the guitar chords take a new, dangerous ca-
dence. The boy smiles. And the familiar, feared sensation
of the bottom falling out of reality gnaws like a cancer at her
spirit: mythlines caught up in a fist and moulded together.

And she understands the nature of their gift. Theirs is the
power of breaching at will the membrane between Earth and
Mygmus, of letting the chaotic images and half-formed
archetypes fountain out into quotidian expression. And she
understands in that same beat of her mind that here under
the spots and strobes, before the Bryghtes and Bootifuls and

Socially Credible of the city, they are going to smash the sluice gates of reality.

Enye bulls her way through the transfixed Bryghtes and Bootifuls and Socially Credibles to the fire exit. Temporarily heedless of the new life inside her, she takes the ice-slick iron steps three at a time. The cars are parked so close together she has to run along the fenders to reach her Citroen, so tight-packed she cannot open the door. She draws her *tachi* and cuts her way in through the sunroof. The Shekinah is in its hiding place under the driver's seat, the personal organiser thrown into the back with empty Diet Coke cans. No time for refinements. She gulps down two tabs of Shekinah. She is halfway up the fire escape when it hits. The lift into mythoconsciousness almost sends her over the handrail two storeys to the cars below. The warehouse is the focus of a hurricane of mythlines; a celebration of derangement. The pull of them is almost enough to tear her from her grip on the emergency exit push-down handle. Dorothy and the tornado. The dance floor is a bedlam of slashing FX beams and mythlines. We certainly aren't in Kansas anymore. No time for strategy. The Gateway has formed. The mouth in the air hovers over the backstage, given phantasmal solidity by the lighting rig. Shapes move through it toward the edge of her world—shapes like dolls' prams that push themselves along with two hairy arms. Shapes like tangles of movie celluloid with an eye in each frame. Shapes like a lung bifurcated at the bottom, shuffling toward the edge of Earth in a way that can never, never be thought of as walking, its yellow crow's beak clacking and snapping. The crammed slammed jammed people clap and cheer—they think it is special effects trickery. And the guitar hammers hammers hammers and the dancer dances like nothing has ever danced before.

She stands by the emergency exit, unable to act. Her hand rests on a rectangular protrusion on the wall. What? *In case of fire* . . .

It had worked for Paul Newman in *Torn Curtain*.

She whips out the *tachi*, shatters the glass with a blow of the *tsuba*.

Never underestimate the power of fear. Spirits are

*contagious, Sleeping may be passed on, Yawning may be
passed on, Fear may be passed on.*

"Fire! Fire!" Bells begin to ring. "Fire!"

The crowd shrieks and surges, wheels to look at itself,
ask itself questions, wheels again toward the exits.

"Fire! Fire!" The warehouse goes up in one great scream
as the spirit of panic passes from person to person: Fire!
Fire! They scream, pointing at flames that do not exist yet
which they can clearly see. She sees Saul's face swirled
away through the storm of mythlines in the blind rush for
the exits, sees feet catch on Phaedra's Marie Antoinette
crinoline and pull her down, down, under the trampling
feet. The alarm bells ring and ring and ring and ring and
ring and ring. Enye leaps up onto the stage, fastens the
computer to her *obi*, draws the *katana*.

The girl dancer applauds slowly.

Enye pushes up her mask.

The guitarist sets down his backpack. Behind him, the
Warped Ones fret at their confinement. The stage area is the
dead eye of a cyclone of mythlines. The guitarist takes off
his mirror shades.

Pale skin covers the sockets where eyes should be.

She understands why she could not find them. She could
not find them because, like her, their control is conscious.
They leave no footprints in the unsurface of the Mygmus,
set no mythlines trembling with their passage because they
are so fully subsumed into the world.

The warehouse is empty. Even the crushed and trampled
have been taken away.

Enye shifts her hold on the *katana* to the light, floating,
intentionless grip taught by the Masters.

In that momentary shift of spirits, the gateway opens.
The Things spill out onto Earth. And the girl attacks. Fast.
So fast. Cartwheeling across the stage. Enye cuts, grip still
unsettled. The sword draws blood only from air. The dancer
tucks and tumbles over the blade. A blast of pain, a kick,
the *tachi* goes spinning from her hand.

The dancer lands on her feet, hands on hips.

Enye thinks her wrist is *broken*.

The falling shadow alerts her. She rolls for the *tachi* as

the guitar falls. It strikes splinters from the wooden staging. The guitar has extruded blue steel blades from its body.

She barely sees the kick coming, rolls with it just fast enough to avoid a broken neck. *Stomach.* She must protect her stomach, protect the child. She slashes out with the *katana. Never slash. Cutting is strong, slashing is weak, desperate.* A crash. A detonation of two hundred-watt bulbs. She must have knocked over a stage-level lighting battery. A smell of burning: hot bulb, the usual back-of-the-monitors litter of paper cups, burger boxes, is smouldering. Wielding the blade-studded guitar like an axe by its machine-head, the eyeless boy advances on her. He does not need eyes to see. He can see her quite clearly by the light of the Mygmus. Blade rings on steel. Enye recovers, uses the Body Strike to fling the eyeless one back across the stage. The pin spots swing and play across the battle. Enye reaches out for her *tachi*. A bare foot deftly kicks the short sword away, comes down on her wrist. Framed by the shock of peroxide hair, the girl looks down at Enye with immense curiosity. Bare foot draws back for killing kick to neck . . . She back-flips away from the blade in Enye's free hand, singing down through the air, crouches, hands and feet flat on the staging, like an animal. The blind guitarist has regained his feet. Enye stands between them.

Across the abandoned dance floor, between the drinkables eatables sniffables smokables, the Things move: things like an ambulatory toadstool covered in hair. Things like a woman dressed in the severely cut grey suit Kim Novak wore in *Vertigo*, except that where Kim Novak's head should be is a single enormous eyeball. Things that look like a dwarf in chain mail with a cannon for a head. Things like a pair of bagpipes walking upon three grass-hopper legs . . . From another world entirely, the Doppler wail of fast-approaching fire engine sirens. The smell of burning is no wishful thinking. A wisp of smoke. A tongue of flame. Fire. Real fire.

Enye uncoils the computer lead from her *obi*, connects it to the *katana*.

The girl dancer grins and purses her lips in poisoned kisses at the sight of the disruptor glyphs anointing the sword.

The eyeless boy launches himself across the stage.

"*Tō!*" She gathers her spirit into one Void-timed "fire and stones" cut: hands, body, spirit, blade, all cutting strongly, rhythmically together. The *katana* shears through the neck of the guitar, encounters the truss rod and is blocked. The back-shock almost knocks the blade from Enye's grip. Glyphs fountain into the neon air. Enye struggles to extricate her weapon. The blind one grins, moves his guitar to trap her blade. She feels the displaced air as the dancer comes tumbling toward her. The girl catches hold of a lighting boom, swings, lands legs locked around Enye's neck. Nylon-smooth thighs crush her windpipe. Enye can hear the girls's breath, panting, excited, in her ears as long, chrome-polished nails seek out the pressure points in her neck and squeeze.

White pain fountains up through her brain; flame, smoke spins around her, but the dumb, mindless motor nerves keep tugging tugging tugging, trying to tear her *katana* free. The air is fire in her lungs. Her blood is molten lead. She can feel the neurons burning and snapping, one by one. She is dying . . .

With the end of her strength she tears the *katana* free from the guitar. The blind one swings his axe in the middle attitude cut. With the dancer choking the last scraps of life from her, Enye reverses her grip on the *katana*.

"Ya!"

She drives the blade upward, at her enemy's head. Howling, the dancer grabs a roof-mounted fold-back monitor and swings away. The warehouse is ringed by the woo-woo sirens and pulsing blue lights of Emergency Services. Cutting to left and right, Enye leaps from the stage into the roaring wall of mythlines, darts between the shuffling Things to recover the *tachi*. The dancer crouches on top of a speaker stack. From her hair, where they have been acting as ornaments, she produces two sets of blades connected to a bar gripped in the fist. Twenty centimetres of steel times six glitters between her knuckles.

With a bird cry, she leaps from the stack over the burning front of the stage, arms spread, blades poised.

And with the perfect timelessness of the masters, Enye cuts her in two with the middle attitude stroke. One cut.

You can win with certainty with the spirit of one cut, for it is the strategy that comes from the heart.

Before the radiance of the dancer's dissolution has died away, Enye has vaulted onto the stage. The Shekinah is a great anthem within. She advances through the whirlwind of mythlines. The blind guitarist raises his weapon, but Enye can see his spirit. He retreats before her until he reaches the other speaker stack. Then he can retreat no farther. Enye rests, reading the time, reading her body and spirit. She disconnects the computer. The glyphs fail and fade. She hefts the *katana* in her left hand. Hurls it.

The guitarist moves to deflect the blow.

Slow. Too slow. Too, too slow.

The sword pins him to a speaker, the blade a line of steel entering just to the left of his nose, exiting through the back of the skull. The thin ichor of the Mygmus-born leaks from the hideous wound, but still he does not die. He does not die because he has never lived. Enye is upon him in a flicker of movement. Short and quick. She can hear the firemen and policemen taking up station around the warehouse. Glyph-light and fireglow illuminate the faces of the woman and the phagus. She plugs the lead from the Sony-Nihon Mark 19 Hakudachi into the socket mounted on the *katana*, poises her finger over the *Enter* key. The flames go up behind her.

"Do not think that because we are the last, we are the only ones," he whispers. "Others will come; others will always come, until you face the Adversary. You have won the battle, but the war is not yet ended."

"Nice speech," says Enye. The blast momentarily out-shines the light of the fire and the banked spots and strobes.

The fire burns hot. The windows crack and shatter in the heat. The smoke tries to choke her, but the Shekinah burns hotter. It touches the edge of her talent and ignites it. With its vision she sees her talent go forth from her, like a great breaking wave, like the ever-breaking hollow of the Deep Sea Wave in the print by Hokusai. She sees the disease-coloured light from that other place beyond the gateway break against it, and fail, and fade. Her talent goes forth from her and it is like a wall, or a rushing mighty wind, halting the Warped Ones in their advance, driving them back, centimetre by centimetre, driving against the power thundering from the Gateway. Its power seems irresistible but little by little, centimetre by centimetre, she drives them back, the Kim Novak thing and the lung thing and the dwarf thing and all the other things that lie within the imagining of humanity, back into the Gateway, back out of the world into the place they have come from.

With the final dregs of her strength, she seals the Gateway and smoothes it away and it is as if it had never been.

As the emergency services people come smashing through the doors with their axes and pneumatic jacks, Enye resheathes her swords and escapes through a window and up onto the roof. While the boys in blue are otherwise occupied, she makes good her escape down the ice-bound fire escape. It catches up with her in the car. She slumps over the Citroen's steering wheel. Hers is the only vehicle in the car park. The slashed roof is incongruous, and cold, though it is not from the cold that she is shivering. She watches the firemen go up their extending ladders to fight the flames that are beginning to lap from the windows. High-pressure hoses knock in the remaining panes of glass. She hopes Elliot has good insurance. Everyone is looking up. Good. She turns on the ignition.

And a cold cold knife turns in her womb.

She cannot breathe. Cannot think. Cannot do anything but lie helpless, paralysed in the car seat as the cold cold knife slowly disembowels her. It is worse, much worse, much much worse, than the pain the dancer inflicted on her, for there she was afraid she was going to die and here she is afraid she is not going to die. Slowly, slowly, the pain eases. She can think. She can act. Fat drops of sweat roll slowly, slowly down her forehead despite the cold in the car. She has bitten her tongue; the brassy taste of blood fills her mouth. She stumbles toward the flashing blue lights of fire police ambulance.

"Help me! God, help me!"

Sparks shoot upward from the conflagration. The ambulances with their pulse-rotating lights and fluorescent orange stripes are light-years away.

"Help! Me! I think I'm having a miscarriage!"

Figures in Night-Glo yellow vests are turning. Too far.

Too slow. Too late. Out of the night, the knife comes tearing with gleeful, vindictive joy; tearing open her womb and sending her crashing to the frost-patched blacktop.

She doesn't know whether to be relieved or disturbed when after a night of tea and tests and trans-sonic scans the gynaecologist (why do gynaecologists always wear bow ties?) pronounces that baby, if not mother, is hale and hearty.

"I can go home?"

"You can go home. If you're careful. The slightest twinge of anything like this again, you come see us. And no more warehouse parties."

The fat friendly nurse with the country accent slips her a card with the address of a Women's Centre on it.

"Leave the bastard," she whispers. "I don't care who he is, what he says, you can't allow him to do things like that to you. There's always someone here." Then, in her professional voice, "Are you staying for lunch? It's pork casserole."

A tall, ectomorphic teenager who is supposed to have swallowed a toothbrush saunters into the ward, stares at Enye's black, hard bruises.

"I think I'll give it a miss all the same," says Enye.

She knows what she is to do now.

The taxi leaves her at the end of L'Esperanza Street. On the first day of the new year she walks past the black iron palings and the high-gloss polyurethane doors and the brass knockers.

She stops dead.

Outside number twenty-seven L'Esperanza Street, like a fragment of the previous night fallen into today, are pulse-rotating blue lights, fluorescent orange stripes, static-blurred snatches of voices on radios.

The police.

The front door of number twenty-seven lies open. A woman officer is standing beside Mr. Antrobus's memorial. By her side is Omry. Two uniformed officers and a plainclothesman emerge from the front door. The uniformed officers are carrying the paraphernalia of her Shekinah factory. The plainsclothesman holds up two plastic Zip-Loc bags, shakes his head.

The woman officer escorts Omry into one of the police cars.

Neighbours peep from behind net curtains, careful not to be seen lest that be mistaken for an admission of complicity.

Enye turns around and walks away. Bursts of police communications crackle from the prowl cars. Engines start and purr. All it takes is for one neighbour to shout, or call. A pointing finger would be more than enough.

She glances over her shoulder.

Two of the three police cars are moving off. One unmarked vehicle remains to await her return. The two cars approach her. Omry is in the backseat between two woman officers.

Enye walks faster.

Faster.

Do not run.

If you run, they will get you for certain.

One of the entries to the laneway that runs along the backs of the gardens is a matter of metres away.

One step at a time. Like the journey of a thousand miles.

She ducks into the entry, presses herself into the back service door of a butcher's shop that fronts the main road. The cars brush past, diesel whispers. She is shaking. She has fought demons, monsters, nightmares, warriors, and she is shaking. She walks away through the web of alleys and entries.

This is how it must have happened. The police bust Omry. Maybe as they arrive, woo-woos blaring, lights flashing, to answer the fire call at the warehouse. Maybe they are coming anyway; maybe they have been tipped. That is certainly what Omry thinks. Omry has been betrayed by that bitch Enye MacColl because she wants Elliot all for herself, after her saying that that bitch Enye can do what she likes with him. Omry takes Enye down with her. Or, Omry decides to plea-bargain. Will His Honour be kind to little Omry if Omry sells him her entire dealership network? One or the other. The former, Enye tends to think.

When she is a safe distance from L'Esperanza Street,

Enye emerges onto the main thoroughfares and flags down a cab. While the driver takes her back across the city to the charred shell of the warehouse and her car, she applies strategy as never before.

The Citroen seems relatively intact. The stock of Shekinah under the driver's seat is untouched. Ten pills. Her entire stock. It is not enough. She has estimated she will need three, four times the amount. It will have to be enough. Her supply lines have been cut. She must face her Adversary before the supply fails entirely.

If your Adversary attacks, are you to die because you have not chosen the time and place at which to fight?

Dull aftershocks seize her womb. She grips the steering wheel, wills them away, pushes them out, out, away from her. The car is slow to start, and cold, so cold. White knuckles on the wheel. Start. Start. *Start*. The heater is at full blast but it does not stop the cold air rushing through the ripped roof. At speed, the fabric flaps and tears further. At the service station where she fills up and buys chocolate, she removes it. Customers stare at her. She smiles at them, but she is worried about making herself too conspicuous. The police will have the number of her car by now. She will answer their charges later. Now she has more important concerns. Thirty kilometres out a green Ford with two peaked caps on the parcel shelf pulls out and passes. She drives very, very carefully until the police car is lost to view. They did not notice her open top. Hah hah, officer. Well, I'm a real fresh-air freak, hah hah.

"Makes you grow up apple-cheeked and roseate," she says to the blind, tumbling blastocyst in her womb. "Sign of high blood pressure. Fancy some music? They do say that the unborn child can recognise external sounds. Of course, you're hardly even a child. Any preferences? Mahler's Fourth?"

The swell of strings and horns spills out of the open-topped car and over the land through which it speeds; across the hedgerows and frost-whitened fields and flooded pastures. Thin, powdery snow has drifted into the windward sides of the furrows. Rooks are dark flopping double-crescents on the eggshell blue sky; clouds of gulls hover over the big tractor rigs ploughing the frozen fields for winter wheat.

"Not that much worse than being on the bike," she shouts to her child. "After a while you stop noticing how cold you are. That's a sure sign that hypothermia is setting in." There may be truth in her joke. She stops at the next roadside bar. Wooden benches where patrons in surfer shorts and surfer shirts had sat swilling lager in the last summer anyone ever expected to see are now scabbed with a leprosy of black frost. Enye orders a coffee and a ploughman's lunch. Rural regulars in sludge-coloured waxed coats look her up and down as if she is a prize heifer and pass comments on her dress. She is still wearing her party gear: hand-painted *yukata* and track bottoms. She stares back at them: *die, peasants*, and they return their attention to the wall-mounted television. A smart young lady on the pale blue screen with pictures of the Happening World hovering above her left shoulder is talking about a series of police raids across the city for Drug-Related Offences following a fire at a New Year's warehouse party last night.

Last night?

It's been a long year.

Onward. Westward. Into the setting sun with Brahms's Piano Concerto Number Two. She shouts at the sun, hold back the night, hold back the night; shouts at the Citroen, faster, faster, she must get there before dark. In the fading light she pushes the needle up into the reckless zone, trying to beat the sun. She shouts and swears at slower traffic; old farmers in Fiats and hats: why do the slowest drivers always wear hats? She takes appalling risks, peels out, swerves in, corners on less than four wheels, screams at the engine while the engine screams back at her: "I'll make it up to you when we get back with a nice oil bath and overhaul, just get me there!"

(When she was a kid and ill in bed, she had dreamed of Paris. Before her mother went out to her job in the Overseas Development Agency, Enye had asked her to pile every book in the house that mentioned Paris at the foot of her bed. Alone with the radio and a glass of orange squash and the comforting intimacy of the blankets around her, she had read and reread those books until she had a Paris constructed in her mind so accurate she could hear the accordion players and smell the baking croissants.)

(The first time she went to Paris as a student, she had walked out of the hostel and within three streets had needed a gendarme to get back again.)

This place is like Paris to her. Since she learned of it from the Midnight Children around their fire of embers under the railroad arch, she has photographed it from every angle, in every light and shade and season, with the f-stop of her imagination.

Fingers, the keeper of the mysteries, had presented it to her with almost sacramental devotion. The heart mystery of the mysteries, the essence of the Rooke archive, wrapped up in a brown paper packet, bound with string. Enye had turned the aged, aged pages, brown and brittle with age, like dried flowers, careful lest even her slightest breath crumble and scatter them. In them she had read of the true name and nature of her Adversary, and the complimentary parts they were both cast to play in the ceaseless unfolding of new mythologies out of the old, like an endless chain of brilliantly coloured scarves from the pocket of a stage magician. New mythologies, new mysteries. Old hurts and pains, old hopes and dreams, played out beneath the Adam ceilings of that house under the shadow of the mountain.

The reality, she knows, will be different.

The Department of Forestry has levelled the ruins of the old house to make a car park. There are wooden garbage bins and a log-cabin toilet block. Two cars are parked outside the toilet block. A man gets out of one, heads to the log cabin. The driver of the other car, also a man, flashes his headlights, then steps out and follows the first man in. There is a signboard with the various nature trails and viewpoints marked out in bright-coloured paints, and a notice about how easy it really is to start forest fires. Her headlights swing across the third notice: *Department of Forestry: Bridestone Wood*.

There is still light in the sky, though the east is dark and the first stars of the winter constellations are beginning to shine out.

She empties out her Junior Housebreaker kit; stuffs the bag with car rugs, chocolate, a flashlight, her computer, her Shekinah. The swords do not quite fit. She leaves them protruding from the half-zipped shut top. The two men come out of the toilet block and drive off in the same direction. The car park is hers and hers alone. She picks her course from the wooden map. The wood is crisscrossed with walks and picnic sites; her way is the one marked with red arrows on wooden marker posts.

She had expected she should feel something—a spirit of place, faces in the trees, souls in the stones, presences seen and unseen. Following the way-marked path up between the naked trees she feels nothing. Whatever spirit resided here, it has been driven far inward by the improving hand of the Forestry Department with its picnic tables and guides to woodland fauna. Or, she thinks, could the picnic tables and split-log garbage bins and way-marked paths only exist here because the spirit of the wood had already withdrawn into monstrous introspection? It is so dark between the trees she needs the flashlight to read the red sign-arrows.

"Up we go, up we go, up we go," she sings to the child within. "Up we go, up we go." The path grows steeper, and she pauses often, the memory of the knife never far. She talks to the foetus about what the video phagus said, the doubts it had cast: that the Warped Ones she has been battling against might only be her own fears returning to her.

"Your grandma did say that Uncle Ewan showed schizophrenic tendencies when he was a boy." She does not tell the unborn thing her conclusion. It already knows, connected to her life by its umbilicus: those same schizophrenic tendencies might have gone undiagnosed in her.

Her own instability, her own fear? she asks the baby. "All the world's queer except thee and me, and I'm not too sure about me." If the spirit of the wood reflects the spirit of the Adversary, is it so deeply introverted that it might no longer be capable of reaching out of the Mygmus into the world? What do you think, baby MacColl? Does baby MacColl think that maybe in its mother's childhood there might be something unremembered but deeply, deeply etched, something branded so deeply into her subconscious that it has found expression in the Mygmus and thus back into the world again in the form of phaguses?

Does baby MacColl know what it might be?

Enye MacColl thinks she does.

"Hey, we're here! Starry, starry night." It is cold—bitingly cold—upon the bare slopes of the mountain. The path leads along the upper edge of the forest. Only at the extreme western fringe of the world is there a lightening in the indigo sky. The stars are huge and brilliant and low enough for her almost to touch. She has never seen so many. Like an ancient god, she could gather a handful and weave them into a plaything for baby MacColl. The stone stands a few metres beyond the viewpoint. The small hollow in which its creators set it has been concreted over and is littered with empty beer cans, chocolate wrappers, foil, and the last condoms of summer.

Small olive-skinned, black-haired Enyc MacColl looks up at the stone, feels it with her fingers. Presses her ear to its dew-slick surface.

Nothing. Only rock.

She sits down at its foot, wraps herself in the blankets she has brought from the car. There is not much heat in them. She chews down the chocolate, piece by piece, bar by bar. She lays the swords, sheathed, on the short turf to her left, lays the computer to her right.

"Sorry, kid, but this has to be done."

She removes the top from the glass bottle and swallows her entire supply of Shekinah. She sits, wrapped in her thin blankets, back to the Bridestone, waiting for something to happen. She wishes she had some music with her. Why doesn't she keep a Walkperson in the car? Mussorgsky's "Night on a Bare Mountain," hah hah . . . And as usual, she has missed noticing when the Shekinah begins to take effect.

When did the hollow in which she is sitting start to get *deeper*?

And the ground beneath her grow soft and insubstantial? She leaps to her feet.

The shallow depression has already become a pit, and is deepening every second. The sky is a disk of stars. What is happening? What is happening? It has never been like this before. She scrabbles at the sides of the pit, clings to the grass, but the gradient increases moment by moment, mythlines pour in, a Niagara of light, like the ocean falling off the edge of the flat Earth. She is drowning in mythlines.

She tries to hold her head away from their downpour to breathe, and all the while the sides of the pit approach perpendicular. The Bridestone has vanished, already fallen into the pit. She reaches for her swords, her computer, cannot reach them. They fall into the abyss. Her grip is failing, the grass between her fingers tearing at its roots. She cannot keep hold, she cannot keep hold . . .

All is lost in the blue shift of infalling mythlines.

Blue shift.

Red shift.

Red.

Times and spaces out of mind no longer terrify her.

Red. All red.

Shifts of reality that would cause others to question their sanity are the warp and weft of the fabric of her life.

Not the red of flames, but the red of wounds, of blood, of flesh.

What is this place her mythoconsciousness has brought her?

She sits on the floor of a great hall that reaches in all directions beyond perspective. Red, all red. Floor and ceiling of red flesh, joined by bone piers and buttresses that splay out into riblike vaulting. Her swords and computer are by her side. Also, a discarded chocolate wrapper.

This is the Mygmus?

It is not what she expected. She had not known what to expect when she took all her Shekinah in one massive, reality-breaching overdose, but it is not this. She fixes computer to *obi*, slings swords comfortably across her back. One way looks as good as any other. She sets off at a slow jog. Thanks to cycling, she can keep this pace up almost indefinitely.

Is she pregnant in here? Just what is the nature of her reality, or nonreality, here?

The pillars and buttresses multiply endlessly. The only perceived change is audible, a distant, slow pulse-beat thud has entered the fringe of her perceptions.

Pulse-beat? She touches a hand to the floor. Soft, warm, vibrating, barely perceptibly in time to the beat beat, beat beat, beat beat.

If the entire universe is her Adversary's body, Enye can understand how this chamber might go on and on forever.

An intrusion into the precise regularity catches her eye—a white something. She holds it in her vision as she jogs toward it; it is easy to lose in the uniformity of the great vaulted space. It seems to be a large white boulder. No, not a white boulder. Closer, she sees it is a tooth. A single molar, three times her height.

Has her Adversary's hold on reality slipped to such a degree that she no longer knows the shape and structure of her own body?

On the other side of the molar she finds a man. He is imprisoned inside a metal gibbet anchored to the molar. Corroded iron bands bite into his flesh. He looks at her from the cage that holds his head upright and fixed, staring out across the endless vaulted arches. Enye recognises him, though her knowledge was not of him in his prime, as he is here, but of his old age.

It is Mr. Antrobus.

"How can you be here?" she asks.

"Because you sent me here."

"But you are dead."

"I am. But in your imagination, I will live as long as your memory of me lives."

"But this is not my imagining."

"Isn't it? We talked about heaven and hell, you recall."

"I recall that I said we make our own heavens and hells."

"Some of us have the power to make heavens or hells for others. I shared with you my image of hell and it was impressed into your dreams and your fears, and became reality."

"My God."

"In a sense, yes. This is, after all, the Mygmus."

He rolls his eyes downward, the only part of him other than his lips that is capable of movement. Between his feet is a dark hole.

"What is that?"

"A way out."

"Where does it go?"

"I do not know. Not here."

"Why should I want to go somewhere else?"

"Because it is not here."

"What will I find if I continue on here?"

"Just the same, endlessly repeated. If you stay, you will be just the same way I am. We will both be prisoners of a place that never changes."

"It would seem that I have no choice."

"No. You have one choice. It is I who has no choice."

"Do I have to throw myself in?"

"Can you see any other way?"

In a moment, Mr. Antrobus chained to the tooth is the only variation in an infinity of flesh and bone.

She falls only a few metres through the stifling darkness before the tunnel flattens into a curve. It is at once exhilarating and terrifying, a Big Dipper ride in absolute darkness, never knowing when the next dip comes, and when it comes, if it will be the end of the ride, or the edge of a final plummet to annihilation; nothing to hold on to, nothing to feel or see, nothing to anchor herself to in any way: a thousand-kilometre scream of free-fall adrenaline.

Wasn't there a scene like this in *Dr. No*? She thinks that this is an incongruous thought to think while sliding through the universe-filling body of your enemy. In such a situation, any thought is incongruous. The darkness brightens, flesh-tone red. The walls of the esophagus grow translucent. Her descent is less precipitous now—she can see the dips and curves and prepare for them. Will she end with a whoop and a splash in the Pancreatic Sea? Beyond the isinglass walls pass arteries and beating, flapping ventricles; ion-blue lightning forks along neurons and jumps synaptic gaps with a crackle of thunder; air sacs the size of small zeppelins swell and contract; floating within, falling free, are all the dreams and symbols of the dark night of a soul, frozen, inanimate, waiting for the breath of life to inspire them.

Disease? Her Adversary's madness, or her own? Trust nothing here, least of all yourself.

Without warning the tube upends and dumps her with a shriek at her destination.

The baby . . .

But the landing is soft, yielding, folds of thick, fingerlike villi. She shakes herself free—the stroking of those, soft, yielding fingers makes her feel violated. What is this elsewhere to which she has been delivered? A small circular chamber with egresses leading from it. The walls resemble close-packed tree trunks moulded from red meat, the ceiling a lattice of interwoven fleshy branches from which yellow luminous sacs hang like lewd fruit. Immediately above her is the portal by which she slid into this elsewhere place.

Chamber of Thirty-Two Doors.

Pick a door. Any door.

And she learns that this elsewhere into which she had slid is the centre of a maze. A maze of faces. As she explores tentatively down the high, narrow corridors, the clear, glassy floor lights up beneath her footfalls. Within the clear, hard substance are faces, eyes closed, lips moving as if talking in their sleep.

A maze.

She has always wanted to visit a maze like the one at Hampton Court Palace her grandmother told her about, where a man in a flannels and blazer and boater hat sat on top of a pair of stepladders and shouted guidance through a megaphone.

"Not now," she says aloud, and at the sound of her words, the sleeping faces open their eyes in surprise and horror.

She could be trapped here. As trapped as the Mr. Antrobus phagus. She is no longer certain she knows the way back to the centre.

A maze. Of faces. Her grandmother.

It is the china maze from the Stone Gardens, the one mapped out with shards of broken pottery, pieces of the faces of the crowned heads of Europe. And in that maze, if you had the gift, you could see the wind. She summons that memory, imagines herself once again a little girl, standing at the centre of the gyre of fragments, trying to see the wind.

Soft as a prayer, a touch on her right cheek. A breath of moving air.

She takes the next opening on the right. A stirring of the

hair on the back of her neck is confirmation and direction: forward, a touch on either cheek, left, right.

There is a key to every maze.

Beyond the maze is a vault so high she can barely distinguish the ribwork that supports the dome. The great space of the vault is filled with towers, some so tall their tops are lost in the steamy vapours that collect under the dome, some only as high as Enye's waist, but so closely arrayed that she cannot see through them to the walls of the vault. The towers are made from dark, black, glossy bones knitted and fused together into suggestions of faces and ribs and contorted limbs. A glazed ossuary; bone totems. The surface beneath her feet is lined and fissured like human skin. As she advances between towers great and towers small, towers lofty and towers least, little creatures go skittering and skidding around her party shoes. She kneels to satisfy her curiosity: whirring and whizzing, they detour around her. No longer than her thumb, they are half pixie, half car, internal combustion centaurs with human heads, arms, and torsos spot-welded into the engine housings of Dinky cars. They rev and roar away from her grasping fingers but she catches one, holds it up to her face. Tiny wheels scream and spin. She drops it with a howl.

The human half of the Henry Ford centaur *bit* her.

It lies on its side, wheels spinning, spinning, trying to heave itself with its arms back onto its wheelbase.

Though she treads carefully and the auto-taurs display startling acceleration and manoeuvarability, she cannot avoid crushing some beneath her muddied party shoes.

Far off between the slick back towers is a shine of white.

And again: closer. Look. Where? There? No. Where? *There*.

Glimpse: a white dress, like an old-fashioned wedding frock. Floating in the air a meter or so above the skin surface.

And a fourth time: closest yet. Lingering for her to be certain she has seen it before drifting out of sight behind the bone totems.

Heedless of the auto-taur traffic, she runs after the white dress. It leads her out of the place of the towers. It leads her through a place where banks and ridges of red gumlike material extrude eyeballs to observe her passage; some tiny and blue as the ol' blue eyes of abalones, some globes several meters across with irisis shaped like crosses, or triangles, or three parallel slits. It lead her through a grove of trees the branches of which terminate in minute, waggling homunculi. It leads her through a place where elephants with sundials growing out of their backs slo-mo across a checkerboard carpet. Enye thinks that she is gaining on it as she pursues the vision across the interior bodyscape: a Chantilly silk bridal gown filled with dried flowers; flowers for head and flowers for hands and the dead brittle stalks of flowers for body and form and substance. She draws nearer, but never near enough to touch, to test its body and form and substance and symbolism with her bare hands.

It is not one of her memories, twisted and reinterpreted. She is certain of that.

She can see where this dream of her Adversary's is leading her. The woven walls and ceiling of the bodyscape flare outward and upward into an indefinite dimension so vast her senses might almost convince her she is in open air. The flesh floor rises gently to break before her into a scree slope of chaotic jumbled shapes, a steeply sloping mountain on the summit of which stands a throne. Phaguses, Enye realises as the slope grows too steep and chaotic for her steady jog, though the wedding dress floats effortlessly over the snarled debris: phaguses, Nimrods, Things from the Gateway, heaped on top of each other. Her hands seek out holds and grips among the projections and protrusions; the phaguses are cold to her touch, hard and colourless as enamel, annealed together by some unknown process of vitrification into one conterminous mass.

She asks, are these phaguses that have been, or phaguses that are yet to be? as she picks her way up. Up we go, up we go, up we go, over things that look like running shoes with trout fins and tails and crystal wine decanters rimmed with feathery cilia and oyster shells with lolling warty tongues and stones with hands with diamond rings on their fingers and Honda mopeds with Mozart's head for handlebars and things that are half shark, half skateboard all ossified and fused together. Then she finds the pig thing she dispatched in the alley behind the convent under her hand, and a ruff of black lace tutu, hard and cold as anthracite, and the lamprey wolf smashed to nothingness on the oil-stained concrete of the QHPSL car park, and a shred of T-shirt decorated with severed heads, pentagrams, and bondage, and a sandalled foot.

Phaguses that have been.

Up we go, up we go. The way grows steep. It seems to her that she has been climbing this mountain forever and still it reaches before her to that unattainable throne on the summit. Up we go, up we go, still the silk wedding dress animated with flowers leads her though she no longer requires its guidance. Up we go, up we go, up we go, until she can go up no farther, she has arrived at the peak, at the summit of the mountain of destroyed dreams.

The throne is a slab of stone standing in a small declivity among the petrified phaguses. Its back is to her. The stone slab is pierced at her eye level. Through the hole she can see the back of a head.

She walks around the throne to see who is seated in it.

It is a man. He wears a business suit of rather old-fashioned cut, a pointy-collared shirt, and a gaudy kipper tie of the kind that was thought most fashionable in the seventies. On the arm of the slate throne sits a girl. Her age is hard for Enye to define. She wears a tiny silk taffeta wedding dress in Chantilly cream that is in every respect the duplicate of the one that led Enye to the mountain of phaguses. The little girl plays with a dried marguerite, twirls it between her fingers.

She looks at Enye, giggles, coyly.

"Hello, Enye," says her father. "Would you like to play, too?"

The child bares perfect white teeth and giggles gleefully again.

And Enye is sent cascading back through time. She remembers. She remembers every little thing.

The times he had got up in the night when he said he had to go to the bathroom for a drink of water.

The times he had come home early from work, and how quiet her mother had been to find him there.

The times she had been sent shopping with her mother

when he insisted that Ewan stay with him while they cleaned out the garage or the attic.

The times she had heard Ewan's bedroom door close in the early morning hours and when the house was silent again, so quiet she could not be certain she was hearing it, the pillow-stifled sobbing.

The times he had insisted on bathing Ewan and drying him by the fire, even though Ewan was big enough to bathe himself, and far too big to dry himself by sitting naked in front of the fire.

The times at the beach when, even after Ewan was old enough to dry himself, he had insisted on rubbing him down with the big striped beach towel with the puffins on it.

The times when Ewan sat, just sat, sat, doing nothing but sitting, watching the rain fall on the garden, when her mother would get up to go over to him and he would say no, let the boy alone, he's got to learn not be a sulk box.

The times when her mother had come to pick them up from school in the old yellow Fiat 127 with suitcases and carrier bags in the back and driven them fast, very fast, almost recklessly, down to Ballybrack.

The times when she had started to grow breasts and hair and feel like she was turning into a wolf from the inside out, when he would come up to her when no one else was around and ask to see how she was growing *up there*. And *down there*.

The times he asked if she minded if he touched?

Up there.

And *down there.*

And his thick, spadelike fingers, stained nicotine-yellow, reaching under the elastic . . .

Up there.

And *down there.*

The times when she was awakened by the sound of Ewan crying in pain and fear and humiliation, and the times the silhouette against the landing light filled her doorway, the shadow fell across her bed.

Be nice to me. There's a good boy. There's a good girl. What's this down here, oh, that's nice, that's good, that's not old and used up, that's new, that's fresh, you love your daddy, don't you? Don't you? Of course you do. Then do *this* for him. Move *this* way for him. Touch *this* for him.

And the doctor is shining his big bright light in her eyes and she can hear him saying, as if he thinks that she cannot hear, or is very, very stupid, "It's as if she doesn't want to remember, Mrs. MacColl. As if she has willed herself not to remember."

But she remembers.

She remembers.

Every. Little. Thing.

"You bastard!"

The swords sing from their sheaths across her back. *Tachi* and *katana*. Here, at the centre, the glyphs blaze and crackle from the blade like nova fire. She raises the *katana* over her head: *Jodan No Kamae.*

Her father smiles, raises a forefinger from the arm of the slate throne.

And she knows what he knows. She knows that if she strikes him down out of the hate in her heart, out of hurt and vengeance and hate, he will become more powerful than she has ever imagined. For if she cuts him down, annihilates him, the hate will go on forever. Hate will have the final say. Hate will be the final word. It will sound forever through the halls of the Mygmus, and so it will never end. The Warped Things, the Nimrods, the phaguses, the Lords of the Gateway, they too will go on forever, created and inspired by the power of her hate, until she is destroyed. By her own hate. And all hope of a new mythic vision, of a new mythology, new heroes, new gods, new demons to sweep away the tired pantheon of Otherworld, will wither in the twistings and perversions of her hatred.

She wants to strike him. For the ten, the twenty, the hundred sins, the twenty, the hundred, the thousand violations and slow, pleasureful maimings, she wants to feel her sword cut into his flesh, she wants to see him annihilated by the God-light of her glyphs.

For her mother.

For Ewan.

For herself. For the Enye MacColls that might have been, the lives they might have lived, the loves they might have loved, but for him.

Action/no-action. Conception/no-conception.

Two samurai, on a hillside, in the rain. The driving, driving rain.

All her strategies fall useless from her hands. The Way has failed her.

Her Spirit is Void.

She rips the connector from the *katana*. The glyphs fade to nothingness. She brings the sword in front of her face. The edge of the blade touches her nose. It is as sharp as the word of God.

With a cry that yields to no simple analysis, she hurls the *katana* away from her, away from the mountaintop. The sword tumbles end over end out into the Mygmus. The light from nowhere and everywhere glitters from the flying blade until it can no longer be distinguished from the void.

She turns to her father. Closes her eyes.

She remembers once again her father's violations of her brother and herself, of their mother, of their family. She cannot bear to look at them, their touch burns like bile, but she gathers them into her arms, embraces them. And takes them into herself. She speaks three words. Each one of the words costs Enye more than anything has ever cost her in her life. The alienation and separation from her mother, losing her job, losing Saul, her unplanned pregnancy, the quest to avenge the Midnight Children—none of these amounts to one fraction of the cost of a single one of the words: "I forgive you."

It is not a complete forgiveness. It is only three words of forgiveness, and it will take the rest of her life to work that forgiveness out, but it is a start.

She opens her eyes.

The slate throne is empty.

The dark place she could never share with any of the people she loves tears as if rent by lightning, from the top to the bottom. A casket of ancient sorrows cracks open and is exposed to the light. The creatures that have swarmed and multiplied within keen and die.

The little girl in the chestnut taffeta wedding dress comes from behind the stone throne. Enye goes down on her knees, beckons the little girl to her. The child is shy and sullen, but comes, curious, a shade fearful.

"I've come to take you away from here. You don't have to stay here anymore."

"I don't want to go. I like it here."

"Here? What is there here for you?"

"Myself."

"Is that what you want?"

"No. But I don't want to go back. Don't make me go back. I won't go back. You can't make me. This is my place. My place. Why did you have to come here to ruin it, spoil my fun, make everything horrible? Why did you have to come and change things? Why do you want to take me away when I don't want to go?"

Enye looks long at the thing she had always thought of as her Adversary: this girl, this child in a woman's dress. She had been wrong. The Rooke archive had been wrong. The Midnight Children had been wrong. Her enemies had spoken the truth. There was nothing here that could possibly have opposed her. The Adversary, as ever, had been within.

Enye opens her arms to the little girl. The child accepts the invitation into her embrace, reaches out its arms to return the affection. Enye hugs the girl to her chest, arms wrapped tightly, protectingly, imprisoning the child within her embrace.

"This is no place for you." Enye whispers. "In my world there is a place for you. A time for you."

The child screams and heaves and thrashes: No no no no no no no no no no no no no no no no no no no no no. . . .

But Enye will not let go. She crushes the child to her breast. The child beats its head against her, again and again and again and again, tries to free its arms to strike and scratch, turn its head to bite.

But Enye will not let go.

And she feels it changing within her grip, feels its human contours soften and run, feels it reform itself. She cries aloud; within her embrace is a snake. But she does not let go. The snake writhes, swells. She is clutching to her soft breasts some impossibly huge, impossibly vile insect. But she does not let go. The insect transforms itself into a chimera of spines and fangs and quills that crucify her flesh. She cries out as the blood leaks from a thousand punctures.

But she does not let go. The child transmutes itself: a white-hot glowing ingot of iron; a pillar of dry ice; a blaze of solid lightning. But Enye will not let go. Claws rend her, acid burns her, vile and poisonous vapours corrode her nostrils, sear her lungs into blisters of pus; leprosy gnaws her fingers and breasts and face to rotted abscesses; maggots and weevils hatch within her belly and eat their way to light and air; she embraces fang and sting and poison and pestilence, but Enye will not let go; through the fiftieth transformation, and the five hundredth and the five thousandth, Enye will not let go.

And in the end, all the changes are run and within the circle of her arms lies something silver and shimmering, like a foetus, and a newborn baby, and a child, and a handsome woman, and an aged, aged crone all at once, flickering from state to state, transient and insubstantial. Enye picks up the silver, dazzling thing. It is slippery to the touch, smoother than glass. It flows over her fingers like quicksilver.

She presses it to her belly.

"Yes!" she cries as the quicksilver thing passes through the flesh of her belly to rest within. "Yes . . ."

A tremor shakes the mountain of phaguses. A crack appears in the slate throne, from top to bottom, runs down through the fused, ossified phaguses. The Mygmus quakes again; the mountain cracks and fissures. Fragments of phagus tumble away down the sheer slopes. The whole unsteady pile groans and settles. The imaginary structure of the Mygmus is coming apart. A third volley of tremors sends Enye clutching for the slate throne. Behind her, the flesh and bone valuting unravels; spans and cables shear and snap; the flesh-stuff from which they are woven breaks into streamers and corpuscles. Whole geographies of bodyscape spin into the unsubstance of the Mygmus, wheeling, shedding ropes and spirals of dream flesh. The mountain of phaguses faults catastrophically across the centre. With inexorable, ponderous slowness the summit, throne, and Enye slide off into the void. Chunks of phagus-stuff fall past her. The bone piers and buttresses that supported the world unwind into their component fibres; those fibres disintegrate into clouds of free-flying cells. Pulsing air sacs tumble through nothingness. Bereft of its shaping and sustaining imagination, the Mygmus is returning to its original unstructured state. In a very few minutes the entire edifice of Emily Desmond's fantasy is reduced to a cloud of corpuscles expanding outward into great and boundless darkness.

Clinging to the wreckage of her father's throne, Enye tumbles through the Mygmus. Beneath her she spies a tear in the unsubstance: a pale dawn light spills through, light in the darkness. The light of a new morning breaks across Enye.

Go there! she screams silently at the stone slab, willing stability and trajectory into its tumbling flight. How did it work in *The Wizard of Oz*? There's no place like home, there's no place like home . . . Don't you need a pair of ruby slippers for that to work? The body-verse is almost entirely absorbed back into the primal state: she alone is the sole remaining quantum of definition and order.

She focuses her desires on that dawn light, that gateway back to her life. She remembers all the things she has ever loved about her life and world, calls them to mind, dwells upon them, touches, tastes, feels them; and while she savours them again, she rejects all that the Mygmus has to offer.

This no place for life.

The vagina-mouth opens; the light of morning shines into the Mygmus, and swallows her.

Light. Primal light.

Cold. Primal cold.

She cannot believe she can be this cold and still be alive.

Because she is cold, she must be alive.

Sometime in the night her body must have fused with the stone against which she is sitting; she is now a frost-glazed outcrop of herself, stone legs stone arms stone hands stone eyes.

She thinks for a moment her eyes have frozen shut.

But she opens them on a still-dark land lying in the darkness beneath the mountain; a giant shadow cast over forest and field and sea. At the zenith the vapour trail of a westbound jet catches the rays of the sun and kindles into burning gold. Light touches the summits of the mountains across the bay, steals with giant, silent strides across the land.

The blankets are stiff with frost. Her attempts to move her frozen limbs makes them crackle and snap. People have *died* in less severe conditions than this. How then has she . . .

. . . unless her voyage to the Mygmus and back had not been the wholly imaginary journey she had assumed.

Immaterial. For now, praise God for light and morning and gifts of *moving* and *stretching* and *feeling*, even if it feels like a rock coming to life after a million years of stillness. The dawning light sends probing fingers over the hilltop, down the mountainsides, calling life and warmth into Enye's body. She bends, stretches, limbers up with the aching slowness of aged aged practitioners of t'ai chi. When she feels at least half human she repacks the hold-all. Imagination? Then where is the *katana*? She shoulders the bag, limps away from the Bridestone. She turns back for one look at her adversary and ally. The stone slab, taller than herself, has cracked through from top left to bottom right. No imagination. She turns back onto the way-marked paths of men. The light is touching the tops of the trees, but an inner light is breaking over whole landscapes of her spirit that had lain long in darkness. Down among the trees, where she can hear the sound of early traffic from the main road, she stops. Of course, it is far too early, it is a biological impossibility for her to feel what she thought she felt, but it had seemed to her that she could feel the baby move and quicken inside her.

Back at the car, she finds that in the night, someone has broken in through the open roof and stolen her new stereo and case of tapes.

She leans back against the car door and laughs and laughs and laughs.

They just won't let you live.

As usual when the phone rings she has to scream at Elliot for five minutes to shut up that damn racket there's someone on the phone. What? Someone on the phone. What? Can't hear. Someone on the phone. Hang on a minute, I'll switch off the music, what? Someone on the phone. Oh. For me? No. For *me*.

Jaypee.

She almost can't believe it. Like getting phone calls from a ghost, or a South American *desaparecido*. He's been meaning to call her for some time but, well, you know, dear heart, this and that and the other, especially the other. How is she?

She is seven months' pregnant, feels the size of a major Jovian satellite, condemned to back pains fallen arches tacky maternity fashions with little bunny rabbits on the breast pocket and Elliot insisting she practice practice practice the breathing techniques they're learning at antenatal class. But it's good.

Finding the courage to tell Elliot she was pregnant had been no trivial quest. She had been tempted to leave it to the incontrovertible evidence of his eyes and time, but then he might have been misled into believing the child was his. Early into the new year they had started sleeping with each other. Sleeping partners do not deserve such shabby deceptions. She wanted him to be in no doubt that the child was not his, even though the price of his knowledge might have been his feet under her duvet and pots of China tea first thing in the morning. Though she bled from the heart at the thought of losing him, she said, "I'm pregnant." For three days he had locked himself away in his attic with the music-making machines he had managed to salvage from the warehouse fire while Enye felt like a sinner condemned by God. He would, he said, Think About It.

And the third day a van drew up outside twenty-seven L'Esperanza Street and out of the back came keyboards QWERTY boards rhythm generators synthesizers reel-2-reels, CD cassette and record decks mixing desks amps mikes posters prints paintings eighteen-gear Shinamo system ATB, and Elliot.

"Every child needs a father," he said. "Seeing as how the real one has finked out on his duty, I would like to apply for the post."

And with the whole of L'Esperanza Street aghast behind their nets at the *brazenness* of it all, Enye, grinning like a synchronised swimmer, opened the doors and let Elliot with his keyboards QWERTY boards rhythm generators synthesizers reel-2-reel CD cassette and record decks mixing desks amps mikes posters prints paintings and eighteen-gear Shinamo system ATB into her home.

The system is cosy and practical. Another communication from yet another set of solicitors left Enye the recipient of yet another bequest—the property and ground of number twenty-seven L'Esperanza Street courtesy the estate of Mr. Antrobus deceased. Elliot has use of the downstairs rooms to make his music. Enye smiles. She sees it as the completion of Antrobus's revenge against the twitch-curtain brigade, a revenge begun when the Drugs Squad raided Enye's apartment and found themselves in possession of two Zip Loc bags of assorted toenail clippings and bleached pubic hair which did not appear to be listed on any of the catalogues of Bustable Substances Euphoriant Stimulant Depressant Hallucinogenic. The folk in forensic had been unable to ascertain an active principle despite the fact that it left odd peaks on the chemical analysis charts. The one cocksure enough of his science to try some of the stuff reported only that it tasted like light bulbs.

Case dismissed.

But it was still the Biggest Event of the Decade behind the lace curtains and vertical blinds of L'Esperanza Street. Until Elliot and his keyboards QWERTY boards rhythm generators synthesizers reel-2-reels CD cassette and record decks mixing desks amps mikes posters prints paintings and eighteen-gear Shinamo system ATB.

Elliot is good. Good enough to be able to do the bikes just three days a week. Good enough to be getting airplay on the FM stations; good enough for the nationwide network to have asked him to cut a session. Good enough to be the uncrowned King of Klubland, Master of the Warehouses, King of the Remixes; Doctor Jive. Even if sometimes Enye cannot hear the telephone.

She tells Jaypee she feels good.

That's good to Jaypee. To hear his voice is like rolling up the years as if they were an old carpet to dance on the floorboards. He has News. Capital N news. Word is up, the skids are under the Blessèd Phaedra. Crossed Oscar the

Bastard on policy decisions once too often. No one knows the exact nature of her transgressions, but Word is Up, So: QHPSL Advertising has a couple of jobs that it's had to put on the metaphorical back burner because right now, dear heart, they're up to metaphorical *here* and rather than lose accounts, they're considering subcontracting. Interested, honey child?

She wishes science-fictiony things like videophones existed so Jaypee could see her smile when she says that *Actually*, she's moving into another area of creative work entirely. Publishing.

Of course, Jaypee asks just what does she mean, but Enye does not want to tell him, not yet, that she posted the revised and edited and corrected manuscript of *The Secret Language of Flowers*, by Enye and Jessica MacColl, to a national publishing house two days ago. She tells Jaypee thanks, but she's really not interested.

Keep in touch, says Jaypee.

She says she will try to, yes, more than try to, she will, and in her voice is a tone of sincerity that says that if they do not meet again it will not be for want of her trying.

Elliot comes bounding up the stairs, shaggy mane flying. He looks so good and fresh and spontaneous that she cannot resist pulling him into the bedroom with tiny squeaks and cries, throwing him down onto the bed and herself on top of him.

"That your mother again?"

"No. An old friend. From advertising days."

He harrumphs. He likes to pretend he is jealous of her advertising friends.

"Oh, by the way, post." It is a postcard, rather, a colour print, somewhat crumpled, with an address scrawled on the back. The message reads, *Love from* and the signatures are illegible. The photograph is of a blocky, thickset man of twenty-wise and a very pretty girl, age approximately ditto, wearing a denim jacket and a T-shirt with the legend "SunMed Capo Blanco." They have a dog with them, a scruffy mongrel. It is jumping up and the man is holding its front paws off the ground, as folk will, with dogs.

"Who's it from?"

"Oh, some folk I haven't seen in a long time." Then she

lifts his hands and presses them to her belly. "Feel. Life. Elliot. Strong life. Feel it kick."

Elliot loves to feel the baby move and stir within Enye's womb.

"Feels like it's going to be a pole vaulter, that one. A little street fighter. Feel that kick!"

"Oh, no," Enye says. "A ballet dancer. She's going to be a girl."

"How can you so sure?"

"Oh, I'm sure."

She rises from the bed, goes to the midi system, clicks on whatever tape is in the deck. Sibelius Five. She crosses to the window, looks out at the garden where late spring is uncoiling from the earth like a slow, silent explosion. It seemed to take a long time to come this year, but it came. It always does.

"What do you think of Emily as a name?" she says.

AFTERWORDS

*"In Fantasy . . . all stories must run to three volumes
and include a mention of the Wild Hunt."*
—David Langford: *Mexicon III* Program Book

THANKS

It's a churlish husband who doesn't dedicate his novel to his wife, so first and foremost, here's to you, Patricia, for encouragement, and when encouragement didn't work, stubbornness, and when stubbornness didn't work, reminding me that I could actually do this thing called *writing*. A great debt of thanks goes to David Rhodes, for permission to plunder mercilessly our mutual childhoods (Percy Perinov lives!), and as inventor of the word *phagus*. Thanks also, and apologies, to the many people who without knowledge or consent may find themselves between these covers. Finally, to the Arts Council for Northern Ireland for awarding me a bursary during work on this novel, and all you nice people at Bantam, hope it was worth the wait: thanks.

ABOUT THE AUTHOR

IAN MCDONALD'S first story appeared in the British magazine *Extro* in 1982. Since then, he's appeared in numerous magazines and anthologies on both sides of the Atlantic. He was nominated for the John W. Campbell Award for Best New Writer, his novelette *Unfinished Portrait of the King of Pain, by Van Gogh* was a Nebula Award finalist in 1989, and his first novel, *Desolation Road*, won the Locus poll as best first novel of 1988 and went on to be nominated for the Arthur C. Clarke Award. His other books include *Out on Blue Six* and a collection of short fiction, *Empire Dreams*. Born in Manchester, England, in 1960, McDonald has lived in Northern Ireland for the past twenty-five years. He lives with his wife in Belfast, exploring odd and diverse interests that range from cats (he has two) and contemplative religion to bonsai and bicycles.

For the summer's best in science fiction and fantasy, look no further than Bantam Spectra.

SPECTRA'S SUMMER SPECTACULAR

With a dazzling list of science fiction and fantasy stars, Spectra's summer list will take you to worlds both old and new: worlds as close as Earth herself, as far away as a planet where daylight reigns supreme; as familiar as Han Solo's Millennium Falcon and as alien as the sundered worlds of the Death Gate. Travel with these critically acclaimed and award-winning authors for a spectacular summer filled with wonder and adventure!

<u>Coming in May 1991:</u>

**Star Wars, Volume 1:
Heir to the Empire**
by Timothy Zahn

Earth
by David Brin

King of Morning, Queen of Day
by Ian McDonald

<u>Coming in June, 1991:</u>

**The Gap Into Vision:
Forbidden Knowledge**
by Stephen R. Donaldson

Black Trillium
by Marion Zimmer Bradley,
Julian May and Andre Norton

**Chronicles of the King's Tramp
Book 1: Walker of Worlds**
by Tom DeHaven

<u>Coming in July 1991:</u>

**The Death Gate Cycle,
Volume 3: Fire Sea**
by Margaret Weis and
Tracy Hickman

**The Death Gate Cycle,
Volume 2: Elven Star**
by Margaret Weis and
Tracy Hickman

Raising the Stones
by Sheri S. Tepper

<u>Coming in August 1991:</u>

Garden of Rama
by Arthur C. Clarke
and Gentry Lee

Nightfall
by Isaac Asimov
and Robert Silverberg

Available soon wherever Bantam
Spectra Books are sold.

AN274 - 6/91

SPECTRA

MM/EARTH